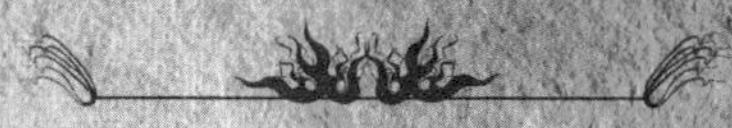

Veri isaakank—veri ekaakank.

Veri olen elid.

Andak veri-elidet Karpatiiakank,

es wake-sarna ku meke arwa- arvo,

irgalom, han ku agba, es wake kutni,

ku manaak verival.

Verink sokta; verink kana terad.

Akasz enak ku kana es juttasz kuntatak it.

SARNA KONTAKAWK

(The Carpathian Warriors' Chant)

Dark Predator

Titles by Christine Feehan

RUTHLESS GAME
STREET GAME
MURDER GAME
PREDATORY GAME
DEADLY GAME
CONSPIRACY GAME
NIGHT GAME
MIND GAME
SHADOW GAME

HIDDEN CURRENTS
TURBULENT SEA
SAFE HARBOR
DANGEROUS TIDES
OCEANS OF FIRE

SAVAGE NATURE
WILD FIRE
BURNING WILD
WILD RAIN

WATER BOUND

DARK PREDATOR
DARK PERIL
DARK SLAYER
DARK CURSE
DARK HUNGER
DARK POSSESSION
DARK CELEBRATION
DARK DEMON
DARK SECRET
DARK DESTINY

DARK MELODY
DARK SYMPHONY
DARK GUARDIAN
DARK LEGEND
DARK FIRE
DARK CHALLENGE
DARK MAGIC
DARK GOLD
DARK DESIRE
DARK PRINCE

Anthologies

HOT BLOODED
(with Maggie Shayne, Emma Holly, and Angela Knight)

LOVER BEWARE
(with Fiona Brand, Katherine Sutcliffe, and Eileen Wilks)

FANTASY
(with Emma Holly, Sabrina Jeffries, and Elda Minger)

FEVER
(includes The Awakening *and* Wild Rain*)*

SEA STORM
(includes Magic in the Wind *and* Oceans of Fire*)*

DARK PREDATOR

A CARPATHIAN NOVEL

CHRISTINE FEEHAN

BERKLEY BOOKS, NEW YORK

THE BERKLEY PUBLISHING GROUP
Published by the Penguin Group
Penguin Group (USA) Inc.
375 Hudson Street, New York, New York 10014, USA
Penguin Group (Canada), 90 Eglinton Avenue East, Suite 700, Toronto, Ontario M4P 2Y3, Canada
(a division of Pearson Penguin Canada Inc.)
Penguin Books Ltd., 80 Strand, London WC2R 0RL, England
Penguin Group Ireland, 25 St. Stephen's Green, Dublin 2, Ireland (a division of Penguin Books Ltd.)
Penguin Group (Australia), 250 Camberwell Road, Camberwell, Victoria 3124, Australia
(a division of Pearson Australia Group Pty. Ltd.)
Penguin Books India Pvt. Ltd., 11 Community Centre, Panchsheel Park, New Delhi—110 017, India
Penguin Group (NZ), 67 Apollo Drive, Rosedale, Auckland 0632, New Zealand
(a division of Pearson New Zealand Ltd.)
Penguin Books (South Africa) (Pty.) Ltd., 24 Sturdee Avenue, Rosebank, Johannesburg 2196, South Africa

Penguin Books Ltd., Registered Offices: 80 Strand, London WC2R 0RL, England

This book is an original publication of The Berkley Publishing Group.

Endpaper design by Diana Kolsky; images by Shutterstock.

FIRST EDITION: September 2011

Library of Congress Cataloging-in-Publication Data

Feehan, Christine.
Dark predator : a Carpathian novel / Christine Feehan.—1st ed.
p. cm.
ISBN 978-0-425-24197-4
1. Vampires—Fiction. 2. South America—Fiction. I. Title.
PS3606.E36D387 2011
813'.6—dc22 2011016465

PRINTED IN THE UNITED STATES OF AMERICA

10 9 8 7 6 5 4 3 2 1

For Brandy Jones,
a small token to make up for the bitter disappointment
of having such a mean boss!
I still can't believe he wouldn't let you
come see me when I was visiting your home.
No worries, I have retaliated and
he has gotten his just reward.
Read on! (But remember all characters are truly fictional!)

For My Readers

Be sure to go to www.christinefeehan.com/members/ to sign up for my PRIVATE book announcement list and download the FREE ebook of *Dark Desserts*. Join my community and get firsthand news, enter the book discussions, ask your questions and chat with me. Please feel free to email me at Christine@christinefeehan.com. I would love to hear from you.

Acknowledgments

Thank you so much to Renee Martinez and Denise Tucker for making the trip down the Amazon and bringing me the research, footage and pictures of the region I needed. I appreciate their guides so much—thank you for answering all my questions and for continuing to do so as I've written this book. A special thanks to their guide Victor Ramirez for answering all the questions we needed on making canoes and the names of trees, flowers and wildlife. You were an amazing help. Thank you to Dr. Chris Tong for all your help; you are truly wonderful! And to Brian Feehan for your wonderful imagination and steadfast dedication to getting it all right. Thanks to Cheryl Wilson and Kathie Firzlaff for the encouragement when I was faltering, and of course to Domini! Special thanks to Lea Eldridge for her contribution to the Jr. Diabetes auction. She won the bid for a character in a book. Thank you so much, Lea, for your generosity.

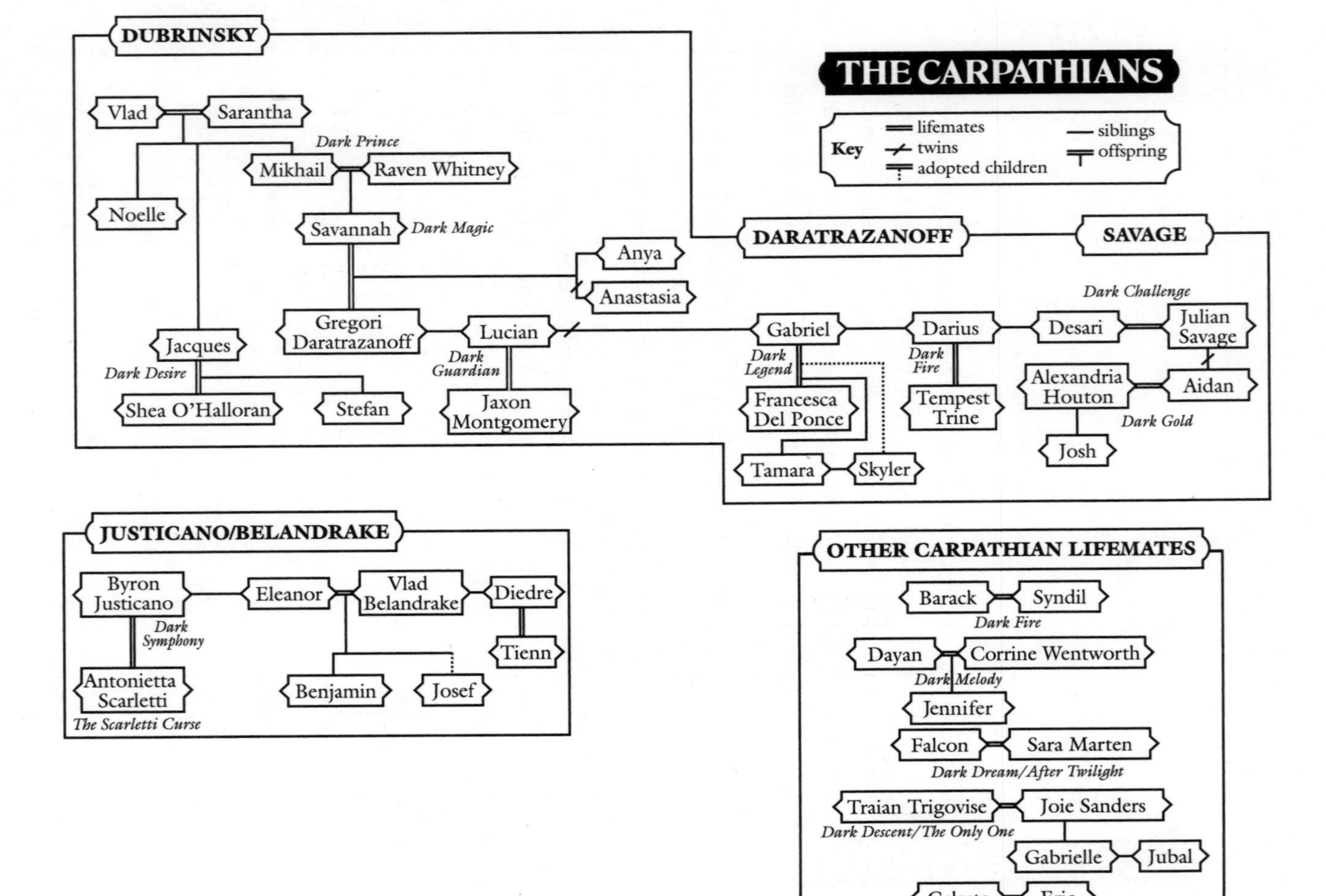

THE CARPATHIANS
Key
lifemates
twins
adopted children
siblings
offspring
DUBRINSKY
Vlad
Sarantha
Dark Prince
Mikhail
Raven Whitney
Noelle
Savannah
Dark Magic
Anya
Anastasia
Gregori Daratrazanoff
Lucian
Jacques
Dark Desire
Dark Guardian
Shea O'Halloran
Stefan
Jaxon Montgomery
DARATRAZANOFF
SAVAGE
Dark Challenge
Gabriel
Darius
Desari
Julian Savage
Dark Legend
Dark Fire
Francesca Del Ponce
Tempest Trine
Alexandria Houton
Aidan
Dark Gold
Josh
Tamara
Skyler
JUSTICANO/BELANDRAKE
Byron Justicano
Eleanor
Vlad Belandrake
Diedre
Dark Symphony
Tienn
Antonietta Scarletti
Benjamin
Josef
The Scarletti Curse
OTHER CARPATHIAN LIFEMATES
Barack
Syndil
Dark Fire
Dayan
Corrine Wentworth
Dark Melody
Jennifer
Falcon
Sara Marten
Dark Dream/After Twilight
Traian Trigovise
Joie Sanders
Dark Descent/The Only One
Gabrielle
Jubal
Celeste
Eric

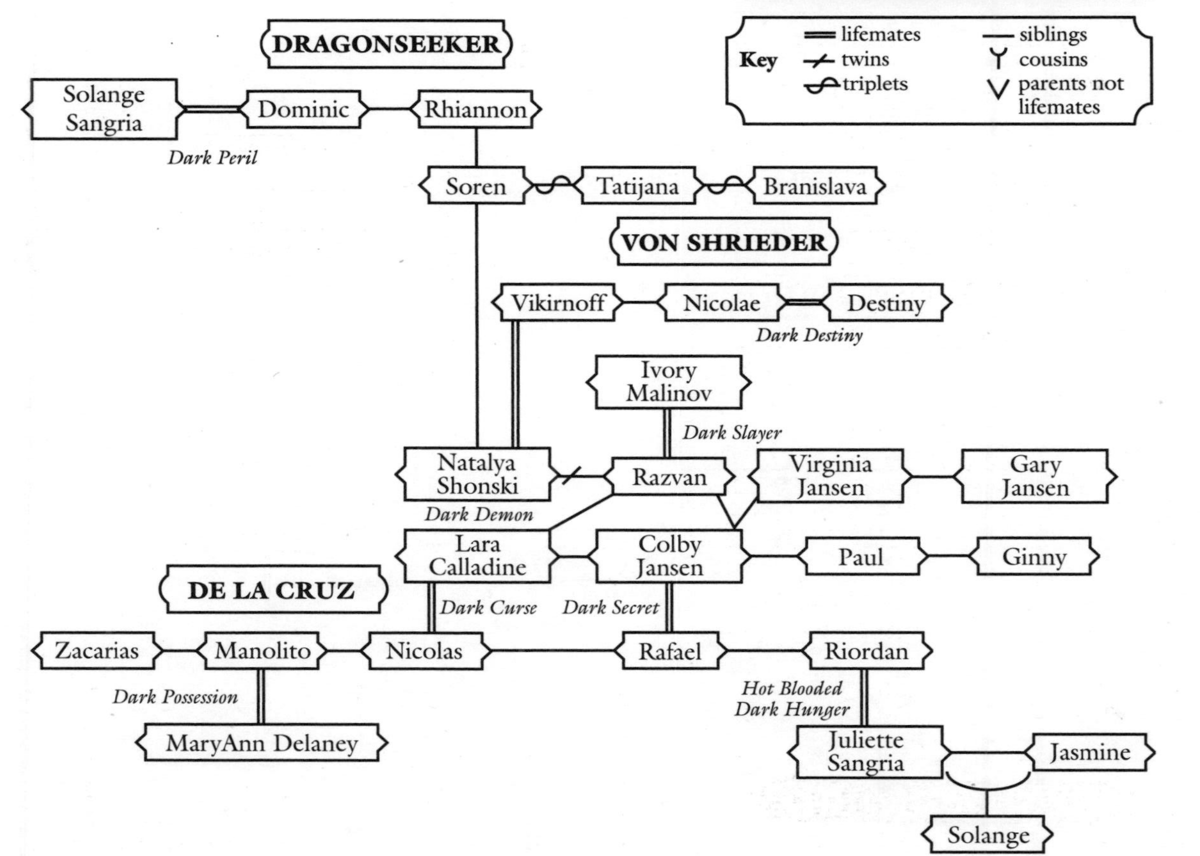
THE CARPATHIANS
Key
lifemates
twins
triplets
siblings
cousins
parents not lifemates
DRAGONSEEKER
Solange Sangria
Dominic
Rhiannon
Dark Peril
Soren
Tatijana
Branislava
VON SHRIEDER
Vikirnoff
Nicolae
Destiny
Dark Destiny
Ivory Malinov
Dark Slayer
Natalya Shonski
Razvan
Virginia Jansen
Gary Jansen
Dark Demon
Lara Calladine
Colby Jansen
Paul
Ginny
DE LA CRUZ
Dark Curse
Dark Secret
Zacarias
Manolito
Nicolas
Rafael
Riordan
Dark Possession
Hot Blooded
Dark Hunger
MaryAnn Delaney
Juliette Sangria
Jasmine
Solange

Dark Predator

I

Smoke burned his lungs. It rose around him in bellowing waves, fed by the numerous fires in the surrounding rain forest. It had been a long, hard-fought battle, but it was over, and he was done. Most of the main house was gone, but they'd managed to save the homes of the people who served them. Few lives were lost, but each one was mourned—but not by him. He stared at the flames with hollow eyes. He felt nothing. He looked on the faces of the dead, honorable men who had served his family well, saw their weeping widows and their crying children and he felt—nothing.

Zacarias De La Cruz paused for just a moment surveying the battlefield. Where before the rain forest had been lush, trees rising to the clouds, home to wildlife, there were now flames reaching to the heavens and black smoke staining the sky. The scent of blood was overwhelming; the dead, mangled bodies staring with sightless eyes at the dark sky. The vision didn't move him. He surveyed it all—as if from a distance—with a pitiless gaze.

It didn't matter where, or which century, the scene was always the same, and over the long, dark years, he'd seen so many battlefields he'd lost count. So much death. So much brutality. So much killing. So much destruction. And he was always right in the midst of it, a whirling, dark predator, merciless, ruthless and implacable.

Blood and death were stamped into his very bones. He'd executed so many enemies of his people over hundreds of centuries, he didn't know how to exist without the hunt—or the kill. There was no other way of life for him. He was pure predator and he'd recognized that fact a long time ago—as did anyone who dared to come close to him.

He was a legendary Carpathian hunter, from a species of people nearly extinct, living in a modern world, holding to the old ways of honor and duty. His kind ruled the night, slept during the day and needed blood to survive. Nearly immortal, they lived long, lonely existences, color and emotion fading until only honor held them to their chosen path of looking for the one woman who could complete them and restore both color and emotion. Many gave up, killed while feeding to feel the rush—just to feel something—becoming the vilest, most dangerous creature known—the vampire. Every bit as brutal and violent as the undead, Zacarias De La Cruz was a master at hunting them.

Blood ran steadily from numerous wounds, and its poisonous acid burned all the way to his bones, but he felt calm steal into him as he turned and walked quietly away. Fires raged, but his brothers could put them out. The acid blood from the vampire attack soaked into the groaning, protesting earth, but again, his brothers would seek that vile poison out and eradicate it.

His stark, brutal journey was over. Finally. Well over a thousand years of living in an empty, gray world, he had accomplished everything he had set out to do. His brothers were safeguarded. They each had a woman who completed them. They were happy and healthy, and he had eliminated the worst threat to them. By the time their enemies grew in numbers again, his brothers would be even stronger. They no longer needed his direction or protection. He was free.

"Zacarias! You're in need of healing. Of blood."

It was a feminine voice. Solange, lifemate to Dominic, his oldest friend, with her pure royal blood, she would change their lives for all time. He was too damned old, too set in his ways and oh, so tired, to ever make the kind of changes to continue living in this century. He had become as obsolete as the medieval warriors of long ago. The taste of freedom was metallic, coppery, his blood flowing, the very essence of life.

"Zacarias, please." There was a catch in her voice that should have affected him—but it didn't. He didn't feel as the others could. There was no swaying him with pity or love or gentleness. He had no kinder, gentler side. He was a killer. And his time was over.

Solange's blood was an incredible gift to their people; he recognized that even as he rejected it. Drinking it gave Carpathians the ability to walk in the sun. Carpathians were vulnerable during the hours of daylight—especially him. The more the predator, the more the killer, the more the sunlight was an enemy. He was considered by most of his people to be the Carpathian warrior who walked the edge of darkness, and he knew it was true. Solange's blood had given him that last and final reason to free him from his dark existence.

Zacarias drew in another lungful of smoky air and continued walking away from them all without looking back or acknowledging Solange's offer. He heard his brothers calling to him in alarm, but he kept walking, picking up his pace. Freedom was far away and he had to get there. He had known, as he'd ripped out the heart of the last of the attacking vampires trying to destroy his family, that there was only one place he wanted to go. It made no sense, but that didn't matter. He was going.

"Zacarias, stop."

He looked up as his brothers dropped from the sky, forming a solid wall in front of him. All four of them. Riordan, the youngest. Manolito, Nicolas and Rafael. They were good men and he could almost feel his love for them—so elusive—just out of reach. They blocked his way, stopping him from his goal, and no one, nothing—ever—was allowed to get between him and what he wanted. A snarl rumbled in his chest. The ground shook beneath their feet. They exchanged an uneasy glance, fear shimmering in their eyes.

That look of such intense fear of their own brother should have given him pause, but he felt—nothing. He had taught these four men their fighting skills, survival skills. He had fought beside them for centuries. Looked after them. Led them. Once even had memories of love for them. Now that he had shrugged off the mantle of responsibility—there was nothing. Not even those faint memories to sustain him. He couldn't remember love or laughter. Only death and killing.

"Move." One word. An order. He expected them to obey as everyone obeyed him. He had acquired wealth beyond imagining in his long years of living and in the last few centuries he had not once had to buy his way into or out of something. One word from him was all it took and the world trembled and stepped aside for his wishes.

Reluctantly, far too slow for his liking, they parted to allow him to stride through.

"Do not do this, Zacarias," Nicolas said. "Don't go."

"At least heal your wounds," Rafael added.

"And feed," Manolito pressured. "You need to feed."

He whirled around and they fell back, fear sliding to terror in their eyes—and he knew they had reason to be afraid. The centuries had shaped him—honed him into a violent, brutal predator—a killing machine. There were few to equal him in the world. And he walked the edge of madness. His brothers were great hunters, but killing him would require their considerable skills and no hesitation. They all had lifemates. They all had emotions. They all loved him. He felt nothing and he had the advantage.

He had already dismissed them, left their world, the moment he'd turned his back and allowed himself the freedom to let go of his responsibilities. Yet their faces, carved with deep lines of sorrow stayed him for a moment.

What would it be like to feel sorrow so deeply? To feel love? To *feel.* In the old days, he would have touched their minds and shared with them, but since they had lifemates, he didn't dare take the chance of tainting one of them with the darkness in him. His soul was not just in pieces. He had killed too often, distanced himself from all he had held dear in order to better protect those he had loved. When had he reached the point that he could no longer safely touch their minds and share their memories? It had been so long ago he could no longer remember.

"Zacarias, do not do this," Riordan pleaded, his face twisted with that same deep sorrow that was on each of his brothers' faces.

They had been his responsibility for far too long, and he couldn't just walk away without giving them something. He stood there a moment, utterly alone, his head up, eyes blazing, long hair flowing around him while blood dripped steadily down his chest and thighs. "I give you my word that you will not have to hunt me."

It was all he had for them. His word that he would not turn vampire. He could rest and he was seeking that final rest in his own way. He turned away from them—from the comprehension and relief on their faces—and once again started his journey. He had far to go if he was to get to his destination before dawn.

"Zacarias," Nicolas called. "Where do you go?"

The question gave him pause. Where was he going? The compulsion was strong—one impossible to ignore. He actually slowed his pace. Where did he go? Why was the need so strong in him, when he felt nothing? But there was *something*, a dark force driving him.

"*Susu*—home." He whispered the word. His voice carried on the wind, that low tone resonating in the very earth beneath his feet. "I am going home."

"This is your home," Nicolas stated firmly. "If you seek rest, we will respect your decision, but stay here with us. With your family. This is your home," he reiterated.

Zacarias shook his head. He was driven to leave Brazil. He needed to be somewhere else and he had to go now, while there was still time. Eyes as red as the flames, soul as black as the smoke, he shifted, reaching for the form of the great harpy eagle.

Are you going to the Carpathian Mountains? Nicolas demanded through their telepathic link. *I will travel with you.*

No. I go home where I belong—alone. I must do this thing alone.

Nicolas sent him warmth, wrapped him up in it. *Kolasz arwa-arvoval*—may you die with honor. There was sorrow in his voice, in his heart, but Zacarias, while he recognized it, couldn't echo the feeling, not even a small tinge.

Rafael spoke softly in his mind. *Arwa-arvo olen isäntä, ekäm*—honor keep you, my brother.

Kulkesz arwa-arvoval, ekäm—walk with honor, my brother, Manolito added.

Arwa-arvo olen gæidnod susu, ekäm—honor guide you home, my brother, Riordan said.

It had been a long time since he'd heard the native tongue of his people. They spoke the languages and dialects of wherever they were. They'd taken names as they'd moved from country to country, even a surname, when Carpathians never had such names. His world had altered so much over time. Centuries of transformation, always adapting to fit in, and yet never really changing when his world was all about death. At long last he was going home.

That simple statement meant nothing—and everything. He hadn't had a home in well over a thousand years. He was one of the oldest, certainly one of the deadliest. Men like him had no home. Few welcomed him to their fire, let alone their hearth. So what was *home*? Why had he used that word?

His family had established ranches in the countries they patrolled throughout the Amazon and the other rivers that fed it. Their range was spread out and covered thousands of miles, making it difficult to patrol, but having established a relationship with several human families, the various homes were always prepared for their coming. He was going to one such home and he had to cover the long miles before dawn.

Their Peruvian ranch was situated on the edge of the rain forest, a few miles away from where the rivers formed a Y and dumped into the Amazon. Even that area was slowly changing over the years. His family had appeared to come into the area with the Spaniards, made up names, uncaring how they sounded as it mattered little to Carpathians what they were called by others, not knowing they would spend centuries in the area—that it would become more familiar to them than their homeland.

Zacarias looked down at the canopy of the rain forest as he flew. It, too, was disappearing, a slow, steady encroachment he didn't understand. There were so many things about modern times he didn't understand—and really—what did it matter? It was no longer his world or his problem. The compulsion driving him puzzled him more than the answers for the vanishing environments. Little aroused his curiosity, yet this overwhelming drive to return to a place he'd been a few times was disturbing on some level. Because the drive was a need and he didn't have needs. It was overwhelming and nothing overwhelmed him.

Small droplets of blood fell into the misty clouds surrounding the emergents, the scattered trees rising above the canopy itself. Beneath him, he could feel the fear of the animals as he passed. Below him a band of Dourouncoulis, very small night monkeys, leaped and performed amazing acrobatics in the middle layers of branches as he passed overhead. Some fed on fruit and insects while others watched for predators. Normally they would screech an alarm as soon as the harpy eagle was spotted, yet as he passed over the family of monkeys they went completely and eerily silent.

He knew it wasn't the threat of the large bird flying overhead that caused the forest to go so still. The harpy eagle sat still in the branches, often for long hours at a time and waited for the right meal. He would rocket down with shocking speed and snatch a sloth or monkey right off the trees, but he didn't, as a rule, hunt in flight. The mammals hid, but snakes lifted their heads at his passing. Hundreds of dinner-plate-sized spiders crawled along branches, migrating in the direction he flew. Insects rose by the thousands at his passing.

Zacarias was used to the signs marking the darkness in him. Even as a young Carpathian, he had been different. His fighting ability was natural, bred into him, almost imprinted before birth, his reflexes fast, his brain working quickly. He had the ability to assess a situation with lightning speed and come up with a battle plan instantly. He killed without hesitation, even in his early days, and his illusions were nearly impossible to detect.

Darkness went deep, a shadow on his soul long before he'd lost his emotions and color—and he'd lost both far earlier than others his age. He questioned everything. Everyone. But his loyalty to his prince and his people was unswerving and that had earned him the undying hatred of his best friend.

He flew with strong wings, fast through the night, ignoring the wounds and his need of blood. As he crossed the border and dropped lower into the canopy, he felt the pull of the compulsion grow. He needed to be on his Peruvian ranch. He simply—needed. The forest stretched out under him, a dark tangle of trees and flowers, the air heavy with moisture. Mosses and vines hung like long, flowing beards, reaching nearly to the watery pools, streams and creeks. Tangled ferns vied for space, creeping over long exposed roots on the dark floor beneath him.

The harpy eagle dropped through branches covered with flowers, liana and all kinds of insects hidden in the jumble of greenery. Far below him he heard the soft call of a tree frog calling a mate and then a coarser, much more grating sound adding to the chorus. An almost electronic trilling joined the symphony as thousands of different voices rose to a crescendo abruptly going silent in unnatural, spine-chilling alarm as the predator approached, then passed overhead.

The dark night sky turned to a soft dove gray as dawn crept in, stealing away the night's powerful reign. The harpy eagle dropped from the canopy spiraling down into the clearing where the ranch house was situated. With his sharp vision he could see the river running like a thick ribbon dividing the land. Gentle slopes gave way to steep ridges, deep ravines cutting through the forest. Trees and vegetation snaked across the rocky ground, a dark tangle of growth determined to reclaim what had been taken.

Neat fences bisected the slopes and as the bird flew over the ravines and valley, hundreds of cattle dotted the grasslands. As the shadow of the bird passed over them, they lifted their heads in agitation, trembling, knocking into one another as they turned back and forth trying to find the danger they scented.

The eagle flew over several fields and at least an acre of gardens, all tended well as Zacarias had come to expect from the extended family who served him. Everything was neat, kept in meticulous repair, every chore done to their best ability. Pastures and fields gave way to the large corrals where the horses whirled and tossed their heads uneasily as he flew over them. Below him, the ranch was laid out before him like a perfect picture he could not appreciate.

As he approached the stable, a rush of heat slid through his veins. Deep inside the body of the bird, where he should have felt nothing at all, his heart gave an unfamiliar stutter. The strange fluttering nearly knocked him from the sky. Naturally wary, Zacarias didn't trust what he didn't understand. What could possibly send heat rushing through his very veins? He was exhausted from the long battle, the long flight, and the loss of blood. Hunger throbbed with each beat of his heart, clawing and raking for supremacy. Pain from the wounds he hadn't bothered to heal ripped through him like an ever present jackhammer, drilling through his very bones.

Weeks earlier, he had been so close to turning vampire, the desire for relief from emptiness so strong in him, the blackness of his soul without the least relief, that his reaction now made no sense. He was in worse shape. Starving for blood. More kills staining his soul. Yet there was that strange reaction in the vicinity of his heart, that heat pulsing through his veins in anticipation. A trick then? A lure set by a vampire? What was he missing?

The harpy eagle slowly folded his seven-foot wingspan, talons as large as grizzly bear's claws digging deep into the roof of the stable while the feathers at the top of his head formed a large crest. The great predator went completely still, sharp eyes moving over the terrain below. He had amazing vision within the harpy's body and his hearing was aided even further by the focusing of sound waves by the smaller feathers forming his facial disk.

The horses in the corral a short distance away reacted to his presence, tossing heads, moving restlessly and bunching together tightly. Several whinnied in distress. A woman emerged from the stable beneath him, a large horse following her. Immediately his gaze fixated on her. Her hair was long, to her waist, pulled back in a braid that was as thick as his wrist. The long rope of hair attracted his gaze. When she moved, the woven strands gleamed like spun silk.

Zacarias saw in the shadowy colors of gray and dull white for centuries. Her braid was fascinating because it was a true black. He was nearly mesmerized by the long, dark hair, the strands shimmering even without the sun. Somewhere in the vicinity of what would have been his belly, his stomach gave a slow somersaulting roll. In a world where everything was the same and nothing moved him, that small sensation amounted to a bomb going off. For a moment he lost his breath, shaken by the strange phenomenon.

The horse following the woman wore no saddle or bridle and once he emerged from the building, he began to dance with restless unease, head tossing, eyes rolling as he circled the woman. The horses were purebred Peruvian Paso, a breed renowned not only for their natural gaits, but for temperament as well. The woman glanced toward the horses running in circles in the corral—it was unusual for them to be nervous—and then lifted a calming hand to the horse half rearing so close to her. She laid her hand on his neck and looked up at harpy eagle sitting so still on the roof.

Those dark chocolate eyes penetrated right through the feathers and bones of the eagle, straight to Zacarias. He felt the impact like an arrow through his heart. *Marguarita*. Even from the distance he could see the scars at her throat where the vampire had torn out her vocal cords because she refused to give up Zacarias's resting place to the undead. She'd once been a carefree young woman, or he'd imagined her to be, but now, someone was using her to trap him.

It all made sense now. The compulsion to come to this place, to think of it as home. Was she possessed by a vampire? Only a master could weave and hold such a spell together—only a master like his old enemies, the Malinov brothers. The five brothers had grown up with him. They'd fought alongside one another for nearly five hundred years. His friends had chosen to be vampire, to give up their souls in their thirst for power. They had chosen to bring together the undead in a conspiracy against the prince and the Carpathian people.

Dominic had uncovered the latest plot and stayed to help defend the De La Cruz properties in Brazil. Knowing that the vampires would test their plan of attack on the ranch before striking at the prince, Zacarias had been waiting for them. No vampire had escaped alive. There were none to return to tell the Malinovs their plan had failed.

Zacarias knew the Malinovs' rage and their bitter, unrelenting hatred of him and his brothers. Yes, this very well could be the payback for the defeat of the Malinov army, but how would they have gotten here ahead of him? That didn't make sense, either.

The harpy eagle shook his head as if ridding himself of unsettling thoughts. No, it was impossible for them to get together another attack this soon. In any case, horses barely tolerated his presence, they would never allow evil to touch them and Marguarita was stroking the powerful neck. There was no possession.

Zacarias wondered at the strange sensation in his chest. Almost relief. He didn't want to have to kill her, not when she'd nearly sacrificed her life for him once. Yet he was incapable of feeling, of any emotion whatsoever. Why did he have these extraordinary stirrings in his body and mind since returning to this place? None of it made sense. He doubled his vigilance, not trusting the unfamiliar.

Warmth seeped into the bird's brain, a soothing impression of a friendly greeting. The harpy eagle reacted, his head cocking to one side, his eyes locked with the woman's. Zacarias felt the bird reaching for her. She was subtle in her touch, so light it was barely there, but she wielded a powerful gift. Even the great predator of the rain forest slipped under her spell. He felt his own mind and body reacting, relaxing, tension slipping away. She had reached past the bird and found his most animalistic, wild nature.

Startled, he pulled back, withdrawing deeper into the body of the eagle, all the while watching her closely as she turned her attention on calming the horses. It didn't take her long to soothe them to the point that they stood quietly, but they didn't stop watching the eagle, aware there was a worse predator buried deep inside the bird.

Marguarita circled the horse's neck and leaped. It was an easy, practiced motion, she seemed to flow through the air, all grace as she slipped onto the animal's back. Immediately the horse reared, more, he was certain, due to his presence than because the girl had gone astride him. Zacarias's breath caught in his throat. His heart accelerated into a thunderous drum—another peculiar phenomenon. The great eagle spread his wings almost before Zacarias gave the order. The movement was more instinctive than thought out, an immediate need to wrench the woman to safety. Marguarita leaned over the horse's neck in a silent command and horse and rider flowed over the ground in perfect unison.

Once satisfied that she was not in danger, Zacarias folded his wings and watched, his talons digging deeper into the roof as the horse sailed over a fence and lengthened his stride. She sat up straight, the elegant gait of the animal a harmonic and rhythmic tapping, so gentle that his center of gravity, where Marguarita sat, was almost stationary.

Intrigued, Zacarias touched the horse's mind. She controlled the animal—yet she didn't. The horse accepted her, wanted to please her—enjoyed the melding of their two spirits. Marguarita wove her spell over the animal effortlessly, holding him to her through her gift—a deep connection with creatures. She didn't appear to realize she did anything special; she simply was enjoying the early-dawn ride—just as the horse was.

This, then, was the reason for the strange stirrings in his mind and body. Her gift. She touched all things wild, and he was as untamed as it got. There was no threat of the undead, only this young woman with her innocence and light. She must have sent the Paso another command, because the animal switched gaits to a graceful, flowing movement, rolling his forelegs from the shoulder toward the outside as he strode forward. The horse's head was up proudly, his mane flying, his eyes bright and exuberance in his every move.

It was a perfect moment—the perfect moment to end his life. She was—beautiful. Free. Flowing over the ground like cool water. Everything that he'd fought for—everything he'd never been. The harpy eagle spread his wings and spiraled overhead, watching horse and rider as they covered ground fast yet unbelievably smooth.

All his life, even when soldiers fought on horseback, even in his youth, there had been far too much predator in him to allow a horse to carry him on his back. In those days he'd tried everything—excluding mind control—to enable him to ride, but no horse could take it. They shuddered and trembled beneath him, even when he sought to calm them.

Marguarita sailed effortlessly over fences, with no bridle or saddle, horse and rider exuding joy. He followed them as the pair rushed over the uneven ground, the horse's smooth gait making it look as if they were floating. Marguarita threw both hands into the air as they cleared a fence, holding on to the horse with her knees and guiding it with her mind.

The Paso switched his gait smoothly as they raced across the field and he turned in a wide circle again. Marguarita gave the eagle a friendly wave and once again, warmth and joy washed over and through Zacarias. He'd given her his blood—but he'd never taken hers. His mouth watered. His teeth filled his mouth and hunger burst through him, radiating need through every cell. He banked the bird abruptly and headed back for the stable. He refused to take any chances with his self-control.

Once before he'd been far too close to giving up what little remained of his soul. He would honor his word to his brothers. No Carpathian would ever have to risk his life to hunt down Zacarias De La Cruz. He *chose* his fate, and he chose to save his honor. He would go to the dawn, head unbent, welcoming his death. His last vision would be of the returning woman—of young Marguarita with light spilling from inside of her as she flowed across the ground on the back of a beautiful horse. He would take the sight of her doing the very thing of his boyhood dreams—riding as one with the animal—with him to his death.

The harpy eagle landed gracefully on the ground beside the stable. Ignoring the terrified horses in the corral attached to the structure, he shifted back to his human form. He was a big man, all muscle, with long flowing hair. Deep lines carved his face. Some called him brutishly handsome. Some said his mouth was both sensual and cruel. Most said he was terrifying. Right at that moment, he felt utterly tired—so weary he could barely manage to look around for a place to sit. He wanted to drop right there in the cool grass.

He forced his body to move as he looked for a convenient place to sit and watch the sun come up over the forest. Very slowly he sank down into the soft soil, uncaring that water seeped into his clothes from the morning dew. He didn't bother to regulate his temperature any more than he had healed his wounds. There was contentment in making his decision. For the first time in his existence he was without the weight of responsibility. He drew up his knees, folded his hands and rested his chin on the small platform he'd made so he could see horse and rider as the Paso went smoothly through the natural gaits that made him so famous.

He felt the sun prickling his skin, but it wasn't the terrible sensation he'd felt his entire life. Solange had given him her blood on two occasions to save him from turning vampire. He had taken great care to avoid her blood once he realized he could spend the dawn hours out in the open without repercussions. Others of his kind could see the dawn and there were some who could actually walk on the morning streets without aid from Solange, but with his soul so dark, he had long ago joined the vampires in their need to hide from even early morning sunlight.

He drank in the sight of Marguarita, as close to happy as a man without emotions might get. She'd traded her voice for his life. He had rewarded her loyalty by saving her life and giving instructions that she be given everything she wanted on the ranch. There were no jewels bedecking her fingers or throat. She wore simple clothes. But she lived for the horses, even he could see that. He'd given her—life. And in some strange way, she'd given him—freedom.

He was unaware of the passing of time. Insects remained silent. The horses stopped circling and crowded as far from him as possible, in a corner of the corral, bunched tightly together, shifting and stamping restlessly, barely able to tolerate his presence. Slowly his body reacted to the rising sun with the strange leaden affliction of his species.

Zacarias stretched out on the ground, face up, head turned toward the sight of Marguarita as she came toward him. Now the sunlight penetrated his clothing and touched his skin like a million tiny needles piercing his flesh. Tiny towers of smoke began to rise from his body as the burning began. He couldn't move, but he wouldn't have. She was beautiful. Fresh. Innocent. Contentment settled deep in spite of the increasing pain. He kept his eyes open, wanting—no, needing the sight of Marguarita riding to be in his heart when he entered his next life.

Perhaps he was watching too closely, his gaze drawing hers, or maybe the strange behavior of the animals and insects alerted her, but she turned her head and her gaze met his. He saw her gasp and the sudden tightening of her knees on the horse, urging him forward.

No! Stay back. Do not come near me. Put your horse away and go.

If there was a small hesitation indicating the words had been forced into her mind, he didn't catch it. The horse sailed over the fence and when he began dancing in fear, she halted the animal and leaped off. The Paso pawed the ground and she sent the horse a dark scowl, then waved her hand toward the corral. At once the Peruvian Paso ran toward the fence, cleared it and joined the other horses in the far corner.

Marguarita approached him cautiously, the way she might a cornered, feral animal, one hand outstretched, palm toward him, her lips moving soundlessly as if she hadn't quite gotten used to the fact that she couldn't speak. Warmth flooded his mind, a soothing balm that told him she meant no harm.

He struggled to move, but the curse of the sun was upon him. She moved closer, her shadow looming over him, her body blocking the rising sun. Her eyes were dark and rich, looking down at him with a mixture of outright fear and alarm for him.

Leave me. Go now. He pushed the order into her head, sending the impression of a snarl, of an absolute command.

Marguarita crouched beside him, touching his smoking arm, frowning in concern and then whipping her hand away, blowing on the tips of her fingers.

This is my choice. Leave me to die. He had no idea whether his commands were penetrating. She didn't blink or look at him as if she heard him.

She'd been trained from birth to obey the members of his family. Surely she wouldn't defy him. She knew how easily a Carpathian hunter close to the edge of madness could become vampire. The undead had torn out her throat. He felt her hand tremble against the heat of his arm. She had to have burned her fingers against his skin. He focused on her and pushed at her mind with a compulsion to leave him. She had too much compassion in her, too much daring to disobey one as powerful as him.

His compulsion fell against a mind he could barely understand. It wasn't as if he found barriers—it was as though his techniques simply dissipated like smoke.

She stripped her short, soft jacket from her body and threw it over his head, covering his face and eyes. He felt her take his wrist and begin to pull him across the wet pasture. In his wake the blades of grass turned brown. He heard the breath hiss from her lungs and knew her hand was burned, but she didn't stop.

For the first time in the long centuries a deep-seated rage coiled in his belly and smoldered there, that someone dared defy his direct order. She had no right. She knew better. *No one ever defied him*—certainly not a human, and definitely not a *woman*. And not one of his own servants from a family that had been given every protection and wealth beyond imagining.

He had chosen death. He had prepared himself. Was content with his decision—embraced his choice. This was the worst kind of betrayal.

You will regret your disobedience, he vowed.

Marguarita ignored him—or didn't hear him. He honestly didn't know which, nor did he care. She would pay. Rocks dug into his back, and then the bump of wood as she managed to get him inside the stable. The sun stopped burning him alive, although the prickle of needles was still penetrating his skin.

Deftly she rolled him into a tarp, not removing the jacket from his face. She even tucked his arms over his chest before rolling him. He felt like a helpless baby. The indignity of it, the wrongness of her actions awakened something monstrous in him. He pulled back like the wild animal he was, waiting for his moment—and there would be a moment. She had known the fear of a vampire ripping out her throat but it would be nothing compared to the terror of Zacarias De La Cruz extracting vengeance for her sins.

She tried to hook the tarp to one of the horses, he knew by scent and by the drumming of hooves as the animal protested being in close proximity to him. He could have told her that no horse would allow his presence, but he held still, now just waiting the outcome of her mistake. The lack of horsepower didn't deter her. He heard the sound of her footsteps and then she began to pull the tarp herself. He knew she was alone by the sound of her breath bursting from her lungs in several repeated small gasps.

He found it significant that she didn't call for help. One yell—okay, she couldn't yell—but she must have a way to attract attention. The males working the ranch would come to her aid if she signaled them, but she must have known he would command them to allow his death—and they would obey. The fierce burning in his gut grew hotter, hot enough that for a few moments he thought he might have burned through his skin to his internal organs.

He could see nothing at all, but he felt each bump of the rocks and the fierce blaze of the sun as she dragged him from the stable to the ranch house. The searing heat was astonishingly effective, driving out all sane thoughts until he wanted to scream with agony. It came on gradually, a slow charring that seeped through skin and tissue to bone.

Zacarias tried to turn off the pain as he'd done for centuries, but the relentless burn of the sun was something he couldn't compartmentalize as he had so many other wounds. Even with the tarp wrapped around him, he felt the piercing blaze like burning arrows dotting his body. The heat boiled his blood and flames licked at his insides. He couldn't scream, or protest, or do anything but be dragged through the yard to what he presumed was the ranch house.

Marguarita huffed hard as she took his full weight up the two stairs leading inside. The moment he was within the thick, cool walls, she dropped the harness and rushed across the room. He could hear her pull the thick drapes into place, covering the windows.

You will suffer as no one else has ever suffered for your disobedience, he promised, thrusting the words into her brain.

Again he had the impression of words falling through cracks, as if she couldn't grasp what he'd said to her, but it didn't matter. He waited while she carefully unrolled the tarp and when the edges fell open, he snapped his dark eyes open and locked his gaze with hers. A long slow hiss, a promise of brutal retaliation, escaped and there would be no mistaking his meaning.

2

Marguarita Fernandez's breath caught in her throat and she sank back on her heels. What she was doing? She could envision screaming at herself to stop, deep inside where no one else could hear her—but as much as she told herself to let him die, as he demanded—she couldn't. There was no turning back now, and he surely would kill her. She dared to disobey a De La Cruz. Not just any De La Cruz, either. She had disobeyed the one the men whispered about. This was Zacarias, no one mentioned him unless they did so in terms of great respect—and even greater fear.

He had already warned her. His voice carved the words forever into her heart. *You will suffer as no one else has ever suffered for your disobedience.* He had warned her repeatedly to leave him. She just—*couldn't.* There was no way to explain that to him. She didn't know the reason herself. And she had no voice. No way to soothe him other than to treat him as she treated the wild creatures around her.

It took great courage and physical effort to wrench her gaze from the imprisonment of his. Pressing her lips together and ignoring her thundering heart, she yanked at his clothing to get the smoldering mess away from his skin. She gasped, nearly flinging herself backward when she saw his wounds. Congealed blood lay thick and ugly over the mottled burns. He'd been in a terrible battle, wounded repeatedly, and he hadn't taken care to heal the lacerations or, judging by his pale complexion, feed.

There was no time for niceties. He was probably being pursued. The undead would be in the ground as the sun rose, but they had all manner of foul servants. She had been drilled since birth on the readiness for assaults by the undead on their home. She ran through the hacienda, securing every window and door and distributing weapons for easy access before rushing to the kitchen to mix a solution to cool her master's burning skin.

She carried the pitcher back to the man lying on the floor. His gaze followed her, but he made no more effort to push fear into her mind. Maybe because she was already so filled with terror there was no room for anything more. Still, his eyes were ferocious with red flames, and a promise of retaliation. She avoided looking into those eyes, a little afraid he could somehow control her and she wouldn't—*couldn't*—step aside and allow him to die. Every cell in her body demanded she save his life—even at the cost of her own.

Her hand trembled as she began to sponge the cooling solution over his body. She knew it had to sting the gaping lacerations, but she had to stop the burn before she could attend his other wounds. She tried very hard not to notice his defined muscle and impressive male equipment. She pretended he was a wild animal, and perhaps he really was, but it was difficult to view him that way when she was stroking the soft washcloth over his very masculine body.

Marguarita was used to being in the company of men. She'd worked on the ranch for as long as she could remember, but none had a body like this. Zacarias was all hard muscle, broad shoulders and narrow hips. He had a fearsome reputation. Few ever saw him in the flesh, but the rumors were terrible. Cesaro Santos, the *capataz* of the ranch, had told her when she'd been attacked by the vampire that Zacarias had saved her life, but she'd never met him, spoken with him or even caught sight of him before. Still, she knew with absolute certainty that this man was the eldest of the De La Cruz brothers and the master of all the ranches.

She carefully cleaned his wounds, all the while soothing him as she would one of her wild creatures, unaware if it helped or not. His body was totally dead, although his eyes remained wide open and fixed on her face. He needed blood. He was far too pale and it was evident from his wounds that he'd lost too much. She could hear her heart begin to accelerate, but she'd come this far already. What would going further matter? He'd already condemned her for her actions.

Taking a breath, she drew the knife from its sheath at her waist and before she could think too much about what she was doing, she sliced her wrist. If she could have screamed aloud, she would have, but even opening her mouth wide, no sound emerged. She positioned her wrist over the master's mouth, allowing her own blood to drip steadily. Silently she demanded he swallow. He could do that much, she was certain of it. When there was no movement, she watched closely and realized his mouth seemed to absorb the blood, as if he was so starved his body took any sustenance it could get. It made sense. He was nearly immortal. His body had been designed to live on regardless of his wounds.

She gave him as much blood as she dared, maybe too much, because she felt a little dizzy when she finally pulled her wrist away and staggered to the bathroom to wrap a bandage around the wound. She had gone past fear and terror now, working on automatic pilot. No one would come into the house now that her father was dead. He had died trying to prevent the vampire from killing her just before Zacarias had arrived. The workers would recognize the signal—the doors and windows locked and covered with the heavy drapes—that a De La Cruz was in residence and must be protected, but not disturbed. Cesaro would put a close guard on the livestock and prepare the ranch for battle.

Marguarita opened all doors between where Zacarias's body lay and the master bedroom where she knew the chamber beneath the earth was situated. She struggled with moving the enormous bed out of the way as it covered the heavy trap door leading down to the darkened chamber beneath the house. She was sweating by the time she rushed back to Zacarias. Her wrist throbbed and burned and her legs felt like rubber.

It was hell dragging him on the tarp through the house. Thankfully, his eyes finally closed and all breath ceased. He appeared as if he were stone-cold dead. Although she knew the basic principles of Carpathian existence, it was still disconcerting to see him lie as if dead when she'd risked so much to save him. For a moment she was in danger of hyperventilating, a condition that often woke her from her nightmares after the undead's attack on her. She recognized panic and forced herself to breathe slowly and evenly while she yanked on the tarp, covering the floor inch by inch until she got to the trap door.

Marguarita bit her lower lip so hard she drew a tiny bead of blood. How in the world was she going to get him down the stairs? She hadn't thought beyond immersing him in the rich dark soil the De La Cruz brothers had brought from their homeland to put in their many resting places. If she called Cesaro to help he would ask questions she didn't dare answer.

With a shrug of her shoulders she went in front of him, pulling him down the stairs on the tarp. She kept his head from hitting each step, but his body thumped all the way down. Although his eyes were closed and his breathing seemed to have ceased, she was certain he was aware of what was happening to him because when she touched his mind with warmth, she felt as if she'd connected to that wild part of him in the way she did with animals. It wasn't as if she could talk as she had no voice, but she sent him the impression of sorrow, of being sorry. Of being afraid. She knew it wouldn't be enough to appease his rage, but it was all she had.

Once she got him on the ground, she began to dig. She wanted the hole deep enough to cover him so the earth could heal him. She could have gone to the tool shed for a shovel, but she didn't dare run into anyone. She didn't lie, not even with her sign language. She wasn't all that adept at it yet and few understood her, so mostly she wrote on paper. Her hands would shake and Cesaro would know something was wrong.

She dug with her hands. The soil was rich and fertile, a black loam abounding with minerals and nutrients. She knew it was so just from the feel of the dirt. It took most of the morning and she was sweating and covered in grime by the time she was satisfied with the depth of the hole. His body needed to be completely surrounded and covered by the soil if he was going to heal properly.

Marguarita dragged the tarp to the very edge of the hole, her stomach churning a little. It did feel as though she was trying to cover up a murder. She could add this day to her nightmares for certain. Crouching, she placed her hands firmly on his shoulder and hip and pushed. Fortunately, she was strong from handling horses since she was a child, but it was still a difficult task to roll him into his resting place.

Zacarias landed awkwardly on his side, like a rag doll—or a dead body. She pressed a dirty, trembling hand to her mouth, feeling limp herself. She rested for a few minutes before she began covering him with the dark soil. When he was completely buried, she sank to her knees beside him and allowed herself a few minutes to have a panic attack.

What had she done? The De La Cruz family made few demands on their people. Very few. Everyone who worked for them was wealthy by any standards. All owned their own lands adjacent to the De La Cruz lands, all because one of the family members had purchased it for them. Cousins, aunts, uncles—everyone related was taken care of. Fathers passed the legacy to their sons. Mothers to their daughters. All had obeyed until Marguarita. She'd disgraced her family name by her disobedience and she had no doubt that she would pay dearly.

She lifted her chin and forced herself to stand. She was a Fernandez, her father's daughter. She would not run from her crime but stay and face whatever Zacarias De La Cruz deemed fit for her punishment. A shudder went through her and icy fingers crept down her spine. He barely seemed human. Or Carpathian. He was terrifying.

She couldn't change what she'd done. She didn't understand it and put it down to her compassion for all things hurt, but that didn't explain why she'd defied him after he'd told her to allow his death. Why would he choose to burn in the sun? It was a horrible death, and how could he think that she could stand by and watch him burn?

He'd saved her life. She touched her mangled throat, stroking dirt-smeared fingers over the scars. Sometimes, at night, when she woke in a sweat, trying to scream but nothing would come out, she thought she had called to him to save her. She could hear the echo of his name faintly in her head, as if she'd managed just his name. Now he was here and he wasn't at all the fantasy figure she'd conjured up in her mind.

Zacarias frightened her in an elemental way, deep down in her very blood and bones. In her soul. She pressed a clenched fist over her heart while it beat frantically out of control. He was handsome, had a rock-hard body, seemed everything a woman might dream of, but his eyes . . . his face. He was terrifying and every girlhood fantasy she'd secretly harbored vanished on encountering him.

Marguarita climbed slowly out of the chamber, dusting every grain of dirt from her clothes and body. She couldn't leave tracks. If a vampire's puppet penetrated the ranch's defenses, there could be no trail leading to Zacarias's resting place. She lowered the trap door and again swept the floor and even washed it, afraid the scent of Zacarias's blood would be detected. It was extremely difficult to push the bed back into place, but she managed, smoothing out the covers carefully.

She refused to dwell on her behavior or the fear building insidiously in her mind. She had work to do and she would remove every single bit of evidence that Zacarias had been outside or inside. Because she desperately needed it, she made herself a cup of *mate de coca*, a tea made with coca leaves. She took her time, savoring the tea for the pick-me-up she needed to keep going.

Marguarita cleaned the entire house, every room, mopping and dusting and permeating the house with a strong cinnamon scent. She armed herself and went outside, following the trail of the tarp back to the stables, carefully removing all signs that something heavy had been dragged through the wet grass. Close to the stable where Zacarias had sat and then laid in preparation for death, she found some of the grass scorched. She very carefully removed every blade.

Exhausted, she had another cup of tea and then showered and changed her clothes again, meticulously washing and drying the outfit she'd been wearing, using perfumed soaps to remove and cover any lingering scent. When she was fully satisfied that she'd done all she could, she went out to help with the stock.

Cesaro spotted her as she came out of the stable on her favorite mare, Sparkle. He waved to her, his face set in grim lines.

"The oldest one has come, hasn't he?" he greeted as he rode up beside her.

Marguarita saw no reason to deny it. She'd signaled by closing the heavy drapes and one of the men had given him the word that a De La Cruz was in residence. It was the only time the drapes were pulled. She nodded her head.

"I knew it. The cattle and horses are uneasy in his presence. Perhaps you should go visit your aunt in Brazil."

She frowned in question.

Cesaro hesitated, clearly not wanting to appear disloyal. "He's difficult, Marguarita. Very different from the others."

She signed a question mark between them.

Cesaro sighed. "I don't know exactly what to tell you. I met him many years ago when I was a boy. He was the only man who frightened my father—frightened all the men on the ranch. And more recently, when we lost your father, when this . . ." He indicated her throat. "He had grown even worse."

She signed the question mark again.

Cesaro shrugged, obviously uncomfortable with the topic. He even glanced toward the main hacienda as if Zacarias might overhear them and—for all Marguarita knew—maybe he could.

"If animals bred as stock horses are terrified when he's around, that should tell you something, Marguarita. When he was here the last time, he saved your life, but he came close to taking mine." He sat for a moment in silence, and then shrugged again. "I would have given my life to save his, but still, there was something not right about him. Even his friend worried. It's best you go."

Marguarita turned the warning over and over in her mind. Had Zacarias tried to burn himself up in the sun because he was close to becoming something he didn't want to be? She ducked her head, unable to look Cesaro in the eye. The idea of running away to her aunt in Brazil was tempting, but she knew she couldn't. She set her shoulders and indicated the animals.

Cesaro sighed audibly. "You're a very stubborn young woman, Marguarita, but I am not your father and I can't order you to go."

She waved toward the horses, ignoring the fact that he was trying to make her feel guilty. She already had enough guilt going. In any case, she noticed that because she couldn't speak, some of the men were beginning to treat her almost as if she were deaf as well. And while annoying, that was somewhat to her advantage in such a male-oriented world.

"Yes, we could use your help settling the horses down. We have three mares close to giving birth and I don't want anything to go wrong. Go into the stable with them and see if you can get them to calm down."

It was highly unusual for a Peruvian Paso to be skittish about anything. They were bred for their calm temperament. Any horse showing signs of nerves wasn't bred. The horses from Hacienda De La Cruz were considered some of the best in the world and yet Zacarias had spooked them all, even their working horses.

She nodded her head, but she feared she'd made a very bad mistake, even as she sent a calming wave to the restless animals huddled in the far corner of the pasture. She gestured toward the sky and made a sign, pointing to her teeth, indicating a possible attack from vampires.

Cesaro understood. He was the best on the ranch at interpreting her strange gestures. "We're aware of the risk of an assault on the hacienda anytime one of the masters is in residence. Everyone is armed, the women and children are under cover—with the exception of you. The moment the horses settle, go into the house and lock it down."

She indicated that she already had done so and she touched the rifle, hand gun and knife she had on her. She was as ready for an attack as she could be, although the thought was nearly as terrifying as knowing she'd disobeyed Zacarias.

Cesaro nodded approvingly. Marguarita, like everyone on the ranch, had been taught to shoot at a very young age. He suddenly stiffened and indicated something over her shoulder, alarm on his face. "Your man has come courting again."

She pulled the pen and paper from her pocket. **He is certainly not my man. Why don't you like him?**

"He's your father's choice, not mine. A city man." There was a sneer in his voice. "He's smooth, but he knows nothing of ranch life. You would be better off with Ricco or my son, Julio." He leaned over his horse's neck, standing a bit in the stirrups. "He does not ring true for me. He looks down on us, even you. Ricco or Julio suit you more."

She loved Ricco, one of the men working the cattle; she'd known him for years. And she'd grown up with Julio. It was impossible not to think of him as her brother. She wanted to please Cesaro almost as much as she wanted to please her father.

He isn't pressing a serious courtship. Since the death of my father, he has only been kind.

Cesaro shrugged, the frown still on his face. "You can't bring him into the hacienda. Send him away, Marguarita."

She scowled at Cesaro. She knew her duty. She turned her mare back toward the stables, waving at Esteban Eldridge as he drove up to the corrals in his truck. She had no idea how the vehicle stayed as clean as it did. Esteban wore his wealth easily. He was a powerful figure, very attractive—at least he had been until she'd laid eyes on Zacarias. Even injured and burning, Zacarias exuded a tough, almost brutal handsomeness, although that seemed too insipid of a description. Zacarias dominated every room he was in. But Esteban didn't scare her, or threaten her in the deep elemental way the eldest De La Cruz did. And she knew when a man was seriously interested in her—Esteban wasn't. But she really enjoyed his sister's company.

Cesaro sat on his horse and watched her. She could feel his eyes burning into her and it made her upset that he would think she might betray their code of honor to an outsider. She ducked her head a little. She'd already betrayed their code, but not in the way he thought she might and no doubt he would know soon enough of her sins.

She swung off the mare, watching as Esteban strode toward her. He made a striking figure as he covered the ground in long purposeful strides. Her father had introduced them and, clearly, Esteban Eldridge was her father's choice for her. He'd acted as if he was courting her before the vampire attack, but he had never been truly serious. Esteban obviously liked to have fun and he was a city boy. Cesaro was correct when he'd said Esteban looked down on the ranch workers, barely acknowledging them. How could she fall in love with a man like that?

He had been kind after her father died, showing up often with his sister, Lea, although after her "accident" that left her without the ability to speak, he treated her like many of the others, as if she was unable to hear or maybe even see. Lea, on the other hand was very genuine.

She smiled and waved a second time in greeting.

"Marguarita." Esteban rolled her name off his tongue easily, taking her hand and holding it briefly to his mouth. "As usual you're looking lovely."

She drew the pen and paper from her pocket and wrote: **I didn't expect you today.**

"I've finally decided I would purchase a few horses and I thought you might come by to take a look at them for me."

She frowned. He lived in an elegant home on the outskirts of the biggest town near them. He rode, but he wasn't a big fan of it. He didn't even have a place to keep the animals. Before she could write down her question, asking what he planned on doing with the horses, he looked around, noting the men out in force, all armed.

"Is something wrong?" he asked.

Marguarita shrugged and went into the stable where the three very pregnant mares stamped and pawed restlessly in their stalls. She was very aware of Esteban following close to her. She could hear him, feel him, her heightened awareness of Zacarias so vulnerable in the ground making her tense. Ordinarily she welcomed visits from the Eldridge family, especially Lea. Esteban was gentlemanly, but sometimes, his overexaggerated flirtations were annoying when she knew he wasn't sincere. The men she'd grown up with knew she could ride and shoot as well if not better than them. Esteban made her feel very feminine, treating her like a fragile woman, ignoring the fact that she was very capable. Right now, all she could think about was an imminent attack on the ranch from the worst, most vile enemy possible and she didn't want Esteban anywhere near the hacienda.

"Your horses have never acted this way," he observed. "Was there a jaguar close this morning?"

She heard the worry in his voice and it warmed her in spite of the situation. He believed she had survived a jaguar attack, and that her father had died saving her, but she'd lost her vocal cords to the animal ripping her throat. In truth, it had been a vampire attacking, seeking Zacarias's resting place. She shrugged again, not wanting to lie to him. Writing down a lie was worse even than speaking it.

"Lea said to tell you hello and she hoped to see you soon."

Marguarita flashed a smile as she opened the stall door and went right in with the mare heavy with foal. She placed her hand on the outstretched neck and sent her waves of reassurance until the horse calmed. Esteban said nothing, just watched as she went from stall to stall, soothing the animals. His presence began to slowly make her uneasy. She felt a kind of dread begin to grow somewhere in the vicinity of the pit of her stomach. It took great effort not to pass her nervousness on to the animals.

Esteban stood quite still outside of each stall, his gaze watchful. The prickle of unease grew until her skin felt as if a thousand pins and needles stabbed into her. She rubbed at her arms as she stepped from the last stall. The horses were eating peacefully and there was no more for her to do. She turned and faced him, taking a deep breath and forcing a smile.

Esteban took her hand and drew her close to him. Strangely the prickling in her skin grew to a burn under the pads of his fingers. She pulled her hand away from him and ran her palms down her thighs to try to rid herself of the sensation.

"I am always astonished at the way you have with horses. They trust you."

She usually enjoyed his compliments, but right now, with the master so close and vulnerable, she wanted Esteban to be gone. She'd never experienced such unease before, and she was beginning to sweat. She could feel dampness growing between her breasts. The burning on her hand faded, but didn't stop completely. She moistened her lips and took out her pen and paper.

I've always had an affinity with animals. Yes, I'll come look at your horses in a couple of days. Why are you thinking of purchasing them? You've never been interested before. She certainly wouldn't want to sell one of the beloved Peruvian Paso to him. He never so much as patted them.

His smile was very wide, showing his perfect teeth. "I've discovered a love of polo. I've been borrowing a friend's horses and I want my own."

He sounded very excited, like a young boy. She wanted to be happy for him, to share in his excitement, but he really cared nothing for horses as she did. And there was the main reason for her reluctance to take his suit as seriously as her father wanted. Ricco and Julio both rode horses every day. They cared for and understood them, and they appreciated her love and need to be around the animals as Esteban never would. Esteban Eldridge seemed an affable, likeable man, but he didn't quite ring true for her. She was surprised her father hadn't realized that.

Where do you plan to keep your horses?

"My friend, Simon Vargos, said I could keep them at his hacienda."

She tried not to wince at that. Simon Vargos traveled to various countries playing polo. He spent a lot of time staring at himself on videos, drinking in bars and picking up women, but no time caring for his stock. He employed grooms, but cared little whether or not they did their job.

"Let's go up to the hacienda and get something hot and discuss a good date," Esteban suggested. "I don't know what anyone is thinking having you outside if a jaguar is prowling around." He put his hand on the small of her back.

Marguarita's breath caught in her throat as pain jolted through her body. She stepped away from him on the pretense of stroking the mare's neck before once more taking out her pen and paper. She handed it to him.

Sorry. Too busy. Cesaro needs me. We'll get together another time.

He frowned, using the same expression on his face when his younger sister, Lea, annoyed him. She'd always thought it rather charming, but now she felt pressured. Nothing seemed right. Her skin was too sensitive, and Esteban was a touchy person.

"Your father would never allow you outside if danger threatened. I need to talk to your man Santos."

His domineering tone annoyed her. She knew Esteban bossed his sister and had a tendency to be just as overbearing with her. Normally she rolled her eyes and ignored him, but she was too worried about anyone discovering Zacarias was in residence—and what she'd done. Esteban had no idea he was encouraging her to enter the very place where the most dangerous predator slumbered.

We all work for a living, Esteban. It is sweet of you to worry for me, but I was raised to do this.

"You were raised to grace a man's side, Marguarita, not work until your back breaks." Ignoring the fact that she was scribbling fast, he continued, "Tell me about this trick you do with the horses. Do you influence them with your mind? Psychically? Lea tells me you can ride without a saddle or bridle and the horse does everything you ask."

She wasn't prepared for the question and had to scratch out everything she'd been writing, something she detested. In a conversation, dialogue was back and forth, but few people had the courtesy to wait until she wrote down her responses. It was very frustrating. She was trying to learn sign language, but she was working out of a book and only Cesaro, Julio and Ricco were even attempting to understand.

My presence soothes the horses for some reason.

It was more than her presence, but she didn't know how to describe communicating with an animal. She'd always been able to calm an animal, to share her emotions with them and they simply responded in kind.

"Can you influence a human being the way you do horses?"

Her gaze jumped to his. Esteban searched her face intently. She frowned as she scribbled her answer. **How could I influence human minds?**

She didn't like the turn in conversation. She was always uncomfortable discussing her gift. Her family simply never discussed her ability. They were happy for her to work with the animals on the ranch, but "talking" with horses was not acceptable in a world where many unexplained things could be evil. Her father had recently become interested in whether or not it might be termed a psychic ability but after his death, she didn't much care what her gift was labeled.

"Don't be defensive," Esteban soothed. "Lea and I had a little argument about this. She said you commmunicate with horses. I thought perhaps it was more a meeting of the minds and you somehow influenced them to do as you wish and that maybe you could do the same with people."

She bit down hard on her lower lip. He was hitting a little too close to the mark.

"Is this some family secret I've stumbled onto?" There was amusement in his voice.

She had many family secrets and this one was minuscule in comparison to the others. She realized she was in a foul mood, not wanting to deal with Esteban and his annoying charm when an impending attack from vampires or their puppets was possible.

I'm sorry, Esteban. I really don't have time for this conversation. I need to get to work. I hope you understand. We can arrange for me to look at your horses another time. To make certain he understood she was finished, she pushed the pen and paper back into her pocket after he'd read her note.

Esteban scowled at her. "I don't think you're behaving very well, Marguarita. Your accident doesn't give you license to be rude."

He was suddenly too close. She could feel the blast of anger pouring off of him. The stable felt too small, and too far away from everyone. He crowded her until she gave way, stepping back before she could stop herself.

"Marguarita." The hard male voice had both of them spinning toward the entrance.

Marguarita breathed a sigh of relief.

Julio Santos sat astride his horse, his piercing dark eyes on Esteban as he held out his hand to Marguarita. "You're needed. Come with me now."

She didn't hesitate, moving around Esteban and catching Julio's wrist. He swung her up behind him. She expected him to start off immediately, but he sat still, regarding Esteban from beneath the brim of his hat. The two men eyed one another for a long, tense moment.

"You good, Marguarita?" Julio asked.

She put her arms around his waist, laid her head against his back and nodded so he could feel the movement. Again she had that strange reaction, her skin burning the moment she made contact with Julio. She jerked her cheek from his back, lifted a hand toward Esteban as if nothing was wrong and, without thinking, silently urged the horse to get out of the stable. Julio was unprepared for the horse's sudden motion, but he was an excellent rider and moved with the animal.

"Next time warn me."

She squeezed her arms tighter to say she was sorry.

"Father sent me. He doesn't like Esteban on the property. He's still shoving the idea of the two of us at me. I got one hell of a lecture, Marguarita, about how I'm allowing such a treasure to slip away." He patted her hands with gloved fingers. "Did he do the same to you?" There was sympathy in his voice.

She nodded her head, once again against his back. That horrible burn was much sharper this time and beginning to spread through her arms, although her skin was covered with the material of her blouse. Uncomfortable, she loosened her grip, using her knees to hold on. Julio's mount was so smooth she doubted if she had needed to take such a precaution.

Julio always made her laugh. She loved him and she had no doubt that he loved her back just as fiercely and protectively—maybe more so. Julio was one of the best men she knew. But they had been raised from birth together and every time someone suggested they pair up, they laughed hysterically together. Although recently, ever since Esteban had come into the picture, Cesaro had pushed them together until it was uncomfortable.

"I've tried to explain to him, but he worries now that your father is gone. Esteban doesn't belong in our world."

She pulled out her pen and paper. Luckily the ride was smooth and made writing easy. **He is incapable of keeping secrets, let alone one as big as the De La Cruz family and what they are.**

If she married outside the ranch, she would have to leave it and she would never be able to divulge her family's secrets to her spouse. Their association with the Carpathians was closely guarded. She knew she wouldn't remember the De La Cruz brothers, all memories would be removed before she left their properties.

"He doesn't belong in this world. Why did he come to our small town, Marguarita? People who come here are desperate for another life. They usually have nothing. He's got money and, to me, that means he's hiding from something."

She thought about it for a moment and then scribbled another message. **He asked me if I could influence people like I do the horses. Why would he ask that?**

"I don't know. I don't like it. The De La Cruz brothers can influence people and have used their abilities to gain more property for themselves and for us than most are able to have here. It's possible he wonders how we were able to get our lands in such large increments."

She trusted Julio's judgment as she always had. Julio wasn't the least bit complicated and he never had hidden agendas. If he tapped on her window in the middle of the night to go riding, it really was to go riding. If he told her he wanted to show her something, it was always something special—usually some wildlife he'd spotted. More than once they'd snuck off together to go into the rain forest to track some animal.

"I'm taking you back to the house once I see him leave," Julio said. "We've got everything settled down, but I'd feel better with you inside. We could be attacked tonight."

The chance of a vampire attacking while a De La Cruz was in residence was far higher than when they were away.

"Did you see him?" Julio asked. "It has to be the eldest or the cattle and horses wouldn't react like they have. I've never actually spoken with him."

She didn't want to lie so she merely nodded her head. Julio glanced at her over his shoulder and raised his eyebrow. He regarded her pale face steadily. She couldn't quite meet his eyes, her gaze sliding away.

"That scary?"

She nodded.

Julio sighed. "Will you be all right?"

She pressed her lips together tightly and penned a short answer. **He won't notice me—I hope.**

She considered telling Julio the truth, but he would go all macho on her and insist on protecting her against Zacarias's wrath. As frightened as she was—she *had* disobeyed a direct order—she couldn't allow anyone else to be punished for her sins. She'd face Zacarias alone and try to explain. Fortunately she had until sundown to find the right words and she'd write it all down. She didn't expect the Carpathian to understand—she didn't understand herself—but she would do her best to let him see she hadn't meant to be defiant.

She nodded her head and Julio turned his attention to riding through the yards, putting his horse through various gaits, showing off that he could control his horse with his hands and knees. She missed laughing. She opened her mouth, but no sound emerged and that took some of the joy away from sharing with Julio.

Only when Esteban's vehicle disappeared down the road did Julio take her back up to the house. He extended his arm so she could dismount easier, but retained possession of her hand when she went to turn away. That same burning sensation snaked up her arm. She looked up at the boy—no, man—who had been her confidante and companion since birth. He regarded her steadily, looking straight into her eyes.

"What's wrong, little sister? I know you too well for you to pretend with me. Did Esteban say something that frightened you? Or is it De La Cruz?"

She swallowed hard. She loved Julio. She refused to lie outright to him. She shook her head slowly as she tried to gently pull her hand from his.

Julio tightened his grip and the burning sensation became more painful, a deep brand that seemed to go to her very bones. She had to fight to keep from crying out and jerking away.

"Tell me."

She pressed her lips together and slowly tugged until Julio allowed her to slip away. She pulled out her pen and paper and scribbled, unknowing if she told the truth or not.

I will be fine, Julio. I love you very much, but you worry too much.

He continued to stare down at her face for a long moment and then he touched his hat. "I love you, too, little sister. If you need me, ring the bell and I'll come running."

She smiled at him, warmth stealing into her cold bones. Of course he would come if she sounded the alarm they'd rigged up. Julio was someone she'd always counted on and she knew he was telling her he would go against the code of their families if necessary to protect her. She put her hand over her heart and watched him ride away, her deep affection for him making her eyes burn and tears clog her throat.

Slowly, she entered the house, her heart beating so hard, she feared she would have a stroke. The empty rooms were silent, accusing, and she wandered around, feeling a little lost in her own home. Eventually, the taste of fear subsided and she cooked herself something to eat and spent the rest of the day writing out long letters to Zacarias, explaining to the best of her ability why she had saved him against his wishes, and then discarding them.

The sun sank and night descended. Insects began their calls in earnest. Frogs chimed in. Horses stamped occasionally and the cattle settled for the night. Storm clouds gathered overhead, dark, ominous roiling masses that blotted out the sliver of moon and stars. Heavy with rain, a few drops fell, a portent of what was to come. Lights went out in windows, one by one, as the workers settled in with their families.

Marguarita took a bath and once again sat at her desk, trying to compose a letter that might save her. The wastebasket overflowed with crumpled paper as she became more and more frustrated. The wind picked up, battering at her window, and Marguarita finally crawled into bed and pulled up the covers, her pen still in her hand.

3

Lightning streaked across the sky, forks zigzagging from earth to sky. The ground rolled, opening a three-inch crevice from pasture to stable. Beneath the master bedroom, in the rich black soil, a heart began to beat. A hand moved, fingers curled into a tight fist and broke through to the surface. Dirt exploded as Zacarias De La Cruz rose. Hunger burned through him, an angry blowtorch, eating through skin and bones to his very insides. It tore through him, relentless, insatiable, a brutal, insistent hunger that was more horrific than any he'd ever felt in all his centuries of existence. Need coursed through his veins and pulsed with every beat of his heart.

She had done this to him. He could taste her life's essence in his mouth, that beautiful innocence exploding against his tongue, trickling down his throat, setting up an addiction, a terrible craving that would never end as long as he existed. His hands shook and his teeth lengthened, saliva pooling along the sharp points.

How dare you!

The ground rolled beneath the house. The walls rippled, a slow undulation, threatening to buckle the entire structure. His vision went red, and he burst through the trap door, throwing the huge four-poster bed against the far wall. Cracks spiderwebbed along the clay bricks right up to the window.

You have placed every man, woman and child in my care in jeopardy.

He could hear the sound of a heart beating, that distinct rhythm calling to him, driving him into a frenzy of hunger, each separate beat pulsing through his own veins. He knew exactly where she was. Marguarita was her name. The treacherous wench who dared to defy a direct order from her *master.* He'd warned her she would pay for her disobedience—her deliberate defiance. He'd expected her to run like a little coward, but the foolish girl waited for him in the very house—*his* house—alone.

The taste of her lingered until he thought he might go insane with craving. He crossed the room in long, ground-eating strides, shoving air at the door so that it exploded open before him, allowing him to move with unerring swiftness through the long living room to the back of the house where her bedroom was. If he hadn't already known where the room was located, he still would have found her. Her heart pounded in fear, thundering in his ears. He didn't bother to turn down the volume, wanting, even needing to hear her terror.

She *deserved* to be terrified. If he'd awoken vampire, he would have broken his vow to his brothers. After centuries of honor, his life of emptiness, his struggle to protect his family and his people would all be for nothing. And it could still happen. He was close—too close to turning. He needed—something. Anything. The anticipation of taking her blood was a rush he didn't welcome—a sign of walking that thin edge between honor and the ultimate failure.

His fingers itched to wrap around her slender neck. These people working the ranch had sworn loyalty to the De La Cruz family, served them, father to son, mother to daughter for centuries, yet she had so carelessly risked them all. He slammed his palm against her door, deliberately splintering the wood rather than opening the door.

Marguarita made no effort to flee, her eyes wide with terror, fixing on his face as he kicked aside the broken wood. She huddled in the corner of the room, her hand over her mouth, her face pale beneath her smooth, golden skin. As he approached her, she held out a placating hand with a piece of paper clutched in her fingers—a poor defense when he was starving.

He jerked her to her feet, aware of how light she was. How soft. How warm. How alive. He was vividly aware of her heart calling to his—that rhythmic pulse setting up such hunger—such want. Through the red haze of madness, the softness of her skin registered. Her fresh, clean fragrance was reminiscent of rain forest mist and the unique and beautiful heliconias that grew up the tree trunks and called to the hummingbirds with their sweetness. The scent enveloped him as he trapped her in arms of steel and bent his head toward her slender neck.

She struggled wildly and he pinned her with one arm and caught her thick rope of hair with the other, crushing the silken strands in his fist as he jerked her head back. He lowered his head toward that sweet vulnerable spot where her pulse pounded so frantically. He didn't try to calm her mind or in any way control her knowledge of what was happening. He wanted her to know. He wanted her fear. He intended to hurt her so she would never forget why she should obey.

Rain battered the windows. Wind blasted the hacienda. Lightning streaked across the sky, illuminating the roiling black clouds. Thunder crashed, shaking the earth so it rolled beneath his feet, feeding his black mood.

Zacarias sank his teeth deep into that soft, defenseless flesh. He bit hard, without a numbing agent, puncturing her neck deliberately close to her throat. She should have remembered the vampire attacking her. She shouldn't have been so careless as to disobey. She needed another lesson in just what a dangerous, uncaring vile creature could do.

Her skin was warm satin, soft and fascinating, the sensation a shock, her natural fragrance alluring. But it was her blood that truly stunned him. Rich. Innocent. Fresh. The taste was exquisite. As addicting as that first taste when he'd been so close to death. She fought him, pushing against him, trying desperately to free her arms, but he was enormously strong and nothing got between him and his prey—and make no mistake, this young woman with her addicting blood belonged to him. He became aware that he was growling, a dark warning. There was no way for her to get free and no one could enter the house—*his* house—without his consent or knowledge. She was completely at his mercy—and he had none.

His every organ soaked up her amazing blood. Every cell sprang to life. There was nothing he'd ever experienced that came close to the perfect richness of her blood. The rush of heat spread through him like an unfamiliar fireball. His veins and arteries sang. Even his groin stirred, filling with the dazzling taste and heat of her blood. He dragged her closer, more animal than man, his arms now bruising bands of steel, his mouth dragging more of that sweet nectar into his starving body.

The gaping wounds on his body began to close. The terrible burning ever present inside subsided and the clawing, raking pain in his gut turned to a scorching fire of desperate need. Even the roaring in his head and the red haze banding his vision diminished. Her legs gave out and he held her weight completely, slipping a hand beneath her knees, all the while dragging her life's essence into his body.

Her head lolled back against his shoulder. She felt light. Insubstantial. Her lashes fluttered, two thick crescents, blacker than the gray he normally saw. The lashes lifted and her dark, almost black eyes stared straight into his with both fear and loathing. Only then did he feel her absolute terror. Horror filled his mind, shook his body and crept like icy fingers down his spine—not his horror—hers. She believed him vampire—and he was killing her.

He swept his tongue across the puncture wounds and lifted his head, never breaking eye contact. Blood trickled from her neck to her breast and, without thinking, he followed the precious ruby teardrop to the soft swell of her very feminine body with his tongue.

She looked more shocked than ever, shuddering, terrified.

"You will drink what I offer." It was a decree, demanding she obey without argument.

He sank down onto her bed, still cradling her to him, and with a wave of his hand, his shirt opened. He drew a thin line across his chest, over his heart. Her eyes widened until they were enormous bottomless pools, stark horror staring at him. She shook her head and tried feebly to push him away. He forced her mouth to his chest and she bit him, still struggling.

Wäke-sarna! Zacarias uttered power words, a curse, a blessing—a vow she would not defy him. He took her mind, ripping it from her ruthlessly, forcing what she would not give him. Her mouth nuzzled his chest, her lips warm and soft, sending a jolt of lightning streaking through his body. He felt a live current electrifying every nerve ending, bringing his body to life as she began to suckle, drawing his blood into her body where it would soak every organ and subtly reshape them, where it would connect them together for all time.

He drew her closer, his hand cradling her head, his mind in hers. Only then, when the wonder of the strange phenomenon of her blood eased a bit, did he know she was screaming. He had commanded her to drink, giving her no other option, but she was completely aware. Her mind connected to his on a level unexpected. He was mostly predatory. An animal. Cunning and cruel. Even brutal. Life and death was his world—his struggle. Her mind raced to that part of him, reached out and melded with him.

He didn't hear a sound, yet he felt her screams, her absolute horror and rejection of him, the numbing fear that refused to subside even when he commanded it to be so.

Be calm. He pushed the command at her, and when it did no good, he forced his order into her mind. She only withdrew further from him.

Marguarita was certainly an intriguing puzzle. His brother had strengthened the barrier in her mind that would prevent the undead and other Carpathians from reading her thoughts, yet she had her own secrets. She had been born with that barrier, after generations of De La Cruz creating it in the families, and now it was even stronger than expected.

She was wholly human. He had no doubts of that. Vulnerable. Fragile. Yet her mind had a natural guard, one that didn't allow her to be easily manipulated. His blood exchange would open the line of communication telepathically between them. He wouldn't hear her voice, so much as see her words and know her thoughts. And, he decided, communication with this particular servant was necessary. She had no concept of obedience, and within his territory, he was the absolute ruler. His subjects obeyed one way or the other.

The longer he held her warmth and curves to him, the more he became aware of her feminine form. Man or woman never mattered, and honestly, he couldn't remember anymore a time when it had. He had no sexual urges, no emotions, nothing whatsoever that would make him care. Yet in the space of a heartbeat—she had awakened things in him best left alone. She should never have drawn his attention to her, never have trickled her addicting blood into his mouth, setting up an insatiable craving.

Rain pounded the roof, and lashed the windows, seeking entrance.

The wild storm reflected his violent nature. The house shuddered under the ferocious wind. For one moment lightning lit up the room and he could see the desperation in her eyes, the very thing he had wanted. Thunder crashed and the room went dark. He continued to stare down into her eyes.

She took his blood into her body because she had no choice, but she rejected his great gift. *Rejected him.* She truly did loathe and fear him, just as she would the undead. He took a deep breath. He just needed to calm her. To make her see reason. She needed to understand the enormity of her sin and the grievous position she'd placed him in. That was all. Why he found her horror disturbing, he was uncertain. It seemed to bother him on a primitive level, although intellectually, he was sure she needed to be afraid. There were terrible, vile creatures in his world and she lived there. Served him. It mattered that she listened to him.

I am saving your life—as I did before. Perhaps reminding her that he'd saved her from the vampire would help.

Marguarita's body shuddered and moved subtly from his, as if touching him was foul. Thunder crashed again, echoing the rioting in his mind. He had chosen life for her. She should be grateful he'd bothered when she was so disobedient. She would not soon forget this lesson and maybe, just maybe, she would know not to meddle in things that were none of her business. And she would obey his commands, which often meant life or death.

The only answer was the rain hitting the roof. The wild beating of her heart. Her ragged breathing. He sighed. Her fear bordered on terror. No, it *was* terror and, quite frankly, he found he didn't like it. There was no letup. Not even now when he treated her with care.

You have taken enough.

He went to insert his hand between her mouth and his chest, to carefully pull her away as one would expect he would have to do, but she jerked away from him so unexpectedly she nearly fell from his arms. He tightened his hold, his fingers digging into her soft flesh. His blood had provided strength for her, and now that he was connected with her, he knew she intended to try to vomit, to rid herself of the substance.

He smiled at her, slowly shaking his head. "My blood flows in your veins already, silly woman. Your body absorbs it. It will not go to your stomach as your foul food does."

Zacarias was prepared for her to fight and he was not going to allow her up until he was ready. Marguarita remained perfectly still, her gaze locked on his face, hardly breathing now, as still as any prey hiding in the trees or grasses might be. A small frisson of unease went down his back. She was exhibiting the exact signs the creatures in the rain forest manifested when he was near. There were no warning alarms, none of the normal shrieking monkeys and birds often used when spotting a predator. Even insects stilled when he was near.

He wanted obedience from her, not stark, raw fear. Well . . . he'd wanted her to be afraid—to learn her lesson. Fear was simply a tool to him, one he wielded easily. Perhaps she was more sensitive than he had considered and he should have toned his message down.

He felt the first slight movement of her body, nothing more than a whisper of space between them, but he knew she was fleeing him. Instinctively he tightened his hold on her, breathing in and out for both of them, his lungs calling to hers to follow his rhythm. His heart beat slow and steady, in an effort to slow the wild acceleration of hers. He barely recognized his need to calm her, or even the reason for it—the need simply existed.

From a place long forgotten, a memory surfaced of a child, a young boy shifting too late and embedding himself in a tree. Zacarias remembered his youngest brother, a fast learner, but trying things he wasn't ready for because his older brothers could. He rocked Marguarita in the same manner as he had Riordan, to comfort her, murmuring in Carpathian, soft words that meant nothing. Noise really. The memory shocked him almost as much as the entire night's events did. He hadn't thought of those days in hundreds of years.

He wasn't a man who felt compassion, but her fear disturbed him. It made no sense and he didn't trust anything he couldn't explain. He set her on the floor. The moment his hands released her, she crawled away from him to huddle in the corner, staring at him with her enormous, frightened eyes.

Tremors wracked her body over and over. She twisted her fingers together, twice reaching as if she might touch the darkening bruise on her neck, yet halting before she brushed her damaged skin. She wore his brand now, color coming up under her skin with two punctures centered almost perfectly. She didn't touch the spot, and he found himself frowning. Puzzled.

As a rule it was easier to use women to feed. His younger brothers moved in political circles in order to achieve the things they needed, such as their larger estates. Decorative women hanging on their arms were always a plus. They had easy access to a food source and cover at all times. It was easy enough to plant memories of wild nights of sex and partying. But Marguarita's mind didn't accept planted memories nor did he particularly want to erase the memory of his moment.

He sighed and stood up. She shuddered, her eyes swimming with tears. The drops formed on her impossibly long lashes, drawing his attention and planting a hard knot in the pit of his stomach. The De La Cruz brothers often strengthened the natural barrier in the mind of those who served them. She had accepted his brother's strengthening of her shields of protection, but she rejected every part of *him*. He knew it was personal. He'd been in her mind. She didn't think of him in the same light as his brothers. He was *hän ku piwtä*—predator.

"Hear me, little girl. You will not *ever* disobey a direct order from me again."

She pressed her trembling lips together, covering them with her fingers.

He took a threatening step toward her. "Are you clear who is in charge? Who is your master?"

She swallowed hard and nodded her head vigorously.

Looking at her fear, the direct result of his actions, something twisted in the vicinity of his chest. He pressed his hand there to stop the strange pain. "For a few days your hearing will be much more acute than normal. It may bother you. Your vision will be sharper as well. You will learn to control it. Do *not* stray from the house. I want you available when I wish it."

Her blood was an amazing concoction and he knew he would forever crave her. He could actually taste her in his mouth and he longed to lick that pulse beating so frantically in her neck, stroking right over his mark with his tongue. He needed to figure out what was happening, what his reaction to her meant. She was broadcasting fear so loud he couldn't think straight. He didn't know why his connection to her was so strong, but he felt her emotions as if they were his own. Long ago, even the connection with his brothers had faded from his memories.

Zacarias shook his head, frowning, stepping closer to her. She shrunk back into the corner, drawing up her knees, trying to make herself smaller. She turned her face away and closed her eyes tightly to block out the sight of him as he extended his hand toward her. He'd been careful to go slow, as he might approach a wild creature, but she ducked slightly as though she expected him to strike her. The idea was ludicrous. He would *never* hit her.

His gut knotted, a physical reaction he couldn't control. He touched her tear-wet face, gathering moisture on the pads of his fingers. His skin absorbed the salty tears, took the glistening diamond-drops into his body and his stomach did another unfamiliar lurch.

Abruptly he turned away from her, striding from the room, unable to bear the sight of her forlorn and frightened figure one more moment. He needed distance. The rain forest. Anywhere but near that absurdly disobedient female.

Zacarias was far more careful with the front door. He wanted to be able to lock that puzzling, baffling, *annoying* woman inside where she couldn't get into trouble while he figured out what to do. He could try again to seek the dawn as the sun came up, but the dramatic end to his life no longer seemed supportable. *O jelä peje emnimet*—sun scorch the woman. She'd turned his world upside down. Everything would be perfectly right again the moment he couldn't smell her scent or hear her heartbeat. The connection between the primal part of his mind would fade with distance and he would be able to breathe—and think.

He stepped out into the rain, waving his hand to calm the storm he'd wrought with his attempt to punish the mortal woman. His breath hissed out of his lungs. He didn't want to take that next step, to spread his arms and summon the harpy eagle for flight. He wavered, nearly transparent, mist and rain becoming one with him, one thing that normally soothed his dark soul, but the reluctance was still there. *O ainaak jelä peje emnimet ŋamaŋ*—sun scorch that woman forever. She had done something to him.

Could she have been mage-born? Had she cast a spell to entrap him? *Him?* Zacarias De La Cruz? Impossible. He was too old. Too cunning. She didn't stand a chance against him, pitting herself against his centuries-old power and experience. He had half a mind to go back into the house and indulge his craving again.

The thought brought the taste of her bursting through his mouth and a rush of heat through his body. Unfamiliar things bothered him. His reaction to Marguarita Fernandez was unheard of. No one, nothing roused his interest in centuries, and now, when he chose to end his life, *she* dared to disturb him. He would not go back to her trap, no longer be ensnared by whatever spell she cast. He would follow his own way, his own logic and she could wait on his convenience.

Zacarias took to the air. The wind rushed through him, through the mist that made up his body, so that he and air were the same—he belonged here—part of the earth itself. He'd developed the trick long years ago when he was so alone and in need of some small solace. Animals and man no longer welcomed him—not even his own kin. They feared him—as *she* feared him. But when he was mist, with the wind moving through his body, sending him drifting through the trees, he actually could feel accepted. Animals and man rejected him but the earth was a constant, steady companion.

Marguarita Fernandez was a puzzle he couldn't get out of his head. The attack of the vampire on her must have unhinged her in some way. There was no other explanation for such blatant disobedience, such deliberate disregard of his direct order. No one would dare such a thing, let alone a little slip of a girl. She had to be a little ill, and if so, he had been a bit hard on her. Satisfied that he'd found the only logical conclusion to her strange and indefensible behavior, Zacarias took to the air to set things straight with her before he sought rest.

Marguarita stayed as still as she possibly could, freezing every muscle in place, terrified he would return. He walked so silently it was impossible to tell where in the house he was, but his presence was so powerful, so strong, she knew the moment he left. Only then did she cover her face with her hands and give into hysterical weeping.

She had never been so afraid in her life, not even when the vampire had demanded to know Zacarias's resting place. She had accepted death and knew she would die with honor. This—this was a terrible, tangled mess she'd created. Everyone was at risk, everyone she loved. Everyone she knew. Because she hadn't allowed a De La Cruz to die.

She knew the truth now. Zacarias had come to the hacienda to die with honor because he was close to turning vampire. She didn't know the process, but she knew loss of honor was the one thing every Carpathian feared. He had risen vampire and *she* had done it.

She spread her fingers and peeked through them to the wastebasket where a hundred crumpled pages from her notebook gave evidence to the fact that there was no explanation. None. She didn't know why she'd committed such a grave sin but she'd been unable to stop herself and now she'd created the very monster Zacarias had tried to avoid.

With a shaking hand she touched her throbbing neck, that spot that burned through skin to mark her bones. She swallowed hard and slowly pushed herself to her feet. Her legs felt like rubber and she couldn't stop the tremors taking over her body. What was she going to do? What could she do? She could never—*ever*—face that monster again. But more than that, she couldn't allow him to kill or use anyone at the hacienda. She'd done this. She was responsible and she had to ensure everyone's safety.

She knew vampires made puppets—humans who did their bidding during the daylight hours when they slept. Puppets craved the blood of the vampire and feasted on flesh. It was a horrible half-life and eventually they rotted from the inside out. She would *not* be Zacarias's puppet, no matter that she had been the one to cause him to lose honor. Certainly that hadn't been her intention.

Marguarita moistened her dry lips and forced her body under control. She couldn't go to Cesaro and Julio because they would try to defend her and they would definitely be killed. No one could stand up to Zacarias De La Cruz. If she went to one of her aunts, he would know. Her entire extended family worked for the De La Cruz family in some capacity or other. As she tried to make sense out of the situation, she yanked open drawers and stuffed the bare minimum of required clothing into a backpack.

She had to formulate a plan. Vampires were cunning, but they did have weaknesses. She couldn't call in the hunters until she led Zacarias from everyone she loved. That much was certain. Vampires killed for the pleasure of it and she couldn't risk anyone on the ranch. If she activated the call sign for a hunter, Cesaro would try to fight Zacarias. All of the workers would. She knew without a doubt she could lead him away from her family because Zacarias would follow her.

Fortunately, she knew the rain forest and she didn't fear it as most did. She would disappear—and he would follow. She didn't know how she knew that he would, but she did. He would find her eventually—and probably kill her—but she had no other real choice, not if she wanted to save her family. She would make her way down river to the next De La Cruz property—a collection of cabins used when moving cattle to various pastures—and she would call in the hunters from there. If they made it before the vampire found her she would be safe, if not, at least she'd saved her family.

She dragged on her boots and ran through the house to find her survival pack. She had a water-filtration system and tablets just in case it was needed, although she knew where waterfalls ran in abundance. She was an excellent hunter, so food wouldn't be too much of a problem, but how was she going to keep Julio or Cesaro from trying to find her?

Marguarita bit down on her lip and tried to still her frantic thoughts. She had to think her escape through. Zacarias showed no interest in reading her note so perhaps it would be safe to leave one for Cesaro. She would have to word it in such a way as to reassure everyone without actually lying. She didn't want them to be so foolish as to question Zacarias. They all needed to stay as far from him as possible. If she was very lucky she would get a good head start on him before he followed.

She forced air through her lungs and wrote a short note. **I took your advice, Cesaro, and left for a few days. Will return shortly. Love to both you and Julio.**

That wasn't a lie. And it gave nothing away. Cesaro would be frustrated with her, but he would think she'd gone to one of her aunts. Julio . . . Now, he was a different matter. He knew her much better than Cesaro and he might consider something was wrong, but once his father reassured him that he'd suggested she go to her aunt in Brazil, he'd settle down and wait a few days to hear from her.

Satisfied that she'd done all she could to keep everyone safe, Marguarita went out her bedroom window. She didn't trust the doors or the fact that

Zacarias had gone out the front. She was *not* going to run into him by mistake. She remained crouched under the window, studying the dark sky with suspicion. Zacarias could be anywhere, in any form. The thought was both disturbing and terrifying. For a moment her heart raced, her blood roaring in her ears. She made herself breathe normally, afraid he might hear her thundering heartbeat.

Before she moved, she touched the animals in the vicinity. As soon as she'd pulled the drapes in the house, the ranch had gone on alert. Cattle and horses had been moved in close where they could be better protected. Everyone was armed and patrols had been doubled, but the animals would know before humans if evil were near. The horses were settled for the night. There was no restless stamping that would have alerted her to Zacarias's close proximity.

The rain settled into a steady drizzle and the ferocious wind calmed as she made her way across the paddocks and pastures to the very edge of the rain forest. She'd always loved the way the natural growth continued to creep back to reclaim what had been taken. Roots snaked across the ground in long tentacles. Creeper vines slid over stones and up fences, even wrapping around rocks in an effort to take back the land.

She slipped into the outer edges of the trees, hurrying along a narrow trail she was familiar with. Insects formed a moving carpet on the thick vegetation, centuries of fallen plants and trees. Large spiders clung to the branches and lizards scooted under leaves for cover. Tree frogs peeped out at her as she hurried by.

Marguarita walked with confidence, knowing exactly where she was going. It was easy to get lost in the rain forest. Most traveling was done on the rivers, but she and Julio had explored the area closest to the ranch almost from the time they could walk and they'd marked their trails with signs both recognized easily. There was a wonderful little cave back behind one of the numerous waterfalls, a small, difficult-to-find grotto where she and Julio had camped several times. It had been their secret place whenever they hid from their parents. Julio often got in trouble in those days. He carried a man's share of work from an early age and traipsing around in the rain forest was frowned upon—especially with a female.

The cave was located on a deep, wide stream that fed the great river.

Julio had carved out a canoe from cedar with his machete. The wood was light enough for the craft to float, yet not so soft that it wasn't strong enough to stand up to the river. They had stashed the canoe behind the waterfall. She could make it there, get the boat and take one of the streams that fed into the Amazon. The De La Cruz camp wasn't far from there.

Marguarita accepted her role in the house and reveled in the fact that she was acknowledged for her gift with horses, yet she loved the rain forest and the way it made her feel so free. She knew Julio felt the same things and together they encouraged one another in running off to explore every chance they got. Julio got in far worse trouble than she had, although she had endured countless lectures about a woman's duties. Now, she was grateful for every trip they'd made.

Fireflies flashed tiny sparkles in the various trees providing her with a little comfort. In the trees, the night was inky black, although the rain forest wasn't completely dark. Phosphorescent fungi gave off an eerie glow. Night monkeys poked their heads out of tree holes to stare at her with enormous eyes and their presence offered her a sign that she wasn't followed—yet.

Zacarias could take any shape in his pursuit of her and he was fast. He could use the sky and cover territory in minutes that might take her hours. She had to run to get to the canoe, and that was extremely risky at night in the jungle, but she had no real choice. She had to keep ahead of him until dawn. Once the sun came up, she could make her way to the De La Cruz cabins and hopefully call in help. Zacarias would be away from the hacienda and everyone else would be safe. It all made perfect sense, but she had to get there fast and that meant running.

She picked up the pace, sprinting, needing to get to shelter. She didn't want to be out in the open, even under the canopy. Where the trees were thick, there was little light and she had to use her headlamp, but it also meant there was little vegetation on the floor. Without light penetrating the canopy, it was difficult to grow much. Saplings had to wait for a tree to fall, providing a gap in the canopy, allowing the sunlight through.

She sent out a wave of energy ahead of her, trying to give the insects on the forest floor the heads-up that she was coming through. Hopefully they would clear the trail. Tiny colorful frogs leaped from branch to trunk, their sticky feet clinging to the surfaces as they followed her on her precarious journey.

She tried not to race, knowing she wouldn't have the stamina. She had to set a grueling pace, but one she could continue for a long time. Hours. It was a long time before the sun came up. She sent out a call for aid, her plea strong enough to wake the animals resting in the canopy above her. Immediately answers came. Monkeys went on alert. Flocks of birds called to one another, all looking for a common enemy.

Centuries of leaves and branches concealed twisted roots that would easily trip her up, and her headlamp caught the animals creeping out of holes to sit on the roots, so that as she ran, she could choose a path with the least obstacles. She rounded a bend, winding her way around a thick tree trunk and a capibara stared at her, crouched directly in her way. She swerved to her right, the only possible direction and realized as she flashed by, that the animal had guided her away from a labyrinth of creeper vines that would surely have sent her sprawling.

She ran with more confidence then, dependent on the animals, feeling comforted by their presence, knowing they would raise the alarm the moment Zacarias came near. They would know he was close. They had to be as sensitive to his presence as the horses and cattle on the ranch. She should have known when all the animals on the ranch had acted so uneasy that evil walked with Zacarias De La Cruz.

Marguarita frowned as she ran. Her lungs began to burn and her legs ached. She swerved to avoid a series of termite mounds her lamp barely managed to pick up before she was on them. Why had she felt so compelled to save him? She couldn't stop herself. Even when he'd demanded her compliance, she hadn't been able to leave him in the sun. She wasn't squeamish. She'd grown up on a working ranch and she did her share of work, no matter how difficult.

She ignored the stitch in her side and jumped over one of the many ribbons of water running downhill to feed into the river system. The ground was muddy as she slipped and slid her way up the slopes, sometimes clawing her way in the mud. All the while her mind continued to puzzle out her strange behavior. She'd been programmed since birth to obey a

De La Cruz. It was life or death in their world and one wrong misstep could spell catastrophe for those living on the various ranches. They all knew the danger of vampires. Monsters were very real in their world.

A small sob escaped. Carpathians fed on the blood of humans, yet they didn't kill. Vampires killed. She didn't fully understand the thin line between them, but she knew it was thin and somehow she had pushed Zacarias over the edge. *And what had his blood done to her?*

She had awakened from the vampire attack with a torn throat, unable to talk, her world turned upside down, but all her other senses were heightened from the blood Zacarias had given her to save her life. Her sight was much better. She could actually spot insects in grass and see birds in the thickest branches of trees. She spotted tiny frogs and lizards hidden in the leaves and creeper vines. Her hearing was even more acute. Sometimes she thought she could hear the men talking out in the fields while they worked. Certainly she could hear the horses in the stable.

With that first blood he'd given her to save her life, she knew he had changed something in her. Her hair, always thick, had grown faster and more lustrous. Her skin had a sheen, almost a glow to it. Her lashes were thicker and longer, everything about her was just *more.* She noticed Julio stayed closer to her and the hacienda whenever the other men were near, and she was aware of them as men, instead of simply people she'd grown up with. She felt the weight of their eyes and at times was uncomfortable, afraid she was reading lecherous thoughts. None of that had ever happened before. And the changes weren't all physical.

She shouldn't be able to run so fast for such a distance even with animals guiding her on the trail. She used her headlamp less and less and was guided more by pure instinct. She could hear her heart beat and it had settled to a slow, steady rhythm. Her lungs had been burning for air, but the farther she ran, the more they began to work efficiently.

Her skin tingled when there were obstacles near her, much like radar warning her which direction to turn, where to place her feet, how to move and slip through the trees without a misstep. She might not be able to speak, but she certainly had acquired other much sharper senses and skills.

She'd been hearing the stream for some time. The rain had fed the water on the ground so that it ran downhill, taking the least line of resistance until it found its way to the narrow stream, deepening the dark water, swelling the ribbon until the banks were nearly overflowing. The waterfall in the distance sounded like continuous thunder and relief flooded her. That meant the water route was open and deep enough to take her downstream rapidly. If conditions were right, she could make it all the way to the Amazon. That would increase her chances of getting to the De La Cruz pastures before Zacarias discovered her. Marguarita increased her speed, running flat out to the falls.

4

The harpy eagle swooped through the canopy, ignoring the sloth, its favorite food, and circled back toward the hacienda, driven by some inner compulsion it couldn't ignore. Deep inside the giant bird's body, Zacarias sighed. He was no closer to the truth than he'd been when he set out. The threads binding him to the woman had grown stronger, not weaker, and he couldn't get her out of his mind.

If he hadn't known better, he would think it was possible she was his lifemate. He'd considered the idea, of course, but then discarded it almost immediately. If she'd been the one woman to complete his soul, he would see in colors and feel emotion. If it was emotion he was experiencing, he didn't know enough about *feelings* to even identify them. Whatever was going on was a puzzle that had to be solved before he returned to his original plan of seeking the dawn. Marguarita Fernandez held great power. She was a potential threat to Carpathians and therefore had to be eliminated. It was that simple.

A piercing pain in the vicinity of his heart brought him up short. He actually looked down at the bird's breast to see if it had been punctured by an arrow. His stomach lurched at the idea of killing her. *O jelä peje emnimet*—sun scorch the woman, she had cast some spell. There was no other explanation for his physical response to the idea of her death. She had tied them together. Or her blood had. Blood was the very essence of life and hers was . . . extraordinary.

He wanted—no, *needed*—to touch her mind with his. Everything in him urged him to reach out to her, to know where she was, what she was doing. He refused to act on the need. He didn't trust it any more than he trusted the way he had to see her, to touch her, to know she existed. Whatever spell had been cast was a powerful one and it had to be a trap.

He had control and discipline, several lifetimes to develop both and no woman, a human woman at that, could possibly destroy those traits in him. He would take his time, prove to both himself and to her that he was far too strong to be brought down by any spell. Before he killed her he would learn her secrets. Every last one of them. She would know what it meant to betray a De La Cruz and try to entrap one of them.

He had fought vampires and destroyed them, the foulest, most vile creatures imaginable; a small slip of a woman had no chance against him. He ignored the way his mind continually reached for hers. The way his blood heated at the thought of her. It wasn't the spell so much as the fact that she actually intrigued him—something that hadn't happened in a thousand years or more. That was all. Interest. Intrigue. Who could blame him when nothing had been a surprise to him—until her. The woman. Marguarita.

He flinched. The moment he thought her name—gave her life—he could taste her on his tongue all over again. His heart gave a strange stutter, and for a moment, deep inside the bird, he thought his body stirred with life. He went very still, a dark predator hunted. His breath felt trapped in his lungs. That was impossible. A trick. An illusion. She was far more powerful than he'd first imagined.

That particular trick would buy her time. He had not been a man for far longer than he could remember. He was a killing machine, nothing more. Nothing less. He didn't have desires of the flesh. He couldn't feel. The strange things taking place in his body and mind weren't real, no matter how good the illusion was, but he closed his eyes and savored the hot lick of need rushing through his veins. Just as fast he snapped open his eyelids, looking suspiciously around. Was this illusion the way to tip him over the edge, allow him to feel, just for a moment, and then take it from him so that he would forever crave the rush?

The harpy eagle slipped out of the canopy and flew high over the hacienda. He refused to give into the ever-present urge to touch Marguarita's mind. Now, more than ever, he had to show strength—and he had to find out everything he could about Marguarita Fernandez.

He spotted the house he was looking for tucked into the mountainside. There were several houses scattered on the property, but Cesaro Santos was the foreman and his status showed in his house. The eagle floated to the ground, shifting at the last moment into human form. Zacarias strode straight to the porch, his body shimmering into a trail of vapor that poured beneath the crack in the door.

The house was immaculate, like most of the dwellings of the humans coexisting with his family. He knew Cesaro to be loyal to a fault. He had offered his blood, even his life, to save Zacarias. The man was above reproach and there was no taint of evil anywhere on the ranch that Zacarias could detect. Cesaro would never steal from the De La Cruz family, or betray them in any way, and if he found one of those working for him to be doing so, Zacarias had no doubt that man—or woman—would be buried deep in the rain forest at Cesaro's hand.

Come to me. Blood called to blood and every trusted employee had been given Carpathian blood—enough that each De La Cruz could read thoughts, protect minds and extract information when needed.

Zacarias knew the instant Cesaro wakened, reaching for his gun. There was satisfaction in knowing he had chosen the family well. Loyalty was the strongest trait within the Chevez and Santos families, both connected through blood. He took his solid form as the *capitan* of the hacienda came out fully dressed and armed heavily in a matter of minutes.

Cesaro bowed slightly and stood, almost stiffly. Zacarias knew no human or animal was ever relaxed in his company. He couldn't hide the killer in him; that was the biggest part of him so he didn't bother. He gestured to the sofa positioned in a strategic location where the occupant could easily see anything approaching his home.

"How can I be of service, *señor*?"

"I wish to know everything you can tell me of the woman." Zacarias kept his gaze on the other man's face, watching his expression carefully, holding a part of himself in Cesaro's mind to ensure he was getting the truth. He read puzzlement and confusion. His question was the last thing the *capitan* expected.

"Do you mean Marguarita Fernandez?" At Zacarias's silent nod, Cesaro frowned. "I have known her since the day she was born. Her father was my cousin. Her mother died when she was quite young and she was raised right here on the ranch along with my son, Julio."

A frisson of something very lethal slid into his veins, a dark shadow protesting the closeness of a man growing up with Marguarita. How close were they? Something very ugly rose up to settle in the pit of his stomach at that thought of Julio alone with the woman. His teeth lengthened and he closed his fingers into two tight fists. Nails like talons punctured his palm.

Cesaro took a firmer grip on the rifle in his lap, his face visibly paling. "Have I said something to upset you?"

Blood trickled across his palm and Zacarias, never taking his gaze from Cesaro's, licked at the line of drops. "Continue."

Cesaro shivered. "She is a good girl. Loyal."

Zacarias waved that away. He didn't want to hear what Cesaro thought of her. "Tell me about her." About any men in her life. Anything he needed to know. The important things.

"She takes care of the hacienda and represents the family with all the workers. She does the ordering and she is invaluable with the cattle and horses." Cesaro clearly didn't understand what Zacarias was looking for. "Has anything happened to her?" He half rose.

Zacarias pushed his palm toward the man in an abrupt motion, not meaning to shove quite so hard, but air slammed Cesaro back onto the cushions. "She is fine. Tell me what I want to know. Is she with a man? Does she often leave the ranch?"

Cesaro's frown deepened. "She has many hopeful callers, some from outside the ranch and some right here. She does not step out with them, especially since the attack on her. She stays close to home, although she does represent the family at charity events as well as going to local dances and events."

Zacarias kept his expression blank. He didn't like the sound of "many hopeful callers," or any of it really. Was she casting her spell wide? He would put a stop to that immediately. "You allow her to go off unaccompanied? A young girl?"

"No, of course not. Marguarita is carefully guarded. Someone from the ranch always goes with her."

Zacarias continued to stare at the man, his locked gaze conveying inquiry and disapproval.

"My son often escorts her," Cesaro admitted. "It has been my hope that the two of them make a match of it. Both serve your family and know what needs to be done to keep our alliance safe. It is a good match, but neither seems to be interested."

The floor rolled. The walls breathed in and out. For a moment the pressure in the room was painful as if all the air had been sucked out of it. Cesaro fought for a breath, his throat closing and his lungs burning. Just as rapidly, the sensation vanished as though it had never been. He coughed a couple of times, one hand going to his throat, his eyes widening in fear.

"Tell me about her gift with animals."

Cesaro shrugged. "No one knows how she does it. I don't think she knows, but every animal, including those in the sky, responds to her. When she was just a little girl, she would tell her father that a horse's leg hurt and where. Sure enough, a few hours later, the horse came up lame. She always knows when a mare will give birth or when there's going to be a problem with a birth. The horses trust her and when she's present, the mares are calm no matter what has to be done."

Zacarias absorbed the information. She'd done such things since she was a child. It was possible she was born psychic, but much more likely she was mage-trained in order to cast a spell powerful enough to entrap him. "Go on."

Cesaro looked more puzzled than ever. "When she was fifteen, a jaguar spooked the herd and the cattle crashed through a fence and ran straight for the children playing soccer. Marguarita stepped in front of them and somehow the cattle veered away from everyone there. They slowed down and stopped without direction." His eyes met Zacarias's once again. "She walked right toward the jaguar and waved me off from shooting it. After a couple of minutes with the two staring at one another, the cat slipped back into the rain forest and we never saw it around here again. Not even tracks."

"What do you know of her mother?" If her father had been a cousin of Cesaro's, perhaps the mother had been mage. There had to be an explanation.

"Her mother was a Chevez from the hacienda in Brazil. You know their family."

He did know the Chevez family, better than he knew any of the others. They were definitely not mage-born, nor were any of them trained in casting spells. The Chevez women had protections placed in their minds from birth. They would be impossible for a vampire to possess or manipulate, not without killing them.

Zacarias closed his fist tight once again as his mind reached for Marguarita. He exercised great discipline to stop himself from touching her. His blood called out to hers. Or was it the other way around? The call was so strong. A compulsion. He swore under his breath in his native language. The woman was a menace.

"If she bothers you, we can remove her from the hacienda during your stay," Cesaro offered, obviously hoping Zacarias would agree to his proposition. "She has many aunts who would love to have her visit."

Another tremor rolled through the ground. Zacarias didn't move a muscle. His tongue slid over the sharpened points of his teeth. His body ached. She had so many sins to pay for, yet he didn't dare go to her—not when he needed to see her—to touch her. He refused to allow his mind to wander, to check, to touch. He was too strong and she could not defeat him.

Cesaro flinched. *"Señor,"* he began uneasily.

"Leave the woman to me."

"I don't understand you. Marguarita is a good girl. She's loved by everyone here. The vampire destroyed her vocal cords, so she can't speak. If that distresses you . . ."

"I do not get distressed."

The very concept of being distressed was foreign to him. But he was disturbed by the need to touch her. To be close to her. To touch all that warm, soft skin and alleviate the terrible craving she had set up for the exquisite taste of her blood.

Cesaro stood up quickly as Zacarias's body began to shimmer and grow transparent. "Wait. Please, *señor,* I need to know you will not harm her."

Zacarias turned glacier-cold eyes on the man. "Do not dare to presume to question me. This is my land. She belongs to me to do with as I will. I will not suffer your interference in this matter. What she has done is between us alone. Have I made myself clear?"

Cesaro gripped the barrel of his rifle until his knuckles turned white. He swallowed hard twice before he very reluctantly nodded his head.

Zacarias had no more time to waste on the man. What was wrong with everyone that they felt it was okay to question his judgment? Clearly a De La Cruz had not been in residence for far too long. His people had forgotten their vows of servitude and *obedience.* This was the very reason why he knew he was obsolete in the world. His ways were long gone. Kill or be killed wasn't fully understood. The world labored under a false illusion that humankind was safe—that monsters such as vampires didn't exist and evil wasn't real. He knew better, but his day was long over.

He dissolved and slipped out of the house, mixing with tear-shaped drops of rain as he made his way slowly back to the hacienda. Even in this form, where he was nearly undetectable, the animals in the stables stamped nervously. Despite his need to find Marguarita, he made himself take a slow sweeping circle around the property, looking for any signs the undead had tracked him to his lair. He needed to prove, not only to her, but to himself, that he was in control, not her.

He had no doubt that one of the Malinov brothers would seek to retaliate after losing so many of their expendable soldiers in their attack on his ranch in Brazil. If they despised anyone more than the prince of the Carpathian people, it was Zacarias. The Malinovs would always believe that the De La Cruz brothers had betrayed them. Instead of turning on the prince and helping to assassinate him, the De La Cruz family had sworn allegiance to him.

Zacarias knew that to kill Mikhail Dubrinsky was to send their people plummeting into extinction. They were as close as a species could get, brushing that fine line, so close to tipping over where recovery would be impossible. With Mikhail alive, Solange's blood and the news of finding out why their women were miscarrying, Zacarias was certain they had every chance now. It was the perfect time to let go of his responsibilities. And he had—until Marguarita Fernandez interfered.

Satisfied that Ruslan Malinov, master of the undead, hadn't had time to find out the reason his soldiers hadn't returned, Zacarias made his way to the main house. His heart accelerated strangely, which only put him on edge. He circled the structure, not once allowing his mind to touch hers. Very slowly he approached the front door, shimmering back into human form and walking inside.

He was *not* going to give in to the rush of heat, the need riding him harder than he had ever imagined possible. He didn't need. He didn't crave. He had been to the top of the highest mountain, traveled to the farthest corners of the earth—looking for—*something*. He had walked the earth for centuries, far longer than most of his kind, killed more undead than imaginable. He had seen treachery at its worst and bravery at its greatest. There were no surprises left to him. Nothing that could change the beat of his heart like this. Nothing that could drive him with such burning need because he simply didn't *need*.

O jelä peje emnimet—sun scorch the woman. There was an answer and he would find it. No one controlled him. He would *not* touch her mind or go looking for her. But he found himself striding through the dark house straight to her bedroom. The door was splintered, hanging on the hinges, the door cracked entirely in half. He frowned, studying the damage he'd done. Wood hung in a series of pieces, the fragments sharp to the point of dangerous.

He waved his hand, mending the mess, not to protect her, or for any other reason such as others looking into her sleeping chamber, but because the sight was not aesthetic. He realized the moment he stepped into the room that her scent lingered behind, but she was in another part of the house, hopefully remembering her duties as a servant in his home.

He looked around her room. It seemed very feminine. It smelled female, but the wash of fear was still present. Although neat and tidy, the wastebasket was overflowing with crumpled paper. He had a sudden memory of her huddled in the corner of her room, her hand out, a piece of paper fluttering in her hand. He looked around. He was almost certain he'd knocked it aside when he'd yanked her to her feet.

A single slip of stationery lay just under the bed. He picked it up and scanned the missive. She had been trying to tell him what happened, why she had been unable to leave him to die in the sun. His gut settled. He couldn't hear the tone of her voice and judge whether she was telling the truth or not by that, but her letter certainly pleaded her case well for her. Like Zacarias, she had felt a compulsion she couldn't possibly resist.

What did that mean? Was someone—*something*—manipulating *both* of them? Perhaps he needed to reevaluate Marguarita's motivation. If she was being manipulated, just as someone was trying to do with him, she was far weaker and would succumb much quicker than a seasoned Carpathian warrior.

He poured the contents of the wastebasket out onto the bed and one by one smoothed each sheet, scanning the contents. Her earlier tries to explain were shaky and lacked confidence, but she kept trying, which told him she was stubborn and determined—and brave. She hadn't gone running to Cesaro who clearly would have been foolish enough to try to protect her. She'd faced up to her crime and waited for him—hoping to explain.

He sighed. It wasn't altogether her fault that she had disobeyed. Compulsions were dangerous and nearly impossible to ignore—as he well knew. He had come to the ranch without reason—the need driving him—and he was experienced in mage treachery. She had no such skills to draw on to save herself.

He shoved the slip of paper into his pocket and waved the others back to the wastebasket before picking up her pillow and inhaling her scent. He breathed her deep into his lungs, giving in to the craving. Her feminine fragrance enveloped him. In truth, it shook him. He smoothed her covers, his hand tracing the image of her on the bed. The source of power had to be close. He could almost feel the warmth of her skin and once again he could taste her exquisite blood on his tongue—better than the finest of wines.

He should have visited every single dwelling on the extensive property and tested each individual. They would all know he was in residence, just by the heavy drapes being pulled. No one would come near the house without an invitation—or they shouldn't. So how was the spell staying so powerful when he was aware of it?

He inhaled the woman's fragrance again, drawing her deep into his lungs. His body responded with a strange tingling, an electrical current that ran through his veins and awakened responses in his body best left alone.

He sighed and went to find Marguarita. He'd fought off the compulsion and proved to himself he was in absolute, total control.

Marguarita pushed the hand-hewed canoe out into the stream and climbed carefully inside. Always before, Julio manned the oars, but she had learned under his watchful eye and knew how to paddle. She thought she'd be terrified in the dark, but strangely, she could see on the water, just as she had in the rain forest. She knew the stream was deep enough to take her all the way to the Amazon. The ribbon of water grew wider, the current stronger as it approached the main river, and she would feel the difference. It was thrilling when Julio was with her, the canoe sliding over the ripples of white water as it approached the roaring Amazon, but alone, with a vampire possibly tracking her, she felt only a terrible urgency to go faster.

Caimans crouched like old dinosaurs on the banks, their eyes glassy and heavy lidded as she swept past. She swallowed hard and pushed the oar through the water. The canoe glided silently along. Under the dark, rolling clouds, the water glistened like an ebony strip cutting through long, hanging trees and roots forming giant cages. She dipped her oar and pushed harder, all the while reaching for the birds in hopes they'd sound the alarm should they feel a predator before her.

As she traveled downstream a strange uneasiness settled over her. Not fear or terror, two things she associated with Zacarias De La Cruz, but a reluctance to continue. She was putting distance between them and with each passing yard a dread filled her. Her heart ached, an actual pain. Intellectually she knew it was not only the right thing to do, but the *only* thing to do, yet her mind refused to believe it. Twice she found herself paddling toward the bank as if her intention was to turn back.

She was fortunate that the rain had swelled the stream so that the current was flowing strong, transporting her even when her arms refused to work to push her faster away from Zacarias. The dread grew in her and the pain spread from her heart to her entire body. Her legs shook. Her arms felt like lead and her mouth went dry.

He was dead. Zacarias De La Cruz was dead, and somehow, by leaving she was responsible. The thought crept unbidden into her mind and once there, she couldn't dislodge it. Grief found its way into her, manifesting itself physically. Her chest became so tight she could barely breathe. Tears swam in her eyes obstructing her vision. There was a terrible screaming in her ears, her own silent protest against his death.

Yet—he was vampire—wasn't he? She was making a desperate run to reach the De La Cruz property ahead of him, to alert the hunters, in effect, call them in to kill him. If he was dead, shouldn't she be rejoicing? Not weeping? Confused, she dragged the paddle into the boat and concentrated on breathing. Zacarias had given her his blood several times. Cesaro had told her that Zacarias had acted fast and saved her life when the vampire had torn out her throat. Was there something in his blood that tied them together in death? He had even forced her to take his blood this last time.

Marguarita pressed her lips together tightly. She was strong, and she would not give in to wild imaginings. She had a mission. Whatever her odd feelings were, they had to be false. The only thing that could matter to her was saving the people she loved at the hacienda. The rain began to pick up again, the steady drizzle turning into a relentless downpour. She had to get to the river and across to the De La Cruz property to call in the hunters. The stream was moving very fast, taking her quickly through the rain forest to dump her into the broad, swollen Amazon.

Her heart began to pound. She had to pay attention if she was going to survive. The sound of the river was thunderous, drowning out nearly everything else. The canoe swept around a bend and the water turned even rougher and faster. She couldn't think about Zacarias or vampires, all that mattered was pushing her paddle into the water to keep from being slung into the series of rocks looming up ahead.

She'd watched Julio maneuver through that treacherous set of drops and rocks leading to the river a hundred times, and she'd laughed with the thrill and danger of the moment. But she relied on his skills and had absolute confidence that he knew every rock position ahead. She wasn't so certain about herself. Julio had allowed her to try it several times, but the water hadn't been flowing quite so fast and it hadn't been dark.

She took a firm grip on the oar and summoned her new reflexes. Her eyes burned with strain as she approached the series of boulders rising through the rushing stream. Forcing her breath out in an effort to relax into the wild ride, she felt the first drop of the canoe as it entered the boulder garden. She called up every intricate maneuver Julio had showed to her. She performed the pattern carefully, as if he was in the boat with her, calling out the moves as she dropped low, shifted her weight back and rounded the first rock to hit the gate perfectly aligned for the next drop.

The water boiled around her, a frothy white in the bleak darkness. Rain pounded the stream and without her heightened vision, she would not have been able to negotiate the tight chute that switched nearly completely back to avoid a particularly brutal stone. The thrill of riding the white water slipped into her frozen veins, easing the terror of vampires. She had always loved the trips into the rain forest with Julio. They'd gone on many adventures and she wished he was with her right then.

The next set of obstacles was the trickiest, the canoe had to go into the gate at the perfect angle to shoot around the surge that could flip the boat. She could hear Julio's voice in her ear, shouting instructions on how to keep the oar in the water to still the canoe for the split seconds it took to turn sharp and then a hard push to send the boat flying forward. She hit the narrow chasm between the two boulders exactly the way Julio had done it, skirting the treacherous roiling water by inches.

The canoe shot into open water and she was on the Amazon. The current caught the canoe and she had to use all of her strength to angle toward the bank. The river was swollen and running fast. It took everything she had to paddle to the edge. As it was, she was slightly downstream from where she wanted to be when she managed to snag a hanging limb and drag the canoe onto the bank.

The slope was extremely muddy and slippery. She was exhausted, cold and wet and miserable. She tried climbing her way up the incline, but kept slipping back. The wind picked up, a ferocious force, slamming into her again and again with such power it tore at the thick braid of hair, tugging out strands so that even her head ached. She gave up trying to climb and crawled instead, clawing her way to the top, sliding back time and time again, until her back and arms ached and she was afraid she'd never be able to lift them again. The rain, driven by the wind, stung her body as she reached the top and lay for a moment trying to catch her breath.

Marguarita didn't bother to get to her feet but crawled across the uneven ground to the shelter of a large kapok tree, trying to get out of the rain. She sank back against the thick fins that made up the root cage and tried to catch her breath. The memory of the vampire washed over her again. Something about the difference between her attacker and Zacarias eluded her, but she knew it was important.

She had been representing the De La Cruz family for years. Most of the families the ranch supported had never set eyes on one of the brothers. She had been the one to bring food and medicine when needed, to arrange to pay debt or allow families to borrow in times of trouble, earning the family loyalty and good will. She had made the De La Cruz family one of the most beloved in the region. Her generosity—okay, it was their money, but she was the one making the effort.

She stood cautiously, forcing her weak legs to work. Without warning the ground rolled, throwing Marguarita to her knees. Instantly ants swarmed over her boots and hands. She suppressed a small cry, knowing Zacarias wasn't dead after all. Why had she been so ridiculous? He had returned to the hacienda and discovered her gone. She leaped to her feet and began to run aimlessly, a stupid, careless mistake.

Giant moths fluttered around her, drawn by her light as she ran. Bats wheeled and dipped catching the insects her lamp revealed. Large eyes stared at her for a moment just feet from her, then the animal leaped onto the trunk of a tree and raced to higher branches. A snake coiled above her and lifted its head.

The ground rolled again and thunder crashed. For a moment she could barely breathe, once again the frozen prey a monster had cornered. The wind rushed through the trees, bending the smaller ones over until they formed arches. Marguarita took shelter in the root cage of the large kapok tree trying to force herself to think—not panic. Clutching the roots, she glared into the forest.

She had been right to believe him vampire. The insects boiled out of the ground and rushed down the trunks of trees at his bidding. Poisonous snakes slithered through wet vegetation and leeches crawled over leaves in an effort to reach her. Everything she'd ever known about vampires came back to her—along with the memory of the one attacking her.

She shuddered, the need to curl up in a ball and hide nearly overwhelming her. She could still smell his fetid breath, see his rotting flesh, and the ugly, twisted claws he had for fingernails. His eyes had gone completely red as they stared at her, trying to rip the information of Zacarias's whereabouts from her mind. She'd concentrated on keeping her mind blank, the shields strong, refusing to give up the eldest of the De La Cruz family.

The vampire had murdered her father and he would kill her—she knew that with a certainty—but she also knew Zacarias or one of his brothers would hunt the vampire down and destroy him. He would never kill again. She had held out even when the horrible creature had shown her his razor-sharp teeth and threatened to tear her flesh out and eat it in front of her. She shuddered remembering his red eyes and his breath. That horrible smell of decaying flesh.

Marguarita sat up straighter. As scared as she'd been by Zacarias, he hadn't been the same. There was no terrible rotting smell. Didn't vampires rot from the inside? He had frightened her—no—*terrified* her. She touched the mark he'd made, rubbing it with the pad of her finger. The attack hadn't been the same. He hadn't felt evil. Or vampire. He'd felt like a dangerous, scary predator, but not evil.

The revelation shocked her. Zacarias was a wild animal, a feral creature that hunted and killed for survival. He was no vampire, not that it mattered. She wasn't going back to the hacienda. Not as long as he was around. She feared few creatures, but Zacarias was an altogether different proposition. The mark he'd left on her throbbed, burning a little, reminding her that no animal in the rain forest was as unpredictable or as violent.

The way he'd come at her, so purposeful, his face an expressionless mask, his mouth set in a cruel, unrelenting line, his eyes flat and cold and without mercy. Her mouth went dry and her heart began to pound again. She couldn't have moved if she'd wanted to, frozen in place like cornered prey. That was exactly how she felt—his prey. She knew he had deliberately frightened her. She'd tried to connect with him in the way she did wild things, and for a moment she thought he'd responded, but then he was worse than ever. He was dangerous, but no vampire.

She had to make it to shelter and determine her next move, and that meant finding the marks on the trees Julio had carved to show the way. She had to backtrack and make her way to the point where they usually pulled the canoe from the water.

She waited for the ferocious wind to die down a little and she pushed herself to her feet to step cautiously away from the shelter of the tree. The branches overhead groaned and creaked and she looked up. Bats hung from every limb, and darted around the tree, vying for space. At first she thought they had come there to eat the fruit, but they weren't eating. More and more settled in the branches, hanging upside down, wings folded, tiny eyes bright—watching her.

A chill went through her. Had she fled from Zacarias only to stumble into a vampire's lair? She knew they used bats and insects as puppets at times. She backed away from the tree and nearly fell over a rotting log. Termites poured out of the wood. She pressed her lips together, refusing to panic. She had to think—make a decision—and she couldn't do that if she allowed herself to go to pieces.

She looked up at the bats. Very gently she reached for them, sending a warm wave of greeting, careful not to push too hard. Her touch was very delicate, but she connected. She should have been able to feel evil if they were commanded by the undead, but they seemed ordinary bats, anxious to go out about their business. They were hungry, needing to feed but something had stopped them—used them—commanded them.

He was using insects and bats to keep an eye on her. He wanted to know what she was up to and had sent spies. An idea took root and she assessed the situation, trying to think logically. Perhaps the bats were the wrong kind of spies to use against her. She had her own gift with animals and insects and it was very possible she could turn them all to her side.

She looked up at the bats again and sent another warm, welcoming wave, urging them to go ahead and eat. She'd slow down so they could do both, follow her and yet eat along the way. Some of the bats gave the impression of fruit while others insects. He'd even mixed species. She smiled up at the little creatures, feeling the kinship that came whenever she touched an animal with her mind. They were connected to Zacarias through fear, through his commands, but she actually formed a bond with them, a kind of empathy that was mutual. Most animals and even some insects strengthened the relationship, feeling the deep tie between them. She wanted to form that affinity with the bats Zacarias had chosen to spy on her.

Marguarita kept the flow of warmth and the invitation to eat. One bat took the initiative, perhaps he was hungrier than the others, but he flew to the nearest fruit and settled to eat. Immediately bats filled the air, many settling on fruit to feast while others went after insects. She didn't make the mistake of hurrying away—that would trigger the need to follow whatever orders Zacarias had given them. She was elated when she found the point where Julio and she usually beached their canoe.

Water was everywhere, dripping from leaves, running down the slopes and mountainsides creating hundreds of small, cascading waterfalls. Water collected in puddles and stood on the forest floor, eventually finding its way to drain in the Amazon River. The sound of it running was ever present—just like the continual hum of insects. She angled away from the loud flow of water heading toward the interior.

Julio had marked branches—as children they'd tried that—but eventually plants anchored themselves to everything—stems, branches, trunks, even leaves of other plants wrapping themselves around the trees. The vegetation was so thick the bark was mostly hidden so there was no point in cutting into the trees. It didn't take long for any marks to be covered. Climbing up the trees were woody lianas, using the trees as gateways to the light above the canopy. Ferns only added to the mix, embedding themselves in the bark as well, climbing toward the sunlight.

Thick roots snaked across the forest floor, anchoring the large trees to earth while the tops reached high into the clouds. The giant buttress roots stabilized and fed the enormous trees, some twisting into elaborate shapes while others formed great wooden fins. Regardless of how they looked, the roots dominated the floor, claiming large spaces and housing bats, animals and hundreds of species of insects.

Julio and Marguarita had slashed marks deep into the roots and both knew where to look, even in the event creeper vines and ferns managed to weave themselves among the branching fins. She swept the brilliant green ferns aside and sure enough, the root had been chipped, leaving a weathered scar.

She moved slowly, continuing to send her communications to the bats. Warmth. Regard. Kinship. No commands. No demands. Zacarias would need to seek the darkness of the soil before the sun came up. It was only a few more hours. She could trick him that long. The bats were very receptive and wouldn't raise an alarm, not when she wasn't running or trying to hide from them.

She tapped into the bats for her own warning system, hoping she would recognize their alert when a predator was close. A fallen emergent with a giant trunk lay in her path, years old, saplings already filling in the void it left. The rotting trunk was covered in insects, fungus and creepers. She studied it carefully, aware of the dangerous snakes and poisonous frogs she could easily touch when climbing over it.

There was nothing else she could do, not without veering from her path, something she didn't want to do at night in a rain forest. She stepped forward and reached up, determined to climb, pushing at the poisonous insects and frogs with her mind in hopes they would move away from her.

Hands caught her waist and jerked her back against a hard body. "Are you dim-witted, woman, or do you simply enjoy placing yourself in danger?" Zacarias's voice purred in her ear, a soft menace that chilled her to her very core.

5

Marguarita went very still. What if she'd been wrong? What if he was truly vampire? The mark Zacarias had left at the side of her throat throbbed and burned. His breath stirred the hair at the back of her neck . . . She stiffened. His fingers brushed her skin, moving aside the heavy rope of her hair. His body was tight against hers so that she could feel every breath he took. He smelled feral, a wild, dangerous creature trapping her far from all aid. His every muscle imprinted on her, every beat of his heart.

His question penetrated her mind. *Dim-witted?* Had he really just asked if she was dim-witted? Fury burned through her, mixing with fear.

Warmth poured into her mind, heralding Zacarias. Earlier when he'd struck, he had penetrated deep, invaded and conquered. This was different. This time he used a slow assault, a heat spreading like molasses, filling her mind with—him. Her breath caught in her throat and she bit down hard on her lower lip. The warmth didn't just stay in her mind, it spread through her body, a thick lava that took her veins an inch at a time, moving lower and lower. Her breasts felt heavy and aching. Her nipples peaked. Her core grew hotter.

Her physical reaction to his invasion was more than disturbing—it was every bit as horrifying as his biting her neck. Every instinct screamed at her to run, but she didn't even struggle, horror and fury holding her in place. His hands caged her, settling on her waist, large hands, shaping her hips, feeling too possessive. Flames licked her skin right through her clothes where he touched her.

She had never had such a female reaction to a male in her life. She'd been told how danger could mask itself in seduction and now she could bear witness to those rumors. Zacarias was as sensual as a male could be, igniting a slow-burning fire inside of her. Marguarita shivered, fearing for her very soul. She made the sign of the cross in a silent attempt to save herself.

"I know you can hear me—whether I speak aloud or inside your mind. Your blood calls to mine. Mine answers. Do not pretend you cannot hear me."

She moistened her lips. *I am not dim-witted.* A little thunderstruck maybe, but she understood him. She just didn't understand herself or what was happening to her body.

She trembled, wanting to wrench herself from his hand, yet she burned for him. She could hear his heartbeat, the sound echoing in her own veins.

He leaned closer until his lips touched her ear. "If you are not dim-witted . . ." One hand slipped from her hip back to her waist, burning through her clothes until her skin was branded with his palm imprint. The other hand slowly wrapped around her throat, one finger at a time. He forced her head back until she rested against his chest, until she had no choice but to stare into his dark, merciless eyes. They stared at each other, locked together in some strange combat she didn't understand.

"Then do you have a death wish?"

His voice didn't just whisper in her ear, but over her skin, touching nerve endings, the trail of fingers brushing gently, shaping her body. The sensation was so real she shivered, fear choking her. She swallowed hard against his hand. Mutely she shook her head. It was impossible to look away from him. His eyes were compelling, so dark and fathomless, heat and fire where he'd looked so flat and cold before. There was something real inside of him—she could see it in his eyes. He wasn't entirely a killing machine, nor was he the undead as she'd first believed—those eyes were too alive. His body was too hot—too hard.

Marguarita reached for the animal part of him—the biggest part of him. He had long ago lost all civility—or maybe he'd been born as he was now, mostly cunning, savage and extremely territorial. She understood animals, even dangerous predators. Pushing aside her fear of the Carpathian, she concentrated on the animal, trying to find a way to soothe him. She didn't expect to be friends, no more so than she would have a jaguar, but she'd encountered one of the big cats and they had both gone their own ways with no animosity. She hoped for the same with Zacarias.

The problem was, he confused her far more than a large cat—or bird of prey. She felt the flowing warmth that always preceded the connection. And it was easier than she'd believed, as if she already knew the path, as if it was well worn. She soothed him as she would a wild thing, a soft approach, touching him gently, stroking with her mind to quiet and calm him.

Zacarias abruptly stepped back away from her, dropping his hands, his eyes glacier cold and more frightening than ever. "You are mage-born."

It was an accusation, a curse, a promise of dark retaliation. Marguarita shook her head vigorously denying the charge. She had no idea why he was accusing her of being a mage—a being who could cast spells. That would be more him than her—*he* was the one bemusing her. If his eyes were anything to go by, no mage wanted to cast a spell around Zacarias De La Cruz and most certainly she didn't.

"What are you then?" he demanded.

She frowned. The answer should have been obvious, but then she was thinking of him as an untamed, feral animal, perhaps she was closer to the mark than she knew. *I am just a woman.*

Zacarias studied that perfect pale face in front of him for a long time. She was streaked with mud. Exhausted. Her heart-shaped face was all eyes, enormous and frightened.

I am just a woman.

Five simple words, yet what did she mean? He knew women—but none like her. She was far more than *just a woman*. He searched his memories and he had many over centuries of time, but no one had ever caught his interest, not like this *woman* had.

They stared at one another for a long time. "You will return to the hacienda with me." He stated it. Ordered it. Gave the command and waited for her typical reaction—disobedience. Perhaps she had some infirmity that made her do the opposite of a direct order.

He watched her throat work, a delicate swallowing and another wave of fear washed over him, hastily suppressed—one didn't show fear to a predator. He knew they were still very much connected and he was feeling her emotions. It was interesting seeing himself through her eyes. He knew, on a strictly intellectual basis, that other animals, including men, thought him a killer, but he didn't have a visceral reaction to the knowledge. Connected as he was to her on that primitive level, he felt her emotions as if they were his own and it was—uncomfortable.

Her small tongue licked at that perfect bow of her lower lip. She stepped back very slowly, feeling with one boot for solid ground. He shook his head and she stopped instantly.

Zacarias read her thoughts easily on her face. She wanted to run and she didn't care if anyone—including him—considered the act cowardly. Her self-preservation instinct was strong now. She'd sacrificed herself once. As far as she was concerned, that was enough. She'd been punished.

"I am not finished with you, woman. You will return to the hacienda with me while I figure out what is going on. And you will not leave again without my permission."

That got to her. He could see the storm clouds gathering in her dark eyes. He couldn't look away even if he wanted to. Her eyes weren't a dull gray like the world around her. Neither was her hair. Both were rich ebony, a deep midnight black, a true absence of color. Her mouth fascinated him. Her lips should have been gray or dull white, but he swore they were a darker pink. He blinked several times to try to rid himself of the impression, but the strange color remained, making him a little dizzy. She fascinated him as no other could possibly do.

Marguarita's chin went up. *If you are going to kill me, do so right here. Right now.*

His eyebrow shot up. "If I am going to kill you, I will choose the time and place, not be dictated to by a woman who does not know the meaning of obedience."

She pulled a pen and notepad from her pocket and began to write. Zacarias swept both items from her hand and pocketed them.

Use our blood bond.

Mutely she shook her head and reached toward his pocket.

He shook his head just as resolutely, no longer shocked that she disobeyed him. He was certain she had an infirmity, some rare, peculiar mental disorder from birth, that made her do the opposite of what any authority figure told her.

"I read all forty-seven missives this night. I do not wish to read another."

All forty-seven? You went into my private room? They were in the wastebasket. Thrown away. Obviously not meant for you to read.

So she would use the blood bond when she chose. Something close to satisfaction rose in him. The fear had faded enough that she responded much more naturally to him. "Of course they were meant for me to read, *kislány kuŋenak minan*—my little lunatic. They were clearly addressed to *Señor* Zacarias De La Cruz." He bowed slightly. "Very formal and proper of you. One would think you would be able to carry out simple instructions."

Give me back my paper and pen.

"You will use the blood bond between us." He knew it made her uncomfortable because it was a much more intimate form of communication, but he found himself craving the intimacy of their bond.

Her eyes went even darker, turned obsidian, flaring like shiny firestones. She clenched her teeth together in a snapping bite. The whiteness of them caught his attention. Without thought, he gripped her upper arms and yanked her close, turning her head toward him so he could see the intense color—gleaming white, like little pearls. Not gray. Not the dingy brownish white he was used to. For a moment there was nothing else in the world, but those small, white teeth and her incredible almost black eyes.

Something smacked his chest, not hard, he barely noticed, but her little yelp made him look down. She had slammed her palms against his chest and had obviously hurt herself. He frowned at her. "What are you doing now?"

I'm hitting you, you brute. What does it feel like?

She had a temper. He recognized the smoldering fire now. She'd hurt herself though, and truthfully, he'd barely felt a thing. "Is that what you call it? You really are a little crazy. No wonder Cesaro tried to remove you from the house. He feared I would be upset with your insanity."

Insanity?

Marguarita closed her fist and took a punch at him. Judging from the way she threw it, someone had taught her how to fight. He ducked to the side before she could land the blow and caught her, spinning her around, crossing her arms over her breasts and holding her tight against his body. His breath came out in a burst of sound that shocked him. He went very still, resting his mouth against her neck, against that warm pulse that beat so frantically and called so loudly to him. Laughter? Had he laughed?

Had he really laughed? That was impossible. He had never laughed. Not that he remembered. Maybe as a young child, a mere boy, but he doubted it. Where had that sound come from? Was it possible this crazy, dim-witted woman was his lifemate? By all that was holy, it could not be. He could not in any way be mated to someone incapable of following the simplest of directions. And his emotions and colors should have returned at once. But truthfully, he felt more alive in that moment than he had in a thousand years.

Like him, she had gone quite still in his arms again, like a frightened little rabbit. She shivered, her wet, muddy clothes clinging to her soft, feminine form. The moment he became aware she was cold, he removed the mud and rain from her clothing, his body heating hers. Such things were natural to his kind, and with her, he had to remember mundane things.

"I will make excuses for you as you did not have a mother to teach you proper etiquette, but my patience will go only so far." He whispered the words against her ear, determined that she would learn who was in charge. Certainly not some little slip of a thing, so silly she went out in the rain forest unescorted and at night. "You have certain duties."

I know my duties. What time is it?

Puzzled, he glanced up at the boiling sky. "About four in the morning."

Exactly. I am off duty. This is my time.

He was tempted to bite that sweet spot between her neck and shoulder as punishment for her continued defiance. "When a De La Cruz is in residence, you are on duty from sunset to dawn. Or whenever *I* tell you.

O jelä peje terád, emni—sun scorch you, woman. Do not argue with me. Have you learned nothing in the last few hours? You will not go unescorted, *anywhere.* You are a woman. A single woman. And you will have a chaperone at all times."

She made no sound, but he felt her absolute rejection of his decree. Deep inside, it came again, that strange sound that started in his belly and welled up like champagne bubbles. By all that was holy, she made him laugh. He *felt* amusement. This slight woman brought laughter into his life. Until he figured out why she had such power over him, he wasn't about to leave her side. She could deny his authority all she wanted, but she was about to learn what and who was the dominant in her life.

He inhaled her scent and found himself fighting the call of her blood. He tasted her in his mouth. That exquisite, rare taste beyond anything he'd ever known bursting in his mouth, trickling down his throat to seep into his veins, pouring through his body like molten gold. Her skin was so warm and soft, her pulse calling to him. He closed his eyes and simply listened to the rhythm of her heart. He wasn't hungry, yet he craved her, like an addiction, wanting to bite down, to feel her soft flesh . . .

His hands slid up over her wrists, stroking, his palms brushing her breasts. Her nipples were peaked with cold—or excitement. He couldn't make his mind stop long enough to find out which. His every sense, his entire being focused on her body. The shape of her. The feel of her. Time slowed. Tunneled. There was only his hands sliding over her, cupping her breasts, his thumbs brushing those hard nipples. His heart hammering. Hers answering.

Heat rushed into him. Filled him. Blood pounded through his center, rushed into his cock, until he was hard and thick and aching—and shocked. His body burned from the inside out. There was a strange roaring in his head. He felt on fire, flames scorching his skin, racing through his veins. Erotic images filled his mind, her body writhing beneath his, a million things he'd seen in his existence, a million ways to make her his. He had seen such things, but never once thought of them. Never once in all his existence had he ever entertained the idea of taking a woman without consent. Never considered burying his body deep in a woman and doing whatever he wanted with her—until that moment. The images and his terrible, brutal need overwhelmed him. Tiny beads of blood dotted his skin, sweat as he'd never known it. He felt edgy, out of control, insane with the terrible craving that had spread from his need of her blood to his body's need of hers.

He shoved her away from him, breathing deep, taking in great gulps of air to stop the madness burning through him. He had known his soul was in pieces, no more than a sieve held together with tiny, fragile threads, but this—this would destroy him—destroy his honor. He wiped the sweat from his face and stared at the blood smears on his hands. "What are you, woman? You have bewitched me."

She shook her head mutely, so pale she nearly glowed there in the darkness. *I didn't. I swear I didn't. I don't know why this is happening to you.*

She'd felt him all right, felt the rising demand of his cock pushing against her body with urgent demand.

"You will not control me."

I'm not trying to.

She took two steps away from him, staring at the large bulge in the front of his trousers. He saw the exact moment when her fear got the better of her and she turned and ran from him.

Zacarias took another deep slow breath and spread out his arms, welcoming another shape, needing the relief from his male human form. Feathers burst along his skin as he shifted. This time the harpy eagle was enormous. He took flight, staying low as he gave chase. The eagle twisted and turned, easily making his way through the trees, hunting his prey. He loomed over her. She glanced over her shoulder, her eyes wide with terror as he dove, his talons reaching for her, snagging her as she ran, and lifting her into the air, Zacarias's enormous strength aiding the large harpy eagle.

Marguarita struggled, but as he took her higher, his giant wingspan beating to gain height, and the ground dropped away, she went utterly still, her hands wrapping around the bird's legs. Once he gained altitude, he sped his way through the rain forest back toward the hacienda. Harpy eagles easily flew a good fifty miles per hour when they wanted, and with the ferocious wind at its back, the bird swiftly covered the distance, reaching the ranch in record time.

Zacarias dropped Marguarita gently in the grass just outside the front door. He shifted as his feet touched the ground beside her. She didn't attempt to run again, but lay quietly, her hands pressed tightly over her waist where the talons had clutched her so tightly. Zacarias bent down and caught her up in his arms, cradling her to his chest.

Her eyes took up half her face and the fear was back, all traces of temper gone. She couldn't scream and her mouth wasn't open to try to call for aid, and that upset him more than it should have.

"Do not look at me that way," he snapped. "Had you simply come with me without a fuss, I would not have had to drag you back in such a manner. Has no one ever taught you consequences?"

She looked away from, shifting her gaze to somewhere over his shoulder, but she couldn't contain the shudder that went through her. Perhaps his voice had been too harsh. He had to remember her infirmity. Her father certainly should have addressed her need to flout authority, but he was there now, and he had no doubt he could get the job done.

He waved his hand at the door and it opened for him. He swept through with Marguarita in his arms and placed her on the sofa while he turned back to employ safeguards. He wove intricate, very strong guards around the entire structure, taking his time, determined no one would enter—and no one would leave while he slept. The workers on his properties knew when a De La Cruz was in residence, they were not to be disturbed during daylight hours. When he was satisfied no one—not even one of his brothers—could get through his weave, he turned back to study the woman who embodied the word *mystery*.

Marguarita sat up slowly. He saw her catch her breath and pain flashed across her face. He frowned and stepped close to her. The scent of blood hit him. Zacarias pulled her to her feet. She kept her hands pressed tightly to her waist. He could see small red droplets trickling through her fingers. Humans didn't heal themselves. He hadn't spent time around humans in years. He'd fed and was gone, a ghost in the night no one ever saw—or remembered.

"Let me see." He softened his voice when her gaze jumped to his. "Take your hands away, woman. I need to see the damage done."

Apparently he sounded just as menacing when he used a low tone because she shivered, but couldn't seem to move.

Very gently he gripped her wrists and moved her hands. The puncture wounds from the grizzly-sized talons of the harpy eagle wrapped around her, front to back on either side. He should have thought about what those talons would do to human flesh, not about her defiance. Watching her face, he spit into his hands. His saliva would not only help mend the punctures, but he had numbing agent that would stop the pain as he healed her. He fit his palms easily over the marks, pressing into her, his hands nearly spanning her midsection.

"You will feel warm, but it should not hurt you," he assured her.

She was trembling so hard he wasn't certain she could remain standing. Her eyes stared into his with the exact look he'd seen on the prey of cobras. She looked mesmerized and terrified, unable to look away from him.

"Stop fearing me." He had wanted her to be afraid, now he wished he could take it back. She looked very fragile, vulnerable, and so very alone. "I will not allow anything to happen to you. It is my duty to look after you." He was telling the truth to her. Nothing would take this woman from him—certainly not death. By some miracle or some devilish trick, he was at long last coming to life, his body reborn, his mind once again intrigued.

He looked around the room and everything in it remained a dull gray. When he looked back at her, he could see emerging color, faint, but there. Her eyelashes were that same amazing black as the rope of her hair. Enormous eyes of deep dark chocolate stared back at him. Her eyebrows were black. Her lips were definitely pink. Colors could only be restored by a lifemate. Emotions—and he was having unfamiliar reactions to her—could only be restored by a lifemate. The fact that his body had reacted physically to her was astonishing, problematic and yet exhilarating—if he could feel exhilaration. But a lifemate would have restored those things instantly.

Mages had infiltrated, occupying the neighboring ranch only a few months earlier, biding their time in hopes of destroying the De La Cruz family. Dominic and Zacarias had stopped them, but there was a slight chance the alliance between the master vampires and the mages had held and mages had found their way back for another attempt. If Marguarita was shadowed by a mage spell—he would have known. As much as he kept coming back to that explanation, a dread was growing in him that he knew the real explanation.

If Marguarita truly was his lifemate, then something had gone wrong, and he feared he knew the answer to what that was. He had not found her in time. His soul was in tatters, already beyond repair. His other half could not seal him to her, could not bring light to the utter darkness within him. It was no surprise that he was a lost cause. He had probably been born that way, but still, there was a time when he'd dreamed of this moment, when he'd envisioned a lifemate and even actively sought one.

His palms grew warm as he pushed heat through his body into hers. Her lungs fought for air and he purposely breathed for her, calming her, the air flowing naturally through his until her body followed the same even rhythm. Her heart pounded so hard he feared she would have a heart attack.

"Just breathe, *miĉa emni kuŋenak minan*—my beautiful lunatic." There was an inadvertent ache in his voice, a mourning for what he'd lost long before he'd ever found it.

Marguarita looked up at Zacarias De La Cruz's strong face. It was a face carved from the very mountains, chiseled with battle and age, yet strangely handsome. This was not a man who had ever been a boy, he was all warrior. For the first time, deep in his eyes, she saw sorrow. The emotion was deep and real and when she touched his mind, she wanted to weep. He didn't appear to realize the depths of his anguish, or maybe he simply didn't acknowledge emotion, but it made her want to weep for him.

He was completely self-contained, not needing anyone. So powerful. And so utterly alone. He inflicted pain, terrified her and then so very gently healed her wounds. Perhaps he was a little mad from being alone for so long. Each time he called her something in his language, his voice softened almost to a caress, his words wrapping around her like strong arms. Sadly for her, that lonely, feral quality in him drew compassion from her. Already her mind reached for his, automatically soothing him, sending him warmth and understanding.

Without thought she lifted her hand to touch those deep lines carved into his face. He caught her wrist, startling her. She hadn't been aware she was actually contemplating touching him. Her wrist ached from the force of his palm slapping her skin. He was as hard as a kapok tree, his flesh not giving at all. His fingers wrapped around her wrist easily, clamping down like a vise, making it impossible to pull away. Her heart slammed hard in her chest and she blinked up at him. Her breath exploded out of her lungs. She'd managed to stir the tiger again, without even thinking.

I'm sorry. Truly.

The suspicion in his eyes was so like a wary wild creature that she couldn't stop that flow of compassion and warmth from her mind into his. She felt as if she needed to calm him. He didn't belong inside a house. There was no way four walls could contain his power or his savage nature. She couldn't imagine anything or anybody being at ease around him. He was too dominant, taking over the room, his aristocratic ways and hard authority adding to the terrifying aura surrounding him.

"Were you planning on petting me?"

There was no sarcasm in his tone, but his question hurt. She licked her suddenly dry lips and shook her head. She didn't know what she had been doing. If she had her pen and paper—maybe she could try to express herself, but she felt cut off from the world most of the time, like this moment. How did she try with mere impressions to convey the way her strange gift manifested?

She wasn't even certain how her gift worked. She only knew that everything in her reached out to the wildness in him, to the tortured soul, stark and lonely and in need. He didn't even know he was in need. How could she explain when she didn't have a voice?

I'm sorry, she repeated, unable to think what else to do.

Zacarias's expression remained absolute stone as he brought her fingertips to his face and held them there. "Do not be sorry. I am not."

Her stomach performed some weird acrobatic somersault at the touch of his skin beneath the pads of her fingers.

"If you wish to touch me, you have my permission."

For the first time since the vampire had attacked her, she was glad she couldn't speak. There were no words. Nothing. She should have been irritated by his aristocratic condescension, but instead she wanted to smile.

She had no excuses. Whatever compulsion he seemed so worried about was obviously working on her as well. And without her pen and paper she felt vulnerable, stripped naked, unable to communicate. She swallowed hard and nodded, wondering a little hysterically if he thought she should thank him for his consent.

He dropped his hand, leaving hers against his shadowed jaw. She pressed her palm into that dark scruff and felt her heart reach out to his. The sensation was so strong it scared her. She dropped her hand abruptly and stepped back, confused at her reactions to him. She was very afraid of him, yet the sadness in him weighed so heavily on her she couldn't stop herself from feeling compassion.

She'd done this to him. She was guilty and there was no getting around that. He had come here to end his life honorably, and she had stopped him, leaving him once more in the loneliness of his bleak world. If there was truly a man who was an island unto himself, it was Zacarias De La Cruz. She couldn't see his entire lonely world, but she felt the tip of it and that was enough to make her want to weep forever. She owed him and a Fernandez always paid their debts.

I didn't know what I was doing when I stopped you from ending your burdens. If I could go back and undo it . . . Would she? Could she stand by and let him die? Her shoulders slumped. She couldn't lie to him. She would never be able to just stand there while he burned in the sun. It was beyond her ability. She raised unhappy eyes to his. *I'm sorry.* Was there nothing else she could say to him?

Zacarias studied her face for so long she began to think he wouldn't speak again. Then his gaze dropped, drifting over her body, studying her feminine form much like one of the ranchers assessing stock. She bit her lip hard to keep from shoving him away from her. She wasn't a horse. She owed him, yes, but she'd apologized more than once. And he didn't have to look at her as if she was a *germ.*

His gaze jumped back to her face, locking with hers. "I am reading your thoughts." His hand dropped to hers. He lifted her clenched fist to his chest and one by one pried open her fingers. "You are a bad-tempered little thing, aren't you? And very confused. One moment you feel remorse and think to offer me your services and the next you think to strike me. You already serve me. I have only to order and you will provide whatever I require. As for striking me, it is not advisable or permitted."

Talking to him was much like having fur rubbed the wrong way, she decided. It mattered little that everything he said was true. She had been about to call a truce with him, to offer her services willingly—not grudgingly. That man was so arrogant he didn't seem to know the difference. And as for striking him—it might not matter whether or not it was permitted if he kept talking like that to her.

A slow, rusty smile, very faint, but real, softened the hard line of his mouth. It was brief, she barely caught it, but his smile was—incredible.

"I am still reading your thoughts."

She frowned at him. *That isn't polite. I can't help what I'm thinking.* Maybe she'd conjured up that smile, it had disappeared so fast—more like ice cracking.

"Of course you can. You will sleep during the daylight hours as I do. You will not, under any circumstances, leave the hacienda without my permission. You will provide for all my needs until I leave. And most of all, you will obey me instantly, without question."

What he needed was a robot, not a woman. She fought not to roll her eyes. *How long will you stay?* God help her if it was longer than another night.

His eyebrow shot up. "You have no need of that information. You will be happy to serve me as long as I choose to be in residence."

He was serious. She could see that he was totally serious. He expected her to be happy—even grateful to serve him—the arrogant, impossible, *dominant* royal pain in the neck. *Should I curtsey, your majesty?*

His brows drew together. The silence grew until the very walls seemed to expand with the tension. His gaze remained locked on hers, unblinking and menacing. She fought not to look away—not to be totally cowed by him. He appeared enormous. He dominated the entire room, his shoulders blocking out everything behind him, making her aware of his power—and her vulnerability.

"Perhaps the alliance between our families has come to an end. If that is what you wish, you have only to say you will not honor our agreement."

Her breath caught in her throat. He wouldn't allow her to leave. She could feel the need in him. He couldn't. He didn't recognize that he had emotions boiling deep below the surface. She tapped into them through their primitive animal connection, but not only didn't he recognize his own feelings, he had no idea they were there. Even if she allowed her fear of him to ruin the alliances between the De La Cruz family and her large extended family, it wouldn't save her.

She pressed her lips together and shook her head. *I wish to serve you.*

"Without question."

She gritted her teeth. He wanted his pound of flesh for her sins. Or maybe she was reading him wrong. He didn't seem to have the least idea how to deal with humans. He probably hadn't been in polite society for hundreds of years.

"Nor did I care to do so," he said, obviously still reading her mind.

She considered taking great delight in stitching his mouth closed while he slept in his chamber. The moment she began to think there was a remote possibility that he could have excuses for his imperious and crass behavior, he opened his mouth and ruined everything.

She flashed him a quick look and saw his lips curve into that ridiculously incredible very brief, faint smile. Her stomach reacted with the same earlier slow-rolling somersault.

"I am getting the distinct impression of someone, who looks suspiciously like you, sewing my mouth closed with a needle and thread. Could I possibly be interpreting your thoughts incorrectly?"

Marguarita tried her best to look innocent. *Perhaps we could communicate more accurately if you gave me back my pen and paper. That way, we wouldn't have these little misunderstandings.* Surely that wasn't a lie. And if nothing else, it might keep her out of trouble.

"I doubt a pen and paper has that much power," he remarked.

She really wished he'd stay out of her head. *I need to sit down, Señor De La Cruz.* She hadn't realized she was swaying. Shock maybe, but suddenly the room was spinning.

He caught her arm and lowered her onto the sofa. "Would you like a glass of water?"

Anything for a reprieve from his overwhelming presence. She nodded her head, trying to look like the fainting type. She was fairly sturdy, so maybe he wouldn't completely believe it, but he was so feudal it was just possible she had a good shot at it.

His mouth did that slight curving twitch that indicated a faint smile. He shook his head and handed her a glass of water. "You are not very good at censuring your thoughts. Tell me what your normal day is like."

She shrugged and ran through her days in her mind. Bath. Brushing hair. Cleaning her room. Breakfast. Cleaning the house. Ordering for the homes on the ranch. Checking horses and cattle for illness or injuries. Making lunch. Taking hot coffee and sandwiches to Julio. Riding with him while they chatted . . .

The air in the room turned heavy. The walls expanded and the floor rolled. She scowled and grabbed at the sofa. *What's wrong? You asked me to tell you a typical day. I do get free time for lunch and riding.*

"Who is this man you laugh with?"

Marguarita frowned. *You don't know Cesaro's son?* When he continued to stare until she swore she felt a burning sensation in the region of her forehead she sighed. *I need a pen and paper. I can't send correct impressions.*

"I think I understand your impressions very well. You will not be riding with this man again. Proceed."

Marguarita rubbed her head. She had the beginnings of a headache. She was exhausted and too confused to be afraid anymore. One moment she was angry with Zacarias and the next amused. She had absolutely no idea how to handle him. The connection between them seemed to be growing stronger the more she was in his mind. She didn't want him in her head, and the more she communicated with him through telepathy, the easier it was for him to slip into her mind without her knowledge. The sensation had become so natural in such a short space of time, she could no longer feel anything but warmth.

I visit any of the ranches that need help, take care of any medical issues that crop up when the men are working, fix dinner and eat . . .

"I cannot tell if you eat alone."

He sounded so grim she glanced up at his set face. He looked like stone. She pressed her fingers to her head. *Most of the time. I clean up the kitchen, bake sometimes, bathe and read before I go to bed—alone.*

He reached down and settled his fingers on her temples. "Close your eyes. I think you have had enough for the night. You need to rest. We will continue this conversation at sunset tomorrow. We shall call a truce between us. Tonight, you will sleep and be unafraid. I have provided strong safeguards. Should a servant of the vampire come, he will not be able to gain entrance to my home."

Her heart jumped. He'd said "my home." She had never heard of any of the De La Cruz family refer to a place as their home. The thought slid away from her before she could hold on to it, the warmth replacing the ache in her head making her slightly fuzzy.

Zacarias bent and scooped her up, carrying her through the house to her room. The bedroom door was perfectly intact. Her bedroom was immaculate, she noted in passing. Her eyelids felt heavy, her body not wanting to move. He laid her on her bed and smoothed back her hair, his touch almost a caress.

She couldn't remember why she thought him overbearing and arrogant and feudal. He tucked her in and reassured her that she was safe. She felt safe. She even smiled at him before she let her lashes drift down. She liked the idea of a truce. She could totally manage a truce.

6

Inside the dark hacienda, beneath the heavy four-poster bed, buried deep in the rich soil, Zacarias's eyes snapped open simultaneously with the first beat of his heart. A shadow passed over the house, barely there, but still, he was an ancient warrior and he felt that subtle disturbance. The sun had sunk from the sky and night had dropped like a heavy curtain over the ranch. The night had brought spies with her.

He normally would have welcomed the hunt. It was what he did. All he knew. He was comfortable in that role. He was a loner. He had no idea how humans lived or worked and he had never wanted to know. They were certainly fragile creatures. Now he had—*her*—the beautiful lunatic who had somehow crept into his life and had no idea how to even protect herself from an eagle's claws.

He had known it was only a matter of time before his enemies would seek revenge. By the very swiftness of their search, he knew a master vampire directed them to each of the De La Cruz haciendas. He had been in existence for far too long to think it might simply be a coincidence. They were hunting him. Ordinarily he would let them know exactly where he was and he would have welcomed the battle—but this time there was too much at stake. He waited until the flock of shadowed birds had passed overhead, circling the ranch several times before moving on.

And then he reached out to touch—*her.* The woman. Marguarita Fernandez. He reached for her before he thought, before he could stop his mind. He wanted—*her.* She should have been sleeping peacefully in her bed waiting for him to wake her. But of course she wasn't. He sighed, no longer surprised by anything she did.

He waved his hand to open the soil, clothing himself as he rose, careful not to disturb even the air so she would not know he had risen. *Emni kuŋenak ku aššatotello*—disobedient lunatic. Did she not realize he would kill for her? She didn't seem capable of learning, no matter how hard the lesson. His enemies were already searching and if they found her, if they knew about her or even suspected . . . He closed his mind to what could happen and ignored that peculiar and very unfamiliar need to smile at the thought of her continual ignoring of his every wish. She really did have to be dim-witted, there was no other explanation.

How strange that this woman could arouse even a small interest on his part. His reaction to her enforced the nagging idea that she could be his lifemate. Before stopping his heart at dawn, he had gone carefully over the details each of his brothers had shared with him about the moment they had recognized their lifemate. They had known instantly on contact. There had been no doubt. Emotions had poured back into them. Colors blinded them.

Even after centuries of existence, Zacarias didn't understand the key to unlocking the mystery of lifemates, but if Marguarita Fernandez was actually his, the universe was playing a joke on him. The woman was positively maddening.

He strode through the master bedroom out into the hall. The scent of her filled the house, an intensely feminine fragrance. He realized she had occupied his home for years, even as a child, her father had lived here, in the main house. The house wasn't stark and bare as were most of his lairs. Marguarita lingered in every corner. She had made this dwelling her home. There was warmth here, the warmth of a woman who cared about her home and took care of it with loving attention to detail.

The rooms were gray and dull, yet he felt the richness of each in the hand-woven rugs and thick lap blankets obviously quilted by hand. He stopped by a heavy chair and rubbed the material of the blanket between his fingers. He felt Marguarita in each of those tiny stitches. She did far more than keep the house. She loved it.

She liked candles. They looked homemade as well. They had electricity and a backup generator but he was certain with the fierce storms they often got, downed trees often took out the electricity and all manner of things could happen to a generator. He had never had to think of such things, but clearly Marguarita did and she prepared for them.

She not only prepared her own home for emergencies, but he saw the list she'd been working on laid out on the coffee table, the name of each family housed on the De La Cruz lands, and what they needed. Lanterns and candles and canned food seemed to be the biggest items. He had never given much thought to how these people lived and worked, but he realized Marguarita took care of them in his name.

The door to the bathroom was open and steam mixed with perfume drifted into the living room. He inhaled deeply to bring her into his lungs. Anticipation stirred. He waited a few heartbeats, savoring that small ability just to look forward to seeing her and there was no doubt now, he was definitely *feeling*, although he couldn't say it was anything like his brothers had described.

His fingers bunched in the quilt and he brought the soft fabric to his face. The material carried a hint of her intriguing fragrance. His body tightened. Not the savage reaction of the evening before, but still, it was a reaction. He breathed his way through shock. His little lunatic was almost assuredly his lifemate and, sun scorch the woman, she'd come along too late. That was just like her. Fate had certainly played a joke on him with its choice and timing.

Zacarias sighed and drew another deep, fragrance-filled breath into his lungs. It didn't matter one way or the other, because he certainly couldn't condemn her to a half-life with him. He was no prize, not with savagery and darkness bred into his very soul. He had been damned from birth and he had accepted that. This was a terrible blow, one completely unexpected.

To be given a lifemate who would always remain just out of reach was the worst torture he could conceive.

Something soft and feminine tickled his mind. Amusement. No sound, just the impression of happiness—a warm glow. He absorbed her into his heart, allowed himself to indulge for just a brief moment. His mind, so obviously tuned to hers, refused to obey him when it came to Marguarita. It needed the contact, that warmth that infused his entire body.

Hunger swept through him, a gnawing, clawing need that beat in his veins and consumed him quickly. He tasted her in his mouth, that unique taste that was all Marguarita. He recognized that he was already obsessed with her, but after centuries of a barren existence, it wasn't too high a price to pay for the ability to feel something.

He slipped further into her mind, craving the warmth of her. Deep laughter burst through his thoughts, an explosion of sound, all male, distinct and familiar to Marguarita. He felt her easy acceptance, the softness in her that wasn't there when he was with her. She was amused by her companion. Accepting of him.

Zacarias moved so fast through the house he was merely a blur, literally bursting into her room. The door splintered with a crash, wood flying in all directions as he ripped it apart. Marguarita sat on the floor by her open window. A man stood on the other side, his head through the opening, his hand on Marguarita's arm. Both turned simultaneously toward him at the sound of the door disintegrating. Zacarias was on the man in a split second in a violent explosive action, yanking him through the window with vicious strength and slamming him against the wall. He held him easily with one hand, legs dangling above the floor as he sank his teeth deep into the pulsing vein in the neck.

No! Stop! You have to stop!

The man gave no resistance after that first stiff struggle. Zacarias made no attempt to calm him, the offense was far too great. He heard a terrible roar and it took a moment to realize the sound emerged from his own throat. He gulped at the rich blood, even as Marguarita's frantic plea burst into his mind.

She caught at his arm and tugged, tried to reach up to insert her hand between Zacarias and his prey. He could see her, far off, through the red haze in his mind, through the need to kill, through the strange animalistic roaring that crashed through his head, but nothing mattered to him but destroying this man who had dared to put his hands on Marguarita.

Zacarias felt Marguarita's warm spirit moving through the ice in his mind and instantly saw himself through her eyes. She was close to panic. He had exploded into violence much like a large jungle cat bringing down prey and was completely and utterly a killer in that moment. On some vague level she realized she was the cause. She was terrified of him, reading his intent, knowing he was acting on instincts rather than intellect.

She flooded his mind with frantic impressions of a wolf pack, and then with dozens of babies as if he was the dim-witted one and couldn't understand the concept of family. Finally she resorted to pushing an image of Cesaro into his mind in a frantic attempt to tell him this man was Julio, Cesaro's son. As if he wouldn't know that. The woman was a menace to herself and to everyone she knew. He swept his tongue across the puncture wounds to close them and dropped the man to the floor, holding him easily with his mind.

Very slowly he turned on the nuisance of a woman. She took two steps back and then made herself stop. She looked small and vulnerable and very, very afraid as she glanced toward Julio.

Is he dead? She took a step toward the unconscious man.

"Do not *dare* to touch him."

She halted instantly, her face going completely white.

"No, Carpathians do not kill when they feed. You should know that. Are you uneducated as well as disobedient?"

She shook her head and looked around the room, her gaze settling on the pen and paper she'd been using to communicate with her lover. When she stepped toward it, he held out his hand and both items flew to him. He pushed them into his pocket for closer inspection later.

"You disobeyed again. Is there anyone you do obey? Or do you simply do whatever you want when you want to do it?" He kept his voice very low, afraid she might faint or fall down. She was so rattled he could see her shaking.

I did not disobey. She was adamant, thrusting her denial into his mind. *I stayed in the house just like you ordered. I didn't do anything wrong.*

Was it possible she didn't understand the enormity of her error? How was that possible? "Having a man in your room is absolutely forbidden. How could you not know that? Do you wish to be taken for a whore?"

She blinked her long lashes at him, her body suddenly quite still. A slow blush infused the pale white of her skin. He could clearly see the color sweeping up her neck into her face and the beauty of it captured his attention so that he almost missed that she stepped into him and swung her hand at his face.

He caught her wrist inches from his head only because of his preternatural speed. They stood toe-to-toe, gazes locked. She was furious. He could feel the rage in her, yet was hyperaware of the smallness of her bones, of the soft skin and lush curves. She was wearing a skirt and blouse, the skirt long, covering her slender legs and emphasizing her rounded hips and narrow waist. He found her pleasing in feminine clothes.

Her eyes sparkled at him, glittering like champagne diamonds. She no longer appeared gray or shadowed, but her every feature was beginning to emerge in color and detail. He had never encountered anything more beautiful in all his centuries of existence.

"I believe we covered the issue of you touching me without permission." *Don't you dare call me a whore.*

He had never seen true sparkling champagne diamond with such pure chocolate and it was an amazing color, especially sparkling as her eyes were now. "I believe I asked if you wished to be taken for a whore. I did not call you one."

He spoke very slowly and distinctly in case she didn't quite grasp the difference. He also noted that along with her anger, she was much more adept at communicating telepathically. He could see her words in the impressions she sent and realized then what it must be like not to have an actual voice to express herself.

His thumb slid over her pulse in a small caress. He felt her shiver in response. "You look quite lovely in your feminine clothes. You will wear them at all times."

She frowned. He thought she would like the compliment, but truly, she was difficult. Her eyes flashed with glinting fire, which was spectacular, but he had wished to please her. Females were difficult to understand.

I won't, you know. I prefer to wear skirts indoors, but not when I ride. And I love to ride, so no skirts. Her chin went up, those eyes sparkling more than ever.

He studied her defiant little face for a long time. She never once looked away from him. Never in his life had anyone defied him the way she did. He was beginning to think there was nothing dim-witted about her after all. "You really are *emni kuŋenak ku aššatotello minan.*" He couldn't help the soft caress in his voice.

What does that mean? I've heard you call me that and similar things.

"My disobedient lunatic," he answered honestly, expecting fireworks. He even took a firmer grip on her wrist.

Her lips twitched, curved into a smile so that her white teeth flashed at him for a moment. He got the impression of amusement in his mind and the feeling warmed him. "You are getting very good at communicating through our blood bond. It will increase in strength when we exchange blood again."

A shadow crossed her face. She swallowed hard and nodded, refusing to look away. She was very afraid but she faced him with courage.

"It will not hurt, Marguarita," he assured. "You will enjoy the experience."

She didn't look convinced but she nodded at him and then glanced again toward Julio. A roaring protest ripped through his body and he felt his teeth lengthen, exploding in his mouth before he could stop the reaction. She gasped, and he looked down at her wrist, still captured in his hand. His fingernails had lengthened into deadly talons.

He could smell the man, until the stench of him nearly overpowered the subtle fragrance that was Marguarita. He didn't want a male close to her, let alone in her bedroom. He recognized he was at his most deadly.

"It is not safe for your friend to be here," he admitted. Evidently some emotions were returning. Rage. The need to kill. Jealousy. Things he hadn't experienced before and therefore had no way of anticipating or understanding what he was feeling, let alone the necessary knowledge to deal with such things.

Marguarita slowly nodded her head. *Should I summon Cesaro?*

His body rebelled, his heightened senses already in battle mode. "That is not a good idea. I will take him to his house and leave him to rest." He didn't want another man around her while he was adjusting to the new, emerging and uncomfortable emotions. He counted himself lucky that he didn't have the same reaction to his lifemate that his brothers had had.

She nodded her head, biting her lower lip a little anxiously.

"Is the word of a De La Cruz no longer good here? I have said I will leave him to rest, yet you are still anxious. Is this man someone important to you?"

He felt her struggle to make him understand. She looked around for a pen and paper but he shook his head. She was his lifemate and they needed to learn to communicate. She sent him one emotion-laden look, and then pushed the image of Riordan, his youngest brother, into his head. She pointed to Julio and then to herself.

"This man is your brother? Cesaro's son?"

She nodded, frowning the entire time. *Not blood.*

He didn't want the man anywhere near her. "It is not safe for him. You understand me?"

Marguarita nodded her head. Zacarias couldn't stand the presence of the other male close to her, or the worried look in her eyes. He scooped Julio up and draped him over his shoulder. He took a step away from her.

Señor De La Cruz?

That soft caressing note in her voice sent a rush of heat speeding through his veins. He looked at her over his shoulder.

Perhaps you would be so kind as to fix my door on your way out.

There it was, that now familiar need to smile. The amusement tamped down his need to destroy every male who had ever come near her. He needed her to use his more intimate first name. "Zacarias," he corrected. "And no problem."

He went out before the urge to heave the offending male through the window so he could yank Marguarita to him and taste her exquisite unique flavor overcame him.

Marguarita watched as he paused to casually wave his hand, weaving the splintered door back into a solid mass before striding out. She took a deep breath and allowed herself to sag onto her bed. Her hand shook as she pressed her fingers to her trembling mouth. She had never seen anything—including the rain forest predators—exploding into violence so fast.

Being in the same room with Zacarias De La Cruz was overwhelming, much like being with a tiger. He took up the entire space, the very air, with his power and energy. He always gave the impression with his focused stare of being alert and ready to strike instantly. When he did erupt into action, it was too fast to even follow and so violent the act was numbing to the senses.

She had done this. Made a terrible mistake. Zacarias had known he had grown too dangerous to be in the company of others and he had taken steps to protect them all. He had made an honorable decision, but she'd inadvertently interfered and placed all of them—including his eternal soul—in jeopardy.

The puncture wounds on her waist were healed, but she would never forget that painful, terrifying ride through the air as the eagle had taken her into the night sky, huge wings beating loud enough for her to hear the *whomp*, *whomp* as they cut through the air. She'd been sick and dizzy, staring at the ground below as it dropped away. She didn't even have the release of screaming. Sadly, and strangely, the only comfort she had was in touching his mind, the mind of a man more feral beast than human.

She touched the mark on her neck and for a moment she couldn't breathe, remembering the way his teeth had burned as they drove through her skin. It had hurt so bad, and she'd been terrified that he would finish the job the vampire had started, or worse, not kill her and make her his living puppet, the very embodiment of evil. She stroked the throbbing mark with the pads of her fingers. She had already made up her mind to serve him as long as necessary—and she knew that included allowing him to take her blood for sustenance.

This evening changed nothing, in fact, it only reinforced her belief that she owed Zacarias her aid, no matter how terrifying it was to her. She covered her face for a moment, rocking back and forth, gathering her courage. She had to find a way to keep him from the workers on the ranch—especially Julio. When Julio awakened and remembered what happened, he would be desperate to make certain she was all right and that was a potential problem.

Resolutely, Marguarita scrubbed her hands down her face, wiping away fear and straightening her shoulders. This was her mess. She'd created it.

She could feel the intense sadness, the heavy sorrow weighing Zacarias down. She felt his emotions—and they were strong to the point of crushing—but she knew he didn't feel them in the same way she did.

He had wanted her to go about her daily routine, so that was what she was going to do, just as if he wasn't in the house. When it came time for him to take her blood she would find a pleasant place in her mind and go there. It was the duty of her entire family to provide whatever a De La Cruz needed—or wanted—and she wouldn't fail her family or herself.

She stared at herself in the mirror. Her hair was in the usual thick braid, but her neck was clearly exposed. Her heart jumped wildly. Perhaps that was too much of a temptation. Quickly she loosened the weave and allowed her hair to spill to her waist. She wrapped a loose tie around the middle just to hold it back from her face so she could work without the huge mass getting in her way. Her hands smoothed the flowing skirt and she took another breath before heading for the kitchen.

Filling the teapot, she turned and nearly dropped it when he was standing there, quite close to her, his hand reaching for the abundance of hair, staring at it as though fascinated. He dropped his hand immediately and stepped back to allow her to get to the stove. Ignoring her pounding heart, Marguarita pretended he wasn't in the room. If he wanted to observe what she did, that was fine. She would make herself breakfast even though it was early evening.

Zacarias leaned one hip against the sink and watched her with that unblinking, totally focused stare that was definitely that of a large hunting cat. She glanced at him from under veiled lashes, unable to help herself.

Would you care for tea?

He frowned. "I have never actually tried human food. My brothers have. To appear human they stock the house with food items and have actually gone to charity events and other large gatherings that made it necessary to appear to eat."

But not you.

He raised his eyebrow. "I do not bother with such things. I make humans uneasy so it was better to send Nicolas or Riordan."

Not even once? In all your years of existence, you never once wanted to taste the forbidden?

"I felt nothing, *kislány kuŋenak minan*—my little lunatic. Curiosity has never been a problem for me. I exist. I hunt. I kill. My life is very simple."

She pressed her lips together. She couldn't imagine such a life. No comfort. Not needing comfort. *You are never afraid? You have never experienced sheer terror?*

"What has there been in my life to fear? I have nothing to lose, not even life itself. I have only a responsibility to protect my people to the best of my ability. I do so with honor."

You've never felt joy? Or love?

"There was a time in my life, when I was a boy, that I loved my brothers. For a time I could touch their memories and remember the affection I had for them. Even that is gone for me."

She wanted to weep for him. He spoke so matter-of-factly, as if having no one—nothing at all to soften his life—was normal. There was no one to comfort him, no one to talk things over with, no one to hold him—or love him. All the while he fought to protect others, there was no one for him.

She realized for all his knowledge, there were huge gaps in his education. Carpathians could regulate body temperatures. They could heal their wounds and minimize most pain. He hadn't considered that she couldn't do those things, which explained why he'd seemed so shocked by the eagle's talon's puncturing her skin. He either didn't know, or he truly hadn't given humans very much thought.

He didn't interact with anyone but the undead. His brothers came to the various holdings and talked with the local governments. Zacarias only came when wounded and he needed a fast fix. The workers were all leery of him. Because her aunts and uncles and cousins worked at the various De La Cruz properties throughout South America, she knew all the gossip on the family and few had ever set eyes on Zacarias. He had been completely alone for centuries.

Marguarita kept her back to him, afraid compassion would show on her face. She might fear him—but it didn't mean she couldn't feel for him. His life had been one she would never have wanted and yet he'd endured for over a thousand years. He had probably welcomed death, and she had taken even that solace from him. She had to find a way to connect more solidly with him so she wouldn't jump every time he came near her. She decided the best course of action was to get to know him, to exchange a little information so she could be more comfortable with him.

How is it that I can feel your emotions, but you can't?

There was a small silence. She braced herself before turning to face him. The battles of many centuries chasing the undead through countries in a ceaseless attempt to protect the inhabitants were etched deep into the lines on his face. He stood there, his head unbowed, watching her with those eyes that held a sorrow he didn't even recognize or comprehend.

There was no place he could go where he could be completely vulnerable. There was nowhere he could be loved or protected or safe. She had a sudden urge to put her arms around him and hold him tightly to her, but she'd have to ask permission first and she wasn't making that mistake again.

Silence stretched between them, filled suddenly by the whistle on the kettle. She carefully poured the boiling water into her mother's small, intricate clay teapot. The body was rectangular and hand-painted with Peruvian Paso horses running free with tails and manes flowing as if in the wind. She loved the teapot her mother had made so many years earlier and was always careful of it. Using it always made her feel closer to her mother and, right now, comforted. She couldn't imagine Zacarias having nothing like that in his life.

"I was not aware you could feel my emotions," he finally, almost reluctantly, admitted.

She turned to face him again, leaning against the counter and studying his face. She found it amazing that he could look so stern and tough, but yet be so brutally handsome. His hair was long, even for a Carpathian, almost as long as hers. A few strands of gray enhanced the deep midnight color. The mass of hair had wave to it—enough wave to spiral into several long swirls from the leather cord he bound it with. The spiraling waves didn't soften his appearance, but only made him that much more attractive.

He didn't appear to be relaxed or at ease. He appeared exactly as he was—a killing machine. No one would ever mistake him for anything else, but maybe she was getting used to his presence because the inner tremors had finally ceased.

I can.

"Explain it to me."

He seemed genuinely puzzled, but how could she explain? She tried to picture a volcano with masses of churning magma. *I can feel what's inside of you. Anger. Sorrow. It's very turbulent and intense, but I can tell you don't feel it in the same way as me.*

His eyes didn't leave her face. She couldn't help the sudden rise of color. She felt a little like an insect under a microscope. Clearly he was studying her—a human specimen.

"Tell me about your friend Julio."

Her stomach knotted. That way lay disaster. His expression hadn't changed, but his eyes had. There was only a subtle difference in his eyes, but she could feel the volcanic emotion roiling inside of him. She turned back to making her breakfast so she wouldn't be afraid.

She did her best to show him her relationship with Julio. *We grew up together. He is but a few months older than me, so we were raised as brother and sister.*

She found it difficult to project that concept, but, glancing over her shoulder at his dark face, she persisted. *There were no other children around. This is a working ranch and even as children, of course, we were expected to help.*

Again, she tried to send impressions of the two of them working in the stables, and in the fields with the cattle. *I could do a better job with my pen and paper.*

"You are doing just fine."

She risked another quick look at his face. She wasn't doing just fine. He still had death in his eyes. She forced down panic, feeling as if she was failing Julio. *My mother died when I was very young and I was inconsolable. I lost myself in the animals. In the rain forest.*

He stirred as if the thought of that little girl alone in the rain forest bothered him, but she couldn't imagine that he could conceive of her pain as a child at the loss of her mother. Or that he might worry for a human child that was of little consequence to him. But Julio had worried. He was only a little boy himself, but he defied his parents and followed her to keep her safe.

And then his mother caught a fever and she died a year after my mother. That created a bond between us. I was careful to stay close to him, as he had done for me. Again she tried to convey the deep sorrow that both of them had felt and the lifelong connection that had been established.

Marguarita turned then and studied his face, the dark turbulence in his eyes. She took a deep breath, feeling a little desperate for him to understand. *Can you see my memories of the two of us?* If he could get into her mind and see for himself, maybe he would be able to feel her affection for Julio and realize it was sisterly, not that of a woman loving a man.

"Of course. Our blood bond is strong, but I would have to go deeper into your mind. You already fear me."

Her heart pounded. They both could hear it. She took a breath as she cut two slices of bread for herself and broke open two eggs to scramble with some ham. *Does it hurt?*

"It would not hurt. It would feel . . . intimate."

The last word whispered over her skin like a soft caress. Marguarita shivered. He was close to her. She could feel the warmth of his body as he stood behind her, watching her cook. It felt dangerous, standing in her kitchen performing everyday tasks with him so close, watching her every move. Breathing when she breathed. She swore their hearts kept the same rhythm.

She swallowed hard and carefully concentrated on sandwiching the eggs between the slices of bread. She placed her breakfast on a plate, ignoring her trembling hands. She was afraid of Zacarias, but when he spoke in that certain tone of voice, her body reacted. Did she dare take a chance on adding to that strange physical attraction by consenting—no—even inviting him deeper into her mind?

She reached for the teapot handle just as he reached around her for it as well. His arm caged her and his fingers settled over hers. A thousand butterflies took flight in her stomach.

"Let me," he said.

That same low caressing note was in his voice. She closed her eyes briefly against the sudden assault on her senses and slid her hand from under his. He didn't move, keeping her caged between him and the counter while he poured her tea. She knew there was a space between them, maybe the width of a sheet of a paper, but she could feel heat radiating from him.

Her body caught fire. Flames danced over her skin, darted through her bloodstream to settle into a burning need in her most feminine core.

Her breath caught in her throat as he moved that scant width, closing the paper-thin distance as he set the teakettle down, so that he was pressed against her, his warm breath against her neck. He inhaled her, drawing the air laden with her scent deep into his lungs. A soft, purring growl rumbled in his throat. The sound seemed that of a feral animal, but there was something terribly sexy about it. She froze, paralyzed with fear, but unsure whether it was of him or of herself. The growl vibrated through her body, until her every sense was completely consumed with Zacarias.

Zacarias De La Cruz was a dangerous powder keg, and she was terribly afraid if she moved or allowed him further entrance to her mind, she would be providing the spark that would set him off. It wasn't his fault that she had such a reaction to him. She'd never had such a reaction to any other male, but it had happened once before with him in the forest. It made no sense, but she couldn't quite catch her breath, waiting . . . wanting . . . what, she didn't know.

Zacarias's lips moved against her ear, his breath stirring her hair and sending an electric shock sizzling through her veins. "I can hear your heartbeat."

She closed her eyes and sent up a prayer that her scent wasn't that of a woman desperate for a man, because if she could feel the dampness in her panties he most likely could smell her feminine call to him. A man so close to animal would have a heightened sense of smell.

I'm sure you can. She could hear her heart thundering as well. There was no mistaking her fear—or her attraction.

His fingers moved the mass of hair she'd so carefully left covering her neck. At the brush of his fingertips her womb clenched, and hot liquid spilled. His mouth moved over her skin, his tongue a velvet rasp, making his brand on her pulse with frantic need. She gripped the edge of the counter, her heart pounding with dread—or excitement—she didn't know which.

Hold very still, mića emni kuŋenak minan—my beautiful lunatic, I have to taste you. It would not be a good thing to fight me. At this moment, I feel on the very edge of my self-control.

His mind slipped into hers unbidden, but she couldn't say unwanted. His touch was sensual, sending a frisson of pleasure down her spine, but his warning frightened her. The thought of his teeth sinking into her was so terrifying she should have fainted, yet her body was suddenly alive, every nerve ending on fire.

I'm afraid. There. She'd admitted it to him.

There is no need. You are the safest person in the world around me. Do not fight me, woman. Give yourself to me.

She wasn't certain what he meant by her being the safest person in the world around him. She didn't feel safe; she felt threatened on every level there was. She forced herself to keep from struggling as he turned her to face him and inexorably enfolded her against his chest. He was enormously strong, his arms like the trunk of a kapok tree, hard and unyielding, a cage she couldn't escape.

Zacarias pulled her tightly against him, fitting her to him as if she belonged there, his body imprinted on hers. She tilted her head to look up at him. He was so beautifully carved, like a statue made of the finest stone, sensuality personified. His eyes darkened with hunger. His teeth glinted at her, white and slowly sliding into place, incisors rather than canines, but his canines appeared very sharp as well. The distinction between vampire and Carpathian was there, but it was slim.

Her heart raced far past pounding, accelerating so fast she feared it would come through her chest. He lowered his head slowly to hers, his mouth brushing the lightest of kisses on the corner of her eye. Her entire body nearly went into meltdown. There was no way to stop the purely sexual reaction to that feather-light touch. His lips trailed from her eye to her jaw, soft little barely there kisses, a leisurely exploration.

Her body went soft and pliant, melting into his. Her temperature soared, her core on fire, burning her from the inside out. All tension drained out of her, her lashes drifting closed as his lips continued down her neck to her shoulder. She felt adrift in a river of pure sensation, floating toward him with her entire being. Her heart and maybe even her soul reached for him.

His teeth scraped back and forth over that throbbing spot and her body reacted, raising her temperature another notch. Her breasts ached, nipples pushing against the thin lace of her bra. On some level she knew she was giving herself up to him, that if she succumbed to him she would never be the same, but he'd woven a sensual web and she was trapped in it—willingly.

He sank his teeth deep, the pain crashing through her, shocking her.

7

Zacarias lost himself in the scorching flames rushing through his veins, and the fireball roaring in his belly. Fire poured into his groin until he burned, heavy and full—for her. For Marguarita. The sensation was overwhelming, complete, shocking even. Nothing in his life had prepared him for the siege on his senses, for the primitive need and the raw hunger raging not only in his mind, but in his body.

This woman had changed him for all time, changed his world, and where there was no feeling for as long as he could remember, now his entire focus, his entire being was centered on Marguarita's soft body, the blood pulsing through her veins and the feminine scent of her calling to the male in him.

He found he couldn't resist the temptation of tasting her, she smelled so good, a lure he couldn't resist. Her body went pliant, molding to his. Immediately his senses became acute, lost, drowning even, in the biochemical signals of a female calling for a mate. He shifted her closer to him, smoothing her hair away from her neck. He bent his head and licked over that strawberry mark that told the world she belonged to him.

His body shuddered in anticipation. Actually shuddered. He felt as if the world stood still, as if he held his breath, waiting a heartbeat, savoring the feel of her, the scent and the incandescent beauty of her color, because—oh stars and moon above—he saw her color. Beautiful, unbelievable color.

Overcome with unfamiliar need, Zacarias sank his teeth deep into her flesh, connecting them together. The pure essence that was Marguarita flowed into his mouth like the sweetest nectar. She tasted exotic, exquisite . . . she *tasted.* Nothing had ever tasted. He fed because he needed life and life was blood. In that single moment, life was Marguarita.

His entire body hummed, his veins sang with joy. She was a musical instrument, playing a song written expressly for him. He knew he was the only man to hear her beautiful notes. He knew he couldn't keep her. He was caught in a half-life and he couldn't condemn her to such a thing. But he'd never truly known life, so right then, in that time and place, it was enough, it was everything to him.

Marguarita was a drug in his system, as fluid as fire, rushing through his veins and filling him with a kind of primordial burst of radiance. The world around him was dull and lifeless, a stark contrast to her jewel-bright glittering eyes and shining blue-black hair. She was color and life, the reason every warrior fought against the plague that was vampire. She was *his* reason. He saw that in an instant. Tasted the truth in his mouth. Felt it vibrate through his body.

He would always know exactly where she was at all times now, what part of the house, and what she was doing—even what she was thinking. He would know how many times she frowned, or raised her chin in stubbornness, bit her delicious lower lip or smiled. He was very aware of her as a woman, with her feminine fragrance, and he would always be aware of the exact moment when she turned her head and looked at him—and when she thought of someone else—because he would never again be out of her mind completely when he was near her—not until he ended his existence.

Lost as he was in overwhelming real emotion for the first time in his existence, he didn't catch the exact moment everything changed for her. One moment she was with him, burning in the erotic fire, and the next, she was fighting. *Daring* to fight him. Rejecting *him* completely. She triggered every hunting instinct he had—and his were honed well over a thousand years. Hunting was bred into his very bones, into his soul. He heard the warning growl rumbling in his throat and felt himself take an unbreakable lock on her now tense body.

She made no sound, but he sensed she was terrified. She struggled wildly and he locked her to him roughly, his body aggressive. It had been well over a thousand years since anyone or anything had ever defied him. In truth, he couldn't remember a time, and she aroused his every need to conquer and control.

His reaction was again more animal than man, but it was all male. He had absorbed her rich fragrance, felt her soft pliant body melting into his, and his world had changed. He didn't want that feeling to ever end, yet it already had and very abruptly. Her scent enveloped him—and this time there was no feminine allure. She was terrified of him. He loathed the scent immediately.

Do not fight me. He was too much the predator and there was no way to ignore the strong instincts demanding he subdue his prey.

Her rich blood flowed into his system, an electrical charge, sizzling through veins and pumping more hot blood into his groin until he was full and hard and even painful. He was experiencing the most pleasure he'd ever felt while Marguarita was utterly and completely terrified. Her body had gone stiff, tense, her mind screaming a protest. Her lungs burned for air. He could tell she was almost shutting down completely with her fear—of him.

Help me, Marguarita. You have to stop fighting or I will not be able to regain control.

His arms were iron bars, locking her to him. Her soundless scream filled his mind. He reached again. *Embε karmasz*—please.

He could not remember a time he had ever pleaded with anyone for anything, but it was imperative she stop fighting him, and even more imperative that she once again feel the things he was feeling. He could override the barriers placed in her mind at birth, barriers obviously strengthened with each generation. But he only used his powers to calm his prey, and she *wasn't* prey. It felt wrong to take over her mind and plant feelings and memories that weren't real.

It must have been the inflection in his voice, that soft pleading in his own language that penetrated her terror, because he felt her sudden resolve, the way she drew a ragged breath into her lungs and forced her body into stillness. Immediately he was able to lift his head, draw his tongue over the punctures in her neck to close the wounds. He held her tight to him, hearing the beat of her heart, feeling the rapid pounding against his chest. He buried his face in her thick silken hair and just held her, breathing for both of them.

He whispered to her in his own language, barely knowing what he was saying to her, feeling the words from deep inside in a place he'd never touched, never been and didn't even know existed. She tapped into some reservoir of tenderness unknown to him—so unknown he had no real idea what to do with it. He was an ancient Carpathian, one of the oldest, one of the most knowledgeable—and he was completely out of his depth.

"*Te avio päläfertiilam*—You are my lifemate, a woman above all others. You hold what is left of my soul in the palms of your hands. I would kill another for you. I intend to die to protect and keep you safe. Do not fear me, Marguarita. I wish only to enjoy a few nights with you. Do not be afraid anymore."

Shocked at what he was imparting to her, even though she couldn't completely understand what he was trying to convey, he kept his face buried in her fragrant hair and held her tight to him, trying to find a way to comfort both of them. He was prepared for any battle—but that of the heart. He was completely and utterly out of his depth for the first time in his life.

Marguarita's heart slowed to the pace of his. Her lungs followed the lead of his. She shifted against him, tilting her head to look up at him. His heart staggered, and then dropped to his feet in a rushing plummet. Tears swam in her eyes.

Tears had never moved him. In truth, he had never thought about what they meant or why people cried. Sorrow was far removed from his existence, but suddenly, those tears were a knife through his heart, far worse than any vampire ripping through his flesh.

I'm sorry. I wasn't prepared for the way it felt. I won't fight you again.

She dropped her head just as quickly, but not before he caught the flash of apprehension.

Zacarias frowned. "Why do you fear my taking your blood? It is natural."

He felt her heart jump against him and he kept her locked in the cage of his arms because he needed the reassurance of her heart beating, the warmth and softness of her. He wanted her capitulation, but not like this. His fingers found her chin and tilted it once again, forcing her to meet his gaze. Her eyes searched his, looking for something—reassurance maybe—that he wouldn't be angry if she told him the truth.

"Tell me," he insisted quietly. "Do not fear the truth." Because he had to know. Understanding her reasoning was as necessary as breathing, which was a strange sensation—to need so much to comprehend why she fought him.

It took her a few moments to muster the courage to answer him.

It is not natural to me, the giving of blood in this manner. The vampire tore at my throat close to the spot where you're taking my blood and I . . . panic. And then you . . .

He caught the impression of a wild beast attacking her. He hadn't considered that his taking her blood would be construed as an assault on her. Her entire family knew the Carpathians existed on blood. They were sworn to provide for him, for his brothers and their lifemates.

"I would not harm you."

Her hand crept up to cover the spot on her neck where his mark was the color of a bright strawberry with two distinct impressions of punctures. *I know.*

The impression she sent him was mixed. She didn't know. She didn't fully comprehend she really was the safest person on the planet. He was her guardian. Her protector. He would see to it that she was safe at all times. Even from herself, which looked to be his biggest job. But first, they had to get past her fears of giving blood.

"You do *not* know. You fear me." Lies between them would not be tolerated, and lying to herself was even worse.

She swallowed hard and reluctantly nodded, pressing her palm harder against his bite as if it hurt her. His frown deepened. Had he hurt her? There was a natural numbing agent in his saliva, shouldn't that keep any human from feeling pain in the process? He'd never really interacted as his brothers had with the species other than to take blood, or if he had done so, he remembered none of it. Perhaps he had felt nothing for so long even his memory was faulty. Even the men and women, who for generation after generation had served his family willingly, avoided him—and he them.

"It hurts you?"

Her first reaction was to nod, but he saw her expression change. It was her turn to frown as if she couldn't quite decide.

"Show me how it feels."

She turned her face into his chest and bit him—hard. The pain flashed through him and he cut it off automatically, shocked that she'd dared to do such a thing to him. No one ever put their hands—or teeth—on him. It just wasn't done.

"What are you doing, *kislány kuŋenak*—little lunatic?"

You said to show you. I did.

A wealth of satisfaction poured off her and he found that strange feeling of happiness—and laughter—welling up out of nowhere as it seemed to do so unexpectedly around her. She bit him and he did find it a little bit funny. "I did not give you permission to bite me. I meant in your head. Show me the feeling of pain."

You felt pain when I bit you.

He stroked his hand down the long fall of silken midnight black hair. Now, even more than before, it was a true black, so shiny he could barely tear his gaze from it. "I do not feel pain."

You do. You just don't allow yourself to acknowledge it. I was connected to you and I felt it.

His hold on her tightened. What was she doing, putting herself in such a position that she would not only feel her own pain, but his as well? "I do not understand you, Marguarita. You make no sense to me. You fear I will cause you pain and then you deliberately connect to my mind to feel any pain you might cause me. Is that in any way reasonable?"

Her gaze remained locked for a long time with his. A slow smile brought his attention to her perfect, sexy mouth. His body responded aggressively again, a surge of hot blood rushing through his system to pool in one place. Her eyes had gone soft, that champagne melting to dark chocolate, a sea of glittering diamonds he feared he wanted to fall into. It was forbidden to him. He knew and accepted that. He was as shadowed as the flock of birds flying over the ranch searching for him—sent by the most evil of creatures walking the earth.

He had never known gentleness or tenderness. There was no give to him, no soft spaces inside of him and there never had been. Indeed, he'd been born without such attributes. Instead, he'd been born pure dominance and he had grown in a time of war and uncertainty into a solitary hunter incapable of caring about hurting another as long as he achieved his ultimate goal—the protection of his species. His belief in himself was absolute and those he protected believed even more.

That a man protected his woman above all else was a sacred law, and that she followed his lead without question was his only way of life, yet in the modern world that was no longer so. Perhaps it never had been. He was without civility and no amount of manners would soften what he was—a killer. He made no apologies for his ways and he never would. Perhaps in another time, long before this one, he would have tried to reconcile what he was with who he would need to be for her—but that time was long, long gone. It was impossible.

Her gaze remained locked with his. He took solace in the beauty of her. And the courage of her. She faced him in spite of her fears. She had saved him and when it came time for him to go, she would face his passing with equal courage. He would make it as easy on her as possible, although she would never know the cost to him. Her gaze searched for something in him, something he knew wasn't there. He couldn't give her gentle reassurance and promises of polite, courteous behavior. He didn't even know those rules. He captured her face, holding her gaze to his.

"Make me understand."

She licked her lower lip and he had a sudden urge to lean down and draw her tongue into his mouth—to savor her again—that indescribable taste he now craved in a new and different way. Because he spoke in commands, it came out that way, but he wanted her to *want* to help him understand.

You hurt me. Scared me. The first time. Like the vampire.

He scowled at her, shook his head in utter denial, in disgust that she would think such a thing. "It was a lesson—and one you desperately needed. He was foul, and he tore out your throat. He would have killed you for his own pleasure. If you were not so . . ." *Dim-witted.* The word vibrated between them, hovered right there in their minds. He cleared his throat as her eyes grew into a stormy brew. "So—stubborn—you would see the difference between us without effort and you would have no further need of a reminder that obedience must be instant and without question. That one lesson should be sufficient for a lifetime. It is not a good thing to cross me."

A lesson? You call that teaching me something? You scared me to death.

"You should be afraid. When a hunter demands something of you, it is for a reason. Usually life and death are involved. Better you remember for all time than to ever hesitate."

And Julio? You looked as if you intended to kill him.

Her eyes had gone wide, dark, enormous, those feathery lashes fluttering nervously. But she didn't look away. His body reacted to her question, his muscles coiled, something deadly moving across his soul. Her mind softened when she thought of Julio. She had warmth in her mind, complete trust. Things that should only be there for one man—her mate—not some childhood friend.

His gaze remained locked on hers. He would tell his woman only the truth. "It is not reasonable for a man to allow other males around his woman. The animals in the jungle do not tolerate such things."

He watched carefully as she caught her breath. She wasn't dim-witted by any means. He was telling her she belonged to him and the understanding was in that quickly veiled expression. She was silent a moment, her eyes searching his for that something elusive he didn't know how to give—would never know how to give.

We are not jungle animals.

He wanted there to be no mistakes between them. No misunderstanding. "*I* am."

She shook her head in silent denial, but she recognized the killer in him.

"You know what I am, Marguarita. I cannot be anything other than what I am."

She blinked. Swallowed. Moistened her lips.

It is a good thing I am not your woman.

He ran his hand down the dark silken fall of her hair and was surprised at the gentleness with which he touched her—and the strange softening inside of him. "You know that is not true."

She took a breath, and he once again smelled fear, but this time, it was tinged with something else—interest perhaps. She was not completely immune to him and it disturbed her.

I am a servant pledged in your service, señor.

"There is more than servant and master between us as much as you wish to deny it. But for now, that will do. I do not want you to fear my taking your blood. I will be more careful of your fragility."

She blinked several times and would have stepped away but he glided closer, without seeming to move, blocking her escape. Her eyes mesmerized him, going from that sparkling champagne to a dark warm chocolate. The difference was striking to him. "I believe you were about to drink your tea and eat your meal."

She glanced at the food on the counter and shook her head. He got the immediate impression of cold. He waved his hand and steam rose from the cup as well as the plate. Her smile was tentative and almost shy, but he found the contrast of her decidedly pink lips and white teeth beautiful. Her eyes were fully brown now, the color rich and melting. Now he could see intriguing flecks of gold. The gold could have been the stars in the midnight sky of her eyes earlier, sparkling like diamonds before he could discern the true color.

She picked up the teacup and plate and he stepped back, giving her just enough room that she would have to brush his body as she made her way to the table. She was careful, her hand trembling just a bit as she set the stoneware down. He knew he would always see every nuance, the smallest detail, stay focused and aware of her every movement, right down to the flutter of her eyelashes.

She sat down and watched him for a moment, still nervous, as if she were trapped in a cage with a great jungle cat. He prowled closer, unable to resist a rumbling growl, knowing her eyes would go wide, and then she would smile at him. It came, that slow, melting smile that seemed to ripple through his body, gentle at first, and then gathering force until she was all heat and fire rushing straight to his groin.

She took a sip of tea. *Stop doing that. You do it to scare me.*

For the first time, the impression of laughter was strong, filling his mind. It wasn't just tentative amusement. *He* had been the one to deliberately tease her and she'd responded. He found great satisfaction in knowing she was aware he'd been teasing her. It was one of a million concepts he'd never understood before, but he wanted her smile and he had to do something to get past her fear.

"You are not really that afraid of me right now," he declared, and continued to stalk through the room.

The kitchen was spacious enough that he had plenty of room, but he had rarely—if ever—spent any real time inside an enclosure other than a mountain, and the walls felt inhibiting to him. He couldn't scent the air. He couldn't continually gather information.

What is it that has you on edge? The shadowed flock?

He stopped moving abruptly. He found it interesting that she had known the birds were tainted by evil and that they'd crossed her mind just after he'd been thinking of them in conjunction with the shadows permeating his own mind and body.

"I am unused to being indoors. Does it bother you to have me moving around?"

She took a bite of her egg, watching him carefully. Eventually she shook her head. *You look very powerful and you tend to dominate the room. I think I'm getting a little more used to you and the fluid way you move, like a hunter.*

"I am a hunter." He wanted to get accustomed to her ways. There was grace in her hand gestures. In the tilt of her head and the way she sat. He liked the quiet rustle of her skirts and the way her thick hair cascaded like a silken waterfall down her back to her narrow waist. Her hair fascinated him. It seemed so alive, always moving, shimmering, the colors deepening the longer he was in her company.

Are we going to be attacked? The birds were looking for you, weren't they?

He read fear for the others. He could see she refused to think about what was going to happen to her. More than anything else, he read fear for him. She was afraid *for* him and that made no sense. She should want him to lead vampires far from her and the hacienda, but he could see her reluctance for him to be found. He even caught the impression of himself in the ground, as if he should hide.

He forced himself to cross the room and pull out a chair opposite her. "Do you really wish to know the truth of the birds? Of the De La Cruz family? If you ask me, I will give you truth, so be careful what you wish for."

She took another sip of tea, studying his face thoughtfully over the rim. Her gaze had gone very serious and in her mind, he felt her weigh his words. Her nod was slow, but quite firm.

"After the attack on you, it was discovered that the masterminds behind the plot to assassinate the prince of the Carpathian people had gathered an army together and they intended to carry out their battle plan against the prince, testing their plans first on one of my family's properties. We were convinced—and we were correct—in thinking it would be on our largest holding in Brazil. Most of my family and their lifemates are gathered there and it was a logical place to try to get us all in one sweep." He bared his teeth. "They did not expect me to be present."

She moistened her lips. Parted them. He lost his train of thought. She blinked several times. Her eyelashes were a thick, long feathery sweep he found himself admiring. He'd never really noticed such details on another being. She frowned at him, her winged eyebrows drawing in, little lines appearing for an instant and dissolving as the indentation in her right cheek was prone to do when her smile faded.

Did they? Catch you all together?

"They thought they had. They had not counted on me or another warrior, Dominic. Nor had they considered that the women would fight—or the humans." Just the brief encounter with Marguarita's wounds after the harpy eagle had carried her through the sky, tearing her flesh with its talons, had made him so much more aware of the fragility of humans—and yet his people there had gone willingly into battle to defend the property.

Did they know what they were facing?

He jerked his head up. "Are you reading my thoughts?"

Your feelings. You feel sorrow for the ones who fell. You admire them.

He shook his head to deny the charge. He *felt* nothing. His mind turned over his new understanding as fact, storing it away with all the other pieces of information he had collected in his long lifespan. But emotions had no place in his world.

Did they know what they were facing? She urged an answer.

He nodded his head. "Nicolas spoke to them all and gave them the option to leave. It was recommended that women and children be moved. They refused. They stayed, although my brother made it clear that we would suffer casualties and any who left would not forfeit their rights to continue to work for us. A full assault had never been planned and launched by vampires, and we knew the battle would be brutal."

Show me.

"I will not." He said the words quietly.

Slow color slipped under her skin. Her gaze jumped to his. He felt her inquiry and there was a tinge of hurt attached.

"War is not for you. You had an encounter with a vampire and one is more than enough. They will never get close to you again as long as I am alive."

Marguarita put down her fork and studied his face. *I work for your family. We are sworn to protect you, señor, and I will, as will the others who work here. We are every bit as courageous and as loyal as those who serve you in Brazil.*

It took him a moment to assimilate the jumble of impressions she sent. He had offended her. "You misunderstand me. I am well aware of your loyalty and courage. I know you have every intention of protecting me . . ." He had thought to find the idea not only ludicrous but dim-witted and simple-minded. A childhood fantasy. But he found his thoughts had changed with knowing her. He couldn't help being secretly pleased that although she feared him, she had in fact raced to call in the hunters to destroy him, that at the thought of vampires coming for him, her thoughts were fiercely protective of him. Feelings were odd things and difficult to accept in himself as well in others. Emotions clearly complicated everything.

She sketched a question mark in the air between them. He shook his head and refused to answer. He wanted her mind firmly in his. He demanded nothing less from her. Their ability to communicate grew each time she formed pictures and impressions of the words she wanted to speak. He would be different than her human companions. With him, she could "speak" without her actual voice. The intimacy of it pleased him.

"You will obey me in this, Marguarita, without question."

He deliberately held her gaze for a moment so she could see there would be swift retaliation if she dared to defy his order outright. And knowing her strange infirmity for doing the opposite of anything smacking of a command, he would be watching her very closely for defiance. He waited until she looked away first before continuing.

"We killed every one of the vampires sent after us, as well as the puppets they created. The masterminds have no time to raise another army to bring against me. Rather, I suspect, they will nip at my flanks to weaken me and then one will come to attempt to destroy me. They will have learned their lesson by now."

This time the question mark was meticulously drawn in his mind. He found that warm bubble of laughter rising. She'd been so obviously annoyed at the word *obey.* The way she squirmed a little in her chair and tried so carefully to hide her irritation from him was rather endearing. He might just have to throw that word into the conversation often to see what eventually happened. If anyone would dare to surprise him, it was obviously going to be Marguarita.

What does that mean? Their lesson? What did it teach them, sending an army after you and your brothers?

"They like to be safe and sacrifice their pawns. Two of the five masters were destroyed. There are three left. If they want me dead, only a master has a chance of defeating me. Not just any master, one of the Malinov brothers must come for me."

A shiver went through her. Her warm brown eyes went very dark. He leaned forward to peer into those enormous, dove-soft eyes.

"There is no need to be afraid. I welcome his coming. Should he defeat me, he will have too great a fear of my brothers to remain close."

Abruptly she pushed her chair back, rose and took her unfinished meal and the teacup to the sink where she meticulously washed and dried them, her back to him. It was a silly human gesture, turning her back, as if that could possibly keep him out of her mind. There was no way to retreat from him now that he had discovered her—shared her mind and exquisite blood with him.

"I speak only the truth to you."

She swung around, her back to the sink, her face so expressive his heart clenched down hard like a vise. This time, when the pain flashed through his body, he made a conscious effort to feel it, to allow it into his mind. Her eyes swam with tears, turning all that beautiful dark to a fathomless pool. It was impossible to fully comprehend the jumble of impressions in her chaotic mind, but she was upset and he'd somehow managed again to be the one to upset her.

Zacarias sighed. Females were difficult at best; one never knew what they were going to do from one moment to the next. They were without logic or reason. At least this one was. He hadn't been around any others for any significant amount of time so maybe others were different, but this woman made no sense to him.

"Stop that," he ordered abruptly, pressing his palm hard over his heart as if he could heal the ache her tears caused.

Stop what? She looked confused.

He watched both fascinated and horrified as one tear tipped over her feathery bottom lashes and ran down her face. His heart stuttered. *"That,"* he snarled.

He stepped close, crowding her. Waves of distress poured off of her. There was no sound, not even a small one, but he was aware of every tiny thing about her and deep inside where no one else would ever see, she was weeping.

Acidic poison from vampire blood could not kill him. Torture. Mortal wounds. He had endured them all and survived, but this . . . this silent weeping by this woman for him—and God help both of them, it was for him—was too much. He might dissolve into a puddle at her feet. Entirely unacceptable and disturbing that she could wield such a powerful sword against him.

He dragged her against him, his body without give, with no soft edges to it, so that the air rushed out of her lungs and she had to catch at his arms to steady herself. He *needed* to hold her to him, without a clear idea of why, but he couldn't look at her tear-drenched eyes another moment. One hand passed over her face, wiping away all evidence. He brought his palm to his mouth and tasted her tears.

You can't order me not to cry.

"Of course I can. And by all that's holy, this one time, you will obey me." Palming the back of her head, he pressed her face tight against his chest.

At first she was tense and stiff, but within moments, as the heat of his body seeped into the cold of hers, she went soft and pliant in his arms. He should have allowed her to step back away from him, but it was easier to maintain some semblance of control over her when he held her. In truth, his arms had become an iron cage and he wasn't altogether certain if he was consciously or subconsciously holding her to him, but found he couldn't drop his arms. He brushed his hand down the length of her hair.

Few modern women seemed to have long hair anymore. A long-ago memory surfaced as he buried his face in those silken strands. Women walking by in long dresses, chatting, vessels of water in their hands as they made their way back to camp. He had noted them because they seemed so happy. Three days later when he retraced his steps looking for where he'd lost the trail of the vampire, the same women lay in a torn and bloody heap in the mud, their eyes staring up at the red moon, their faces like wax, their hair in twisted dirty hanks.

Don't. Marguarita suddenly wound her arms around him and held him to her.

The gesture was so unexpected and shocking he nearly stepped away from her. He had held her captive, but now, although she was far weaker than a male Carpathian, she seemed to have taken him over.

Please don't remember. It hurts you. I know you say you don't feel it, but you do. It washes through you and settles deep inside you. Just don't remember anymore. Not right now.

He rubbed his chin on the top of her head. Strands of hair tangled with the heavy shadow on his jaw, almost as if her hair could weave them together. "Why are you so upset?"

You accept your own death so easily. You look forward to fighting a master vampire. You would have burned in the sun. You just act like nothing touches you, but it's destroying you from the inside out. All those deaths. You think they don't affect you, but they do. You see your own death, not because you fear becoming vampire, but you can't live with the pain of who and what you are anymore. And you aren't like you see yourself, not really.

Her fist clenched and she hit his chest in a small rhythmic drumming. He doubted she even knew what she was doing, or surely she wouldn't dare to strike him. It was hardly more than a tap so he chose to ignore her indiscretion, puzzled by the things she said. He covered her fist with his palm and pressed until she became still.

"I do not feel, Marguarita, as much as I would like to. I have even lost my memories. These things you speak may have existed in another lifetime—long ago—but I no longer have recollection of them."

That's not true, Zacarias. I swear to you, it is not the truth. I am inside of you and I see the battles, the memories, and I feel the pain. The sorrow is so intense and overwhelming, unlike anything I have ever experienced—and I have lost both of my parents and know sorrow. I can't make something like this up. I wouldn't.

How could she feel his pain when he didn't feel it? Was she simply projecting her own feelings onto him? The connection between them grew stronger each time they used it, but still, it would be impossible for her to feel what he did not.

"Show me," he whispered against her ear. "Show me what you see in me."

One minute he was Zacarias De La Cruz. Carpathian warrior. Hunter. Alone. He was ice inside. Brittle and cold. Glaciers moved in his veins. And then she poured into him like warm thick honey, filling up every empty space inside him. Finding every dark corner, every secret tear and rip inside his mind. That warm honey spread through the ice, finding every broken connection, building bridges, filling the holes, restoring broken connections.

Electricity sizzled, arced and snapped in his head. He felt her every breath. Inhaled with her. Her heart beat and it was inside his own chest. *She* was inside of him until everything he was, everything he was about was filled with Marguarita, filled with all that warmth. With her blinding light. The heat melted the ice encasing him, melted faster than any barricade he could throw up to stop it.

He blinked rapidly, feeling her holding him close, filling more and more spaces with herself until for the first time he was complete. He wasn't alone. Stars burst in his head, opened like a primordial mix, rushing at him so fast at first he couldn't grasp what he was seeing.

8

Zacarias's brothers crouched among the rocks, shock on their faces. Riordan was little more than a newborn babe, but there was nothing young about his awareness or intellect. He stared with the same shock and horror at the approaching vampire as his older brothers. Above them, dark storm clouds churned in the sky, nearly obliterating all the stars, but the full moon shone bloodred, right through the towering, turbulent clouds.

Spread out, behind him. When I tell you to run, get out of here and do not look back, Zacarias commanded. *You are responsible for Riordan, Manolito. Fall back with him. Nicolas and Rafael, protect them. All of you, get out of here.*

We will help you, Rafael said, his voice shaking.

You cannot do this alone, Nicolas stated, sorrow dripping from each word.

Run, Zacarias. Run with us, Manolito pleaded.

Zacarias heard their protests, but when he gave an order, they knew to obey. Their mother lay dead, her body torn and bloody, crushed against the rocks. There was no time to mourn her or think of her as she was in life. His father had arrived too late to save her, but the vampire who had made the kill lay in strips beside her, the body literally torn apart. The sheer savagery shown in the killing should have warned Zacarias before his father turned around to face them, but still, those jagged teeth and red-crazed eyes were a shock.

His father's hands were raised toward the mountains where the boulders were set so precariously. The ground shook. Zacarias hadn't expected the attack on his brothers and he was that second too late in countering. He threw a shelter around the boys to protect them from the avalanche even as he raced into the attack. He knew his father hadn't expected aggression and it was the only thing left to him. His father was far older, stronger, more experienced, but he was a newly made vampire and wouldn't be used to the high the kill had given him.

His father was skilled in battle, a legendary hunter whose name was whispered in awe, but he'd taught those same skills to his oldest child. Zacarias was still considered young as a Carpathian, but he'd fought vampires and battles often. He'd already begun to lose his emotions, colors had long since faded from his vision and he wasn't even close to the age when that should have happened.

He struck through his father's insubstantial form, stumbling forward. The blow took him hard in the back and sent him flying forward into the pools of blood from his mother's body. He skidded across the gore facedown, landing nearly on his mother's head. Her lifeless eyes stared accusingly at him. He planted his hands to lever himself up only to find they were buried wrist-deep in her blood. His stomach lurched. His heart nearly stopped.

Zacarias!

With Nicolas's warning filling his mind, he rolled, dissolving at the last moment, remembering that he could. His father's fist slammed deep into the ground, right through his mother's lifeless body.

Zacarias was shaken to the very core of his being, and he had to pull himself together if he was going to survive. And if he didn't survive, neither would his brothers. He breathed away his mother's blood covering his body and the sight of her eyes staring at him, accusing him of trying to kill his own father. Not his father. Vampire. The undead. An evil, foul creature who would destroy everything and everyone in its path. Even now, the very grass withered beneath its feet. It. Vampire. Not father. Not the man he loved and respected above all others.

Zacarias felt the familiar coldness sweep through him, the chill he'd noticed early, even as a young boy, but now it was a glacier consuming him, pouring into his body, icing his veins. When other boys were carefree, running and playing, he had been quietly observing ways to kill, to battle, to outwit. His senses were acute, his reflexes faster. He had soaked up information, worked on concealing himself even from his parents. He had practiced over and over his ability to sneak up on others and observe them for hours without being seen. He had known even then that he was different, that the cold seeping into his veins gave him an edge others didn't have, he had known, but he had fought that knowledge.

He reached for the cold this time, instead of working to stay ahead of it. He embraced the shadows within himself, allowed, for the first time, the darkness to take him. It settled over and into him, fitting like a glove, that pure predator being. He'd always known it was there waiting to take him. He had fought that path, desperate to stay whole, but he knew there was no other option if he was to survive and survival was essential to protect his brothers. He chose that being for himself in order to choose life for his brothers.

He moved with the turbulent wind, sliding in behind the vampire in silence, gathering his strength, as stealthy as the most seasoned of hunters. The undead looked around and, not seeing or hearing any threat, spat on the ground and turned his attention to the four boys caught in the cage of rocks. He showed his teeth in an evil smirk.

"He has left you to me. I will tear off the head of the little one and feed him to you, limb by precious limb, before I devour you alive."

Nicolas and Rafael stood, two young Carpathians, shoulder to shoulder in front of their younger siblings.

Deliberately Zacarias sent a small rock rolling behind him. The vampire spun to face the sound, presenting a full-frontal target.

Look away, Zacarias ordered his brothers. *All of you, look away. Do not watch this! Nicolas, cover Riordan's eyes. None of you witness this.*

With his heart in his throat, with tears burning a hole in his soul, he shifted, assuming his physical form with blurring speed, then drove his fist into his father's chest, using every ounce of strength he possessed. He stood toe-to-toe, looking his father straight in the eye as he smashed through bone and muscle and grasped that beating organ. His father tore at his flesh, digging great chunks of skin and muscle from him, but Zacarias closed down all feelings of pain and all emotion so that he could save his brothers and his family's honor.

The sound was horrendous, a terrible sucking blended with his father's scream of pure agony. The vampire hissed promises, begged and pleaded for his life, raged and snarled vows of vengeance and death on the children, promised to tear off his brothers' heads and feed them to him. Spittle and acid burned over his skin as he dragged the heart from his father's chest and flung it a distance away.

His father grasped Zacarias's forearms, staring at him with shocked, blood-filled eyes. "Son," he whispered. "My son."

A silent scream welled up. It took every ounce of courage he possessed not to put his arms around that torn body and hold his father to him. Zacarias watched the man he loved most in the world teeter and fall, first to his knees in front of him and then fall facedown in the mud. He stepped back and called the lightning from the sky.

He was more shaken than he knew. The first bolt of sizzling electricity missed the pulsating organ. The heart rolled, and landed in his mother's blood. The sight was so loathsome, he steadied himself and sent the next bolt slamming directly into his father's heart, incinerating it.

Zacarias bent double, no longer able to block the excruciating pain, a sheer physical reaction he could no longer control. His scream of denial tore up from his churning belly through his shattered heart to break the blood vessels in his throat. He didn't feel his wounds, some to the bone, or the acid burning through his skin left behind by the vampire blood, only the agony of his parents' deaths, of the kill forced on him by fate, by destiny. Of the loss of all innocence, of being thrust into a role he'd been born for but did not want. He didn't want to ever face the knowledge that all that darkness consumed him—remained inside of him.

"Zacarias." Nicolas was there, wrapping an arm around him, trying to pull him away from the scene of death.

Zacarias stepped away from him, afraid of tainting his brother with the shadows that were now solidly a part of him. Grimly he incinerated the bodies of his mother and father, the vampire, before taking care of the acid on his skin.

He turned to study the pale faces of his brothers. "None of you will ever think of this again. You will not dishonor our father or me with this memory, do you understand? Not *ever.* You will not think of it or speak of it again. Do your crying now, because when we walk away from here, it is done. Finished. Tell me you understand. Each of you. Say it. Swear it on the life of our mother."

His brothers each swore to him they would obey his wishes and reaffirmed their allegiance to him. Only then did he leave them to let them mourn while he went a distance away and sank into the earth and cried for the last time in over a thousand years.

Zacarias touched his face and his fingertips came away smeared with blood. He could feel Marguarita in his arms, feel her inside of him, all around him. Her heartbeat was rapid and her breathing ragged. She was crying, and he felt her pain as though it was his own. Startled he looked down at her shoulder. Her blouse had droplets of crimson staining the material. His throat felt clogged and aching. Shocked, he shoved her away from him, throwing her out of his mind, rejecting her, rejecting the memories, rejecting the agony of such of things.

The adrenaline and absolute refutation of the memory—of the emotions—put far more strength in him than he intended, and Marguarita went flying, stumbling back away from him to land several feet in a small heap on the floor. She looked up at him with resignation, making no attempt to stand.

Zacarias took a deep breath and expelled the terrible taste in his mouth—in his mind. He was Zacarias De La Cruz and he was . . . alone. Completely, utterly alone. Without her in his mind, filling those torn, shadowed places, he had never been so alone. He could feel it, that emptiness yawning like a great endless hole threatening to swallow him whole. He backed even farther away from her—this witch who had turned his life upside down.

The agony of remembrance was unbearable. Tremors ran through him. He took another step away from her, putting the length of the room between them. Inside there was a terrible wrenching, as if he was tearing his own body apart in order to separate from her. He couldn't afford her. He was pure predator, born that way, shadowed from birth, encased in ice. She was melting each of his shields, destroying his ability to function properly.

A slow hiss of warning emerged. Fear slid into her expression and instead of the satisfaction he should have felt, his stomach took a plunge and something vicious squeezed his heart.

You asked me to show you.

He *felt* her plea, although this time he wasn't certain she did. She held out an unsteady hand to him. Zacarias studied her, his eyes flat and cold, his expression deliberately remote. "Of what use is this to me? This memory was never meant to surface and yet you bring up something that has been buried over a thousand years. For what purpose?"

But the memory is still inside of you and so is the pain. You lock it away instead of letting go of it.

"If I do not feel it, it is gone."

She shook her head, dropping her hand. *If it was gone, I could not have found it or felt the agony you felt.*

He despised her logic. She had uncovered a long-buried secret no one in the Carpathian world, let alone the human world, knew. He took a step toward her, his teeth snapping together in a vicious warning. "I should break your neck for such an indiscretion. You dare too much." He actually twisted his hands together as if he had her neck between his palms.

She tilted her chin at him. *I'm tired of being afraid of you. Do it then. Get it over with.*

He was on her so fast she had no time to do anything but blink up at him. His fingers wrapped around her throat, dragging her to her feet. Her pulse beat into the palm of his hand. He knew the moment he touched her that he was lost. There would be no killing this woman, no harming her in any way. She was fast losing her fear of him and she had every reason to be afraid. Each time he got near her, inhaled her, *looked* at her, his body reacted, full and hard and so aching with need it rivaled the hunger throbbing in his veins for her.

"Sun scorch you, woman," he whispered, dropping his hands. "No one controls me. *No one.*" He turned his back on her, striding from the room.

Zacarias dissolved before he reached the front door. He needed to be outdoors where he could breathe. He didn't belong in any enclosure. The world had long since moved on without him. He was a predator long outliving his time and he understood nothing about the modern world—nor did he want to. Modern houses and conveniences meant nothing to him. He had the rain forest and the caves, the earth itself was his home. He was meant to be alone. He had been born to a different life and he had no place in a world with houses populated by humans.

Marguarita was a complete mystery to him. She was like some beautiful lure he couldn't resist, drawing him deeper and deeper into her spell where he would have to . . . He slammed his mind closed, refusing to bring her with him out of her dwelling. She would stay there, where he put her and he would return when it suited him. In the meantime, he had other much more pressing problems than a woman who refused to leave things alone that should never be brought into the light—such as Zacarias De La Cruz.

He slipped through the crack beneath the door and streamed out into the night, out into the world he understood where it was kill or be killed. He took the form of the harpy eagle and rose into the sky, circling the ranch several times before retreating into the forest. There was no doubt in his mind that evil was out and spreading through the great forest and down the winding Amazon and all its tributaries looking for him.

Ruslan Malinov, eldest of the Malinov brothers and their acknowledged leader, would not take his defeat lying down. He would need vengeance and he would be unable to pass the task to another, not even one of his brothers. The lesser vampires would be watching, waiting to see if he exacted his revenge. He had to come after Zacarias or lose control of everything he had built. He would come, but he would not come openly.

The harpy eagle soared to the highest point above the ranch and settled into the branches of a tall kapok tree. He had extraordinary eyesight, was able to see anything tiny, even less than an inch, from a good two hundred yards away. As a rule, the harpy had poor night vision, but Zacarias was born to the night and his night vision coupled with the harpy's made for excellent sight. Ruslan had sent the tainted birds, and it wouldn't be the only thing he sent looking for evidence of Zacarias's passing.

Leaving the battlefield in Brazil, he'd been severely wounded. He'd left a blood trail leading straight to this ranch. Ruslan's spies would have had no problem following the scent. It hadn't mattered because he had intended to end his existence and Ruslan would have led the fight away from his brothers. The master vampire would have been satisfied knowing Zacarias was finally dead. But now, because he was alive, Ruslan would come and he would bring every foul thing with him he could possibly conjure up in a short time. Deep inside the harpy eagle, Zacarias smiled, a grim, welcoming smile.

Destroying the undead was familiar territory, one he was very comfortable with. He found he welcomed the coming nights. A game of wits. Ruslan had always been intelligent and arrogant and that had led to his inevitable downfall. He had considered himself far above the Dubrinsky lineage and believed that by assassinating the prince he would become the leader of the Carpathian people.

There had been a time far back when Ruslan and Zacarias had been best friends. They fought together, side by side, watched each other's back as close as blood brothers, but Ruslan had crossed a line impossible to retreat from. Ruslan had never once admitted to making a mistake, and his arrogance had grown over the centuries. Until now, he had avoided direct confrontation with Zacarias, but he would come.

Zacarias glanced toward the house. The pull of the woman was growing stronger by the moment. She crept into his thoughts and refused to leave. He wasn't going to escape, not even within the body of the eagle. She was there in his mind, wrapping him up in her silken web. He wanted to see her, to know she was safe, and his mind kept trying to tune itself to hers.

Marguarita Fernandez was his true lifemate. There was no denying that fact now. He had found her and the danger had increased a thousandfold. His father had been born with that same taint of shadow Zacarias had in such abundance. He had found his lifemate, lived many centuries, but in the end, none of it had mattered. With his lifemate torn and bloody before him, he had turned into . . .

He slammed his mind closed on that atrocity. Sun scorch Marguarita Fernandez. She had opened Pandora's box and there was no closing it now. He was lost no matter what. If he claimed her, if he didn't claim her, and how could he not? He was tied to her irrevocably and the strength of those ties grew with each passing hour. He had to protect her at all costs and the moment Ruslan found out about her he would use every weapon in his arsenal to get to her. He would know the danger to Zacarias's soul. Zacarias was already so close to turning, losing Marguarita would tip him over the edge just as assuredly as it had his father. Ruslan would do everything in his power to bring about Zacarias's downfall through his lifemate.

The moon had begun to wane, although light spilled down, bathing the ground in silvery beams. Stars glittered bright and a few clouds drifted very slowly across the sky, more wisps than real. It took a moment, as he looked out over the ranch, before he realized some of the dull gray of the grass and fences had deepened to other hues. Eagles, like most birds, saw in color, and the harpy was no exception, but even inside the raptor, Zacarias had never been able to distinguish any color whatsoever. He nearly fell off the tree branch peering down at the grass in the field. The gray had taken on both green and yellow tints. Enough that in the gleaming light from the moon, he felt a little dazzled by the sight. The corrals and fences looked a drab wooden brown, but definitely brown versus the gray he was used to. Before, he had begun to see only Marguarita in color. Now the world she lived in was coming alive to him.

He forced his gaze away from the hacienda and back toward the fields. Spies came in all forms and it was good to be prepared. Only Cesaro, Julio and Marguarita had actually seen him and they all knew to go about their daily routines with added vigilance. Every single worker on the ranch had been equipped from birth with protection for their minds. No vampire could penetrate those shields. They were also trained from the time they were toddlers in fighting the undead. The games taught to the children were actually skills needed to slay a vampire.

Each man and woman working on any of the ranches knew if a De La Cruz was in residence, the danger was very high and they took precautions. Animals were moved into protected areas and all riders carried both modern and ancient weapons, usually concealed so any spy watching wouldn't realize they were armed with more than the usual ranch tools.

The rain forest had a way of continually creeping back to reclaim its own territory and already, in spite of the ranch workers fighting to hold back the growth, creeper vines snaked their way along the ground to sneak beneath the fences and take root in the fields. Some of the woody vines wound their way up posts and around fencing. In the corner of the far field, where cattle roamed, several thick plants broke through the ground in places. The harpy eagle took to the air and circled above the field, his sharp gaze fixing on the plants.

The vines were twisted, thick braids of wood, dark and running with a thick sap. They appeared to be growing at a rapid rate, eating through everything in their path. Even as the eagle watched, a curious mouse scurried across the grass and ventured too close. The sap beaded along the vine and dripped into the ground. The mouse sniffed the substance curiously. The sap seemed to reach for the inquisitive rodent, splashing up, surrounding the little mouse, encasing it in the dark, oily substance.

The mouse screamed, lifting its head for air as the sap encased it, eating the hapless creature alive, right through the fur, through the walls of skin and tissue, to devour the tiny bones. That sap could devour a steer, horse or human—just as easily. Zacarias noted every place the vines had grown and headed toward the small home where Cesaro and his family lived. It would be necessary for the humans to recognize the plant and mark it without going near it as well as ensuring all animals stayed away from it.

Cesaro answered his call immediately, coming out onto the verandah, still buttoning his shirt and closing the door hastily on the growling, cowering dog behind him. "Is something wrong, *señor*?"

He looked as uneasy as his dog acted. Zacarias stepped off the porch to put a little distance between him and the dog now at the window, snarling and nearly foaming at the mouth. There was no doubt animals were disturbed by his presence.

"Unfortunately I have found evidence of evil creeping onto the ranch. I want you to come with me so you can identify the plant to all those working under you before I destroy it. It will kill, not only plant and animal life, but human as well."

Cesaro immediately nodded his head. "Do you need my son?"

Zacarias first thought to shake his head. As a rule he avoided contact with the workers, knowing he made them every bit as uneasy as he did the livestock, but maybe he needed to spend some time with Julio. Zacarias knew he was far too much of a predator to allow his woman to be with a man she felt genuine affection for, so to keep Cesaro's son safe, it was best to ascertain his intentions toward Marguarita.

"Yes. We want to make certain there is no place on the ranch that this plant grows. Your son spends a good amount of time in the saddle and he covers a good deal of territory."

"I'll just be a moment." Cesaro disappeared into the house.

The dog was annoying. Zacarias put up with the irritating snarling a couple more minutes and then he waved his hand and the noise ended abruptly. The dog continued to stare out the window, but when he opened his mouth to bark or growl, no sound emerged.

Cesaro hurried out followed by Julio. The boy looked younger than Zacarias remembered. In truth, he'd barely glanced at the kid when he'd yanked him through the window, intending to kill him for daring to put his hands on Marguarita. Julio touched his neck and then straightened his shoulders.

"We won't take the horses," Cesaro told his son, shooting a quick glance toward Zacarias. "Not until we've seen everything Señor De La Cruz needs to show us."

Zacarias led the way toward the back field. Already, the vines had circled the fencing and had grown thick along the back corner. He waved his hand toward the plant. "That is deadly to anything living that comes near it. I will incinerate it, but you will have to be very vigilant. All of you. It will continue to return as long as I am in residence."

"How long do you plan to stay?" Cesaro asked.

Zacarias pinned him with a cool gaze. "Indefinitely." The man paled beneath his bronzed skin, so Zacarias took pity on him. It had to be said eventually. "There is an unforeseen complication."

Cesaro glanced at Julio.

Zacarias sighed. "I do not like it any more than you do. As much as you are disturbed by my presence, I am disturbed by yours."

"You misunderstand, *señor.* This is your home and certainly you should stay as long as you wish," Cesaro corrected hastily. "It is just that Marguarita is needed with the animals and our regular routine is important to keep to. We have a couple of mares ready to give birth any day now and with you present, the cattle have to be watched continually. She's good at soothing all the animals."

"I am afraid you will have to get along without her."

Julio glanced at him sharply. He pulled his hat down closer over his eyes. "Is she all right?"

"Why would she not be all right?" Zacarias challenged.

"She is always out with the horses," Cesaro explained. "It is worrisome that she hasn't gone to the stable and at least checked the mares."

"She is fine." That wasn't altogether the truth. He had thrown her across the room and hadn't even checked her out. He was always forgetting how fragile humans were.

"I'd like to see her," Julio said.

Zacarias halted abruptly. He felt the familiar cold sweep through his body. His gaze focused on the younger man, a direct, predatory stare. He felt the need to kill building, that raw desire to remove every obstacle from his path. "Why?"

Cesaro edged closer to his son but Zacarias stopped him with a flick of his gaze. Tension stretched. Julio refused to be intimidated, ignoring his father's restraining hand.

"Marguarita is like a sister to me. I love her and I need to know she is safe and well and happy. She would never willingly avoid checking the horses. The horses are her passion and the fact that she hasn't come out to the stables is not a good sign."

"Marguarita is my lifemate."

Cesaro drew in his breath, shaking his head in denial, his shock plain. Julio frowned and looked to his father for an explanation.

"That can't be, *señor*," Cesaro protested. "She is one of us, not Carpathian. There is some mistake."

"What does that mean?" Julio demanded. "I don't understand what that means."

"It means she belongs to me. She is my woman. My wife. And that puts her in more danger than you can possibly imagine. If it becomes known that she is my lifemate, every vampire and his puppet the world over will be looking to kill her. It is far safer for her to be inside the dwelling until I can remove the immediate danger to her."

Julio shook his head. "You can't just come here and decide that Marguarita is your woman. She may work for you, but she has rights. What does she say about this?"

"Julio," Cesaro hissed in warning.

"She has no say in the matter," Zacarias said, pitching his voice low—a velvet warning. "In our world, the man claims his woman and she is bound to him. There is no going back for either of them."

"It's a mistake."

"It is impossible to make a mistake," Zacarias said. "She is mine."

"You don't sound happy about it, *señor*," Cesaro said quickly, interrupting his son before Julio could speak. "Perhaps in this instance, something could be done to free her. Surely you don't want to be saddled with a human woman—one that can't speak."

There was a short silence while Zacarias turned the idea over and over in his mind. All along, he had been thinking that exact thought—he didn't want to be saddled with a human woman—any woman—but especially one who didn't know the first thing about obedience. He had considered walking away from her, just leaving her without a word. He'd thought to stay a few days just to see color and feel just a little before ending his days. Hearing Cesaro give voice to his own thoughts changed everything.

He felt his gut tighten, his body react physically to the thought of losing her. His mouth went dry, something viselike squeezed his heart hard in his chest. Everything he was rebelled against the idea of breaking the ties between them. Marguarita was *his* woman. He wasn't about to find a way to be free of her. He didn't believe there was a way, but even so, she belonged to him and he would never give her up willingly. Not to the humans, not to the vampires and certainly not to another man.

So there it was. He had a lifemate, as crazy as the woman was, she belonged to him and he was keeping her. He flashed his teeth at Cesaro, allowing a flare of absolute predator to show in his eyes as a warning.

"I will not give her up. There is no discussion. If you both care for her as you say you do, this will stay between us. No one else can know, not even other members of your family. It is the only way to keep her safe."

"Is she a prisoner?" Julio dared to ask.

Zacarias touched his mind. The man's barrier was intact, but Zacarias had taken his blood and pushed harder to gain entry. Julio pressed his fingers to his temples, shaking his head.

"Just tell me what you want to know."

Zacarias was already getting the impressions he needed. Julio did love Marguarita as a sister. It was a relief to know he wouldn't have to kill Cesaro's son. "Who is this man you do not like that keeps coming around to visit Marguarita?"

Julio looked startled. "Was I thinking about him?"

"You do not like the idea of Marguarita being my lifemate, but you like the idea of her being with this strange man even less," Zacarias said. "Tell me about him."

They were approaching the vine and Zacarias waved both men to a halt, not wanting them too close to the treacherous sap. "Just in the time I have spent with you, the vines have been busy."

"I've never seen anything like it," Cesaro said. "The plant looks alive, eating everything in its path."

Zacarias nodded. "The vampire bends everything to his evil purpose. He knows I am in residence and he will be nipping at my heels in the hopes of weakening me before he shows himself. Do not try to kill this plant yourselves. If anyone spots it, let me know immediately."

Both men stepped well back when Zacarias waved them away from the destructive vines. Above their heads, clouds gathered, churned and boiled, silver veins flickered inside the turbulent patches. Lightning leaped along the ground, forks of white-hot energy traced the path of the thick vines, incinerating the wood, leaves and thick sap everywhere it touched. A foul smell much like rotting eggs permeated the air.

"Do not breathe it in," Zacarias cautioned.

The trail of burning ash grew long and wide, racing over the ground and under it, following the path of the vines back to the original source—the edge of the rain forest. It was clear, seeing the blackened ash, the vine had been traveling toward the hacienda, searching for Zacarias's resting place.

"Tell me about this man you do not like, the one you believe is courting my woman," Zacarias commanded as they turned back toward the hacienda.

Light was just beginning to streak across the night sky, fading the stars and moon. Zacarias quickened his pace. Safeguards would be necessary throughout the ranch now.

"Esteban and his sister, Lea, moved here a few months ago," Cesaro said, glancing at his son for confirmation. Julio nodded with a small frown. "Very wealthy and very arrogant. This is not the kind of man who settles here. He has no real interest in ranching or raising horses. I ask myself, why would this type of man come here to this remote part of the country when he is so obviously a city man?"

"That is a good question," Zacarias affirmed. "Have you an answer?"

Julio sighed and shook his head. "We've talked it over several times. Either they're hiding here, on the run from something or . . ." He trailed off and looked at his father.

"Or they're hoping to get to a De La Cruz," Cesaro admitted. "It is no secret who owns this land. It is far larger than any other holding here in our country, and although on record it looks as if each of your brothers has bought land to put together, one family having so much acreage is unusual. Your family has a certain reputation and many men would wish it to be known that you are friends. And the man, Esteban, often brings up the De La Cruz name, asking questions we do not answer."

"It is possible they have knowledge they shouldn't," Julio added reluctantly.

"Did you express your concerns to Marguarita?" Zacarias asked.

"Marguarita is completely loyal to the De La Cruz family," Julio snapped. "She would never betray you, certainly not to an outsider."

"That is not what I asked," Zacarias said.

Julio hung his head when his father sent him a dark scowl.

"No. Marguarita regarded Esteban and his sister as friends, no more than that," Cesaro said. "She knew he was courting her, but then so were a lot of men. She showed no real interest so we thought it best to just tell her that he was an outsider and didn't belong here. That is as far as it went."

Zacarias nodded. "Do you really need her for the animals—the horses?"

Cesaro nodded. "Especially now. They are . . . disturbed."

Zacarias broke away from the two men, heading back to the main ranch house. "Tomorrow evening then, she will help you."

He didn't wait for their response. It mattered little to him what they had to say. Marguarita was his woman, and for as long as he chose to remain on earth, no one else would direct her but him. He safeguarded the house, paying special attention to the foundation and the ground beneath the house before he added protection to the doors and windows. Only when he was completely certain Ruslan's spies couldn't penetrate his guards did he allow his mind to seek Marguarita's.

She hadn't moved from the floor in the kitchen. He found her sitting with her knees drawn up and her chin resting on top of them. She looked small and forlorn. His heart stuttered when her eyes met his. There was no condemnation in her expression or her mind. She simply looked at him with her dark chocolate eyes, her gaze drifting over his face, as if trying to read his mood.

Are you all right?

He found her warmth filling his mind. She didn't pour into him as she had before, but drifted in just as her gaze moved slowly over his face. His heart found the rhythm of hers, slowed her frantic pace so that they beat in sync. There were tear tracks on her face and the sight offended him. He crossed to her side and reached down to lift her into his arms, cradling her against his chest. She made no protest, but curled into him, resting her head against his shoulder. Her hair spilled around her face, hiding her expression, but she couldn't hide her mind from his.

I'm sorry. I shouldn't have been meddling in things I don't understand. Truly, Zacarias, I'm very, very sorry.

She was worried for him. She wasn't thinking of herself or his reaction, the things he'd said and done to her, she was worried about how the memories had affected him.

"People do not worry about me, Marguarita."

Someone should.

There was a hint of a smile in her voice and it warmed him. He turned her response over and over in his mind. "If I put you in your bed will you stay there?"

This time there was no mistaking the laughter. *Probably not, but I'll try.*

He laid her on top of the bed and stared down at her for a long time. Her black hair spilled across her pillow, like a fall of silk skeins. Her lashes looked thicker and darker than ever. Color added so much to a world, even the dull colors he was seeing. He wanted to lean down and taste those perfect lips, but he knew it wouldn't end there. The call of her blood beat in his veins and he was done scaring her for the day. Not when she was so obviously worried about him.

"Sleep well, Marguarita."

I almost miss those strange names you call me.

He touched her hair once, feeling a shift in his heart, one he feared would change his life. He moved back away from her without another word, unable to decide what he was going to do about her. He could not remember a time when he hadn't known exactly what he was going to do. Abruptly he left her room, left her fragrant scent and the terrible need clawing at his veins. He was still in control, but for how much longer was anyone's guess.

9

Marguarita rolled over and stared at her window. The heavy drapes were drawn, but a sliver of light told her it was the middle of the day. A rain of pebbles hit the glass and she sighed and pushed herself up. Her body felt leaden, not wanting to cooperate, but resolutely she slipped out of bed and crawled across the floor to the window pushing the drapes aside just as Julio sent another light spray of small rocks rapping against the glass.

Trying not to laugh, Marguarita shoved the window up. Sunlight spilled into her room, burning her eyes. She hastily covered them, shocked at how she was already so used to being up all night. She dragged a pen and notepad from the bedside table.

Are you crazy? He might kill you if he finds you here again.

"He's sleeping. I made certain to wake you well before sundown. I had to make certain you were all right."

She shaded her eyes and looked him over carefully. There was a thick bloody wrap around his forearm and he looked upset.

What happened to you?

"The dog went crazy about an hour ago. *My* dog. He suddenly started snarling and growling. He hadn't made a sound since . . ."

She sketched a question mark between them.

"De La Cruz came to our house last night. Max went berserk. All the animals do when he's around, you know that. He was barking and snarling at the window and then abruptly he went silent. Not a peep until a little while ago and then it was like he went crazy. He started snapping at my horse's heels and one kicked at him. I dismounted to calm him down and he attacked me."

Marguarita climbed onto the windowsill, sitting with her legs dangling, and indicated Julio come closer so she could inspect the lacerations.

Julio took off his shirt to show Marguarita the scratches across his chest. The dog had gone for his throat and he had held him off with sheer strength. Her heart sank. Julio had thrust his forearm into the dog's mouth, sacrificing his arm to prevent the attack on his throat.

You had to shoot him? She knew the answer before he spoke. Julio had loved his dog.

"Ricco shot him. He didn't have a choice, Marguarita. I think De La Cruz did something to my dog."

She shook her head rejecting the idea, frantically writing on the notepad.

He wouldn't do that, Julio. Everything on the ranch is under his protection, including the animals.

"The animals are terrified of him and you know it. The longer he stays here, the worse it's going to get. Even the horses are upset, Marguarita. They're hard to control when we're out patrolling. I think he's staying here because of you. He's got to go."

She glared at him.

This is his home, Julio. That's a mean thing to say.

Julio shook his head, crumpling her note. "This is our home. They're never here, especially him. He's the worst of them. He can't just come here and tell us all that you belong to him. We work for him, but you aren't his slave. He's got to go, and you have to get out of there. Now. Before he does something to make it impossible for you to get away from him."

He needs me, Julio.

Julio scowled at her. "He's not one of your broken animals to rescue, Marguarita. He's dangerous to you. You can't treat him like a wild animal."

That's exactly what he is. He's alone, and he needs me. I'm not going to abandon him the way everyone else in his life has done. He pushes everyone away and they go. I'm staying.

"What if he wants more from you than you're willing to give?" Julio demanded. "Because he thinks you're his woman. Do you have any idea the demands he could make on you? You're playing with fire, Marguarita. If he's a wild animal, then he's the most dangerous one you've ever encountered and you aren't going to tame him. Get out while you can. I'll help you. We all will. He doesn't own you. He doesn't own any of us. We have choices here, and you do as well."

My choice is to see him through this. You have no idea of his life, Julio. He came here to end his life with honor and I ruined that for him. He's lost right now and I need to help him. I want to help him. I know that I can.

Julio cursed under his breath. "You've always been like this, Marguarita, so stubborn no one could make you see reason." He started to put his shirt back on, but stopped when she shook her head.

Marguarita slipped back into her room and rummaged around until she found the first-aid kit she'd made up years earlier for the workers. Over time she'd become somewhat of a nurse with all the lacerations and accidents that occurred on the ranch. She smeared antibiotic cream over the deep scratches and handed him some tablets.

Julio obediently took them and dragged his shirt back over his head, smoothing it over his chest. "I'm telling you, hon, De La Cruz is no ordinary man. You have to let this one go."

She unwound the bloody rag and gasped when she saw the wound on his arm. She mimicked sewing, frowning at him. Julio shrugged and shook his head.

"It'll heal. Just do whatever you do so it doesn't get infected."

Marguarita had to blink several times. The sun seemed unusually bright and her eyes kept watering. She shook her head and indicated she needed to at least put butterfly strips across the wound to try to close it.

"Get on with it, then. I've got to get back to work. You have to get to the stables tonight and settle the animals down. Someone's really going to get hurt if you don't, Marguarita."

She nodded as she carefully applied the antibiotic cream and then began to meticulously close the wound.

"He can't keep you," Julio reiterated. "You don't owe him your life, honey. Seriously, think about leaving this place."

He would find me. I want to stay anyway, Julio. I know I can help him.

She had almost written *save* him. Zacarias needed saving from himself. Perhaps it couldn't be done. She wasn't even certain he wanted saving, but someone had to care about the man. He didn't seem to care much about himself. He was arrogant and had complete confidence in himself, but he also believed he was tainted with evil.

I'm sorry about your dog, Julio, but whatever happened, Zacarias had nothing to do with it. You be careful today. I'll come out this evening.

She hoped Zacarias would be cooperative. He knew the ranch work had to be done. If it took her going to the stables to calm the animals, she was certain Zacarias would agree to it. She waved to Julio and resolutely closed the window and pulled the drapes. She was tired, but a few hours to herself sounded good, so she decided to stay up.

In the bathtub, she laid with her eyes closed and allowed herself to think about Zacarias. He was such a mystery—a man who had no real idea of who he was. Her heart went out to him, a man so utterly alone. No one should be so alone. And he had no real idea of his own feelings. He'd buried his memories so deep, never forgiving himself, refusing to acknowledge he even remembered that terrible tragedy in his life.

Marguarita sighed as she sank down into the hot, scented water, soaking the long, thick rope of hair. She felt exhausted, and it was difficult to keep her mind away from Zacarias. In the short time she'd been around him, she'd mostly been afraid, so it didn't make sense to her that she was so determined to help him. She hated that he was so alone. No one should be alone, not like he was, not cut off from anything soft and gentle. He had so little humanity left that he no longer believed he could overcome the predator in him.

She saw inside of him, but every time she tried to show him he was different inside, he rejected her. It was almost as if he was afraid of that softer side of himself. It made him vulnerable and Zacarias De La Cruz had never really been that way—or if he had—he certainly didn't remember it. Nor did he want to remember it.

Zacarias had lived so long as a dangerous hunter, always alone and always apart, that he really had no way to fit into modern society, with humans or even with his own people. He had supreme confidence in himself as a hunter—a killer—but not as a man. And he was wrong. As arrogant and as dangerous as he was—there was someone gentle and loving deep inside him. His tremendous loyalty and sense of duty were admirable. He didn't see it that way. Everything was so black and white to him.

She dried herself off slowly, taking her time, enjoying the feeling that she had her home to herself and she could feel as if it belonged to her. She'd been mistress of the hacienda a long time and now, with Zacarias home, dictating to her what she could or couldn't do, where she could go and what she should wear, she had forgotten how peaceful she found the house. It was her sole domain. She kept it clean, decorated it the way she wanted and was in total charge of her own life. She had suitors courting her, which was a nice boost to her ego, but she knew she wouldn't want any of them for a husband.

Zacarias. Thinking of him made her feel alive. She loved riding horses, the freedom of flying over the ground, one with her horses. Zacarias gave her that same thrill only more so. He wasn't peaceful by any means, but being in his company was exhilarating. She sat at her vanity and brushed her long hair into a semblance of submission while she thought about him.

He was handsome in a rough, brutal sort of way. His body was fit, that of a warrior. Physically there was no doubt she was attracted to him, but that wasn't the draw. She imagined most women would be unable to resist his looks. He was mesmerizing and had an animal attraction as well. But still . . . There was so much more to him, right there under the surface, and quite frankly, he intrigued her.

She pulled on her usual house clothes, a blouse and long skirt, frowning a little that she was conforming to what Zacarias liked. It would have been childish to wear jeans just because he'd stated she should wear feminine clothes. She *liked* her skirts. She wasn't going to change for him—one way or the other. No one had dictated to her, not even her father, and having Zacarias speak in such commanding tones all the time was a little humorous.

Someone walked up onto the porch and knocked on the front door. It was a timid knock, not at all like Julio or one of the other boys would make. Her stomach jumped and she glanced toward the master bedroom. She took a loaded gun from the trunk in the hallway and pushed it into her skirt pocket. They didn't get many visitors, and with Zacarias vulnerable during the day, she was determined to protect him.

She peered out and was a little shocked to see Lea Eldridge, waiting for her alone on the porch. Lea had never once come to the ranch without her brother. She was a tall, blond woman, very chic. Her hair was never out of place, her makeup perfect and her clothes obviously designer. Where Esteban talked down to the workers, Lea always seemed open and friendly. She was a beautiful woman, and Marguarita liked her more than she did the women she'd grown up with. Lea seemed a genuine, giving person. She always had time to speak to the older workers and children, not just the handsome single men. Marguarita liked that about her.

She opened the door and frowned when she saw Lea's face. There was a faint bruise on her cheekbone and obvious signs of tears. Lea's skin was flawless, as porcelain as peaches and cream, and even with her careful application of makeup, it was impossible to hide the purple. She stepped back to allow Lea entrance.

Lea glanced around behind her, a covert, stealthy perusal of the surrounding area and roads before she ducked inside and hastily closed the door. "My brother doesn't know I'm here. No one does."

I'll make tea. I'm glad you came to visit me.

Marguarita handed her the note and led the way into the kitchen, gesturing for Lea to sit at the table while she prepared tea. It was obvious Lea was very upset. It was times like this that Marguarita was especially frustrated that she couldn't speak. Writing things down took forever. While the kettle was heating, she sank down into the chair opposite Lea, touched her hand and slid a paper across to her.

What happened? You're safe here, Lea.

Lea blinked back tears and shook her head. "You don't understand. My brother's friend, Dan, we call him DS, has found us here. He's . . .

awful. Everywhere we go, he finds us, and Esteban does whatever he says. I thought if we came here, he'd never find us, but he's here and he's going to do something terrible. He always does."

Who hit you?

Lea ducked her head, touching her cheek with her fingertips. "The truth is, Esteban does whatever DS tells him to do. I thought we'd moved to this place to get away from him, but he was the one who instructed Esteban to come here and get friendly with the people on this ranch." She raised sorrowful eyes to Marguarita. "I swear I didn't know. I really thought we had a chance here to get away from him. He's the devil, Marguarita. Esteban does terrible things around him. And if he's planning something to do with this ranch, it isn't going to be legal or good," she confessed. "I'm so sorry."

Marguarita tapped the note again and sketched a question mark in the air between them.

Lea rubbed her temples. "DS hit me because I refused to do what he wanted." A sob welled up. "Esteban just stood there while DS shoved me around."

What does DS want from you and Esteban?

"He wants to meet a member of the De La Cruz family. He's obsessed with the idea. He wants me to seduce one of them. He says if I don't, that he'll kill Esteban. I tried to talk to Esteban but he just laughed and said I'd better get it done then." Lea wiped at the tears and shook her head. "I don't have anywhere to go and no one to talk to. I can't trust anyone. And I didn't want to betray our friendship, but I don't know what to do."

The teakettle was steaming, so Marguarita rose to pour the boiling water into the teapot. She hastily scribbled a note as she did so and shoved it under Lea's nose.

The De La Cruz family rarely visits this ranch. Why would this man think you could possibly seduce one of them when they never stay longer than a day or so and are gone for years? That makes no sense. What does he think seducing one of them would gain him?

Lea shoved both hands through her hair and shrugged her shoulders. "Wealth, maybe. Thrills. I don't know. DS runs drugs and weapons though. Esteban got caught up in all of that. He likes the idea of being on the inside of some underground gangster-type organization. DS talks about some secret society he belongs to—that all the members are in the know, and that kind of thing appeals to Esteban."

Your parents?

"They're both dead. We have a trust fund our uncle controls. Esteban is never satisfied. I keep thinking he'll mellow out, but he keeps looking for that next thrill. Since he met DS, our lives have been insane. DS hangs out with some very scary people."

Why do they believe a De La Cruz will come here?

"You." Lea accepted the teacup and small plate of biscuits. "Your accident. Something that bad was bound to bring one of the owners to the ranch to check on things. Esteban probably sent for DS." She took a sip of tea and regarded Marguarita over the rim of the steaming teacup. "I thought I would have a chance at a real life here. I like it here. And there's . . . Julio." She watched Marguarita's face carefully. "Are you two involved? He's very protective of you."

We were raised as brother and sister.

"He doesn't like us, does he?" Lea asked. "He doesn't even look at me."

She sounded so sad, it wrenched at Marguarita's heart. Julio was right about her, she fell for every wounded thing, man or animal. She sighed and shrugged a little as she wrote.

Julio said it was strange that you and Esteban came here. You have money and you're used to the city life. Neither of you seem to fit in here. But he looks at you, Lea. You're beautiful. How could he not?

"I want to stay. Even after Esteban moves on, I want to stay here. I like our home and I'm beginning to love the horses. I know I could make a life here. And Esteban will move on. He gets bored easily. I've done my best to try to save him from himself, but I know I can't. He won't listen to me anymore. If one of the De La Cruz brothers doesn't show up here soon, DS will want to go to another of the ranches where he might have a better chance of meeting one of them and Esteban will do whatever he says."

The brothers keep to themselves. Even when they do show up at one of the ranches, they rarely talk to anyone but Cesaro. They stay a night or two and are gone again.

"Have you met them?"

A couple of them, once or twice, but I don't really know them. Lea, whatever this man, DS, wants with the De La Cruz family, he won't find it here. Does he want to do some sort of business with them?

Lea nibbled at a tea biscuit, a small frown on her face. "I don't honestly know. Esteban won't talk to me about it. He just tells me to do whatever DS says."

Marguarita allowed the tea to slide down her throat. It was hot and sweet and her stomach rebelled a little, but settled after a moment or two. She'd found it difficult to eat food lately. Nothing tasted good, and often, she felt as if she might get sick when she put solid food in her stomach. The scent of meat particularly offended her. She feared it had something to do with the vampire attack on her and her torn throat. Of course Lea thought a large jungle cat had attacked her as most people did. She touched her throat and immediately felt the throb of the mark Zacarias had put on her. Without thinking, her fingertips brushed a caress over the spot.

"Does it hurt?" Lea asked. "Your throat?"

Marguarita shook her head. It didn't hurt anymore, but it was still difficult to accept that she couldn't speak. Lea had stayed her friend. Esteban had always acted as if he was courting her—until the accident. He continued to come around, but he was careful not to flirt too much with her anymore. She realized he didn't want her to get the wrong idea. Without a voice, she wasn't up to his standards. Perhaps that was judging him harshly, but she had always known he wasn't seriously courting her.

Lea impulsively leaned across the table and put her hand over Marguarita's. "We're such a pair. Me with nowhere to go and you with a torn throat."

Marguarita smiled at her. She raised her teacup and took another sip.

"I don't suppose Julio would have tea with us?" Lea ventured, trying to lighten the mood. "Maybe you could find a secret love potion and slip it to him."

Marguarita smiled and shook her head.

Ask him to show you the horses. Get him talking about them. He loves the horses. I've never seen you ride. Do you know how?

"I hired this man to teach me, but he never shows up. I love to watch you ride, and when I'm on a horse I feel so free. I love the wind in my face and the way the horse moves, flowing across the ground. I know I could live here, even without my brother. I don't spend much out of my trust fund, Esteban blows through his portion every month, but I could buy property here and be happy."

There's no city life here, Lea. It can be lonely for a woman.

Lea sighed and stroked her finger down her bruised cheek. "It can be lonely in the middle of a crowd, Marguarita. I just don't feel I fit anywhere. Not until I came here. I know I seem sort of prissy to you, but I'm a hard worker. I can learn. I just want to find peace."

Why do you travel with Esteban when you know he's involved in illegal activity?

"He's all I have. We have the family business and I could go back and work there, but my uncle is the only one alive that's family other than Esteban. I didn't even know him before my parents were killed in a small plane crash. He's older and very rigid. Esteban can't stand the sight of him and unfortunately, my uncle lets him know at every opportunity that he's a spoiled rich kid. That just seems to egg Esteban on. I was hoping if I was with him, he'd stop doing such dangerous things."

Is he hooked on drugs?

Lea bit at her lower lip. "He uses cocaine. At first it was recreational, and I tried not to get upset about it. Really everyone we knew used it. But Esteban can't go a day without it now. I've tried to talk to him about it, but he says I don't know how to have fun. He thinks I'm a workaholic. I used to work for my parents. Esteban was rather spoiled by my father and dad encouraged him to be a playboy."

He must have taken your parents' death very hard.

Lea nodded. "I think that's what made him so vulnerable to DS. He started doing more drugs and partying hard. He jumps out of airplanes, skis very hazardous mountains, anything that's dangerous, he does it. No matter what I say to him, I can't stop him." She rubbed her temples as if she had a headache. "I can't keep following him around the world trying to keep him alive. He won't listen to me."

I'm sorry, Lea. I wish there was something I could do to help.

Lea sent her a small smile. "I appreciate your listening. It's been a long time since I felt like I had a real friend I could confide in. I have absolutely no idea what I'm going to do to get me and Esteban out of this mess, but you've made me feel better."

Is it safe for you to go home?

Marguarita wanted to invite her to stay, but with Zacarias in residence and knowing Esteban and DS were looking to meet a De La Cruz, she felt she had to protect Zacarias. But still, she felt afraid for Lea.

Lea shrugged. "Esteban loves me. He doesn't believe DS would really hurt either one of us, but if it came down to it, I believe he would protect me. And I plan on avoiding DS. I just wanted you to know not to trust them when they come here. And they'll come. I just don't know what they're up to. Once I'm back home I can try to get Esteban to tell me."

Marguarita shook her head quickly.

There's no need, really, Lea. Even if they come here, what are they going to see? The boys at work. Me. You don't see a De La Cruz anywhere around, do you? They won't, either. They'll look around and then go home.

Lea nodded. "I guess I shouldn't worry. And the De La Cruz family is very powerful. They probably have people like DS targeting them all the time."

The warning siren went off alerting Marguarita that something had happened somewhere on the ranch. Marguarita leaped to her feet, racing toward the front door. She could hear the pounding of hooves as horsemen approached the house at a wild gallop. Marguarita flung the door open. Julio stood with his fist upraised, face white beneath his tan, his clothes covered in blood.

"We need the helicopter pilot, Marguarita. Ricco's been gored. His horse threw him and the cattle stampeded. It's bad. Really bad."

She raced back into the bathroom and grabbed the first-aid kit while Julio made the call for the pilot.

Julio was swearing when she reached his side. She sketched a question mark.

"Charlie's drinking again. He's gone just when we need him most." Julio shoved his hand through his hair. "He won't make it if we don't get him to a hospital."

"I can fly a helicopter," Lea said. "I have a license. I can fly small planes as well. My father owned a charter service, and we all learned to fly."

Julio swung around to scowl at the woman as if she'd grown two heads. "You better know what you're talking about. Ricco's going to die if we don't get him medical attention."

Color crept up Lea's neck into her face. "I can fly him to the hospital. I've logged hundreds of hours in a helicopter and more in small planes. I can fly just about anything. It's what my family did."

"Then you're the pilot," Julio said. "Let's go. Come on, Marguarita, you're going to have to try to keep him alive until we make it to help."

They ran toward the big hangar housing the aircraft. One thing she had always been grateful to the De La Cruz family for was the first-class equipment they always supplied. The ranch was out so far that they used aircraft for medical aid as well as for checking the cattle and horses in the hills and fields.

"Is your helicopter kept in good condition?" Lea asked, running to keep up with Julio's longer strides.

"Yes. It's always serviced after every run. But you'd better double-check. I have no idea how long Charlie's been drinking this time," Julio replied grimly.

Several men rushed toward the hangar, carrying Ricco on a stretcher. Marguarita raced to intercept them, trying to inspect the wound as they took him to the helicopter. The steer had caught Ricco in the abdomen and it looked bad. Very bad. She didn't think, even with a surgeon standing by, that he had much of a chance. She glanced at the sky and looked over the stretcher at Julio, a question in her eyes.

Julio looked as grim as she felt. He wasn't stupid. He'd seen what a maddened steer could do before. The sun was still a ball in the sky, but it was dropping slowly. The sky was clear with few clouds. They had a good hour before sunset. Ricco didn't have that kind of time. She'd seen what the sun had done to Zacarias. She shook her head. Julio glared at her as the men carefully loaded Ricco into the helicopter. Marguarita climbed in beside him and tore open his shirt.

She gasped and put pressure on the wound. There was no way he could possibly make it, no matter how fast they got the helicopter into the air.

Zacarias. She didn't want to force him to tell her he couldn't help, but the wound was ghastly and no way would Ricco make it alive to the hospital. *I need you.* She had no idea if he would answer her call or even care, but she had to try.

The stirring in her mind was instantaneous, as if all along he had been aware of her awake and out of the house. *Are you hurt?* His voice was filled with concern for her and strangely it warmed her.

Not me. Ricco, one of the workers. We're going to take him to the hospital, but he won't make it if you can't help us.

You wish me to do this for you?

Her heart leaped, stuttered and then began to pound. His voice was so matter-of-fact and in truth, she wasn't entirely certain what she was asking of him—but he'd managed to save her and she never should have lived.

What is the risk to you? She had to know. She bit at her lower lip, suddenly terrified of what she was asking of him. *Nothing can happen to you.*

There was a moment that she felt him in her mind, touching every part of her, a brushing caress completely at odds with his lethal presence.

Show me the wound. Look directly at it.

Marguarita steeled herself. The horn had penetrated deep and she was certain the tear had all but killed Ricco. It was fortunate he was unconscious because she had nothing to stop the pain. She forced herself to stare at Ricco's torn stomach, trying to send her own impressions to Zacarias.

Put your hands on the wound and apply pressure. Go deep, Marguarita.

She'd dealt with lacerations, but never anything like this. She was no nurse, but she was all Ricco had. She closed her eyes and did as Zacarias instructed. Her hands sank into blood and gore with a horrible sound.

Soft laughter teased her mind. *I have to see, kislány kuŋenak minan—my little lunatic. Keep your eyes open.*

Swallowing hard she did so. She felt heat move through her body. Her hands tingled and grew hot. Her fingers moved of their own accord and somehow, for one moment, she was no longer inside her own body, but tied to Zacarias and moving through Ricco's body. It was an odd wrenching sensation leaving her physical body behind and streaming through another human. Her stomach rebelled, but she fought hard to stay in control, breathing deep.

Just as abruptly she was back, a little dizzy and feeling weak. She could tell Zacarias was even weaker than she was.

That should hold him until he gets to a surgeon, but he's lost too much blood, Marguarita. I will have to give him mine or all of this is for naught.

Do you want us to bring him back into the house? Can you make it up this time of day?

Do not take the chance of moving him again. I will come to you.

But you can't. He couldn't. The sun would burn him. What had she done? *Please don't sacrifice your life.*

Again she felt that brushing caress go through her mind, as if he'd trailed fingertips over the inside of her skull.

Lea was in the pilot seat, already going through the checklist, preparing for flight. Marguarita lifted her hand to attract Julio's attention. Frantically she wiped her hands and scribbled a note to Julio.

Tell her we have to stabilize him before she can fly him out of here. Zacarias did what he could through me, but he says he needs his blood to survive the journey. He's coming out and Lea can't see him. She can't know he's in residence. I'll explain as soon as I can.

Julio nodded. She was grateful he understood the gravity of the situation and didn't waste time arguing with her. Outside the sky darkened and ominous clouds gathered and spun as if angry.

"We've got to go," Lea shouted.

"Not yet," Julio protested. "Marguarita has to stabilize him or he won't make it."

"The weather's turning ugly," Lea said. "If we don't get moving we're not getting him to the hospital."

"The storm will pass fast," Julio assured. "Trust me on this."

I will be out in a couple of minutes. Zacarias's voice entered Marguarita's head.

I'll tell you when it's safe for you. There's someone here who shouldn't see you. She's not one of us and I think her brother is a danger to you.

She will not see me.

Marguarita felt close to panic. She might not want to betray their friendship, but Marguarita didn't know her well enough to count on her to remain silent if her brother insisted on the truth.

She handed Julio the note.

Take Lea somewhere for a few minutes.

Julio bent down and whispered into Lea's ear. She nodded and tossed her headphones aside, sliding from the helicopter. They both ran toward the house. The sky darkened even more, the turbulent clouds casting dark shadows across the ground. The horses began to act up, half rearing and pawing the air, tossing their heads and dancing around. Marguarita waved the men away from the area, sending a calming touch to the horses.

In the midst of the storm clouds, she made out a stream of vapor moving through the shadows, staying beneath the canopy of trees and the various rooflines. Zacarias made his way through the yard to the large hangar.

He moved quickly into the large building, staying to the darker corners as he approached the helicopter. Marguarita moved to allow him inside. There wasn't a lot of room with Ricco lying so quiet and still, taking up a good deal of space.

He's barely breathing, she pointed out.

Zacarias took his human form, his wide shoulders and larger frame crowding Marguarita as he bent over the wounded man. "His lungs sustained damage." Using his teeth, he opened the vein in his wrist and pressed it against Ricco's mouth. "You will drink what is offered and you will stay alive. Do you hear me?"

Ricco's mouth moved against Zacarias's wrist. Marguarita couldn't look away. It was repelling and fascinating at the same time. She knew Zacarias's blood flowed in her veins; it was only because of him that she had lived through the vicious vampire attack. If Ricco lived, he would owe his life to Zacarias.

No, emnim—*my woman, he will owe his life to you. I did this because you asked it of me. I do not meddle in the affairs of humans.*

Thank you. He's important to me. Ricco has served your family since he was a child and he's always been loyal.

"It is enough that you asked me, Marguarita." He whispered again to Ricco and took his wrist from the man's mouth, closing the laceration. He ran his hand down the length of Marguarita's hair. "Come back to the house and allow them to take him to the hospital. If he fights, and they have a good surgeon, he will live."

You can't be seen here. I'll come as soon as Julio gets back. She was anxious for him to stay out of sight.

Zacarias flashed her a careless smile and her heart stuttered in her chest. He looked virile, so strong, it was hard to conceive that in the daylight he was vulnerable and even weak.

"You think I cannot handle a mortal? A female at that?"

She made a face at him. His ego was going to get him into trouble. The door to the house banged and she knew Julio was warning them that he was on the way back with Lea.

They're coming back. Go now. Hurry. Disappear. She felt desperate. She didn't trust Lea, or anyone else for that matter, not to talk about seeing him. He was too mesmerizing, too different. Too dangerous. *You have to go.*

Zacarias's smile reached his eyes. He wrapped a length of her hair around his hand. "I like when your hair is a mess. You look as if we have been hours playing in the bedroom."

He'd *never* said anything like that to her. No one had. She felt the blush start and go all the way down to her toes. Anxiety poured through her. She pushed at the wall of his chest. *You have to go. I'm not joking.*

He captured her hands, pressing her palms tight against his chest. Her heart accelerated until she thought it might jump out of her skin. He laughed softly. "There you go again, touching me without permission. How should I punish you? I wonder . . ."

She looked over his shoulder at Julio and Lea. Lea carried an armload of blankets. *Please. Just go. Please hurry. You can do whatever when you're safe.*

"I can do whatever?" His eyebrow shot up. "That leaves me a lot of room."

Julio glared at her, signaling frantically.

Zacarias!

He dissolved right in front of her. One moment he was solid, his heavy muscles under her palms, and the next he was gone and she was alone. She stepped quickly from the helicopter, giving Julio room to leap in beside Ricco.

"Has he helped then?" Julio whispered.

Lea handed in the blankets and climbed into the pilot's seat. Already the clouds were dissipating just as fast as they'd formed.

Marguarita nodded and hurried back to the house while the helicopter rose into the sky.

IO

Zacarias stood in Marguarita's bathroom, inhaling her unique fragrance. The clawed tub was deep and the scent of peaches and cream wafted up from the porcelain. His slumber had been disturbed by the pebbles hitting her window. He was so tuned in to her now, so much a part of her mind, that even in his sleep, he was aware of her.

He was a little stunned at the excitement flaring, his nerve endings alive and sizzling with the anticipation of being in her company. He was looking forward to sparring with her. He'd even teased her a little about touching him without permission and as shocking as he found that—he'd enjoyed it.

He'd been all over the world, climbed to the highest mountaintops, descended into the deepest of caves, lived in the rain forests, roamed free and never once in all that time, in all those centuries, had he felt alive—until now. Standing in a small room drawing the scent of Marguarita deep into his lungs made him feel more than he ever had—or could ever remember.

He looked forward to seeing her, touching her. Hunger beat in his veins, a raw, frantic need that echoed through every cell in his body. His physical body took up that call, an urgent demand for the taste and feel of her. Marguarita, his beautiful lunatic. His woman. He allowed the thought to seep into his bones and settle in his soul. He couldn't remember a time when he had called anything his. Warriors were never attached to anything or anyone. But Marguarita had somehow found her way inside him—become a part of him. He didn't even know how it happened. She was just there, in his mind, filling all those shadowed places and connecting broken threads he hadn't known—or cared—existed.

He knew the moment she entered the house. She washed her hands in the kitchen and then went to her bedroom. He heard the rustle of clothes and moved silently into her room to stand behind her, just observing. She stood in front of a full-length mirror, and as he came up behind her, he made certain his reflection didn't show in the glass.

There was something beautiful about a woman doing the simple task of undressing. The skirt pooled at her feet and she stepped free of the material, revealing her slender, shapely legs, and her rounded bottom encased in a very sheer scrap of lace. His breath caught in his throat as she slowly opened the buttons of her blouse and inch by slow inch revealed the creamy swell of her breasts molded by another sheer, lacy undergarment.

Her skin was flawless, so soft it was difficult not to reach out and run his hand down her back. He liked her hair wild, a black cloud of silk cascading like a waterfall to below her waist. Zacarias stepped close to her, his hands sliding around her to link just below her breasts. She inhaled in a kind of shocked delight, her eyes jumping to the mirror. He allowed his own form to materialize behind her. He was a good head taller than she was, his shoulders much wider than hers. He cupped the soft weight of her breasts in his palms and leaned down to bury his face in the cloud of her hair.

"I love how you smell," he whispered into all that silk. He loved how she felt, how her hair felt against his skin. How they looked together, her feminine body so completely engulfed by his masculine one. Simple things. Pleasurable when there had never been pleasure.

She didn't tense or push him away as he expected. He would have allowed her freedom, but she leaned back into him and closed her eyes, relaxing against him. Such a small thing, but for him, intense.

He nuzzled her neck, his fingers moving over her breasts, the sensation astonishing. He felt the softness beneath the pads of his fingers and each touch fueled more heat in his body, driving his temperature up. He did nothing to control the rush, allowing it to spread through his body, marveling at the miracle of woman. He stroked caresses over all that soft skin. His shaft swelled, became full and heavy, and he pressed closer to her soft body.

"I want to exchange blood with you. This time it will not hurt. I will make certain you will enjoy it. Will you trust me?" He whispered the words, a blatant seduction. He wanted her to agree, to give herself to him. To be part of him willingly.

She went still, but there was no rejection, not from her body, or in her mind. She slipped her arm back over her shoulder, hooking her hand around his neck as she tilted her head back. The action lifted those soft, full breasts, her nipples tight and pushing at the lace.

Kiss me. A soft wisp of heat curling in his mind. Sheer temptation.

His cock jumped. Pulsed. She was sensual without even knowing it, enticing him when he no longer had the will to resist her. He had known when he answered her call that he was making a commitment to her. He hadn't considered that he would make her fully his. She had never been in so much danger and yet she didn't seem to have any self-preservation.

"If I kiss you, *kislány kuŋenak minan*—my little lunatic—I do not know if I will stop there." The ache was there. The need. The hunger clawing deeper than it ever had.

She nuzzled his neck. *You would stop if I asked you to.*

There was complete confidence in her voice. She should have been afraid of him. He had given her reason to fear him—deliberately had done so, yet he felt her confidence. She was giving herself into his keeping and he didn't understand why. He truly didn't trust himself with her—so how could she? She was every bit the lunatic he had named her, yet now, it was an endearment. Now, he thought her beautiful and brave. He thought her—*his.*

Kiss me, she whispered again into his mind. An enticement. A seduction.

Her fingertips traced his earlobe and his body tightened. He felt the breath leave his lungs. There was no resisting that soft lure. He turned his head to find her mouth with his. He brushed his lips gently, almost reverently over hers. He felt the impact right down to his toes. Electricity sparked along his nerve endings.

He took his time, tracing her lips, committing the shape and feel of her to memory. He had refused for so long to retain anything in his memory that didn't add to his fighting abilities, but now, learning all about her was as necessary as breathing. He didn't want to hurt her. Not again. He'd spent a great deal of time thinking about how she felt his emotions when he couldn't. How she saw inside of him when he was unable to do so.

Her fingernails traced around the upper curve of his ears. She turned her head a little more and found his earlobe with her mouth, biting gently, and then suckling, her tongue a velvet rasp, sending spiraling heat to his aching groin. Her fingers found his thick hair in an erotic massage that added to the sensations streaking to his cock.

The physical feelings were intense now, gathering like a fireball in the pit of his stomach and spreading through his body like a wildfire. He hadn't felt anything for so many centuries and now she had brought his icy body to volcanic, fiery life. And she knew what she was doing. She wanted him to feel.

It doesn't hurt you to feel. Her voice slipped seductively into his mind, proving she was lodged deep in his being—proving she knew his thoughts. *Feel me, Zacarias. Feel what I'm feeling when you're touching me.*

"This is dangerous," he whispered, knowing he was already lost.

His hands, of their own accord, pushed aside the flimsy scrap of lace covering the soft weight of her breasts. He tugged at her nipples, his mind already firmly entrenched in hers. He could feel exactly what each tug and roll did to her, the sizzling streaks of fire racing to her core. He could become just as addicted to feeling her pleasure as he was fast learning about his own. "*You* are dangerous."

I won't hurt you.

The words brushed in his mind like silk against his skin. He felt her smile, that tender, outrageous, amazing gift of a smile.

"*I* am afraid of hurting *you*. You have no idea what I am capable of." He was fighting for her, yet he couldn't stop his hands from exploring all that creamy flesh. She was so soft and warm and beautiful. The heady scent of her arousal enveloped him and fed the fires burning and clawing at his belly.

Her fingers continued that slow, erotic massage along his scalp. Her lips whispered over his ear, his neck, her tongue tasting his pulse. She was temptation and he was too weak to resist.

I see you. I'm inside your mind just as you're inside my mind. I see inside of you, Zacarias. You would never hurt me. Never. It isn't in you.

I did hurt you. Several times.

Her soft laughter rippled through his groin, so that he felt himself swell more. Felt the first drops of need weeping for her. *You were striking at yourself, Zacarias, not at me. You know what I say is truth.*

He hoped she was right, because there was no way he could stop himself from tasting heaven. Not now. Not with her soft body moving against his and her wild hair brushing like silken skeins over his skin. Not with her breasts in his hands, his fingers rolling and teasing and tugging at her sensitive nipples. Every shiver that went through her body, every electrical spark, he felt in his own. He heard himself groan as she bit down on his neck, that sweet sensitive spot where his shoulder joined. She was killing him slowly.

Hunger beat at him, raw and desperate. The sound of her pulse throbbed in his own veins. He didn't hide his need from her. He wanted her to see who he was—what he was. She had to accept the truth, not some girlish human fantasy. He was pure predator. He had no gentle edges, or soft spots. She was rousing the devil, and if he took her, he would never let her go.

"I need your blood." He said it deliberately, his mouth moving over that sweet pulse that called so deeply to him.

He waited for her to panic, to pull away from him, to save herself. Instead, her lips moved back to his ear, tugging on his earlobe and sending another streak of fire straight to his groin.

Kiss me. I won't be so afraid of you taking my blood if you kiss me. You can't lie when you're kissing someone.

Did she think he would lie to her? He knew nothing of relationships. He'd long ago buried his mother and father from his existence, refusing to ever allow them into his mind—or heart. They were gone along with every scrap of humanity that had ever been in him. On some level, he recognized that this woman, this *human* woman who had no reason to even like him, was fighting to save him. It was in her mind, in her heart.

Kiss me, Zacarias.

His heart felt brittle. He feared it would shatter in his chest. Kissing her again would be claiming her. Making her irrevocably his. Her body was amazing, a sensual lure he doubted few could ever resist, but it was that tenacious determination, her resolve that she would pull him into the light that drew him like a magnet. She mesmerized him. She had no thought for herself, and she refused to abandon him to the fate of all predatory Carpathians.

How did one fight that? How did he find the strength to walk away from someone that courageous? He was lost for the first time in his life. And for the first time, he wanted to fight for his existence—for her. To match her courage.

He drew her close, his breath settling over her, into her. His heart picked up the frantic rhythm of hers and automatically took charge, matching her pulse beat for beat. He watched her lashes drift down to veil the desire in her dark eyes. Her lips parted. He took her breath into his lungs. She was so warm and soft, heating him from the inside out.

He let his mouth settle leisurely over hers. A part of him was desperate for her, so hungry he could barely think, but he wanted to take his time, to feel her every heartbeat, to taste her every breath, to know the shape of her mouth, the velvet depths, what made her breath catch and what made her body crave his. His kissed her lightly, a slow exploration, absorbing every separate sensation until need overcame him and he simply lost himself in her fire.

He kissed her over and over, stealing the breath from her lungs, breathing for her, his tongue taking possession of that inviting, scalding velvet paradise. His thumbs traced her nipples, as he took her mouth over and over. She melted into him, all that fire, scorching him, searing his very heart.

What happened when fire met ice? He feared he would cease to exist, yet there was no other path for him now. His body was in flames. His hunger beat at him like a thunderous drum. The pounding need filled his groin and ate at his soul. Marguarita. *His.* He had to take her now. Had to make her his. Had to fill his veins, his body with . . . her.

His mouth drifted over the corner of hers. He kissed his way down the curve of her face to the small indentation at her chin. He swept back her cloud of hair from her neck with one hand, his mind firmly settled in hers. He allowed himself to experience all that she was feeling and she was completely aware of his every need—of every urgent demand of his body. His growing hunger. Still, she didn't pull away from him, but he could feel her holding herself very still.

"Do not fear this, Marguarita. There is great courage in you." He whispered the words against her collarbone as he kissed his way along her smaller frame. He turned her in his arms, his mouth continuing along the swell of her breast.

It's hard to be afraid when you make me feel so alive, she confided. *But it is a little frightening after the last time.*

He would make certain a blood exchange would be erotic, not painful. She had been born with a barrier, a product of evolution, so many generations of her family having served the De La Cruz family. That barrier in her mind had been reinforced, so controlling her was difficult at best. And he didn't want control. He wanted her to be willing.

I am willing, she whispered in his mind. *I'm just a little nervous, but I've never been with a man, so all of this is new to me.*

He knew that, he was locked in her mind with her. He knew her every insecurity, and right now, she was holding herself together for him. Because he needed, and she provided. It was the Carpathian way, but she was human and yet instinctively, she knew what he needed.

He pressed his forehead against the soft temptation of her breasts. He had walked the earth for well over a thousand years, had a vast wealth of knowledge, yet knew nothing of humans—or of women. And this woman was everything—would be his everything from this moment forward.

She didn't see him the way the rest of the world did. She didn't even see him the way he saw himself.

I see what and who you are. I see your heart and soul.

She terrified him. Her courage matched that of every warrior he knew. He was no normal man. The hard edges inside of him, the driving need to hunt and kill should have sent her gentle nature running, screaming from him. Those dark shadows, the one tainting him from birth, the terrible legacy handed down from his father scarred his very soul. The light in her shining so bright should have diminished, should have shunned him and yet she faced him, faced her own fears—to save him. To offer him life. She knew what she was doing. She knew he planned to allow the sun to take him—but she stood in front of him, deliberately seducing him with her soft, giving body and her amazing courage.

"It would take a miracle to save me, Marguarita."

She was a miracle to him. He was long gone from this world. He'd never belonged, and now modern society had passed a man such as him up centuries ago. Miracle or not, courage or not, how could she possibly live with such a throwback to ancient times? His world was kill or be killed. Survival of the fittest. Women weren't a part of such things, and if they were, they were used and forgotten quickly, or held captive, close where a warrior could always protect her.

"Do you see who I really am, or who you want me to be?" Because, God help them both, he would rule her. He would hold her too close. He would destroy both of them. He would damn them both to hell, but it didn't seem to matter. He couldn't break free from her, not even to save his honor. He burned like fire. He needed. Desire ruled him. Craving. Aching. Pure need. Pure hunger. He was predator, and she was prey. He was locked on, focused his entire attention on her. She would forever bear the cross of his shame, his inability to resist taking what he now had to have.

I want to be yours, Zacarias. I need you to stay with me. Please stay. Please choose me. Whatever this is—it isn't shameful. I'm giving myself to you freely.

He heard his own groan. There would be no escape for her. How could he refuse her plea? Her gift? He couldn't resist her soft breasts, her dusky nipples teasing his lips. He closed his mouth over temptation and suckled. He wanted this to be real. More than anything, he wanted what she was offering to be real. By all that was holy, let him have a miracle.

Her body arched into him. Her arms crept around his head, cradling him to her.

I see you. All of you.

He couldn't give up the amazing sensations streaking through both of them. The characteristics she saw in him, he wasn't certain they were really there, but he wasn't going to stop what he was doing to use his voice to tell her that. He tugged on her nipple with his teeth, heard her gasp, but fire streaked through her—through him, the blood rushing to both their centers, as if she had a pathway to both leading straight from her nipples.

You know what I am. Yet you are not afraid?

He tugged again, a little rougher, his hands kneading soft flesh, rolling that taut peak, using tongue and teeth mercilessly. He needed her to understand he was a rough, dangerous man, all hard edges and steel. It didn't seem to matter how he touched her, she tightened her arms around his head, her breath ragged, her arousal permeating the air between them.

I'm giving myself to you, Zacarias. Freely. Without restrictions. I don't know what your women do, but I can only be me. I know of no other way. I don't want you to go. The thought of you alone, fighting an evil enemy night after night with no one to hold you, is abhorrent to me.

If I walk into the sun, I will not be fighting an enemy.

No, but you will always be alone and that is unacceptable to me. I can't find impressions to show you why, so, yes, I'm giving myself to you of my own free will to entice you to stay. I want you to stay with me. What you do with me is entirely up to you. But you will not go alone if you choose to leave.

His mouth was filled with her, his hands sliding possessively over her curves and hollows. How could he give her up? And yet, he was no man of honor if he did not. *You did not answer my question. Are you not afraid?*

Yes. She was absolutely truthful. *Of course I have fear of the unknown, but that fear is small compared with my need to keep you safe.*

His heart clenched. *Do you fully understand what you are offering to me, Marguarita?* Her body called to him. Her blood. The taste of her burst through his mouth, through every cell in his body. His groin swelled until he was so full and hard the ache was intolerable. The thought of this woman giving herself so completely to him was intoxicating. His to command. His every wish fulfilled. Marguarita with her soft skin and her doe eyes. His.

He lifted his head to look into her eyes. They stared at each other a very long time. He felt himself falling, drowning in those dark pools of courage.

Be very certain. You will think only of me. Your life will be my life. My happiness will be your happiness. I know no other way. If you are mine, if you wish me to continue this life, then you will bind yourself to me for all time. Forever.

He sighed, his voice sinking to a whisper of sarcasm. *Not so long, forever. Marguarita, the years will be endless if you are unhappy.*

I know what I ask of you, she said. *I know you're weary and you fear who and what you are. But I want you to stay—with me. I want you to live. To know happiness for whatever time we have together.*

There was no more resistance in him. She was going to be his world, and he would fight with every breath in his body to keep her.

"Then give yourself to me."

His whisper was against the soft swell of her breast, right over her heart. He felt her heart jump and then begin to pound. His hand drifted down her body to slide between her legs. She was damp for him, her arousal evident, but as his fingers skimmed over her panties, her heart accelerated and he felt her force herself to stand still for him. He hesitated, his teeth already lengthened, the taste of her bursting through his mouth. He didn't want her afraid. And she had to be certain.

Once I claim you as mine, there is no going back.

She drew a breath. He felt it in his own lungs. She caught his face in her hands and looked him straight in the eye. *Stay with me.*

She was afraid, but determined. He wasn't about to be a saint and turn away what she was offering. Life. Emotion. Color. Something for himself. Something all his.

He bent his head and ran his tongue over her frantically beating pulse. He felt the echo of that throbbing beat deep in his own veins, pulsing through his thick cock. His teeth rasped back and forth over her skin, his tongue easing the small sting. Each time his teeth bit gently, he felt the liquid heat dampen her panties in welcome.

"I will say words—powerful words that will unite us. Our souls will become one. I will take your blood and give you mine in a full exchange. This will not bring you fully into my world, but it is our second exchange and you will be more than halfway there. There will be—repercussions."

I don't understand.

"Unlike human marriages, ours are irreversible. Once the words are said, there is no retracting them." His mouth teased her pulse and moved to her nipple, suckling a little roughly, tugging with his teeth, once more moving his tongue in a velvet rasp to ease the ache. "You will always need me near you. I will always need you close to me. Our minds will forever seek to remain locked within the other's. I will never be able to let you be free. Nor will I be free. There will be no Zacarias without Marguarita. No Marguarita without Zacarias."

She took another deep breath, her fingers burrowing into the thick mass of his hair. She closed the strands in her fist and held tightly.

He took that for her assent. There would be no going back for either of them. She was giving him life when she gave herself into his keeping. He pulled strongly at her breast, allowing himself to get lost in the sensations of pure pleasure.

"Te avio päläfertiilam," he whispered against her pulse. "You are my lifemate." His body shuddered, the fiery streaks of need turning his groin into an inferno. He shed his clothes with a thought and drew her closer, removing the lacy scraps shielding her body from him in the same way. *"Éntölam kuulua, avio päläfertiilam."*

What does that mean?

His teeth nuzzled that pounding pulse. "I claim you as my lifemate." He kissed her soft skin along the curve of her breast and bit deep. Pain flashed through her. He pressed his hand between her legs, caressing with his knuckles, sending shivers of excitement coursing through her. The pain gave way to an erotic rush. She threw her head back and held him to her breast, her fist pulling at his hair.

The essence of her life poured into him, feeding his addiction. He craved that unique, sexy taste that was all Marguarita. All his. Only for him. Created for him.

He switched to the more intimate form of communication while he drank. *Ted kuuluak, kacad, koje—I belong to you.* He would always belong to her. He always had.

Élidamet andam—I offer my life for you. Pesämet andam—I give you my protection. Uskolfertiilamet andam—I give you my allegiance.

Her blood flowed into him, rejuvenating every cell. Filling him—with her. He could feel the powerful ritual words doing their work, binding them together with millions of tiny, unbreakable threads.

Sívamet andam—I give you my heart. He did give her his heart such as it was. Shadowed. Damaged. But it was hers to keep for all time.

Sielamet andam—I give you my soul. His soul was in shreds. So many holes had pierced it. All those kills over the centuries. He had lived for them and each one had taken a toll on the soul he was giving to her.

Ainamet andam—I give you my body. His body craved every inch of her, and he could feel that same craving rushing through her for him. He felt it in her welcoming wetness as he pushed one finger into her, feeling her muscles clamp down on him, desperate to draw him inside of her.

Zacarias lifted his head and watched the ruby beads run down the slope of her breast before dipping his head and following the trail with his tongue. He used his saliva to close the puncture wounds before shifting her in his arms, lifting her and cradling her close to him. Very gently he carried her to the bed where he sat, holding her naked body in his lap.

She was beautiful. Her rounded breasts were streaked with marks from his hands and mouth. *His.* His mind couldn't believe that someone so much of the light could look at him with such smoldering desire. With such a need burning in her to be with him. A gift. His miracle.

"You will drink, Marguarita. I know it feels wrong to you, but this is our way. You've put yourself into my keeping." He drew a line over the pulse beating in his breast and pressed her mouth to him. "Trust in me now."

Marguarita tried. She moved her lips over the laceration, her tongue tentatively tasting him. He groaned, his erection pressing tightly against her bare buttocks. He had not expected the terrible raw demands of his body, the way she would get inside of him, all heat and fire, melting the ice in his veins, bringing back floods of memories, good and bad, bringing him fully to life. Bringing his body to such a fevered pitch of sheer need. He uttered a command to make it easier for her to accept his gift of immortality.

He whispered the next part of the ritual binding words into the cloud of her hair. "*Sívamet kuuluak kaik että a ted.* I take into my keeping the same that is yours."

Her body would always be in his keeping and he would spend his nights worshiping her in every way he could. He filled her mind with erotic images. His hands roamed over her, massaging her rounded bottom, sliding up the clean line of her back to the flair of her hips and her narrow, tucked-in waist.

One hand tugged and rolled her nipples to keep her stimulated while she drew the essence of his life into her body—while the very blood of the Carpathians claimed her for his own.

"*Ainaak olenszal sívambin*—your life will be cherished by me for all my time." *Cherished.* He knew the meaning of the word now, where he never had before. He would cherish her. Protect her. Keep her.

Marguarita was the meaning of life, his holy grail at the end of the centuries-old battle between good and evil. She was the reason. She was what he had been looking for all of his life and never once realizing it. "*Te élidet ainaak pide minan*—your life will be placed above my own for all time." He knew the moment he uttered the words that he meant them. Her life would always be put above his own. His woman. His personal miracle. A human woman who had found a drowning man and served herself up as a lifeboat.

"*Te avio päläfertiilam*—you are my lifemate." Colors shimmered before his eyes, glittering and bright. Vivid, dizzying colors. For a moment his world tilted and then righted itself. Those colors pulsed and throbbed in his heavy erection, sending spirals of electrical currents charging through his body.

"*Ainaak sívamet jutta oleny*—you are bound to me for all eternity." He had tried to save her, but it was far too late now. They were tied together soul to soul for all time. She would stay with him through both good and bad and he feared, for her, it would be far more difficult than she could ever imagine with her modern mind. She could not conceive of the kind of monster he truly was.

"*Ainaak terád vigyázak*—you are always in my care." That was the one thing he could give her. He could promise her. He would never go back on his word. There would be absolute loyalty to this woman and he would always, *always* see to her care.

Gently he slipped his hand between her mouth and his chest. Her tongue rasped one last time over the laceration and his body clenched, shuddered, the feeling so erotic he knew he would want the experience over and over. He closed the wound and took her mouth, his hand on the nape of her neck, holding her still while he fed at the rapture there.

Heat poured through him. He shifted her, turning, laying her out on the bed in front of him like a gift. Her eyes were slightly glazed, brilliant champagne diamonds glittering with lust and need. He'd put that look there. It was all for him. She was all for him.

He knelt over her, his hands in between her thighs, pulling her legs apart so she was open to him, so he could enjoy the sight of the glistening evidence of her need of him. His hands went to her breasts, roughly kneading, rolling and tugging on her sensitive nipples. Every streak of fire that went to her core shot straight through to his cock. He took her into his mouth, suckling strongly, his teeth teasing that taut peak, tugging and biting while she writhed and gasped beneath him.

Her hips bucked with every sting of his teeth, with every lave of his tongue. He sucked hard, reveling in her body, in the soft, pliant offering. His. All for him. Her arms came up to circle his head, she arched into his mouth, pushing deeper, her hips lifting to rub over his body. His heavy erection pressed against the V at the junction of her legs and she widened her sprawl to try to get closer to him. Her smooth thighs rubbed against his body, driving him past sanity.

He captured her nipple and tugged just to feel the wonderful sensation of streaking fire, filling his groin, vibrating through him. His mouth found hers again, a little brutally this time, taking her response, demanding she give him everything she was. He wanted nothing less than everything from her, nothing less than complete surrender.

Marguarita never so much as pulled away from him in her mind. His hands grew rough as they shaped her body, claiming her, wanting her to know and accept him as he was. He would give her everything he was, pour himself into her, give everything he was to her—it was all he had.

She was incredibly responsive to him, her body writhing and bucking as he stroked caresses over her belly and thighs. He inhaled, wanting to forever remember this moment, wanting to savor every new separate experience and emotion. He'd never had such a sensual, tactile experience. Pure sensation. Pure pleasure. Lust was deep and driving, in his blood, pounding with need, clawing and raking, yet at the same time, spreading like fire through his body—and through her body. The dual sensations were overwhelming and irresistible.

He completely indulged himself, exploring every inch of her soft, curvy body. Every streak of fire that went through her, went through him. He felt drunk on the building hunger, this time for her body, for that scorching hot sheath that begged and wept for him. He was just as addicted to the rush of electricity streaking through his body and filling his heavy erection as he was to the taste of her blood.

He had no idea of passing time, only of her body, of her taste and texture. Of knowing her gift was real. Never once did she protest, even when he took her too high and she was gasping and pleading with him for release. She stayed connected, wanting his pleasure, giving herself to him without reservation, keeping her word.

And he found her pleasure was just as important to him, if not more, than his own. Each gasp, every plea in his mind, the score of her nails raking down his back, her fist in his hair—all of it added to his pleasure. He loved seeing her needy for him, seeing her eyes dazed, her mouth open, the soft cries in his mind. The mindless chant of his name. He was rough, yes, but he made certain that she felt nothing but pleasure. He wanted her to want to be with him in every way he could conceive, and hurting her or ignoring her needs felt repugnant and wrong to him.

He indulged himself for the first time in his life, taking this time for himself—for her. The two of them were one now, soul to soul, and as long as he was in her mind, he felt. He saw in color. His world was rich and emotional. There was no ice in his veins, no shadows in his heart. Her bright light illuminated him inside and he felt as if he could soar to the heavens or run in freedom across the land. She made him free.

When he knew she was more than ready for him, slick and hot and gasping, he knelt between her legs and lifted her hips, pushing into that tight hot space created just for him, joining their bodies in the same way their minds were joined. He was careful, feeling her response. He was thick and long and she was tight. He could feel the burning and stretching with his invasion just as she could feel the sizzling pleasure racing through his body as her sheath grasped him in scorching pleasure.

He had to fight a battle to control himself. He needed to plunge into her, bury himself deep, and had he not been in her mind, feeling what she felt, he had no doubts that he would have selfishly done so, but the burning was bordering on pain for her. He forced his body to go slow, whispering to her in his native language, soft words of encouragement. He found himself calling her *sívamet*—my love, or more literally, of my heart.

He hadn't known until that moment of pure revelation that she was of his heart. She had given him so much, this small slip of a human woman with more courage than good sense and she had somehow slipped inside of him and wound herself tightly around his heart. He was more careful than ever, slipping into her inch by slow inch until he felt that thin barrier.

"Take a breath, *kislány kuŋenak minan.*" Deliberately he leaned closer to her, pressing on the spot that brought her the most pleasure and translating what had become an endearment, "My little lunatic, you have given yourself to me, and I accept you into my keeping."

He took her then, making her fully his, burying himself inside that tight cauldron of heat, claiming his home, his sanctuary. The ice was gone from body and mind to be replaced with Marguarita. He had found home and he never wanted to leave.

He took his time, careful to allow her to catch up to him, at first setting a slow, excruciating rhythm, and then, as her body became more receptive to his invasion, as pleasure sizzled through her, he picked up the pace and drove into her as he needed to do, hard and fast, his hands biting into her hips, his body plunging home again and again, burning light into him.

He threw back his head in a kind of ecstasy, fire burning him through the inside out, driving him higher and higher. All the while, he was aware of her, every caress, her fingers in his hair, her soft little gasps, her hips bucking under his, that exquisite tight sheath, grasping and milking, just as needy for him as he was for her.

He could hear her soft gasp in his mind and knew the exact moment the building tension in her body hit that shocking point where she was stretched on a rack of intense pleasure that touched pain. He pushed her over the edge, her body taking his with it, her muscles massaging, milking and grasping so tight he burned for her.

He lay a long time over her—in her, mind to mind, connected, forever wanting to live there—knowing the moment he withdrew, he would be that *köd, varolind hän ku piwtä*—dark, dangerous predator, filled with shadows and tainted with evil. The brilliant colors would fade and his vivid, intense emotions would fade. He hoped to hell his care of her wouldn't do the same. They were tied now, for good or bad. He couldn't undo what he'd done and she could not survive without him—or he without her.

II

There was no going back. Marguarita had known that when she'd offered herself to him and she didn't want to take back her offer. He'd taken her to paradise, but still, she could have used a brief respite from his overwhelming, intense personality. Zacarias seemed to love the scent of her bath. He'd insisted on pouring her fragrant oil into the water, and now he sat on the edge of the sink, watching her with that unnerving, focused stare of his. He knew he was making her uncomfortable, but he made no apologies, nor did he stop staring so possessively at her.

Are you going to stare at me forever? She touched her hair self-consciously. It was piled on top of her head to keep it out of the oily water, and she knew she looked a mess. The room was lit with candles, so the light was soft and flickering, but still, she didn't look her best.

He suddenly smiled, robbing her of all breath. "You will have to get used to me staring. Watching you take a bath brings me pleasure." He folded his arms across his chest, never taking his gaze from her. "And you look sexy with your hair messy. It is my favorite, when it's down and all over the place, but this look is a close second. I like when you have all those curls falling around your face and down your back when you're trying to look very severe, putting it up. It is wild, like you. Very sensual and pleasing."

She felt color creeping up her neck into her face. *You're easy to please.*

His eyebrow shot up. "I assure you, I am anything but easy to please. And you are covering yourself again. Please take your hands away from your breasts. I enjoy looking at you. Your body is beautiful and I am certain it will be an everlasting source of pleasure."

She hadn't realized she was covering her body for the second time. He had already asked her to stop once. She felt her color deepen. Really, she was trying to do what he wished, but his stare was so possessive and intense, she felt a little as if she were under a microscope. Reluctantly she put her hands under the water, grateful for the steam rising. It didn't exactly provide protection, but at least there was the illusion of it.

Marks of his possession covered her body, and between her legs, she was definitely sore, but the water was soothing, and he had been incredibly gentle, carrying her into the bathroom and filling the tub for her before placing her in the hot water. Her heart was pounding so hard she had to fight not to press her hand over her chest. The enormity of what she'd done hit her hard after she'd floated down from subspace.

She had thought long and hard about what she was going to do to save Zacarias De La Cruz. He was so far on the other side, already with one foot out of the world she knew. If she didn't do something drastic, she would lose him. Wherever one went after death, she didn't want him alone for one more moment. She'd made up her mind to seduce him into staying with her—but now it was clearly a case of beware of what you wish for.

"You have every right to fear your new life, Marguarita."

She closed her eyes. His voice was so mesmerizing, so sensual she felt it like fingers brushing over her body.

"But do not try to hide your fears from me. I will not always do the things you will need and I will make many mistakes, I am certain, but you have to talk to me. Tell me when you are hurt by things I say or do. I will only make the mistake once. I am not asking this of you, so do not make the mistake of treating what I say lightly. I am commanding this. It will take great courage to confront me, and even more to live with me, but I expect nothing less from you."

She went back and forth from being annoyed to amused with his commands. He had spent centuries giving orders and expecting—and receiving—obedience that of course she knew he would continue to do so. Sometimes it made her want to laugh. He truly *expected* her to do every little thing he said. As if that was even possible. *It isn't necessary to make everything an order, Zacarias.*

"Perhaps with others, but you defy logic and reason. I have never known any other who disobeys direct orders the way you do. Even today you were sitting on your windowsill bandaging your friend Julio. Did you think I would not know exactly what you were doing?"

Her lashes lifted and she stared him straight in the eye. She would not be intimated by him. She saw inside of him—better even than he did—and she was safe. She just had to have the courage to stand up to him when he was being unreasonable.

I know you don't mean to make me feel like a prisoner, Zacarias, but it does feel that way just a little bit when you say things like that. I have a duty to those on this ranch . . .

He held up his hand. "Not anymore. Your sole duty is to see to my needs. I think I made myself very clear on that."

Yes, well, I still had to see to Julio's wounds. It wouldn't do to have them get infected. Did you do something to his dog? His dog suddenly went crazy, attacking the horses and then attacking Julio.

"I stopped the animal from snarling at me, but that would not explain his behavior. Where is the dog now?"

They had no choice but to shoot it. Julio asked me to see to the horses and cattle. Something's wrong. She rubbed the little dent in her chin, frowning a little, hating that everyone on the ranch believed the dog's behavior had something to do with Zacarias's presence.

"Your eyes are sad. Do not feel sorrow for me, my beautiful lunatic." He shrugged. "You believe they all think I am causing this reaction in the animals. It is probably the truth. Animals sense the shadows in me. Even my own people call me *köd, varolind, hän ku piwtä*, which means dark, dangerous predator, and even the most experienced hunters call me *hän ku tappa*—which means violent, but more. I am used to others fearing me. It does not bother me. I expect it."

It bothers me, Marguarita admitted, shivering. *The water is growing cold and I need to get out.* It wasn't the cold water, but more the realization of the enormity of her decision. She had made up her mind to save this man—to love this man—without fully understanding just how different and dangerous he truly was. She didn't regret the decision, but she was feeling her way through a minefield.

He reached almost lazily for a towel and held it, clearly expecting her to step out of the bath in front of him. She had asked for this, she reminded herself. She had wanted to belong to him and she'd told him she would do whatever it took to make him happy. Standing naked for him didn't seem too much, not after the way they'd had wild, abandoned sex, yet she felt herself blush from head to toe as she stepped from the tub and allowed him to envelope her in the large towel.

"Why does it bother you, Marguarita?" he asked, his voice dropping an octave. "These people are nothing to me. What does it matter if they think I am the devil?"

These are my people, Zacarias, she explained carefully. She stood very still as he gently wiped the beads of water from her body. *I love them and I don't want them thinking untrue things of you. I want them to accept you as my choice.*

His hands stilled. "Why do you presume they think untrue things about me? Animals are restless in my presence. No horse has ever tolerated me near them. I am certain what they say is true—the cattle and horses are all edgy with my continued presence. I rarely stay near humans or animals. Long ago I noticed the reaction."

His voice was expressionless. Even. Factual. But she felt the little catch in his heart when he specifically mentioned horses wouldn't tolerate his presence. He didn't mind humans shunning him, but it bothered him that horses did. She drew in her breath. Another secret buried deep in his subconscious, one he didn't acknowledge, but she saw it so clearly. She loved horses. Only another horse person would understand the deep need in her to spend time with the proud, beautiful animals. And she understood that unsaid, unacknowledged hunger in Zacarias.

She wanted to put her arms around him and comfort him—but the irony was—he didn't know he needed comforting. He was Zacarias De La

Cruz. He felt no pain. No emotion. He was the ultimate killing machine, shadowed and tainted with evil and he accepted that with no self-pity in his heart. He simply was.

How did one stay annoyed with such a man? It wasn't in her to do so, no matter how many silly orders he threw out or how skewed his thinking was. She turned to face him and circled his neck with her arms, linking her fingers behind his head. She leaned her body against his, her breasts rubbing tightly against the towel as she turned her face up to his throat and kissed him. Her heart felt as though it was melting in her body when he simply stood there for a long moment as though shocked by her action. Then his arms came around her, locking her against him and it felt like—home.

I know I did not ask permission to touch you, but I couldn't help myself. She deliberately pushed a teasing note of mischief into his mind. *I know how important these rules are to you, but that particular one is very difficult for me and may take some time for me to fully obey it. I ask for your patience.*

His hands immediately swept down her back to her bare bottom, shaping and kneading her firm muscles there. He lifted her a little, tilting her hips so that she rubbed against his thick groin. "Perhaps I will have to overlook your need to touch me."

Butterflies took wing in her stomach at the small note of happiness edging his voice. *Thank you, Zacarias. I have a great need to touch you often. I know I would always forget to ask first. I appreciate you relaxing your rule.*

"Just the one," he pointed out, a hint of laughter creeping into his eyes.

Her heart stuttered. For one brief moment, there in the steamy room, with the soft light of the candles, his eyes, always so black, appeared a dark sapphire. As his smile faded, so did the deep, true color from his eyes. She had been looking at the real Zacarias as he should have been before the world shaped him into a killing machine.

She held him tight to her, resting her head against the steady rhythm of his heart. He didn't seem in the least impatient, he simply held her close. She waited until the silly emotions choking her were firmly under control before she lifted her head.

I'd better get dressed. I need to check the animals and see what's going on.

He buried his face in her hair, nuzzling the top of her scalp. "I suppose

I did agree the other evening when I spoke to Cesaro. I do not like you endangering yourself. If the animals are as vicious as the workers claim, letting you around them is inconceivable."

I love my horses, Zacarias. I need to ride every day. It clears my head and makes me feel so free. You'll have to try it so you can understand.

His hand rubbed her buttocks, lingered, so that her body began to heat. She hugged him tighter and then stepped back.

"No horse has ever tolerated me that close and I refuse to use mind control on them."

You won't have to, she assured with confidence. *I know you like skirts, but when I ride, I prefer jeans. It's safer.*

His smile was a small quirk of his lips, but the action sent her pulse tripping. It also gave his eyes that dark sapphire glint that robbed her of her breath. His eyes were beautiful in their true color. She couldn't stop herself from tracing that small smile.

You really are beautiful, Zacarias.

He caught her wrist and pressed her fingers to his mouth. "Men are not beautiful. And you are simply trying to distract me from the fact that you are trying to break another rule."

She sent the impression of laughter into his mind. *I wish that were true. I wish I wasn't so enamored with you that I could think so quickly on my feet. Was dressing in a skirt really one of your rules?*

"I prefer feminine clothing. You are to please me in all that you do. So dressing in skirts is naturally preferable to men's clothing."

She went up on her toes and brushed a kiss across his mouth. She loved his sensual mouth. She was afraid she could stare at it for hours and just fantasize. She didn't even care that he was in her mind reading her thoughts. *I could you know, just make up fantasies for hours. But I think men's clothing can be quite sexy as well. Let me try.*

"I will not have access to you."

She smiled at him, rubbing his shadowed jaw. *Fortunately you can do that thing with your mind.*

"What thing?"

Make my clothes vanish. I rather like that little perk.

"This is seduction, Marguarita. Pure seduction to get your way." Once again his hand shaped her bottom. "I suppose I will have to get used to you occasionally getting your way. Men's pants are more practical for riding, although a divided skirt would work."

She stepped away from him and deliberately walked to her dresser, her hips swaying. *Just reserve judgment.*

She took a pair of lacy thong underwear, the sexiest she had, from her drawer. The sachet of lavender scented the panties.

Zacarias followed close behind her and he held out his hand to inspect the little scrap of black lace. The thin strip would barely cover her crotch, the lacy strap would disappear between her cheeks and four black cords hugged the curve of her cheeks.

"This is underwear?"

She nodded.

"I will see you in these men's clothes and know this is what you wear beneath them?"

She nodded again. The building lust in his eyes sent heat rushing through her body. His gaze settled on her high, rounded breasts and then swept lower to the triangle of black curls guarding his personal treasure.

"And what will you wear to cover your breasts from the eyes of other men?"

His voice rasped over her and instantly her nipples grew hard. Her breath turned ragged, but she obediently pulled a matching black bra from the drawer. She had nothing quite as daring as this particular set she'd bought on a whim. Sheer black lace stretched over her full breasts, edged with black satin. Her nipples would show right through all that lace, peeking at him through the thin material. The underwire gave support and at the same time pushed her breasts up and out.

He accepted the bra and turned the fragile material over and over in his hand before raising his gaze to her breasts.

"Come here."

The command in his voice nearly brought her to her knees. She loved the way he sounded so male. She loved that husky note that told her he belonged to her in that moment. There was no one else in his world. Everything and everyone else disappeared for her when his voice took on that note. There was only Zacarias and the growing hunger in his gaze. She loved the idea that he could want her after just taking her so thoroughly earlier.

"It pleases me when you are aroused," Zacarias said as she approached him.

His hands went to her breasts, rolling and tugging on her nipples. He leaned down and the mass of his long hair slid over her bare skin, sending electric currents straight to her core. She could feel her body dampen, growing moist for him. She was aroused, just looking at him, thinking of him, hearing his sexy voice. It didn't matter with him that she had no voice, he was in her mind, reading her thoughts, and the intimacy of that communication was every bit as sensual as the way his fingers teased her nipples. The edge of roughness only added to her desire, his hard body such a contrast to her soft one.

Zacarias didn't allow her to hide from him, not in her mind and not sexually. She hadn't known she was capable of such lustful thoughts, but everything she'd ever read, or heard, or imagined, went through her head when she was with him. She wanted his body to belong to her alone, as she knew hers did to him. The idea of another man touching her in the way Zacarias had was repugnant to her.

"I cannot believe these scraps are undergarments, but I will enjoy knowing you wear them for me."

He had definitely picked up on the fact she'd never worn the black lace before.

You want me again. There was an invitation in her mind.

"Yes. I will always want you, Marguarita, but before my needs and wants, I must put your health. You are very sore."

Can't you do something about that? She infused the idea with blatant temptation.

"Until I know more about how your body reacts, I wish to see how you respond naturally. You are very small and tight. I realize it was your first time and there was stretching along with taking your virginity. You bled."

She fought the blush stealing up her body. *That's normal when a woman is a virgin.* He didn't mind discussing sex with her, or her body's response, which she was grateful for. It allowed open communication, but still, she'd never done that before with anyone, let alone a man she was fast becoming obsessed with. Still, she went warm knowing he would deny himself just to make certain she was fully healed.

"I can ease the soreness if it is too much," he offered.

She shook her head. She liked the feeling of his possession, but wasn't certain how to give him that impression.

He seemed to understand. He touched the dent in her chin with a gentle finger. "Dress in your male clothes and let me see how seductive such clothes can be."

The teasing note in his voice played havoc with her senses. Every nerve ending was already raw and on alert, totally tuned to him, completely aware of him. When she inhaled, she felt as if he was the very air she breathed. How had it happened without her realizing he was slowly creeping into her head—and into her heart? She had been so afraid at first, mixing him up with her memories of the vampire. His behavior hadn't helped—until she'd taken that plunge and allowed her mind to connect fully with his. He'd melt the hardest heart if they could see inside of him. He was noble, loyal, a man of honor. He deserved love.

"Sívamet." He whispered the Carpathian endearment aloud and pushed the word deep into her mind. "You see someone who does not exist. I wish he did. I would give anything to be that man you have given such a gift to. I am a warrior. Nothing more."

Marguarita slipped on the black lace panties, as provocatively as she was capable of being. The protest welling in her mind spilled into his. *You are more than worthy—to me you are worth everything.*

He shook his head, but clearly the sight of that scrap of lace sliding between her firm, shapely cheeks distracted him. He cleared his throat and she smiled as she reached for a pair of her favorite jeans. They were worn and faded to a vintage light blue, the material soft and distressed on her thighs and over one knee, but they fit like a glove and when she rode, they were the most comfortable pair of jeans she owned.

She felt his reaction more than saw it. His face was as expressionless as ever, although his eyes were alive with heat and desire. Very casually she clipped the bra on, allowing it to cup her breasts. The marks from his mouth and hands were visible through the peekaboo lace. He stepped close to her and bent his head to brush first her left breast and then her right with a soft kiss.

"Did I hurt you?"

You know you didn't. You made everything perfect for me. He had. He had been rough, yes, but he had more than ensured she felt nothing but pleasure.

Marguarita sank down onto the edge of the bed and pulled on thin socks and then her riding boots. She lifted each foot into the air to pull on the tanned leather boots, taking her time, enjoying the hunger in his gaze. Truthfully, the very act of dressing in front of him, having his focus so completely on her, was sexy beyond her imagining.

She smiled up at him, noting his eyes were midnight black. He looked so larger than life, his body hard and scarred, well muscled. He flowed across the room, his shoulders filling the space, his eyes penetrating, his mouth sensual.

I like looking at you. She admitted it shyly. She wanted him to know she was in his world, however he wanted her—that he wasn't alone and that she had chosen of her own free will to be with him.

"That's a good thing, my beautiful lunatic, because you will be doing so for a very long time."

She noticed the indentations around his mouth. At first she thought them lines, but they were far more and she smiled to herself. Her tough man had a softer side after all. She didn't mind being his lunatic. Quite possibly, she was one. She hadn't looked at every aspect of her decision before making it. She'd jumped in with both feet and damned the consequences, but right now, as she pulled a thin tank over her head, her stomach cramped.

She actually bent over to ease the pain. Instantly Zacarias's hand went to the small of her back and she felt him moving through her. He did it so quickly, so easily, Marguarita was a little shocked. She lifted an eyebrow at him in inquiry.

He rubbed her back gently. "We have had two blood exchanges, Marguarita. As a rule, it wouldn't matter how much blood I gave you, such as I gave Ricco, but if we make an exchange, that will begin to work on your organs and the inside of your body, reshaping you in the way of the Carpathian people."

She slowly straightened up and looked him in the eye. *You knew this?*

He shrugged. "Of course. It is the way of lifemates."

She heard her own heartbeat, its pounding rhythm. The hum of voices outside the house. The stamp of horses and low murmur of the cattle. Insects drowned out everything, the volume of noise horrendous. Marguarita pressed her hands to her ears, her gaze jumping to his for an explanation.

"I have been careful to keep the volume turned down for you, because we were otherwise occupied, but you can do this yourself. Think about it. Think how soft you want the background noises. Humans do this automatically. Your refrigerators run and you no longer hear them, but the noise is present. Your vision and hearing will be far more acute. You have to control it consciously and eventually it will become subconscious."

Marguarita reached behind her to find something to hold on to. It had not occurred to her that her world would change so drastically. She'd given herself into Zacarias's keeping, but her physical body was human.

Zacarias wrapped his arm around her waist. Solid. An anchor. "Breathe, *sívamet,* as frightening as this all sounds, I am with you always. I will not allow anything to harm you."

She took a deep breath. *Tell me what this means to me.* She would not regret her decision. She had known all along it would take sacrifices. Physical sacrifices hadn't occurred to her, but she could deal with it.

"You will need to drink water and juice, Marguarita," he instructed.

Her stomach lurched at the idea of putting anything into it. She pushed her hand against her belly and shook her head. *I cannot. The thought makes me feel sick.*

"Nevertheless, it will be necessary. No meat, of course. The thought of eating meat is repugnant to us."

And yet you own a cattle ranch. She sent him a faint smile, desperately trying to find a balance. She accepted the responsibility of what she'd done, and had known there would be consequences. She could live without meat. Millions of people did so every day, but the thought of taking blood as sustenance was disturbing to her.

"I will help you when you need to eat or drink something."

She couldn't imagine doing either at that moment so she simply nodded her head. She moistened her lips, rubbing her arms a little. What else did having his blood mean to her? She had to be able to go out into the sun, but her skin felt strange at the thought. She was certain it was her imagination, but earlier, with Julio, her skin had been sensitive and her eyes really hurt. With a second blood exchange, would that grow worse? What had he meant when he said she was becoming like him? Panic began to edge her thoughts.

I'm changing inside my body? Becoming like you? She rubbed her hands up and down her arms more vigorously as if she could change her skin's composition. *If I am like you, will the sun harm me?*

He nodded his head slowly. "The sun will burn you. Not in the way it does me, but you cannot go out in it without great peril. You would blister, and the burn would be severe. It will not kill you as it would me. You will need to cover your skin and eyes all the time."

Her heart nearly stopped beating. She actually felt faint. She loved horses. Loved the Peruvian Paso breed. They'd been her obsession before Zacarias and she couldn't imagine never flying over the ground, jumping fences and feeling one with the horses. She enjoyed their personalities, their quirks and the gentle temperaments. She loved every single thing about them. Just watching them filled her with joy. She couldn't imagine not caring for them, riding them, spending her time with them.

The Paso retained its natural, inherited gait, when so many other breeds had been diluted. It had been kept true to its lineage. In her experience, her horses had passed their gait to one hundred percent of their offspring. The breed's center of gravity remained nearly immobile. *Paso Ilano*, a broken gait that was a rhythmic and harmonic tapping, was very gentle, pleasing and extremely comfortable. She could ride her horse for hours, moving in harmony across the land never tiring or getting sore.

She hadn't considered that she might become sensitive to the sun. Her breath felt trapped in her lungs. Her throat clogged with tears. Never to ride again. Never to feel that amazing experience, the sharing between horse and rider. The Paso also possessed a unique pace aptly named *termino*. To Marguarita, nothing was more graceful. The movement was flowing, the forelegs rolling from the shoulder toward the outside as the horse strode forward. She was part of the horses and they were a huge part of her.

Zacarias studied her averted face. Deep inside her mind she'd gone suddenly quiet and then she'd completely withdrawn from him. The world around him instantly dulled to barely-there color, pale and drab. Ice poured into his veins, into his heart. Her sudden exit left him more alone than he'd ever been—ever conceived. She filled his body with warmth and light, with color and emotions and the moment she was gone, so was her radiant heat. Once able to see vivid colors and experience real feelings, the warmth and brightness of her filling every broken, jagged, *shadowed*, space, thrown back into that ugly, stark, bleak existence, made it utterly unbearable.

He realized what his father had lived with. His mother had filled up those broken spaces with her warmth and bright light. Without her always residing within, the color and emotion within his father had faded just as it had done with Zacarias. The contrast was sharp and ugly and impossible to bear—not after so much joy. He stepped toward her, unable to resist that bright beacon when his world had gone so cold. His soul actually shuddered.

"Do not seek to leave me." He said it sharply, much harsher than he intended. His fingers bit down like a vise on her wrist, shackling her to him. He jerked her body close to his. The scent of a predator prowling for prey permeated the room. She tensed, looking as if he'd struck her.

I don't know why you would doubt me. I am adjusting to the things you're revealing to me and I'll admit they frighten me, but I am a woman of my word. I gave myself to you freely and I meant it. Whatever the future holds for me, I will find a way to deal with it and be happy.

He felt her determination, but still, he was alone. Sun scorch the woman, she didn't get it. He wasn't about to plead with her, or take what she refused him. Would he stoop that low? He jerked her even closer, forcing her chin up so that her eyes met his.

"You will not leave me again." He gave her a little shake. He let her see the killer in him, that dark force that was more of his soul than any other part of him. "Do you understand me?"

Marguarita looked confused. He had to give her credit; she was courageous when most men would have gone to their knees. She met his gaze without flinching. He felt that first, almost tentative reach for him and the relief was overwhelming, almost driving him to his knees. Her warmth slipped into his mind, seeking answers. He felt that hot flow filling him up, bridging those broken circuits, restoring vivid color. Emotions poured in. Fear amounting to terror. Hers? It had to be her fear of him. He didn't know fear.

The taste of terror was in his mouth. The horrifying emotion beat at his heart, and invaded his lungs so that his breath was trapped there.

"You are all right. Take a breath." He could barely get the words out.

Marguarita shook her head, never taking her gaze from his. *I am not afraid of you, Zacarias. I fear letting you down, but never that you will harm me.* Her eyes never wavered, locked on his, forcing the truth into his mind. He feared losing her. He feared turning vampire. He—*feared.*

Zacarias groaned out loud. Sun scorch her. She really was going to have him on his knees. She had reduced him to this. He hadn't known fear, and now it consumed him. He'd never had anything worthwhile to lose. Certainly not his own life. But Marguarita with her soft body and her bright light and her mind filling his with life was worth everything to him. A treasure he wouldn't—*couldn't*—lose.

He knew he would hold her too tight. He would smother her. He didn't belong in a world where women made decisions for themselves, wore male clothing and dared to look at a predator such as he with such terrifying courage.

A slow smile lit her amazing eyes. That sparkling champagne turned to a warm, inviting chocolate. *You are not prehistoric, silly. Just as I have to learn about your world, you have to learn about mine. It's an adventure we're going on together and I'm looking forward to it.*

She made everything so simple when he knew it wasn't. He knew what he was and even if she found a gentle side to him, he would rule her with an iron hand. A human woman could have no idea of the dangers in the world he lived in. Every vampire around the world would seek to target her at Ruslan's insistence. Ruslan knew the shadows in him. He might not know how it worked, but he would know that Marguarita made Zacarias incredibly vulnerable.

His hand slipped to the nape of her neck, his fingers curling around that fragile stem. He could hear her heartbeat. The air in her lungs. He inhaled her feminine fragrance, and she *his.* He bent his head slowly toward hers. She didn't look away. She didn't flinch. His woman, with more heart and courage than good sense. His fingers slipped around to the front of her throat. He could feel her pulse beating into the palm of his hand.

He could crush her by simply tightening his fingers, but she leaned into him, trusting him in that disarming way she had that sent his heart melting into a puddle at her feet. His breath hissed out in annoyance and still she didn't recoil from him. He bent his head to hers. She stared directly into his eyes and it was him falling into her, not the other way around. He could feel that now-familiar heat grow scorching hot, burning through his veins, spreading like a wildfire, roaring in his belly and settling into a fireball in his groin.

His mouth took hers. There was no gentleness, he was too far gone for that, caught up in the tangle of emotions he needed to sort out. He fed his addiction to her, craving the taste of her, needing her submission, her surrender, needing her to give herself to him without reservation. She had turned his world upside down. Brought memories best buried deep to the surface. She had placed him in an intolerable position as a hunter.

I wish I could say I was sorry for wanting you to stay with me, for stopping you from seeking the dawn. I should be sorry and I'm ashamed that I can't let you go. I need you to stay with me.

Her voice was soft and a little sorrowful, turning his heart over. Her slender arms crept around his neck and she leaned her entire body into the shelter of his. It was a form of paradise to a man who had never known happiness. Or joy. There was joy just in holding her. His tongue danced with hers, probed and explored and claimed her. His teeth tugged on her full lower lip, biting down gently, just enough to feel her breath catch before kissing her again and again. He took his time devouring her. He kissed his way down her neck, leaving dozens of little bite marks, tiny stings he eased with his tongue and half a dozen strawberries he left just because he could.

He raised his head and waited for her lashes to lift so he could look into her eyes. So she would know he meant what he said. "I would not have missed being with you for the world. Whatever happens in the nights to come, Marguarita, never think that I will ever regret any moment spent with you. Hopefully it will be hundreds of years, but if not, I will not regret that you kept me alive."

Thank you for that.

She smiled at him, her lips swollen from his kisses, her neck and throat red with his marks of possession, and happiness shining in her eyes. She took his hand. *Come meet the horses.*

He didn't have the heart to tell her there would be no meeting her beloved animals. He scanned the ranch to ensure no vampire was near and went out into the night with her. Stars glittered overhead and the moon spilled her silvery light across the grass.

Zacarias reluctantly followed her toward the stable. It was a long, well-built building. As he approached, he could hear the horses stamping and blowing, dancing in their stalls, aware that a predator was near. At the entrance, there was no doubt that he was wreaking havoc with the even-tempered animals. Several reared and plunged, raked the air with their front hooves and tossed their heads, eyes rolling.

Zacarias caught her arm. "No farther. You will not go in there with those animals."

He felt her mind expand, reach out and connect with the horses. It was a strange sensation, not unlike what he experienced when he took the form of another creature but even more so, as if they were joined not only in mind, but in spirit.

You smell like a predator to them. You are not evil to them. Or tainted.

She had found his fears once again and he tried not to react with anger. He didn't ever look that closely at the why of the animals not accepting him. They didn't. It was a fact. Anything else he simply pushed away. What did it matter—the *why*? He didn't know if it was true that he feared they found him evil and tainted, but if she saw that in him—it was most likely there. She was uncovering secrets he kept even from himself. The more she found, the more reluctant he was for her to find more, yet he couldn't live without her mind connecting completely with his and that gave her access to everything he was—everything he had been.

"It does not matter why they will not accept me, only that they will not," he pointed out.

She tightened her fingers in his. *They will accept you just as they do me. After all, we're one, aren't we?*

His heart jumped and inwardly he cursed himself for being such a fool. It was impossible. He knew the horses wouldn't let him near and yet somewhere inside of himself—he believed in her.

12

Zacarias tugged Marguarita to an abrupt halt, by the simple act of ceasing to move. They stood together at the open doors of the stable. The horses were rolling eyes and tossing heads, watching the door in mounting terror.

You smell menacing. I find it quite sexy, but the animals are afraid. Give me a moment to calm them so they can connect with you in the same way I do.

The soft amusement, the caressing "I find it quite sexy" slid into his mind like massaging fingers over his body, but he refused to give in to her. Danger was danger, no matter where or who the threat came from. He locked her to his side.

"I will not allow you into that building with the horses riled up. You saw what happened to your friend Ricco."

She rubbed her cheek against his arm much like a cat. *It would be easier for me to calm them inside, close to them. It would only take a moment.*

"I said no." There was steel in his voice, in his heart.

He would give her the moon if she asked. He'd walk through fire, but this—*this*—never. She could plead with him, look at him with her incredible eyes and it would only serve to harden his resolve. Her safety was paramount. At the moment, he wanted to throw her over his shoulder and haul her back inside where no harm could come to her.

Amusement teased his senses. He felt his cock stir and his nerve endings come alive. That little whisper of laughter, not heard, but felt, never failed to arouse him.

Were you alive during the caveman days? I could see you dressed in animal fur, hauling your woman into the cave by her hair.

Her teasing would always be erotic to him. When a man had never had such things, they became treasures when he found them. Laughter had never been a part of his world, certainly not teasing. She didn't fight his commands. She didn't pout or get angry. She laughed softly and rubbed along his body with hers, just as if she felt those snapping electrical sparks in the same way he did.

"Do not tempt me, my beautiful lunatic. Dragging you to your bed by your hair is not out of the question." His voice came out gruff, husky even, not at all menacing like he intended.

Her soft laughter teased his groin into semifullness. The sweet ache permeated his body, his temperature going up a few degrees. He was Carpathian and always in control, but what she did to his body was so exquisite, he allowed the sensations to pour through him, savoring every ache, every degree of mounting desire.

I want you to stay in my mind very quietly. Feel the way I pour myself into the horses. I do it very slowly, a soft warmth, like this . . .

His entire body shuddered as she came inside of him. Not just his mind, but invaded his soul. Her presence was far more intimate than she intended, but already, that same hunger and need was clawing at her, just as it raked at him. Her presence was light, almost delicate, but with him, very sexual.

"I would prefer that only I feel this connection with you—in fact I demand it."

A dark swirling shadow rose to the surface. His teeth lengthened and something deadly rose with the shadow. He made no attempt to hide it from her. She had to know what she had tied herself to. Life was full of unexpected moments, and this was a surprise to both of them, but no less lethal.

Everything in him stilled. For the first time that he could remember, he *felt* the predator rising. He felt the deadly menace spreading and growing and the ice building to cover his emotions, to obliterate all feeling, making him a much more efficient killer.

Of course I don't feel that way about anyone—or anything else. The only sexual feelings I've ever had have been toward you. I don't know what you've done to me, but the feelings are very strong and hard to control around you. When I'm inside you, I can't help but want to be with you in any way. I'm sorry if that upsets you. I promise to try to do better.

She struggled to give him the correct impressions in her mind and heart. She was very sincere, and very concerned *for* him. Again, there was no fear, no pulling away. She didn't flinch or look at him with contempt or anger.

Her palm moved up his chest. She looked him straight in the eye. *Whatever you need, Zacarias, I will provide. If that means we wait to do this, until you understand you are my one and only, then that is what we'll do. Just tell me.*

He could feel her intense need to show him the truth, even though it embarrassed her a little. The sheer courage in her, the way she kept her word, giving herself to him fully and without reservation in every situation no matter the cost to her, astounded him.

Zacarias knew how much she loved the horses. He could feel the joy in her when she spoke of them or thought of them, yet she was willing to turn around and walk back to the house with him if that was what he needed. She humbled him with her gift. With her serenity. With her efforts to put him first. She simply stood in front of him, quietly waiting his decision.

Zacarias drew her into his arms and buried his face in the thick mass of her hair—the hair she'd left wild and messy just for him. How small a thing was it for him to allow her to calm the animals, especially if he was the one making them edgy and perhaps even dangerous?

"You shame me, Marguarita."

No! She shook her head violently and stepped back to look him in the eyes again. *Don't do that. Don't ever do that. You are my choice, just the way you are. I am not asking for changes. I will do whatever you wish.*

She wasn't asking anything of him for herself that he could see. In truth, she had asked for the life of a friend. He had saved the man because she'd asked him to, but her motives weren't selfish.

He gestured toward the stable. "Continue. And do not worry about the way you feel. It pleases me that when we are together you are aroused by me."

She smiled at him. *I am aroused by the mere thought of you, Zacarias. I don't have to be in your presence. That's how pathetic and obsessed I've become.*

He frowned at her. "Not pathetic. I am pleased."

Marguarita studied his face as if seeking something—reassurance perhaps. He was certain she didn't want him going berserk and destroying her horses in a jealous rage.

Again that sweet amusement slid into his mind. *It never occurred to me that you would do such a thing.*

There it was. Her naivete, her innocence didn't allow her the imagination to see the true depths of the monster she had tied herself to for all time. He refused to lie to her. To look away from her. "I am quite capable of such an action given the right provocation."

She frowned. *What would that be?*

He squared his shoulders. She had courage and she deserved truth. "Jealousy. A threat to me—to you. To us."

There. It was out between them. The truth of what he was. Let her try to pretend she wasn't appalled, sickened even, wishing she could shun him as the rest of the world did—and should. He watched her expressive and transparent face closely. At the same time, he held himself still inside of her, wanting to know every thought in her head.

Marguarita sighed and brought his hand to her mouth, kissing his scarred knuckles. *You have a very skewed vision of who you are and what you're capable of, Zacarias. It's a good thing I can see inside of you. I think you are deliberately trying to frighten me. Do I see that you are capable of great violence? Of course. I have access to your memories—all of them—even the ones you refuse to revisit. Are you capable of murder? Killing for killing's sake? No. Solidly no. Firmly no. All the arguing in the world won't change what I know to be true.*

He heard himself groan. He leaned his forehead tight against hers. "I have no idea what I am going to do with you, Marguarita."

Again her soft amusement filled his mind, bringing that heat that kept growing and moving through him, chasing out shadows and replacing them with light.

Fortunately for you, I have all kinds of ideas. Let me take you into the stables, Zacarias. I want to share this with you. It's the one thing I have to give you—a gift. My gift to you.

She made him feel as if he could do anything. Was this love? Was this what he had been searching for all over the world, through centuries, never knowing such a thing really existed? He felt he could endure the warmth of the sun as long as he had her. She had brought colors to real, vivid life. Maybe there was nothing she couldn't do, no miracle she couldn't work. Maybe the horses would accept him into the stable as long as he had her by his side.

"If it means so much to you, *sívamet*, then we will try."

Her face lit up and he felt everything in him settle again. She took his hand, threading her fingers through his. *Let yourself drift with me. Stay inside me. You'll feel what you need to do eventually.*

Once again he felt her pouring into him, all that heat and fire, all that fascinating light spreading through him like a million candles. The fire turned molten, spreading slow and thick through his mind and body, until he felt that connection deep. Spirit. He often left his own body and became nothing but spirit in order to heal a fellow warrior. He had done that very thing to save Marguarita when the vampire had torn out her throat those months earlier. He should have suspected, yet it came as a surprise.

Marguarita was entirely human, yet she possessed strong psychic ability. Her connection with animals—and her first connections with him—had been spirit to spirit. She shed her ego, what and who she was, and became a being of welcoming light. Even for a Carpathian, shedding what he was, shedding his physical body, was a difficult task, yet she did it so smoothly and easily, he hadn't realized what, within him, she was bonding with.

His spirit. He was very aware of it as he never had been. He felt her bathe him in scorching heat, dispelling the deeper shadows that had taken hold. They fled before her as if she would destroy them with her brightness. He felt light. Different. *Saved.* But he knew his salvation would last only as long as she was connected to him.

He closed his eyes, understanding now what his father had endured through the centuries, trying to find a balance of keeping his lifemate close to him, yet safe from danger. In the end, he had killed her, putting her life in jeopardy by taking her with him on a hunt for a master. He'd known better. Zacarias had pleaded with his father, fought with him. He had offered to go, but leave his mother behind. He had blamed his father for her death. He had been responsible. She should have been kept safe. That was their law; their duty to their lifemates. His father had taken her and had been outmaneuvered. His mother had paid the price and, ultimately, his father had, too.

And you, Zacarias.

"Do you understand now?" he whispered, wanting to save her.

Not all the way, but I'm getting there.

"I will face the shadows and the cold before I will ever allow danger to you." It was a promise. A threat. A declaration that dared her to try to defy his orders.

She didn't give him sympathy, not exactly, more it was a stronger connection, as if she poured more of herself into him. He felt her warmth invade his heart and he caught her shoulders and gave her a little shake.

"She loved him too much. She should never have gone with him."

There is no such thing as loving someone too much, Zacarias. Whatever happened, I know it wasn't because they loved each other too much. I have told you I will obey you, but I cannot stop my heart from loving you. You can't ask that of me.

He let out his breath, unaware he'd been holding air trapped in his lungs. He caught her face in his hands and took possession of her mouth. There was nothing to say. He was already lost. If this was love, he was too far gone to take a different path. He would put her above himself and his own needs. She would never be placed in jeopardy just so that he could shut out the cold, see in color and feel emotion. He could handle being utterly alone if it meant she was out of harm's way. He vowed to himself he would always be strong enough to put her safety first.

He kissed her long and hard, making a thorough job of it. He had nothing to say to her, no way to reassure her. He hadn't expected their connection. He hadn't expected the emotion to be so intense, and he certainly hadn't intended to feel something close to love for her and he feared that was exactly what was happening. When he lifted his head, his gaze burned over her. Her eyes were wide and a little glazed, but she had kissed him back without reservation.

"I will do this with you, but if I say we leave, do not question me."

She nodded her head and took a step through the open door. The horses watched curiously, stamping occasionally, but she'd touched them, spirit to spirit several times and they knew her, were used to that strong connection. They trusted her. Because they felt Zacarias's spirit mixing with hers, the horses were more curious than alarmed.

We breed the best, the horses with even temperaments as well as brio, that elusive quality that shows arrogance and exuberance in every move. Look at them. The way they move, the steps they take, the tossing of their heads. They have steady eyes and beautiful gaits. They are loyal and hard workers. They will place their body between an enraged steer and a fallen rider. They have great courage, Zacarias.

She drew Zacarias farther into the stables. He had never been so close to a horse, not without it rearing and plunging, throwing its rider and running full speed away from him.

People misjudge them because they are not a really large horse. They stand fourteen to a little over fifteen hands in height, which isn't terribly tall, but never underestimate them. They have such noble heads.

He was beginning to feel what she meant about the spirit or brio of the Peruvian Paso. Marguarita approached a stall where a beautiful chestnut-colored mare watched them carefully. She didn't take her eyes from Zacarias, those amazing large, intelligence-filled eyes.

She has a long official name but I just call her Sparkle. Isn't she gorgeous?

Zacarias couldn't look away from the mare. He was within touching distance and the horse wasn't screaming a protest and kicking her stall door, eyes rolling in terror. He found his hand was trembling. He had never understood why he had been so drawn to this species, the horse. He often had watched them running free over the land, manes flying in the wind, their muscles flowing, necks stretched out, and hooves thundering over the earth and it was one of the few things that brought a semblance of peace to him.

He looked down at Marguarita. All those centuries ago, had she been there, a whisper in his soul keeping him from falling into that dark abyss? He didn't understand how it could be so, but that rapt look of joy on her face when she observed the horses, echoed in his own heart. Horses. Simple creatures, yet complex at the same time. Each had their own personality. Most had a wild spirit he understood and now, with his spirit connecting with the horses in the stable, he realized they weren't so far from him after all.

"Thank you, *sívamet.* You have given me another gift beyond measure."

We are nowhere near finished. There's so much more. Come with me.

He didn't want to ruin this perfect moment. He stood just behind Marguarita, his arm wrapped around her waist from behind, his spirit floating with hers through the stable and mingling with the spirit of the horses. The ride was exhilarating, and yes, because he was so tightly woven into Marguarita's spirit, even sensual. His every sense was alert and alive. He smelled what the horses smelled. Felt what they felt. The wild freedom of just being, and the affection pouring from them for Marguarita—and now for him. He was tightly entwined with her, the two becoming one and the horses accepted his presence.

"You have done more for me than I ever thought possible," he whispered into her ear, nuzzling her, his teeth tugging on her sensitive earlobe. "You are my miracle."

Her soft amusement brushed like a caress. *I am your lunatic, remember, so I say there is much more. And I want so much more for you. Let me give you this, Zacarias. Trust me. I put myself into your hands, put yourself into mine.*

His arm tightened around her. She was already so much to him he couldn't imagine what would happen if she gave him more. Being alive was extraordinary. Feeling joy was immeasurable. His world had been a dull gray. The colors of the horses gleamed bright, almost like glittering diamonds. The scent of the hay and stamp of hooves were etched into his soul for all time. He would always have this moment Marguarita had given him. If things went wrong, nothing could mar this perfection.

He brushed his mouth across her ear, breathed warmth against that perfect little shell. "Then continue. I'll follow where you lead."

He took the time to once again scan the ranch for vampires, that sign of shadows, or even blank spots where the undead tried to cover their tracks, but if Ruslan was close by, or if he'd sent his lesser pawns ahead of him, they weren't anywhere near the ranch.

Marguarita opened the door to the stall and stepped right in, close to the mare. Zacarias found he was holding his breath again. She looked quite small beside the horse. She was right, the animal wasn't particularly tall, but she exuded power and held herself nobly. She nuzzled Marguarita with her nose and, if Zacarias hadn't stepped in, right behind her, the gentle touch might have pushed her back a step. His arms went around her waist from behind to steady her with his taller, stronger frame.

Her hands came up to caress that inquisitive nose. He noticed how, with every stroke of her fingers, she did the same in her mind, brushing her spirit against the horse's spirit just as lovingly.

Marguarita reached down, took his hand in hers, and brought it to the mare's arched neck. His body went still as he felt her press his palm against that warm, smooth neck. For the first time ever in his endless existence, he was actually touching a horse. He had steadfastly refused to control the animals down through the centuries. If they refused to give him allegiance, then he would rather not get near them.

His hand trembled. His belly knotted. A thousand butterflies took wing. He had been all over the world, sailed the seas, raced through meadows and fields of flowers and had resided in enormous, beautiful caves, yet he had never done such a simple thing as touch a horse. The enormity of what Marguarita was giving to him shook him. What had he done for her? He'd scared her nearly to death and he'd put her life in jeopardy by tying them together.

Stop, silly. Marguarita rubbed the back of her head against his chest while she slowly stroked his hand over the horse's neck. *You said yourself that I don't obey very well. Do you think I would do something so life-changing if I wasn't fully committed? That it wasn't what I wanted? Stay with me, right here. Be in this moment with me and let everything else go.*

He nuzzled her neck and then bit down gently. "Did you just call me silly? I do not think I have ever, in all my existence, been referred to in such a disrespectful manner."

Really? She sent him a smoldering look over her shoulder, one eyebrow arched and mischief sparkling in her eyes. *Perhaps others don't know you in quite the same way I do.*

He bit her again, this time with a little sting so he could bathe her pulse with his tongue.

Do you want to go for a ride?

His heart leaped. "On a horse? Do you think one will tolerate me?"

Do you feel fear from any of them now? They know you the way I know you, spirit to spirit, and they accept you as they do me.

He was more worried about Marguarita now, not about ruining the moment—Marguarita on the back of a horse, flying over fences at night. A small hole in the ground could cause a misstep and break the horse's leg, sending her tumbling to the ground. A thousand possibilities crowded into his mind. She had become as essential to him as the rich earth he rejuvenated himself in.

She leaned her head back against his chest, snuggling into him. *I need to ride.*

His first thought was that he didn't care. *Need* was a word she didn't truly understand; he knew what it meant and it wasn't the dream of riding a horse. Need was elemental. Need was the ability to feel emotion and to feel alive. It was Marguarita forever in his mind, lighting up every shadow, connecting those broken paths so he could feel life running through his body, feel it with every breath he took. He'd forever been damned to a kind of living hell. She'd dragged him out and, by all that was holy, he wouldn't—couldn't—go back there. That was need. True need.

Zacarias felt her grow still. She didn't pull away—or protest. He heard her heart accelerate. She had put herself into his keeping, under the rule of a dictator. He knew better than she just how much of a dictator he would be. She made no move to influence him; she simply waited for his decision. A part of him wanted to see her reaction if he denied her. Would she sulk? Argue? Be angry with him and try to retaliate.

Look into my mind, Zacarias, she offered. *I do not go back on my word. I knew this wouldn't be easy for either of us. I asked a great sacrifice of you. Would I expect less of myself?*

Sun scorch the woman, she was definitely bringing him to his knees. He wrapped his arms tighter around her, threatening to crush her fragile, feminine, *human* bones. "You are impossible. And you make no sense. If you wish to ride, then you will ride. But Marguarita, if your life is threatened in any way, I will kill whatever threatens you. You will not hold that against me. Do we have an understanding?"

Her lashes fluttered. She knew what he meant; he could see it in her eyes. She turned to face him, her fingers brushing over his face with the lightest of caresses, but he felt that touch all the way to his very bones, as if she branded him with her name, with her spirit. She nodded slowly. *There will be no need, Zacarias.*

He shrugged. If one of her beloved horses threatened her, there would be no question as to what he would do. Just as if one of her beloved workers threatened her. Man or beast, he would destroy every enemy. It was what he was good at. This—finding a balance with a woman was an altogether different proposition.

But enjoyable, she pointed out.

"Enjoyable," he echoed. "More than I can express." Although another woman might have made it a mindfield for a man such as Zacarias, a throwback to medieval days.

Further, my man, much further. Try caveman, she teased as she opened the stall beside the mare. *This is Thunder. He moves as if he has wings. There is no better horse on the ranch to ride.*

He could feel the pride in her. She was offering him one of her greatest pleasures. Her eyes shone again like the sparkling champagne. If he'd never wanted to ride a horse, he would have done it, just for that look. He pushed his worries for her safety to the back of his mind. He was powerful and he could watch carefully, a small price to give them both this special moment.

You use your connection with Thunder to guide him into doing what you wish. There's no need of a saddle or bridle. I just ride bareback and think where I want to go and they take me. If I'm just riding for the beauty of riding, I let them go to their favorite places on the ranch. They like sharing the control.

Zacarias didn't like sharing control with anyone or anything. He nodded his head and laid his hand on Thunder's neck. Instantly he felt the horse's spirit brush against his. He knew he could do nothing to hide his nature from the animal. He was born to lead, and if the horse didn't accept the dominance in him, there would be disappointment for Marguarita.

Her soft amusement slid into his mind. *There you go again. You disregard your own feelings. The disappointment will be yours. You want to do this. Thunder knows and he'll do as you wish. I want this for you, because you want it, not for myself. It's all right if you'd rather just watch me ride.*

"Not a chance. I will be at your side every moment you are outside and exposed to danger." He couldn't help the hard edge in his voice—the one that should have told her there was no give to that side of him.

Marguarita smiled at him, caught the horse's neck and leaped on in one smooth, practiced movement. He could see how her male jeans were an asset. The moment the thought entered his head, so did the memory of her body encased in nothing but black lace. A thick erection was not going to be an asset on the back of a horse and he willed the erotic picture of her out of his mind.

It was easy enough to slip onto Thunder's back—after all, he was Carpathian and could levitate—but it wasn't quite as easy ridding himself of the picture of Marguarita's body, bare but for those small wisps of lace, her cloud of blue-black hair tumbling like a waterfall down to her waist. He raised his head and looked at her. Her eyes met his, full of mischief, sexy, dark desire flickering in their depths.

She was temptation. And she was fun. Her soft amusement stroked him like fingers, and the flow of her spirit into his was suggestive, sensual, erotic, her mind circling his thickening cock like a fist and stroking. Her eyes transformed to dark, melting chocolate, filled with lust—for him.

Her horse turned abruptly and exited the stables. Horse and rider flowed over the ground, not at a particularly fast pace, but a ground-eating four-beat gait that was breathtaking. He urged Thunder to follow, and the horse immediately responded, taking them from the stable. Zacarias felt almost as if he were floating through the air. He felt every muscle of the powerful animal beneath him, felt the joy in the horse as it trotted over the ground, gathered itself and sailed over the fence right behind the mare.

As connected as he was, spirit to spirit with Thunder, he felt the way the earth seemed to rise up to meet the dancing hooves, he felt the wildness as the wind blew the mane across the horse's face as he trotted. They flew across the field and then the next one, riding the edge of the rain forest where the tangle of fern, trees and wildflowers winding up trunks added to the beauty of the moment.

He urged Thunder to Sparkle's side so that the horses moved in perfect unison. Marguarita sent him a smile and his cock stirred again. The moon spilled down a silver glow over her, pushing moonbeams into her hair. Her skin was gorgeous, and her spirit was alive in his, all that hot flowing magma, slowing working its way through his mind and deeper, into his soul. She filled those empty, jagged holes with her brightness.

He looked for her smile. He watched carefully for the desire rising in her eyes. He waited for the moonlight to shine through the silken strands of her hair. Moments of beauty. Of pure delight. He'd never known such things and now, in her, everything he needed was there, in this strange human woman. He was beginning to realize life with another was lived in moments. Heartbeats of time, and this was one of them. A perfect moment. It would last centuries, stored in his mind to be pulled out again and again as if it were brand-new.

She reached out to him and he linked his hand with hers. They walked the horses along the fence line and he found he was at complete peace. The sound of the hooves hitting rock and ground added to the rhythmic beauty of the horses' easy gait. The wind blew gently and the stars vied for space in the sky.

"You keep giving me incomparable gifts, Marguarita. What have I given you?"

She was silent a moment, her dark eyes moving over his face. *You. Your life. You stayed with me against everything in you telling you it was time to go. You stayed when I asked. You know better than I the future we face together. You were weary of fighting, and yet, when I asked, you stayed. Thank you.*

"I meant every word of the ritual binding vows. I will cherish you and place you above all others. I am a dominant being, I cannot change what is fundamental in me, Marguarita, no matter how much either of us would wish it, but I will see to your happiness."

I see into your heart, Zacarias. I know you will.

"The things I demand of you will not always be easy," he warned.

I was aware of that the moment I realized you were not vampire and I had condemned you once again to this world. I took the time to see who you are. I know you are not a modern man and it worries you that I will one day rebel against the chains you put on me. Her fingers tightened around his and they locked gazes. *If it is what you need—truly need—my obedience to your will in that moment, it will be the most important thing in the world to me. No matter how hard. I meant what I said when I asked you to stay. I serve you out of choice. I want your happiness.*

He knew the truth of her words. She was prepared for his dominance, but she also realized things he did not. She had taken into account his feelings for her. He didn't recognize those emotions ninety percent of the time, or acknowledge them, yet she knew they were there and that the feelings were growing each moment in her company.

He tried one more time to let her know what it would be like with him. "I will rarely leave your mind, Marguarita. You will never be alone, never have a thought I do not know. Every breath in your body, I will feel. I will know where you are, who you talk with. There will be nowhere that you can go that I will not be with you."

She smiled at him and let go of his hand to lean forward and pat the neck of her horse. *I am growing used to feeling your eyes on me and it's becoming lonely when I am without you in my mind. I had not realized how truly alone one can be until I felt you inside me.*

Zacarias took control of both horses, turning them back toward the stables. He wanted to be inside more than her mind. He wanted to see her body without the denim hugging her skin so lovingly. He needed the feel of her hands on him, the hot velvet of her mouth fitting tightly over him. He looked at her, knowing she could see the hunger in his smoldering gaze.

Her answer was that small, mysterious, all too sensual smile that teased his cock into hardness. He urged Thunder forward, needing Marguarita. She'd given him this night, a gift, and he wanted more. Maybe he would always want more.

Marguarita contemplated Zacarias's thoughts as she quickly rubbed down the horses and led them into their stalls with a small mixture of hay and feed for thanks before turning to face her man. Excitement had been building in her from the moment she'd slipped the lacy underwear on right in front of him. It had been a daring thing to do and made her damp just thinking about it.

The erotic images in Zacarias's head made that dampness grow into distinct wetness. He couldn't fail to scent her welcoming call to him, but she took her time, letting the sexual tension stretch out right there in the stable while she washed her hands and dried them carefully before she turned to him.

How can I please you? She loved the sound of inquiry, that soft submissive questioning. She didn't need a voice or words to indicate she wanted her hands and mouth on him, that she wanted his every desire met—by her.

"I want you to touch me. Explore my body as I explored yours."

His voice was mesmerizing, the command in his tone so masculine. She didn't understand why she felt the need to ease his burdens the way she did, but there was a drive in her to meet his every need. This man had battled alone for centuries. Entirely, utterly alone. He was wounded in places no one could see and in all his lonely life, he had only let one person close enough to see inside of him—her.

Her heart stuttered with pleasure, knowing he found solace in her body, that he found peace. She would do anything to bring him that and she would find her own enjoyment in every act, every compliance.

Just like that his clothes were gone and she was gasping at the size and shape of his heavy erection. He was so thick and long, much more so than she believed possible in a man. She found it impossible not to touch him. Her hands had a life of their own and really, after all, he'd given his permission.

Amusement slid into her mind. "More than permission, my beautiful lunatic, a command. Please me."

She couldn't have refused that teasing note, or the edge of hunger she felt pushing against her mind. Her fingers slid up his thigh, all the while she watched his face and kept her mind firmly planted in his. She wanted to feel his every reaction. She needed to observe him as well. The breath leaving his lungs in a rush was an aphrodisiac. She touched the fiery head, a thick round knob with a single pearl leaking. She used the tip of her finger to spread that lubrication over the head until it was glistening. His eyes burned with heat.

I trust that no one will come near. Even as she expressed her fear, she obeyed the pressure of his hands on her shoulders, sliding down to her knees.

She could feel his pleasure at the mere sight of her kneeling in front of him, hair spilling wildly down her back, her eyes bright, her lips slightly parted. "You are beautiful, Marguarita. I wish to see those wisps of lace covering your body. I thought about them on our ride together and how your body would look covered in those little scraps of lace."

She had known and she'd helped to feed those fantasies with a few of her own. She half smiled, her attention on the heavy erection so close to her face. She wrapped her hand around the thickness and tilted her head toward him. *How is it possible that you fit inside me?* How could she possibly take all that into her mouth as she saw in his mind?

Her tank vanished as if it had never been and the cool night air teased her nipples through the black lace into twin peaks. She found herself kneeling on something soft and the air teased her bare butt as her jeans and boots went whichever way her tank had. She'd never felt sexier. He was so beautiful to her, his masculine body all hard, defined muscle.

"I just do. I was created for you."

His hand slipped to the back of her head. She felt the breath trapped in his lungs as he urged her forward. She didn't resist, but her hand leisurely explored the size and shape of him, enjoying the texture and heat. She leaned forward and took an experimental swipe with her tongue. He tasted of her favorite tea. He must have tasted it when he'd kissed her in the kitchen and he'd remembered.

Pleased and shocked that he'd taken the trouble to add to her pleasure, she was as honest as possible. *I've never done this, Zacarias. I don't want you to be disappointed.* She was trembling as she licked around that broad silken head. The moment she felt him shudder, the pleasure that burst through him, it steadied her.

His fist bunched in her hair, and her mind firmly in his, she could see what he needed. The stroking lap of her tongue from base to head to get him wet. She fast was developing a taste for him and the exotic mixture of rich tea and Zacarias. Her mouth slipped over the wide head of him, her tongue swirling, the fit tight and hot.

Without warning he suddenly jerked her away from him by her hair. It hurt, her scalp tender, but it was more upsetting that he rejected her ministrations. His face was an expressionless mask, his eyes glittering almost red.

Ice poured in, glaciers of it, impenetrable barriers locking her out. She was rejected both physically and mentally. He had virtually thrown her away from him without telling her what she'd done wrong. Shocked and humiliated, she sank back on her heels, struggling not to cry.

13

Zacarias dragged Marguarita to her feet, clothing her quickly in the garments he preferred, a long skirt and blouse covering the temptation of her body. His fingers closed over her upper arms like twin vises and he forced her to look into his eyes.

"You will do exactly as I tell you, Marguarita. You are my greatest vulnerability, the biggest liability to me. There can be nothing of you within me. No trace. No scent. Nothing. Once I withdraw, you cannot reach for me, no matter how long, or what occurs." He gave her a little shake. "Do you understand me?"

She shook her head, tears swimming. It couldn't matter to him. He couldn't look at those tears and ache inside. There could be only ice and stone, no traces of this woman who had the potential of getting thousands of people, both Carpathian and human, killed. He could have no trace of her in him or on him. He needed to shed the scent of her beloved horses as well.

Marguarita blinked several times, shock and pain in her eyes. He'd put that there, but he couldn't comfort her. He couldn't be part of her. She was not yet Carpathian and she didn't understand the way their world worked. She looked around her, as if coming out of a dream, dazed and confused.

He couldn't blame her, his entire body felt as if it had been going up in flames. He'd been very lucky he was so tuned to danger.

The horses reared and pawed the air, slashed at their stall doors and screamed a protest. Marguarita turned toward the horses, her face going pale.

Her breath caught in her throat. *Do you feel that? They're afraid—but not of you. There's something else, Zacarias, something deeper. There's a thread, a tendril . . .*

He reacted instantly, jerking Marguarita around to face him, half shaking her, his fingers biting into her shoulder like a vise. "Do not try to follow it. It is vampire. The undead has spread his tentacles out and is reaching for you even now through the very animals you love."

I'll sound the alarm and the boys will help fight.

"You will trigger the alarm that tells them to seek shelter. They would be in my way and witnessing a battle will only make them fear me more."

The tears spilled over and fear shimmered in her enormous eyes. *Nothing can happen to you. They could help. I could help.*

He gave her a little shake. "You will do as I tell you without question. I will take you to the house quickly." He wrapped his arm around her waist and lifted her feet from the ground. "You will stay there until I come to get you, no matter how long that takes. Do not speak to me. Do not connect with me. I expect your obedience in this."

He felt the urgency consuming him, the one that told him the battle was close. He had to weave safeguards over the houses and stables to prevent destruction of life and property, which vampires were prone to do just for fun. Most of all he had to banish every trace of Marguarita from his mind and body, from his heart and soul. There could be no hint of her where the enemy could catch even the faintest of scents.

He flew with dizzying speed, masking them as he took her into the house. He went right on through to the master bedroom; the walls were the thickest there and shoved her into a tight little alcove against the wall. "Do not move. If you do, Marguarita, there will be severe consequences."

She drew up her knees, nodding, wrapping her arms around her knees to hold herself tight. Her face streaked with tears, but the fear in her eyes was all for him, not for what he might choose to punish her with if she disobeyed.

Zacarias couldn't think about the taste of her breath, or how she felt pouring into his mind, he had to shut down completely and become empty, a warrior alone and without anything to lose. He turned his back on her and hurried out to weave his strongest safeguards over every building on the property. It took strength and stamina to hold such strong weaves in the face of the approaching vampires.

He inhaled the night. Three of them. Ruslan would not send his best on the first outright attack, but he would send seasoned vampires. They were coming from three directions, trying to box him in and pick the battlefield. Zacarias wanted them far away from his woman and everything she loved. He took to the air, streaking toward the far end of the De La Cruz ranch, where the rain forest met the clearing, where Ruslan had tried to infiltrate with his poisonous plant and set a trap to aid his advancing vampires.

A game of strategy then. Ruslan was a master at strategy and he would do his best to manipulate Zacarias into a trap. This attack would be the opening gambit to test his strength and resolve. He had stayed too long in one place so Ruslan would assume, since he hadn't moved on, that Zacarias had been mortally wounded in the battle in Brazil. It would have been reported that there were droplets of blood in the air. Ruslan's hounds would have followed that blood trail to Peru, to the De La Cruz hacienda. Ruslan would be thinking his recovery was slow and that he was vulnerable.

Zacarias was vulnerable, but not for the reasons Ruslan believed. He made certain that he removed all scent from his body, and all traces of her from his mind. Loneliness hit hard, nearly unbearable, now that he knew what it was like with her inside of him, filling him up. Without her connection to him, the world went gray and dull. Everywhere he looked, the vivid color was gone. The bright vibrant greens of the rain forest, the bursts of brilliant colors of flowers winding up the trunks of trees, even the hues on the lacy ferns all had disappeared to be replaced by a dreary gray.

Resolutely, he turned his mind away from Marguarita. It took a great deal of discipline to do so. Lifemates needed one another. Once those threads were woven, they were unbreakable, and his mind would forever seek to touch hers. Add to that the need to see in color, the ability to feel only when she was connected to him, and he felt tremendous need.

Fortunately, he was an ancient warrior, and his priority above all else was Marguarita's safety.

He turned his back on the human structures, homes that meant so much to them. He had never understood before. He was a nomad, continually moving for self-preservation, not even allowing his brothers to know his resting places or his secret lairs. He had dozens throughout South America, places he could retreat to and rest in when necessary, but now, he understood what a home was. Not the structure. Not the place. The woman.

He took to the sky, a thin stream of vapor, drifting with the slight breeze, riding the drafts, feeling his way, searching for the exact location of his enemy. In the distance, he could see a single black cloud churning madly, heading toward the pasture where the herd was bedded down for the night. Angry red ropes of lightning lit the edges of the black, turbulent cauldron.

He marked the cloud, but remained a distance from it. Ruslan would have coached his vampires. He would warn them of Zacarias's personality. He was a fighter and unlike Ruslan, he didn't hesitate to face his enemy. The master vampire would have told his pawns that Zacarias wouldn't run, that in fact, he would go straight for trouble. The giant storm cloud, looking so very evil in the otherwise clear sky, was merely a calling card to draw him out—and a rather weak one at that.

He sent an illusion streaking toward the cloud, a mere replica of himself that was more air than substance, but he was embedded in that vague shape, just as a master was in all illusions. He felt the puppet of himself hit something unseen, something solid and sharp. His illusion shredded. Instantly he grew one long nail and tore a laceration in his wrist. He called a soft breeze and shook droplets of blood into the wind, sending it out over the battlefield he'd chosen, that smooth field where Ruslan had so carefully arranged a trap with his foul plant.

His blood was powerful. He was ancient Carpathian, unquestionably one of the most powerful hunters alive. The scent of his blood would draw the vampires like hounds. They would sniff those droplets and the power contained in a single drop of blood would be a prize to fight for. They would also transmit triumphantly to their master that Zacarias was indeed wounded and that they had scored the first coup with their simple trap.

Ruslan would believe that Zacarias was still hurt, but he would know the ruse of a storm cloud had not drawn him out.

He hovered over the field, allowing the breeze to take more droplets of blood into the air and scatter them wide. It was a call that would be irresistible. A newly made vampire would have already crawled out of the bushes to try to find a precious bead and lap it up quickly before it was taken from him. The fact that there was no stirring right away told Zacarias that Ruslan had sent experienced fighters after him.

Instincts rose. The primal hunger for the fight. He lived for it. Knew the rush as intimately as he did the kill. He waited with endless patience born of a thousand such battles. It took seven minutes and the first of the three vampires showed himself. The brush just inside the rain forest nearest the fence withered, turned brown and shrunk away from the unnaturalness of the undead as he parted the long fronds and peered into the field.

Zacarias had seen this one before, only a few years earlier, or perhaps it was more—time passed now and meant nothing—but even then, before the Carpathian had turned, Zacarias had known he was already lost to honor. Zacarias had avoided him, as he did all Carpathians. He was a hunter, no friend to any of them. He didn't want to know them before he killed them. This one was no more than five or six hundred years old and someone turning at that age was beneath even contempt. What could possibly drive a Carpathian who had not suffered the full ravages of time to turn away from honor?

The vampire raised his nose and sniffed the air, drawing the potent scent of ancient Carpathian blood into his lungs. His tongue flicked out greedily, his nostrils flared. He grimaced, showing the rotting, pointed teeth, already blackened and sharp. His name had been something to do with the forest—Forester, or something close. It mattered little. Before, Zacarias thought of him as *man of little honor*; now it was *man of no honor.*

Zacarias allowed the breeze to cease, so that the air became very still, the potency of his blood-scent increasing. Man of no honor shrank back into the withering ferns, his head turning first one way, and then the other, a wary, animalistic gesture, before he again found the courage to stick his head out into the open.

Zacarias studied the battlefield. Nothing else moved. Not a single blade of grass, or the leaves on the trees. Two of Ruslan's undead pawns had enough discipline to resist the call of such potent blood. They believed him wounded, but still, they were patient enough for him to show himself, and intelligent enough to use their more impatient partner as bait.

Zacarias recognized that his trap could easily become one for him. The ice chilled more, a blue glacier adding layers as the chess game progressed. This was his world. He understood it. He watched the man of no honor crawl from the shelter of the dense shrubbery, a mere shadow sliding across the field. In his wake, the light-hued grass turned a murky dull brown, creating a swath of destruction the vampire didn't notice. He was so caught up in collecting the drops of blood on his tongue that he had forgotten how nature rebelled against such an unnatural being, creating a path that pointed straight to the undead.

The shadow stretched as the vampire slithered on his belly, lapping at the blades of grass, eager for the powerful rush giving him a dangerous high. Careful to keep every movement so small that it was impossible for the two hidden vampires to detect the stir of power, Zacarias sent a sudden massive wind shooting through the field of grass. At the same time, he edged the individual blades, turning them to vicious saw grass.

The vampire screamed and rolled over, holding his bleeding mouth as a thousand cuts streaked his blackened tongue and lips. Zacarias didn't bother to look at his handiwork, he studied the ground and trees and even the sky. A shadow moved in the dark roots of a kapok tree, just the slightest of movements, but it was enough. Zacarias closed the laceration on his wrist and removed all scent of blood. He allowed the shifting winds to take him in the direction of the rain forest, right to that tall, imposing tree rising like a sentry above the canopy emerging into the night sky.

No bats clung to the roots. No birds rested in the branches. The leaves drooped and shivered. There was no telltale sap running down the trunk, no hint of tree cancer, just that vague movement he'd caught out of the corner of his eye. The wind had died down to a soft breeze and he let himself drift right into that large root cage. The foul stench told him he was close to his prey.

Once in the shelter of the spacious enclosure, he was painstakingly cautious to remain very still. The dirt floor had bat droppings and small fruits scattered over the dirt. He studied the root system. He could see where the undead had entered. As careful as he'd been not to touch the tree itself, he'd brushed against one of the thick fins reaching out over the forest floor, slightly blackening it. The blight on the root was faint, indicating the vampire was cunning and much more careful than most.

Zacarias knew he was in a small confined space with another predator, one evil and cunning, one willing to sacrifice his hunting companion to the hunter in order to kill a Carpathian. One wrong move and he was dead, yet there was no fear, no apprehension. He was in full warrior mode. He understood kill or be killed—and he didn't make mistakes. He had endless patience. Sooner or later, this vampire would stir to check what was happening on the field. He would see his companion crawling through the saw grass, cutting his legs and belly. By now, man of no honor had had a taste of Zacarias's powerful blood and the subtle compulsion would be working on him, growing his addiction until nothing mattered but another taste of that blood.

Zacarias waited there in the darkness, trying not to breathe in the stench of the undead's rotting flesh. The tree groaned, the only sound other than man of no honor's continual weeping as he continued to quarter the ground, seeing the elusive droplets of blood. The saw grass cut his hands, his arms and belly, even his face and tongue, but the compulsion was on him now, the terrible need for more of that precious blood.

A careful stirring just to the left of Zacarias gave away the position of the enemy. The creature moved silently forward in order to get a better look at the field. He was growing tired of waiting. Zacarias knew he was beginning to question whether or not Zacarias was really there at all. He hadn't rushed to the storm cloud as Ruslan had said he would. He hadn't shown himself. They had followed the blood trail and scented fresh blood. Zacarias might have fled to find another place to heal what was most likely a mortal wound.

As a Carpathian hunter, Zacarias had seen it all, he knew the workings of the minds of his opponents. Patience was never a strong suit of the *nosferatu*, although, so far, the third conspirator had not given himself away. He moved into position behind the foul-smelling vampire, careful not to disturb the air in the now rank cage of roots. The air was so still, the slightest draft could warn his enemy. Once in the perfect location, he positioned his fist a scant inch from the back of the undead and slammed through bone and sinew, straight to the heart. At the same time, he trapped the vampire's throat, preventing him from crying out.

The acidlike blood, thick and black, poured over his hand and arm as he slowly extracted the pulsing, withered, organ. His fingers of his other hand dug into the throat, ripping out the voice box, so no sound could emerge and betray his presence.

Overhead, in the sky, whips of lightning began to strike the field, hitting the open meadow where man of no honor crawled. Hundreds of strikes shook the ground, lightning rained from the sky, great jagged swords slamming again and again, a dizzying attack that was everywhere. It was impossible to see where every strike hit, the range was so wide, yet none exploded the trees, only struck near them.

One of the whips hit the heart just outside the cage of roots where Zacarias flung it. The heart incinerated immediately. Ruthlessly, Zacarias tossed the vampire carcass through the bars of the thick woody fins, allowing the lightning to burn that as well. He rinsed his hands and arms in the white-hot cleansing energy, allowing the lightning strike to continue a few more moments over the field, so as not to give away his location.

All went dead quiet again. The sky cleared, stars shining above, and only the single rolling mass of turbulence indicated there was trouble. The grass appeared blackened in spots and there were a few small burning blades that sent sparks along with spiraling black smoke into the air. The fire leaped and danced, multiplying quickly, just tiny little blazes sending that wispy black smoke into the air. Several fires sprang to life around man of no honor.

Zacarias allowed the breeze to slide over the canopy so that the leaves on the trees rustled and stirred along the fence line a hundred feet away from him. Instantly the ground burst open near the tree with the glittery leaves, the dirt rising like a geyser, a tangled vine exploding upward, wrapping around the tree, strangling the trunk and rising higher, toward the canopy, smothering everything it touched, everywhere it reached. It wound tighter and tighter, choking the tree so bark popped off in strips and with alarming force, shot from the tree. Limbs cracked under the weight, eventually shattering into pieces and falling to the forest floor.

The vampire had struck quickly and precisely, but he hadn't given away his position. Impressive. Ruslan had sent one who was possibly a worthy opponent. Zacarias allowed the breeze to expand and blow out over the field so that the plumes of smoke began to stretch over the area and join together, partially obscuring vision. He drifted into the smoke, his color identical to the smoke, nothing but grayish-black, nearly transparent vapor that merged more and more together from the small fires until the smoke became a solid veil, nearly impenetrable, obscuring all vision.

Below him, man of no honor wept, his tears burning blades of grass, but still he continued, frantic now, slithering like the lowest worm, desperate to find more of the powerful blood. He couldn't live without it now, and nothing else mattered to him, certainly not Ruslan and his threats and empty promises. Only the blood. He needed the blood. He whimpered and slobbered, uncaring now of the thousands of cuts to his face and body, seemingly unaware the saw grass had sharp serrated edges that cut deeper and deeper into him. Only the blood mattered, only that next drop.

Man of no honor didn't notice the flames on the ground or the smoke layered thick over his head. He scented the treasure—that wonderful, amazing, *powerful* treasure that only he could have. He would never share and it would make him invincible, impossible to kill, more powerful even than Ruslan—after all, this lone hunter was the one Carpathian Ruslan feared above all others. He would be ruler of the vampires and eventually Carpathians. Humans would be nothing but puppets and cattle to him.

He sniffed the air. Was that a droplet above his head? He rolled over, his tongue frantically trying to find it in the smoky air. If the Carpathian would show himself, he would rip out his heart and devour it, and then consume every drop of blood the hunter had in him. He needed that blood. His tongue found nothing, but his nose scented more. Rich. Tantalizing. The droplets had fallen directly into the wounds in his chest and belly. The Carpathian had to be close and had to be bleeding.

His sharp fingernails lengthened to razor-sharp talons and he began tearing at his own flesh, ripping and peeling to get at those precious drops of blood. The sounds were horrendous, shrieking cries of agony, desperate whimpers of hunger and need that resounded through the night. The horses in the stables reacted, kicking and stomping, in a frenzied attempt to escape the sound. The cattle in the distant fields came to their feet, nearly all at the same time as though an electric charge had run through the herd.

In the distance, Zacarias heard the *whop-whop* of the helicopter blades. Cursing in his native tongue he struck hard and fast, extracting the heart of man of no honor and flinging it far out into the field. He moved under cover of the smoke, careful to float with the breeze and not give his position away by trying to hurry. He knew the other vampire would strike at his screaming partner, certain Zacarias was somewhere in the smoke next to him. Again, lightning lit up the sky, streaks of it, looking to all the world like a modern war zone, the spears of white-hot energy slamming to earth. One bolt struck the heart, incinerating it, and then jumped unerringly to the vampire's body, destroying that as well.

The cattle were going to stampede. The vampire would realize instantly that the people in the helicopter worked for the De La Cruz family. The ranchers would pour out of their homes in spite of the order to remain inside, their instincts to save the herd overriding the command. More bait for the vampire—he would expect Zacarias to protect them.

Zacarias reached for the turbulent cloud the vampire had spun to use as a trap, rolling and spinning in the sky. It was heavy with moisture, spinning larger and growing into a lumbering tower, a dark malevolent funnel of spinning rage. Zacarias opened the floodgates, allowing the trapped drops to pour down over the field and extinguish all the flames. The black smoke mixed with gray vapor, growing dense and churning with the wild wind until the air was thick with smoke, dust and debris.

He streaked through the haze toward the helicopter, cursing as he did so. The vampire surely would attack the craft first. It was far easier being a Carpathian warrior uncaring of anything but killing his enemy. Protecting humans added a huge risk factor and his mind kept turning resolutely toward the reason. He shut it down fast and hard, but a knot began to grow in the pit of his belly.

He slipped into the helicopter right behind Julio. *Get out of here fast. A vampire is here.*

As soon as he'd pushed the warning into Julio's mind, he was gone, throwing a protection ring around the craft. The strike came just as expected, a missile streaking through the air, leaving behind a trail of vapor. The projectile hit the protection ring and exploded. Lea, the helicopter pilot, screamed and banked sharply. She had not seen Zacarias, nor was she aware of the warning. Looking below, she couldn't fail to see the thick smoke.

"Get us out of here, Lea," Julio demanded.

"I'm trying," she shouted back, although they both wore a radio.

The helicopter lurched as something exploded very close to them.

"Someone's shooting at us," she cried.

"No, it's an explosion from the fire. Can you see?" Julio asked.

"The smoke is so thick," Lea responded. "How can it be so thick everywhere?"

Zacarias could hear the humans' frantic discussion as he followed the trajectory of the missile back to the origin. The vampire would have moved as fast as he'd delivered the attack, hoping to bring down the helicopter, but his moving left a trail. And Zacarias could follow any trail no matter how slight. He streaked across the exact vapor trail left by the missile, using the line of trajectory to scan below.

Above, caught in the smoke, the helicopter seemed to be in trouble. The vampire fed the smoke, pouring more into the sky and field so that it was dense, nearly impenetrable. Zacarias went after him. If he stayed and tried to help the two in the helicopter, the men rushing from their homes to get to the cattle would be in danger. He had to stop the undead.

The vampire had been very clever, hiding almost out in the open. Once straight overhead the hiding place, Zacarias could see where he had utilized the natural terrain as it dipped below the sloping fence line. Bushes were thin there, but he had managed to secrete himself in the sparse vegetation without touching a single leaf. The grass where he had stood was shrunken and a dull brown, some blades shivering, testifying to the fact that the undead had recently abandoned his hiding place.

The vampire moved under cover of the thick smoke, hastily changing his position, passing close to the vine-covered post on the outer fence. The leaves and tangle of shrubbery recoiled subtly. Zacarias followed that faint path. In the distance, he could hear the frightened bawling of the cattle and the sounds of men rushing to horses. The undead had a target. Stampeding the herd, bringing out many potential victims, would give him advantages.

Above Zacarias the helicopter lurched awkwardly as another projectile exploded against the protection ring. He soothed the wild wind, sending it out and away from the funnel cloud to disperse the smoke, giving the helicopter pilot a way to see an open spot to bring the metal bird to the ground safely.

Men poured from the houses, leaping onto the backs of horses, racing wildly toward the far fields where the cattle had been semisheltered by the gently rising slopes and tall shade trees. Zacarias streaked ahead of the vampire, throwing up a barrier so the undead hit it hard and bounced back, finding himself sitting in the middle of the burned field.

Zacarias materialized a distance from him. "I know you. You should have known better than to hunt me."

The vampire picked himself up slowly, dusting off his clothes with meticulous care. He bowed low, and then stood straight and tall. "Who could resist pitting wits against the great and all powerful Zacarias De La Cruz? You are the thing of legends. Any who defeated you would be known for all time."

"And you are just the man to manage it," Zacarias said softly. He kept his voice pitched low, melodious even, a stark contrast to the vampire who had to work to modulate his voice. All the while he listened to sounds of the frantic men trying to calm the restless herd.

The buildup of electricity in the air told him the vampire would attempt to use a lightning whip to prod the cattle into stampeding. Zacarias waved a casual hand toward the sky countering the electrical charge. The air stilled, all clouds disappeared.

"An old trick," the vampire said. "But you cannot protect them all from me."

Insects burst from the ground, thousands of them, a plague of starving bugs, desperate for food. They took to the air, flying straight at Zacarias, the migration heading for the cattle, horses and men behind him. He seemed a small obstacle in their path.

Zacarias shrugged. He stood calmly, not moving as the insects approached him. "What does that matter to me? I have one purpose. One."

He smiled as his wind shifted, picking up, driving away from him straight at the vampire. Blades of serrated saw grass speared through the air like a thousand knives. The insects tried to devour it in midair, the force of the wind blowing them backward along with the grass. The blades struck the vampire with such force they went through his body before he even realized they were concealed in the mass of insects. Hundreds of grass spears impaled him from his head to his feet. At once the insects covered him, desperate to feed at the wounds.

Zacarias materialized inches in front of the vampire, slamming his fist through bone and muscle, through the acid blood. Insects rained to the ground, dying as they touched the hideous unnatural blood of the undead.

"I destroy vampires," Zacarias whispered, looking him straight in the eyes, his dispassionate gaze saying it all. "That is my one purpose." He extracted the blackened, wizened heart and tossed it into the mass of wiggling, dying insects.

Lightning forked across the sky and slammed into the mountain of bodies, incinerating the heart as well as the insects. Zacarias stepped back calmly and allowed the body to fall so the white-hot energy bolt could incinerate the remains.

He stood for a moment, allowing the cool night air to take the stench of the undead from his nostrils before he turned to make certain the helicopter had landed safely. Julio ran across the open ground just in front of the hangar, Lea's hand in his, both headed toward the stables, presumably to help with the herd.

In spite of the way the ground shook under the pounding hooves as the cattle began to run mindlessly, Zacarias's gaze was pulled unerringly, even compulsively, to the hacienda. She was there. Marguarita. Huddled inside. Alone. He had ruthlessly abandoned her, and he would do it again and again, over and over. He ran his fingers through the mass of thick hair.

There were no lights on in the main house—the only structure still dark on the property. As soon as the alarm had gone out that those guarding the cattle would need help, every home on the property had come to life—with the exception of Marguarita's home. He could have touched her with his mind—certainly every cell in his body needed her, needed that deep connection—but he refused.

The moment he touched her, he would feel. Fear mounting to terror would crawl through his body—fear that she would regret her choice, fear that she would want to sever the ties between them. Standing alone in the middle of the empty, burned field, he didn't have to feel anything.

Behind him he heard Cesaro shout. The massive herd sounded like thunder approaching. Cesaro, Julio and two others were trying to turn the running animals. The steers were large, big muscular animals, heads down, eyes rolling as they pounded toward the fence separating Zacarias from danger.

Cesaro fired his rifle into the air in a last-ditch effort to turn the cattle. They crashed into the fence with their broad chests, snapping wood like twigs. The cattle bellowed and bawled, dust rising into clouds as they tore through the fence.

Zacarias could hear the shouts of Cesaro and his son, warning him to run. He turned to face the huge steers, one hand in the air. Allowing the predator to rise to the surface, he hissed a warning into the air between them, pushing the scent of dangerous predator with it. He sent that intimidating threat in a straight line out just feet from him, a long wall of deterrent.

The lead animals abruptly turned, swinging around in a semicircle, suddenly more afraid of what was in front of them than the animals pounding behind them. More animals rushed toward him, but the scent of danger was overwhelming. It didn't take long for the cattle to become confused, bawling and slowing, circling, allowing the cowboys to take control.

Julio rode closer. The horse danced sideways, trying to get away from Zacarias. "The pilot, Lea Eldridge, isn't one of us. She saw things I can't explain to her."

Zacarias nodded his head. Julio remained stationary, controlling his horse with his knees and hands. Zacarias arched an eyebrow in inquiry.

"It's just that she saved Ricco's life and she's Marguarita's friend."

Julio's voice told Zacarias much more than Julio was prepared to give away. He might say the woman didn't belong in their part of the world, but secretly, he wished she did.

"I will be careful which memories I remove when the time comes," Zacarias said.

"Are you all right?"

"Why do you ask?"

Julio hesitated. "Your eyes, *señor*, they're glowing. Do you have need of . . ."

Zacarias shook his head. Destroying the undead took a toll on every hunter. The taking of lives was not done lightly or without consequence. Julio already feared him—all the workers did—even Cesaro. He couldn't explain the dangers he faced each time he took a life—even that of the vampire. Taking blood was a temptation, a very dangerous one after the taking of lives. He inclined his head in thanks, and then turned away from the man. In truth, he turned away from the sight of the nervous horse.

Marguarita had pointed out that the Peruvian Paso, at least those bred on his ranch, were bred for temperament as well as abilities. They were renowned for their steady natures in the face of adversity. He'd finally been able to ride, flowing over the ground, his spirit connected to the animals, yet now, the horse didn't even recognize he was the same person. The killer was far too close to the surface.

Zacarias turned away from the battlefield, the lingering smoke and drifting scent of death, and walked back to the main house—back to her. Marguarita. *Susu*—not his birthplace, but home was a woman he called *päläfertiil*—lifemate. The only place he could find peace was in her. The only time he truly came alive was with her. The only way he could leave the half world of shadows was by filling his empty spaces with her bright light. Marguarita was *sívam és sielam*—his heart and soul. There was no getting around the fact that without her spirit brushing his, he had no heart or soul, just places that were now sieves, filled with millions of holes no longer connecting to anything worth saving.

He hadn't wanted this. He was too far gone and, while he'd been searching for the undead, a solitary hunter, living in strict isolation, the world had long since passed him by. He didn't understand modern ways. So many centuries of walking the earth hunting prey had kept him remote, removed from other species. He knew nothing of humans and certainly nothing of women, but after feeling her inside of him, after being inside of her, there was no going back.

He walked the worn path to the front steps, noticing the flowers and shrubbery. All were a dull gray, no bright colors for him until he stepped inside and joined his mind to Marguarita's. A part of him resisted this new path, but she was already a drug in his system, an addiction he couldn't defend against. He needed the vivid colors, the rush of emotion, the pure pleasure he'd never experienced. Marguarita was laughter and frustration. She was an intriguing puzzle he couldn't solve.

He walked up the stairs, a simple act, yet something inside him, something hard and edgy seemed to settle. He felt her close. She was still closed to him and he didn't allow his mind to seek hers. He needed to see her face—to know that she could accept this part of him. He was the predator the animals recognized. He knew his face was honed in battle, rough and etched with the stamp of a killer. His eyes would still be glowing, his canines would be sharp and a little extended.

She had to see him as he was. It was difficult to accept the Carpathian, but the hunter was terrifying. He had no idea what he would do if she rejected him. Take her off to his lair and try to find a way to make her happy, perhaps? Impossible. He shook his head, his palm resting on the door, just the height of her head. This was an impossible situation. By all that was holy, what was destiny thinking? A Carpathian woman, an ancient, would have had difficulties with him. But a human? A woman with no experience with a rough, dominant male who would rule her without the tender things a woman needed? How could she possibly cope with him?

He was careful to remove all safeguards. The Carpathian men could leave their houses, but getting back inside would have been difficult—painful—and dangerous. He opened the door and went inside. Normally, inside a structure, he found it difficult to breathe. Outside, the wind kept him apprised of danger. Inside, the scents of the humans and the way they lived overrode everything of value to him. Now, when he inhaled, he drew in—Marguarita.

Her fragrance was all woman. Soft and subtle. She smelled like a miracle. Clean and fresh and belonging to the rain forest—to him. He padded silently down the hall, not wanting to give her time to prepare herself. She needed to see him as he was and he needed to see her face, her true expression. Touching her mind would tell him everything, but once her mind was in his, the lifemate bond would take over and mask her fears and her initial true reaction to him.

He stepped into her bedroom. The room was completely dark. The drapes remained closed, blocking out the moon. Marguarita huddled in a corner, on the floor. Her face was streaked with tears, her hands were pressed tight over her ears. Of course she'd heard the sounds of the battle, the screams of her beloved horses and the bawling of the cattle. She couldn't fail to know the herd had stampeded, not with the crashing, thundering hooves pounding into the ground. His blood had heightened all of her senses.

Her long hair was down, all those silken strands and even now, in his worst predatory state, he could see that thick mass was a true black, gleaming without even light to show the hidden blues. He watched her for a long moment, prolonging the wait, not wanting to know the truth, but needing it at the same time. He took a breath, drew her into his lungs and willed her to look up.

14

N*ow. See me now.* He pushed the compulsion into the room and held his breath as Marguarita lifted her head.

Her eyes were drenched in tears. Enormous, beautiful, chocolate eyes. Her gaze locked on to him, and he saw her catch her breath. Her breasts rose and fell in a soft, feminine movement. She swallowed as if something was lodged in her throat. Her fingers were twisted so tightly together they were white. But it was her face he focused on.

She stared at him for what seemed eternity. Very slowly she stood up, feeling her way up the wall, her eyes wide, moving over him inch by inch, looking for damage. Carefully inspecting him. When her gaze returned to his face, she took the few steps to stand in front of him. Her hands framed his face and then slid over him, a touch of her fingers, feather light, but the obvious caress sent a jolt through his body.

A mixture of emotions crossed her face, so easy to read. She couldn't speak, but her feelings were transparent. Relief. Joy. Fear. It was all there, but his heart took up a rhythmic beat when he hadn't even realized it was stuttering along with his ragged breathing.

He wrapped his hand around the nape of her neck and drew her body close to his, holding her head against his chest, slipping his arm around her to feel her body against his. She melted into him, her arms circling his waist. She held him as if comforting him, or comforting herself. And maybe both of them needed comfort. He rested his head on the top of hers and let her peace seep into his mind and heart. She hadn't looked at him as if he was a monster. She was afraid, but *for* him, not *of* him. Perhaps having a beautiful lunatic for a lifemate was the perfect solution for a lost man like him. She didn't know enough to fear him.

Holding her wasn't enough. He needed her inside of him. "Come into me, *sívamet*. I need you inside me." He whispered the invitation into the cloud of midnight blue-black hair.

She lifted her head and looked into his eyes. He felt himself falling. The ground under his feet shifted. She came into him slow, like warm molasses, thick and perfect, filling him with her brightness, filling the holes in his heart and soul, bridging the broken connections and driving the shadows out. She filled him with—her. Her spirit moved against his. His soul recognized hers. She became the rhythm of his heart.

Zacarias had never needed anything or anyone. Now he couldn't do without her. She made him as vulnerable as a new baby. He knew forever. He'd lived forever, but now, with her, with Marguarita, everything was different. Forever wasn't going to even be close to long enough with her. He blinked several times, the colors in the darkened room so vivid and bright they hurt his eyes. Marguarita was color, all those intense, beautiful hues that burst in front of his eyes when she was in him.

Using the hand wrapped around her throat, he forced her head up so that her dark eyes were compelled to meet his. His heart stuttered in his chest. His body trembled. He felt as if he'd been hit by a tsunami and he was being swept away, drowning. Perhaps he'd been drowning all along and had never noticed the sensation until her mind connected all the dots, but now, he knew the water had closed over his head and he was under.

There was only Marguarita in his world. Marguarita with her soft skin and the light she poured into his dark soul. It was a strange thing for a man who had spent lifetimes utterly alone to need. It was uncomfortable and unfamiliar, but the need was greater than anything else in his world. She was so fragile, so vulnerable. He could crush her easily, yet she had all the power.

Drowning in her eyes, a rush of fire swept through him. Need became physical, leaping from his mind to his body, a dangerous flame, so hot and so raw every muscle tensed as hot blood rushed with the fire from every point in his body to fill his groin with a terrible, clawing demand. Lust burned deep and gut-wrenching. Where before, his need had been hunger, now it was for Marguarita. All of her, her blood, her body, mind and heart and soul. He needed.

She brought him life. She made him experience what he could not. Pain. Pleasure. Sorrow. Laughter. Rage. Joy. She was life. She was now *his* life. His everything. He couldn't live without the emotions and colors she brought to him, or the soft slide of her mind against his, the warmth that melted all that ice in his veins. He needed.

She caressed his shadowed jaw with her fingertips and that slight touch, that whisper of a burning caress, ignited something raw and primal deep within him. Lust and hunger hit with a brutal punch, a vicious clawing need in his belly, filling his groin until he hurt beyond all reason.

He lifted her chin and took her mouth without preamble. No soft kiss. No gentle tenderness. He took what was his, claiming her mouth for his own. "I need to be inside of you. Deep inside you. Do you understand, Marguarita?"

It was an impossible question. How could she possibly understand? The world he lived in and the one she offered him were in complete contrast to one another. He understood one and needed the other. For a Carpathian hunter, needing was the worst possible obsession.

His kiss roughened as hidden emotions welled up, a volcano, long suppressed, building and building inside of him. Anger at her for having such a hold on him. She had claimed she was no witch, but the spell was stronger than any he had ever encountered, the web more beautiful but no less lethal than any trap ever sprung on him. He was caught. By this. By her. Marguarita. His fingers dug deep into her shoulders and he gave her a little shake, the anger building by the moment.

She had dragged him away from eternal rest, forced him to face his past, the memories long buried—and forgotten. He'd put those things in a vault and locked them up tight never to revisit them. She opened floodgates and, sun scorch her, he was addicted to her and those vivid intense emotions she allowed him to feel.

He realized those few moments after killing the vampires, when the horses rejected him, when the cattle turned away, shunning him, preferring the unknown to coming near him, he had been terror-struck. He hadn't connected those feelings until she'd poured into him, but she'd reduced him to that. A warrior beyond all measure, and he'd been nearly brought to his knees at the thought that she might turn away from him.

His mouth took hers over and over, long hot, rough kisses. He didn't give her a chance to breathe, to pull away, to be anything but what he wanted her to be. *His.* Only his. All his. She leaned into him, giving herself, but it wasn't enough for him. He could hear the growls rumbling in his throat, but he couldn't stop. The force inside him demanded she give him everything.

He used his hands to rid her of her clothing, his enormous strength, brutally ripping her blouse and tearing off her skirt to get at her soft skin. He became a frenzied madman, desperate to remove every barrier between him and her body. She didn't question him, but stood still under his rough hands, until he'd stripped her bare.

He paused for one moment looking down at her naked body, all soft curves and feminine heat. This woman was his only salvation, his only way to go on living and stay sane. She was his sanity, his life, and he would demand impossible things of her, but he couldn't give her up, no matter that it might be the honorable thing to do. He was too far gone. With a small groan and a wave of his hand to remove his own clothes, he took her mouth again.

He sank into all that heat and silken promise. His tongue slid along hers. He filled her mouth the way he wanted to fill her body, hard and deep, holding her still for his assault on her senses. He kissed his way down her face to her throat, his tongue flicking over the bites he left along her skin, a trail of his possession. His hand found the soft weight of her breast and he cupped paradise in his palm, his teeth and tongue and lips finding the path to the creamy swell.

He lapped at her frantic pulse. Her felt her grow still, her body trembling. He lapped at her nipple and bit gently with his teeth, then harder, tugging, arousing her, sending lightning streaking through her body. He felt that reaction, and lifted her, growling, desperate for her.

"Wrap your legs around my waist and lock your ankles. Put your hands around my neck." His gruff order was barely audible.

She sucked in her breath, knowing how open she would be to him, but she obeyed without hesitation. He closed his eyes, feeling her warm, slick heat on his belly. She pulsed against him and he felt the answering jerk in his cock. He was desperate to be inside her haven, to bury and lock himself there, away from the rest of the world. Away from blood and death. He chose life and he chose Marguarita.

His fingers flexed on her hips, her only warning, and he slammed her down over this surging erection. He was so thick and hard, he drove through her tight folds. The feeling burst through him, the moon rising over the river, spreading through his body to take over every cell. Her sheath was scorching hot, searing him to his soul, driving out every shadow, the exquisite pleasure pounding through his veins. He held her, his hands driving her down over him mercilessly, his hips rising to meet that velvet soft fiery paradise. He was lost for a time, lost in the ecstasy, pounding into her, turning so he could lean her back against the wall and continue driving like a jackhammer, feeling every stroke through his body, every ripple of hers.

Her breath turned into ragged gasps, her breasts bouncing against him, nipples rubbing over his chest. Her hair was everywhere, brushing over his skin in a sensuous fall. He let himself go, let the monster reign, gave him power. He took her savagely, taking everything for himself, his pleasure, his need driving him.

He nuzzled at her neck, wanting more, but he couldn't get to her with her head lying on his shoulder. *Put your head back,* he commanded.

She complied immediately, throwing her head back. Her breasts jutted toward him, a beautiful sight, bouncing with every hard surge and thrust. She had no choice but to ride him, he refused to allow her respite, even when her body tightened and spasmed around his, again and again. He simply drove her higher. Taking her without inhibition. Needing this. Needing—everything, wanting to feel her orgasm again and again, wanting the pleasure bursting behind his eyes and rushing up his legs to center in his groin.

More. Give me more. Again, Marguarita. Again.

His head was filled with erotic lust, need driving need. He managed to remember to swipe his tongue over her neck before he bit deep. The taste of her burst into his mouth, his mind, rushed like a fireball into his groin. Her body went into another orgasm, one right after the other, her sheath gripping so tight she was strangling him. He could hear her gasps, and pleas for mercy from somewhere in his mind, but it wasn't enough. He needed more. He couldn't leave that inferno of pure, unadulterated pleasure. His haven. He was lost there. Mindless.

He wanted to consume her, be part of her, live inside her skin. Feel this. This perfect place, perfect moment, with her pleas for mercy and his body serving hers, giving her more pleasure than she'd ever dreamed or imagined. She would always know she was his. No one else could ever do these things to her body. Make her feel as he did. He could take all the power back, leave her stripped and as vulnerable as he was.

This was his obsession. This was his brand of ownership. This was—love. The realization of what he was doing swept over him. Shocked him. Utterly shocked him. He was loving her. Trying to say without words the intensity of what he felt for her. How could he possibly say it when he didn't recognize the feeling? It was only here, deep in her body, that he knew absolutely the stark, raw truth. This wasn't punishment for giving him life. This wasn't ownership or possession or obsession. This was love. His love, as rough and raw and untamed as it was. The rage inside of him, welling up like a volcano, threatening to explode, to destroy both of them—*that* was his love for her. He was saying with his body what he didn't know how to say with his words. He was worshiping her. Giving himself to her, burning up in her fire.

He swept his tongue across the bright strawberry on her neck and lifted his head to look into her eyes as he felt the volcano take him, sweeping him up in a rocketing eruption, killing him with fierce, hot pleasure so that he was reborn, remade. A phoenix rising from the ashes. And sun scorch him, he should have been more careful with her.

Her soft admonishment slid into his mind. *Love me any way you want, Zacarias. I feel your love in everything you do to me. I don't need the words. I don't need gentle. Yes, sometimes I'm a little afraid, but I know you won't ever hurt me.* She rested her head on his shoulder, her body surrounding his, almost melting into him so that they did feel as if they had the same skin. Her hair was damp. So was his skin.

He held her close until their hearts slowed from the dangerous high to a more controlled beat. He kissed that sweet spot, the junction between her neck and shoulder, over and over and then swept up her throat to find her mouth.

He had never apologized to anyone in his life. *I am sorry, I should have been more careful with you.* It was easier to push the words into her mind, rather than say them aloud. He felt so much a part of her, his cock still deep inside her, still throbbing while her body pulsed around his with continuous aftershocks.

Her hands caressed his ears, and she lifted her head to look at him before she initiated another kiss. Her lips slid along his, her tongue finding the seam of his mouth, teasing for entrance. He let her take control, let her explore his mouth, loving the way she gave herself unconditionally to him. She would be sore. He'd been a savage, his cock a jackhammer. He had spent a long, mindless time losing himself in her.

I loved every second of it. Feel free any time. I might be sore tomorrow, but it will feel wonderful knowing it was from you making love to me.

You were thoroughly loved. He had given everything he was to her. He demanded no less of her. And it seemed easier to refer to their bodies than their hearts.

Her teeth tugged on his lower lip. He felt her amusement as he slowly allowed his body to separate from hers. Very gently he lowered her feet to the ground, holding her until he was certain her legs were steady enough to hold her. In the distance, outside the house he heard footsteps.

"We have company," Zacarias said. "Your friend Julio and the woman who flew the helicopter." He cupped her breasts, reluctant to give up even a few moments with her. He wanted this night for himself.

Lea Eldridge. Marguarita's hands went to his bare chest and pushed. *I'll have them leave as quickly as possible. She can't see you. Her brother and his friend are too interested in you. Go. Hurry, Zacarias, while I dress.*

He smiled, his palm shaping her throat, tipping her head up toward his. "I am your protector. I will stay and meet this woman."

Her face paled, her eyes darkened and went wide with shock. He couldn't resist bending his head to brush her parted lips with his. She blinked at him, and then shook her head frantically.

It's too dangerous to let her see you. If she accidently slips up and lets her brother know you're in residence, he'll tell that awful friend of his. Seriously, don't stand there smiling at me, you have to go.

She looked around for her clothes, pressing both hands to her mouth as a blush started up her entire body. Her clothes were in ruins, shredded by his urgent hands earlier. He loved the way she looked, helpless and vulnerable. She was all soft skin and generous curves, her wild hair tumbling in all directions around her body, the silken strands catching sensuously on her nipples and traveling in waves to the curve of her very sexy butt. The marks of his possession were everywhere, all over her skin, red marks, dark smudges, his fingerprints, his bite marks. She was beautiful to him. He couldn't resist sweeping his hand over her creamy breasts, watching the breath catch in her lungs.

He loved the way her stomach muscles bunched under his palm and as he dipped lower, the way she widened her stance to accommodate his searching hand letting him know she accepted his possession of her body. She was hot and slick from their lovemaking and smelled of him. He was stamped deeply into her now, and that knowledge pleased him. No matter that he lived in modern times, he was a throwback and the ways of his world would always be a part of him. He wanted other males to know she belonged to him, that she was protected and taken.

His fingers delved a little deeper, into that hot, damp passage and her hips bucked in response. Her body trembled. He loved to feel the shiver of need move through her mind and body. He bent his head to the temptation of her nipple, taking his time, letting her know she belonged to him and it mattered little what the rest of the world was doing while he took his pleasure. And it did give him pleasure to see her little gasps, the flush spreading and the dazed look in her eyes. He loved the desire smoldering there, the need and hunger for him.

He pushed two fingers deep into all that scorching heat. He thought of that tight fiery hot sheath as *his.* All for him. All that intense desire and need gathering in her eyes was for him. Her half-opened mouth. That glazed look of wonder. Her ragged breath. His thumb found her most sensitive spot, flicking and teasing, while his fingers plunged deep. He left a wet trail with his teeth and tongue and lips down her neck and chest to his ultimate destination.

He couldn't resist taking her breast into his mouth and biting down on her nipple with exquisite precision. Her entire body jumped and shook. He moved back and forth between her breasts, taking his time, uncaring of the knock on the door, lost in a world of pleasure, his mouth going from peak to peak. His fingers pushed deep and retreated, then buried deep again while his thumb tapped and tugged on her now engorged button. She shattered, her breath hissing out, her body bucking, rippling, muscles gripping hard as he threw her into another orgasm.

The knock on the door was polite but persistent. He glanced toward it, supporting her weight when her knees buckled. He smiled at her, pleased with her heightened color and wild hair. She looked like a woman who had been made thorough love to. She raised one hand to her mass of hair and he caught her wrist and pulled it down.

"Leave it. I like the way you look. I will get the door while you go to the kitchen and prepare refreshments for our guests."

She frowned, still fighting to breathe, to think logically. *I'm naked. And Lea can't see you. Please, Zacarias. I can barely think straight.*

"There is no need to think. Just do as I tell you."

I have to clean up.

He looked at the mixture of his seed and her cream glistening on her thighs and the intriguing V of curls at the junction of her legs. "I asked you to go to the kitchen and prepare food for our guests, not argue with me. It is a relatively simple request, Marguarita. As usual you seem to find it difficult to follow instructions."

She pressed her lips together. He saw the flash of fire in her eyes. Her chin went up. Without a word, she turned her back on him and walked away, naked, barefoot, her long hair caressing the curves of her butt. He felt his heart jump. She had courage—and fire. And she kept her word no matter how difficult.

"Marguarita." He said her name softly.

She half turned, her left breast, red and covered with his marks, nipple still hard and taut, peeked out at him through the veil of long hair.

"You forgot your clothes."

She frowned, puzzled, glancing at the shredded strips of cloth on the floor. He flashed a grin and waved his hand. Her feet remained bare, but a long skirt fell gracefully to her ankles and a soft peasant blouse clung to her breasts, the loose neckline nearly off her shoulders. A wide belt cinched her waist. Gold glittered at her earlobes and around one wrist.

She touched the bracelet. *It's beautiful. Thank you.* Her hands smoothed the full skirt over her hips. *Umm. Zacarias. You sort of forgot my underwear.*

He flashed his teeth at her. A wolfish smile. "I do not forget—anything."

The blush stole up her neck into her face. She shook her head, her gaze dropping from his. She went on through to the kitchen without another protest. He enjoyed teasing her. He enjoyed the flashes of temper he caught simmering in her eyes—in her mind. As if he'd ever allow another man to look at her body. It wouldn't happen and she should have known that.

Warmth flooded his mind, soft laughter. *I knew. The moment I turned and started toward the kitchen and felt your laughter and your smug, arrogant male satisfaction. I knew then that you were teasing me.*

Little lunatic of a woman. I am far too possessive of you to let another man see what is mine. You should have known at once. I do like watching you walk away from me naked. It gives me great pleasure.

He sent a fresh breeze through the entire house, and added scented candles burning low. He would have left Marguarita's shredded clothing on the floor, but it would have embarrassed her. Neither visitor would fail to notice that he had made love to Marguarita. The evidence was all over her body. In any case, it wouldn't take them long to realize she belonged to him, because he planned on making that very clear.

He flung the door wide and Julio gasped and took a step back, putting his body between Lea Eldridge and Zacarias. "I didn't know you were here, *señor*," he said, his tone apologetic.

"Come in. Marguarita is making tea and some sort of wonderfully smelling cake," Zacarias greeted, stepping back to allow them entry.

Julio looked more confused than ever and gave a brief shake of his head, slightly jerking his chin toward Lea. His protective instincts toward the De La Cruz family had kicked in. He had been born into a family that guarded their symbiotic relationship carefully from all outsiders.

Lea peeked around Julio's shoulders, her eyes going wide. Zacarias could read the excitement in her eyes, the appreciation and stark, raw fear. She put her fingers in Julio's back pocket, a gesture Zacarias was certain she didn't even know she'd made. It told him several things without penetrating her mind. She knew he was a De La Cruz and she was very interested in Julio Santos.

Zacarias swept his hand toward the interior, and Julio reached behind him and took Lea's hand in his, before stepping inside.

"Señor De La Cruz, this is Lea Eldridge. She did us a great favor tonight by flying Ricco Cayo to the hospital. I had no idea you were here. When did you arrive?"

Julio was fishing for Zacarias to set the lead on what to say and how to act.

Zacarias bowed, an old-world, courtly gesture that had Lea blushing. He flashed what he hoped would pass for a smile as he closed the door behind them. "I cannot stay away too long from my woman . . ." He frowned and shook his head. *"Päläfertiilam."* Again he shook his head and lifted an eyebrow at Julio. "How do you say this? *Esposa.* Wife. My wife."

He was very pleased by Julio's shocked look. Zacarias had married her, in the way of the Carpathian people, and it was far more binding than any other species he knew of. They could not live now, one without the other. Marguarita was his wife in every sense of the word.

Lea gasped. "You can't be talking about Marguarita."

"Of course Marguarita," Zacarias said smoothly. "She is mistress here."

"But—" Lea pressed her fingers to her mouth as if trying to hold back her question. She blurted it out anyway. "Why wouldn't she tell me? I'm her friend. Why wouldn't she say anything to everyone around here? You can't be married to her."

"I assure you, Ms. Eldridge, she is mine." Zacarias spoke quietly, but his tone brooked no argument.

Lea looked to Julio, hurt, offended, and excited all at the same time.

Julio shrugged his shoulders, in an effort to look casual. "You can appreciate how this would not be a good thing to get around. Marguarita has to be protected. The De La Cruz family has a great deal of money and many kidnappings take place. It's better if no one knows."

Lea flashed him a look of pure annoyance, but she was obviously intimidated by Zacarias and didn't say another word until they were in the kitchen.

Zacarias entered first and stopped, his gaze on Marguarita. She stood by the stove, pouring water into the teapot her mother had made. To him, there was no more beautiful sight in the world. The colors of her skirt were vivid and bright, her skin gleamed and her hair was a shiny waterfall of blue-black silk. Her movements were graceful and fluid. He knew his blood had enhanced her already beautiful looks when the humans looked at her with such awe, as if they were seeing her for the first time. He could see appreciation in Julio's eyes. He would have to teach her how to turn down her allure.

His blood also enhanced her senses. She couldn't have failed to hear the conversation, not with Carpathian blood running in her veins, and her face was very still as she looked at him, not at their guests. He went to her side and lifted her left hand, remembering the human tradition of wearing a circle of gold. He lifted her fingers and kissed the ring he'd fashioned for her.

She pressed her lips together and frowned a little, looking at the band. *What are you doing, Zacarias? What game are you playing?*

He detected hurt in her voice. He'd done something to hurt her. His fingers tightened around hers and he tugged, pulling her into the shelter of his larger frame, uncaring what their guests might think. He wrapped his arms around her from behind and held her locked against him.

"Have you tea ready for our guests?"

He had made certain the kettle boiled so there would be no waiting. He brushed his mouth over the top of her hair. The contrast between her brightness and the way he saw Julio and Lea was astonishing. Lea was an attractive woman and he could see her in color, but those colors were dull in comparison. Julio's colors were there, but again not rich and vibrant, and he could see his beating heart, the arteries running like a road map through his body. Lea's heart and arteries were there, but much fainter.

Soft amusement poured into his mind. *Targets, my man. You're identify-*

ing targets. He's a friend, not a target. That's how you always see everyone. Even me at first. You don't see them as people, they're all potential enemies.

He realized it was true. He hadn't thought about anyone as human or Carpathian in centuries. He lived in a kill or be killed world. Julio's skin and features were the dullest because he was the biggest potential threat. It was those broken connections Marguarita had filled, the shadows, so many, so large, throughout his mind, that she had provided bridges for that allowed him to recognize Julio was more than a potential enemy. He was a man. Maybe someone who would not be a friend, Zacarias had few in the world, but someone he could respect.

Zacarias realized how he saw the world without Marguarita. There hadn't even been knowledge of identifying others as targets, it was so ingrained in him. He knew every pressure point on a body, every place one could deliver a mortal blow. He had been that disconnected from civilization.

Marguarita's hands suddenly crossed over his tightly, as if holding him. She was reading emotion in him that he wasn't aware of. He searched for it. Shame. He was ashamed that men like Julio, good, courageous men had fought for his family, some dying for his family, and he had never acknowledged them. Not once. Not to himself.

Please sit down and tell us how Ricco is doing, Marguarita wrote and invited.

Julio's gaze jumped to Zacarias's face and he took another step back, toward the door as if he might flee, his grip on Lea tightening.

Zacarias took another deep breath to draw Marguarita's scent into his lungs. He didn't need any others in his life, but she did. He made an effort to feel her emotions toward Julio and Lea. They were important to her—so that made them important to him.

"Yes, please sit." He indicated a chair, looking straight at Julio. It was a clear order, couched in polite words.

Julio immediately held a chair for Lea and sank into the one next to her.

Try not to sound so intimidating, Marguarita advised.

Sun scorch them both, woman. They are taking up my time with you, he said, but there was a teasing note in his voice that surprised them both.

He toed a chair around and straddled it while Marguarita put the tea and cakes on the table. She started to sit opposite him, but Zacarias caught her wrist and tugged her down beside him. She blushed at Julio's raised eyebrow.

What are you doing? This isn't a good idea. Seriously, Zacarias, you shouldn't be here and you shouldn't let anyone know that we're . . . It isn't safe for you.

You are lucky I do not make you sit in my lap where I can feel your soft body against mine, he teased wickedly. He rather enjoyed this part of company. His woman wasn't embarrassed around him, but she was shy about their relationship in front of others. That made no sense to him, but he enjoyed her fussing at him.

"Why didn't you tell me that you were married, Marguarita?" Lea asked, hurt in her voice. "I thought we were good enough friends that you could have confided in me. And you let Esteban think you were available."

Marguarita drew the notepad to her and began to write. Zacarias put his hand over the pad the moment he saw the apology.

"I know you do not wish Marguarita to apologize for something that is a safety issue. Your brother was never seriously entertaining the idea of courting her, and she knew that. I am a very wealthy man and I have many enemies. Marguarita would have told you if she could. If you need to be angry, please be angry with me. I put her in the position of secrecy. And certainly, Julio is not to blame. He knew I was in residence, but he was not privy to our marriage."

We are not married.

Zacarias flicked her one look, daring her to deny him. There was a promise of retaliation in that look. If she didn't acknowledge what he was to her . . .

We have not stood before a priest.

I do not understand. We are married. I spoke the ritual words to bind us.

"Let me see your ring," Lea said, by way of forgiving her.

Zacarias frowned. Marguarita had done nothing wrong, and Lea's magnanimous tone bothered him. Before he could react, Marguarita laid her hand very gently on his wrist in warning.

It's a human thing. Please let it pass.

He didn't fully understand, but then it didn't matter, not when he could do something so simple for her. He would demand much of her and small things that meant a great deal to her—as this obviously did—was easy enough to give her.

Marguarita slid her hand across the table to show Lea her ring. It was actually braided gold, Renaissance antique, wound in several braids and forged together. Intricate, when one looked closely, there were ancient words in a beautiful scroll wrought into the gold.

Marguarita rubbed her finger over the letters. *Sívamet andam. Sielamet andam.*

"What does it say?" Julio asked, frowning at the unfamiliar words.

"I give you my heart. I give you my soul," Zacarias translated. "I have done so, and once given, a De La Cruz doesn't ever take them back. Both belong to Marguarita and are forever in her care."

Lea made some kind of noise of approval, beaming at him.

"Congratulations, *señor*." Julio made an effort to look Zacarias straight in the eyes, but couldn't hold his gaze, looking at the ring instead. "Marguarita is very beloved on the ranch. Do you plan on taking her away from us?" Julio demanded.

Zacarias felt the shock spread through Marguarita. She hadn't considered that. What had she thought? That he would come and go as he always had? It mattered little. Where he went, Marguarita would be with him. She had given herself into his keeping—and keep her he would.

Marguarita pressed her lips together tightly, but he felt her fear shimmering in his mind. This was her home, her world. These people. The horses. The ranch. He wasn't attached to anyone or anyplace nor could he imagine ever feeling that way. His gaze returned again and again to Marguarita. She was home to him and a part of him didn't want to compete with people, animals and places for her. He wanted to take her far from them all so she would always turn to him for her every need. He would be all things to her.

You are everything to me. There was calmness in her. Acceptance. Her spirit moved against his, a soft caressing brush that weakened him. *If you wish me to leave this place, I won't lie to you, Zacarias, it would be difficult and wrenching, but I would choose you over this place in a moment and I would not regret my decision.*

His heart hammered in his chest for a few beats before settling into a steady rhythm. There was truth in her quiet declaration. He was a man with no trust—and a centuries-old code of honor that had kept him alive but alone. She was changing all that. Her truth was becoming enough for him. *Why? Why are you so certain, Marguarita? I can be very rough.*

She reached for him, right there in front of the others, her heart in her eyes. *You need me, Zacarias. I see the real you, the one I love with all my heart. You can't see him without me.*

So she knew. He should have realized he couldn't hide the truth from her any more than he could hide his memories. Her fingers trailed over his face and he caught them, holding her hand to his heart.

Lea ducked her head, glancing at Julio. It wasn't that difficult to read the longing on her face. Zacarias forced a smile, hoping he looked friendly, not wolfish.

"Do you plan on staying in our little corner of the world, Lea? Marguarita enjoys the company and we intend to make this ranch our home base, although we will have to travel at times." He could give that much to Marguarita.

Lea put her teacup into the saucer and nodded. "I hope to. My brother plans to move on soon, but I've been making arrangements to stay. I like it here."

"You can't stay alone," Julio objected. "Your brother wouldn't leave you alone, would he? Who would protect you?"

Lea made a face. "I don't need protection. I'm a big girl." She sent Marguarita a small, apologetic smile. "I'm not married to one of the richest and most elusive men in the world."

"You're a woman," Julio muttered, his face darkening. "What kind of brother would leave you to fend for yourself?"

Lea's chin went up. She stared coolly at Julio over her teacup as she lifted it toward her mouth. Zacarias detected the slight trembling. It was so subtle he doubted if Julio noticed, but Lea Eldridge was a little more nervous of being on her own in a strange place than she let on.

"My brother doesn't enjoy it here, it's too remote for him. But I like it, and who knows, if your helicopter pilot doesn't show up, maybe I can have his job. I've already interviewed for it."

"Where is the helicopter pilot?" Zacarias asked before Julio could make another retort.

Julio sighed. He wiped his hand over his face and glanced anxiously at Marguarita. She pulled the notepad toward her, but once again Zacarias laid his hand over it.

"I am asking you, not Marguarita," he said quietly, once again a command in his voice.

"Charlie Diaz has a drinking problem, *señor.* He's good for months and then he falls again, goes off and stays drunk for three or four months before coming back."

Zacarias narrowed his eyes. "Knowing this, Cesaro kept him on? He is a danger to all of you. Ricco Cayo would have died without medical attention. Had Ms. Eldridge not been here to fly him to a hospital, we would have lost him." The censure in his low voice was as alarming as his ice-cold eyes.

15

Marguarita felt the tension rise in the kitchen. Zacarias looked more intimidating than ever. Lea moved a little closer to Julio and looked as if she might cry. The air in the room became very heavy. She threaded her fingers through Zacarias's and smiled at Julio in an attempt to ease the sudden tension.

What's wrong?

Zacarias's focused gaze continued to bore into Julio, demanding an answer.

Julio's face darkened. "My father and I have had many talks about Charlie and how best to handle his situation. We thought he would make it this time." He ran a hand through his hair. "No one's seen him for days."

"And neither you nor your father thought this might be something I should know?" Zacarias's voice was very quiet.

Not in front of Lea. Don't do this, Zacarias, Marguarita pleaded. Julio would be more embarrassed than ever to have his boss take him to task over something he knew was wrong in front of both Lea and Marguarita. *Julio is a proud man and very loyal to you . . .*

He is loyal to his fellow worker. And he endangers both of us.

Zacarias never took his predatory gaze from Julio's face, staring him directly in the eye, locked on, focused and very frightening. Marguarita felt her stomach begin to churn. She hadn't realized just how tense she was getting.

"Yes, *señor*, you should have been told. Charlie has a family, children. We hoped drying him out would work this time."

"He is a liability to everyone on this ranch. Cesaro should have known that."

Julio's face flushed nearly crimson. "He's aware of it."

"I want this man found and brought to me."

Lea cleared her throat. "My brother talked about a man named Charlie he met in a bar."

A chill went down Marguarita's spine. Her gaze jumped to Julio's. If Charlie was drinking heavily and he was talking to Lea's brother in the bar, had Esteban's friend been there as well—the one so interested in the De La Cruz family?

Connected so deeply with Zacarias, he couldn't fail to read her concern. His mind slid against hers in a brushing caress that shocked her. He didn't often show tenderness and the gesture felt just like that—tender and caring.

"Tell me about that conversation," Zacarias commanded, his voice a low velvet persuasion.

Marguarita recognized the buried compulsion. The Carpathian blood flowing in her veins heightened every sense and she knew immediately that Lea would be unable to resist that gentle push to obey Zacarias. She wasn't certain how she felt about the manipulation, but above all, she wanted Zacarias safe so she pressed her lips together to keep from protesting.

Lea rubbed her temples as if she had the beginnings of a headache. Marguarita actually felt the pressure slowly exerted on her. Zacarias was trying to be gentle, a concept new to him, she realized. Ordinarily he would have ripped the information from Lea's head and never looked back. His gentle touch was in deference to Marguarita.

She glanced at him. He looked so incredibly handsome and dangerous. It was no wonder both Julio and Lea were intimidated by him. Even trying to be friendly, Zacarias looked what he was and in total command. No one would ever fail to notice him.

He sent her a wave of reassurance, but kept his gaze on Lea, wanting her to remember details she probably didn't think were important.

"Esteban came in very late, about three in the morning, and he'd been drinking, more than I've ever seen him. He just doesn't do that. I had to help him into the house. He couldn't make it up the stairs to the porch. DS had just shoved him out of the car."

"You were waiting for your brother?" Zacarias asked.

Lea nodded. "I was worried."

She rubbed her temples again, and then twisted her fingers together anxiously. Julio reached up and covered her hands with his in a gesture of comfort. His eyes met Marguarita's. He knew exactly what Zacarias was doing and he was ashamed that he'd put Lea in such a position. Cesaro and Julio ran the ranch. The men and their conduct were their responsibility. Charlie had been a liability for a long time, but for his family's sake, they had kept him on.

"I sat outside on the porch steps waiting for him. Dan—DS—laughed when he pulled up the drive and saw me sitting there. I stood up and started for the car and DS leaned across the seat, pushed open the car door and shoved Esteban out onto the ground. I could hear him laughing and he looked right at me . . ." She trailed off, shivering.

More. Tell it all, Zacarias pushed relentlessly.

Marguarita couldn't help frowning at him. Lea was obviously scared of Esteban's friend. Anyone could see that. She started to reach for the notepad, frustrated that she couldn't find a way to comfort her friend. Very casually, Zacarias's hand got there before hers. He pocketed the notepad leaving Marguarita feeling cut off from the others in the room and a little hurt. The notepad was her only means of communication and Zacarias had just declared it off limits to her.

Lea cleared her throat and twisted her fingers to meet Julio's as if for strength. "DS sort of grabbed his crotch and yelled 'later' to me. He pushed out his tongue and made several suggestive gestures. I hesitated, not wanting to get too far from the house in case I had to run, but he drove off laughing."

Clearly she's humiliated for having to tell us this, stop now.

Zacarias shot her a warning glance. His eyes focused for a moment on her. There was no ruby red indication that the predator was riding him hard. There was no midnight sapphire their lovemaking brought out, there were only hard black diamonds glittering at her. A chill went down her spine. She didn't understand the driving need in him to interrogate Lea, but nothing was going to stop him, certainly not Marguarita.

She tried not to feel hurt. She didn't understand him yet. He had never answered to anyone and he believed she should trust him and follow him in all things, but he didn't understand the rules of polite society and how what he was doing could hurt Lea and Julio. She feared they would never be comfortable looking at one another again if he continued to force things from Lea. In the end, Julio would forever be upset and distrusting of Zacarias and it would color her relationship with him.

Marguarita looked into her teacup. She didn't really feel like drinking tea when she'd always loved it. Nothing tempted her, other than water the last few days. She was losing her world and going into his, little by little. She had made that choice, but she wasn't quite prepared to give up everything she loved so fast.

"My brother was on the ground, facedown in the dirt. I could hear him laughing and it really upset me. I'm pretty certain he didn't see DS, and he probably didn't hear him, but I didn't like him laughing, not when I'd been so scared," Lea admitted.

Julio shifted his body toward her. "Of course you were scared. Who is this man, DS?"

Lea shook her head. "Don't go near him, Julio. He's bad news. Ever since my brother met him, we've had nothing but trouble. He persuades Esteban to do things that are wrong." She ducked her head, avoiding eye contact. "I've barely managed to keep Esteban out of jail more than once."

"That night," Zacarias prompted, keeping her on track. His voice was pitched very low, a velvet persuasion no one could resist.

"I helped Esteban into the house. He was really drunk and he kept talking about Charlie and how DS had recruited him. He bought him drinks all night. Esteban bragged how he kept up with Charlie who was knocking them back. He kept talking crazy, making no sense at all. They played some crazy game. A shot for truth or a dare."

"What do you mean, he talked crazy?"

Marguarita's mouth went dry. Suddenly her heart began to pound. She was very, very afraid. It was the purr of Zacarias's voice, a stirring of a dangerous predator, one who clearly had caught the scent of prey and was locked on.

Drink your tea, mića emni kuŋenak minan—my beautiful lunatic. Allow your heart to follow the rhythm of mine. Zacarias shifted slightly, the movement subtle and probably impossible for any other to track, but his body was closer to hers, his heat seeping into the cold of her skin. *There is no need to be afraid. Your friend is safe from me. There is no evil in her.*

"Crazy things." Lea rubbed her temples again. "Staking vampires. He kept calling himself Van Helsing. It's a name from the book *Dracula*. He said he was going on a hunt. That he needed a stake and garlic. And then he'd laugh like a maniac and tell me to make necklaces of garlic." She covered her face with her hands, shaking her head. "The next morning he acted like he didn't remember anything at all, but then he told me not to tell DS that he'd said anything about vampires and garlic and stakes, so I knew he was lying to me again." She looked at Julio a little pleadingly. "Honestly, insanity doesn't run in our family. He was drunk. I have no idea what he's into, but Esteban likes the idea of secret societies and gangsters. He's very susceptible to bad influences."

"What did Charlie tell them?" Zacarias persisted.

Marguarita felt tears burning in her eyes. The penalty for betrayal was death. Everyone knew that. You could ask to leave and memories could be removed, but if you were part of the families serving the De La Cruz for generations, the barrier in the mind, the shield protecting the brain from invasion was present at birth and removal was a difficult thing to endure. Charlie had talked in his drunken state to Esteban and his friend DS.

Lea frowned and this time rubbed at the little lines on her forehead as if that would help her remember. Power stirred in the room. It was so strong, Marguarita was shocked that neither Julio nor Lea seemed to notice the crackle of energy in the air.

"Esteban said Charlie drew maps to the sleeping chambers and it would be easy to stake the vamps during the day because they wouldn't be able to move." She blinked rapidly and looked around the table, embarrassed. "He was really drunk and he wasn't making sense."

Again Marguarita felt Zacarias probing Lea to insure she was an innocent and not probing for more information. She didn't believe in vampires and thought DS and her brother had likely taken drugs along with their drinking. She was certain Charlie was having drunken hallucinations. She was very humiliated and didn't understand why she couldn't quit talking about a subject very painful to her. She wanted to go home and pull the covers over her head.

"Thank you, Lea," Zacarias said quietly. "I know that was difficult. Charlie is responsible for the lives of his coworkers and we needed to know how ill he really is."

Marguarita drew in her breath. She heard the soft note of a sentence pronounced. Charlie was likable when he wasn't drinking, but how did one tell a man like Zacarias that? Zacarias had lived centuries in a stark, lonely unbearable existence, but with honor, never breaking his code. He wouldn't understand weakness. In his world, the weak didn't survive.

Zacarias suddenly reached out and wrapped his arm around her, bringing her into him, under the protection of his shoulder. His chair was beside hers that fast, with no one the wiser that he had moved again to cover the short distance between them.

My world is difficult for you. I am sorry, Marguarita. You should not have to know these things. I cannot keep them from you. Charlie gave my family up to this man. He talked of our sleeping chambers and revealed locations at several of the ranches. I will make certain before I destroy him, but he has put my entire family—and you—in danger. I will not permit that. He cannot be trusted.

She knew that. She knew that a few of the members of the main families—Chevez, Santos, Fernandez and Diaz—all knew that the sleeping chambers lay beneath various rooms in the ranches. They were used only when the De La Cruz family kept up appearances of being human and living in human society. Zacarias was the one member of the family that rarely showed himself at any of the ranches, yet if Charlie had given any forbidden details—and it sounded suspiciously as if he had—Zacarias would be in danger because of her. He was only staying at the hacienda because she was there.

You have to go, Zacarias. It will be safer for you.

She could feel her eyes burn. He wouldn't listen to her. She knew he wouldn't leave. He would hunt his enemies. She tried again.

You already have vampires hunting you.

Very gently now, knowing Lea was pushed close to her limit, Zacarias murmured softly into her mind. *Tell me what else your brother and DS have discussed.*

Lea pressed her fingers to her mouth, guarding a secret. She looked at Marguarita guiltily. Ashamed.

Marguarita could feel triumph rising in Zacarias. He didn't feel it, he only kept pressing Lea, peeling back the layers until he found the secret she guarded so carefully.

"I'm sorry, Marguarita. Esteban made us come here because of you. It wasn't just because this hacienda is owned by the De La Cruz family. I feel like such a fraud. According to my brother, there is a worldwide agency called the Morrison Agency, or something like that . . ."

Marguarita's heart jumped. She pressed her hand tight over her mouth. *My father heard of such a place several months ago. They test for psychic ability. He thought my gift with horses was a psychic talent.*

He was correct. Did they test you?

I filled out their questionnaire but I never did their follow-up because my father died and I . . . Marguarita touched her scarred throat. *I lost my voice and how could I explain it anyway? You have to feel the connection. There is no other way.*

"We know of the agency," Zacarias said. "Marguarita did initially begin the interview process, but went no further than filling out a questionnaire. What did that matter to your brother?"

Marguarita realized that by Zacarias answering for both of them, he appeared to know all about her, as if she'd shared all the details of her life with him.

Lea looked confused. "I'm not certain exactly, but it is the reason we chose this remote area. Esteban was avoiding the law, but I'd never really heard of this place. I overheard him on the phone talking about Marguarita and this Morrison Agency and he agreed with whoever he was talking to . . ."

"Was it this DS character?" Julio demanded.

She nodded. "I think. They thought it likely that if Marguarita did have a psychic talent then the chances of a De La Cruz showing up was much higher than on any of their other properties. Esteban was to come out first and strike up a friendship with her."

"So you weren't really friends with her." Julio's voice turned hard. He glared at Lea.

Tears immediately sprang to her eyes. "That's not true." Lea reached out for Marguarita imploringly. "I swear to you, the friendship between us is real. I felt at home here. For the first time in a very long while, I was happy."

Marguarita took her hands, her gaze flicking to Zacarias. *I don't have my notepad. Please assure her we're good, that I understand and am her friend.*

Zacarias smiled at Lea, a mere baring of his teeth that was obviously supposed to serve as a smile. "Marguarita knows your friendship is real. Have no worries." He pushed a small compulsion at the woman.

I don't understand what Esteban would want with me just because I filled out a questionnaire. What does this mean?

I will explain later.

"It sounded so silly to me," Lea continued. "I knew you were good with horses, but really, psychic? I didn't care why we came, just that we had. Even Esteban seemed happy for a while—until DS showed up. It doesn't take long before he ruins everything. Now our house is just plain scary."

"You shouldn't go back to that house," Julio told Lea. He glanced at Marguarita, pointedly prompting her to invite Lea to stay.

"You are welcome to stay, Lea," Zacarias said for both of them, surprising Marguarita. He brought her hand up to his mouth and brushed his lips lightly over her knuckles. *She will not stay here. She still believes she can save her brother.*

But you don't think she can?

I am sorry, sívamet. He is too far gone.

You don't know that. But he did. Zacarias had been in the world too long. He had seen too many friends, family members, humans fall. She saw it all in his mind. She felt his terrible sorrow like a weight pressing on his chest, on his heart—yet he refused to acknowledge it.

She closed her eyes, allowing herself to take it on, that weight that never left him. What would it be like to spend her days hunting people who had meant something to him at one time? Having to kill the people that had mattered? To know you could never make a friend, trust anyone, love anyone or be loved? She wanted to understand him and it was here, in this sorrow, in the memories he refused to acknowledge she would find her courage to stand with this man.

"Take me home, Julio," Lea said. "It's very late and I need to sleep. I'm glad Ricco is going to be all right."

Marguarita signed thank you and blew her a kiss.

Julio rose with her. "Thank you for the tea, Marguarita."

Zacarias kept his hand on Marguarita's shoulder as he rose, too. "I will see you out." *I have to remove her memories of the conversation with us about Diaz. It could put her in danger.*

She was surprised that he had added the last after a brief hesitation. In his memories, she had never found an instance where he explained himself to anyone.

I am a fast learner. You need reassurance that your friend will be all right.

She felt as if he'd wrapped her in a protective cloak of warmth—more than warmth—he surrounded her with protection and filled her mind with love. She hugged herself, trying not to smile. She wasn't even certain if he knew what he was feeling toward her, but she knew and, right then, when she felt a little out of her depth, she needed him just the way he was.

Marguarita collected the cups and dessert plates and took them to the sink to wash up. Looking at the crumbs made her think of hunger, but she didn't feel it. The thought of eating anything was disturbing. She drank water, hoping that would assuage her growing thirst. There was a strange throbbing in her veins, a beat that refused to go away, a soft insistent call that steadily grew stronger. A need. A longing. A hunger.

The entire time she'd spent with Lea and Julio, she'd been uneasy and had convinced herself it was because of Zacarias, afraid of what he might say or do. But here, alone in the kitchen, with no one to witness, she could admit to herself, it was the call of their hearts, the steady ebb and flow of the blood in their veins. She could hear it, and although she'd turned the volume down as Zacarias had helped her learn to do, she found the temptation beating in her own veins—beating in Zacarias's veins, in his mind and heart.

It would never stop, not as long as her mind was immersed in Zacarias—as long as he filled her up in the way she filled him. The hunger didn't stop for Zacarias, not when he could hear the drumming call of a pulse, not when he could smell the rich scent of fresh blood. That was his world and one she had to become accustomed to.

When she was alone, trying to analyze how she felt about taking blood, the human in her was frightened and even utterly repulsed. Strangely, after first being terrified, Zacarias had somehow turned the act of giving or receiving blood into something natural and even beautiful, a sharing of the very essence of life as long as he was with her.

Marguarita knew the exact moment Zacarias entered the room. He moved in utter silence, but she was immediately aware of him, every one of her senses springing to life. Her body sang. Her heart fluttered and a million butterflies took wing in her stomach.

He came up behind her, so close she felt his heat, the warmth of his breath on the back of her neck where he swept her hair out of the way and bent to brush his lips over her skin. A whisper of a caress, and yet she shivered in reaction, her blood turning warm—her body welcoming.

"I know that was difficult for you as well as for your friend, and I am truly sorry."

She turned around. He didn't step back. She was pinned between the sink and his body. Tilting her head, her gaze found his. She smiled at him.

Did you know that when we are alone and you're looking at me like that, your eyes are a deep, dark sapphire, like the blue in the midnight sky?

He kissed the tip of her nose. "If that is true, you are the only one who sees my eyes in color. I have only seen them dark, like the shadow of death."

She circled his neck with her arms, linking her fingers at his nape as she leaned into him. *I assure you, they are a beautiful blue when you look at me that way.*

"What way is that?"

With caring. She couldn't bring herself to say love, but it felt like love.

He caught her chin so she couldn't look away from him. "Will it feel like love when I take you away from everything you know? Everyone you love?"

It was never your decision, Zacarias. It was mine. I insisted you live. I asked you to stay for me. I chose you. I will always choose you.

His eyes stared into hers. All midnight blue. So beautiful her heart fluttered.

"You humble me."

Because I am human and female does not make me stupid. I thought this through from every angle. I didn't just jump into it with both feet. I had all night just to think. I know it will be difficult for us to merge our two worlds. I know sometimes it will be wrenching. But Zacarias, you told me you would make me happy. You vowed that you would and I believe you. I absolutely believe you will.

"I will rule you." He said it starkly, shadows sliding into the blue of his eyes.

Hopefully you will choose to do so with love. I can't imagine being happy and feeling cherished if you are not thinking of what pleases me. Life is filled with choices, Zacarias. I choose you and I choose to be happy. When the earth is shaking and I'm terrified, I plan on holding on very tight.

A slow smile softened the hard edge to his mouth. "I will expect you to keep your word. Do not ever keep your fear or your anger from me. I want all of you."

Laughter spilled into his mind. *Ask Julio and Cesaro before you ask for that. I have a very bad temper. It doesn't happen often, but I'm not reasonable when someone is silly enough to push me too far over the edge.*

Zacarias looked down into those melting-chocolate eyes and knew he was lost. He was not a man who trusted, yet he trusted her word. She would stand with him. He took her hand and tugged, leading her through to the main room of the house.

"I want you to come with me, Marguarita. I want to show you our world." He smiled down at her, his eyes more blue than ever. "With you, I will be seeing it for the first time."

She sketched a question mark.

"In color. You will provide the colors and emotion. I have never seen the night and the moon and rain forest in vibrant color." It seemed a miracle that she could do that for him. Just being with her gave him a different world altogether.

He'd lived in a kind of void. A hell that was stark and barren and very ugly. The rich colors and even the emotions—both bad and good—made everything a kind of miracle.

She had given him such a gift, allowing him to ride a horse with her, exploring the ranch, flowing over the ground, one with the animal, and he could give her this. He hoped to woo her a little, court her, show her he had something to give as well.

It's close to dawn, Zacarias, she reminded gently.

What I wish to show you requires the dawn.

The night was his, what little was left of it. His world. His domain. It mattered little that for centuries it had been a hell. She was with him now. Marguarita. The flip side of hell was paradise and he would take her there, find it with her, experience it with her. *Through* her.

Marguarita didn't hesitate. She tightened her fingers in his and reminded him gently. *I'm not wearing any underwear. Will I need different clothing?*

He groaned. He'd been steadily ignoring the temptation of her body. He wanted to spend time with her, give her something besides his continual hunger.

"I will keep you warm." His gaze drifted possessively down her body. He loved her hourglass figure, all those lush curves just for him. "You are a beautiful woman."

She blushed, glowed. Her smile was a bit like the moon rising and the stars joining in. He went out the door before he lost his control and they didn't make it out of the house. She seemed to have that effect on him.

He wrapped his arm around her waist and took to the sky. She gasped and clung. He laughed softly and buried his face in all that hair. Silken strands were everywhere. She tried to tame it by tightly holding the arm locking her to him and reaching cautiously with her other hand to bunch the mass into a thick twisting knot held to the nape of her neck.

"You have to actually open your eyes to appreciate this," he whispered.

Joy burst through him. Fireworks. Vibrant colors. Speeding light zipping across the heavens. A glittering wonderland spread out below him and Marguarita was in his mind, sharing it all with him. She was more than a miracle, she was a little piece of heaven. What would it matter if he had seen this without her? It would have meant nothing at all. Now . . . his rain forest . . . his country—was everything, because she was there.

He felt her fingers dig into his arm. He bent his head to put his mouth against her ear, although he didn't use words. He wanted the more intimate form of communication. He felt every breath she took. Felt every beat of her heat. *Show me your trust, mića emni kuŋenak minan.*

Her breath hissed out, although he felt laughter, nervousness and excitement at the same time, filling his mind. *You just called me a lunatic again, didn't you?*

Well, he teased, *you are flying through the air above the canopy of the rain forest with me. You have to be a bit of a lunatic to do that. I did call you beautiful though. And mine. Does that make up for it?*

She opened her eyes. Below her was every shade of green on the color spectrum, with the bright silvery light of the moon spilling over the canopy. Instead of looking up at it from the forest floor, she was looking down at it. A breathless sigh of wonder filled his mind. He dropped down fast, taking her through the branches, to show her the spectacular find he'd run across years earlier.

Few people, if any, have ever seen this sight. I have come here once a year to see these macaws. In the early morning they flock together for their morning meeting, stirring just before dawn. I found a small cave near this spot and hollowed out a chamber, just so I could see them take flight.

He felt the wonder of that sight from so long ago, and knew now why he had returned year after year to make certain the flock was still there. He hadn't felt the rush back then, but he felt it now, the beauty and majesty of the large birds all roosting in the hollows of the grove of trees. There were so many, great imposing birds.

He had always felt at home in the rain forest and had felt more of a kinship with the animals than he had with people populating the world.

Like me, Marguarita confirmed. *That's why we connected so quickly and deeply, Zacarias, we both have a kinship with animals.*

The impression of her soft laughter teased his mind. *Of course you're more like a great jungle cat, all teeth and claws, and I'm more like the hummingbirds buzzing around the flowers.*

She looked up at him, her eyes bright with joy, with the thrill of what he was sharing with her. Deliberately he showed his teeth, baring them at her much like a wild animal. More laughter spilled into his mind. All that warm honeyed molasses poured through him, a kind of molten gold, filling the cracks and spaces and driving away more of the shadows.

His arm tightened around her. How had he gone from being completely alone to being completely filled by a woman? A human woman at that?

More laughter spilled brightness through him. *A lunatic of a woman.*

My lunatic, he agreed, finding himself smiling.

She had changed the world. Brought him to life. Brought the world around him to life. He couldn't resist teasing her. *You do know that hummingbirds fight all the time. They are vicious little creatures.*

Perhaps that's why I have such an affinity for you.

He laughed out loud. The sound startled him—pleased him. He had heard the word *fun*, but didn't really understand the concept until that very minute. Sharing with Marguarita was fun.

Are you cold? Had he detected a little shiver?

You're keeping me very warm, thank you. I'm just excited. It's so beautiful, Zacarias. I've seen macaws, but not so many poking their heads out of the hollows in the trees.

Everywhere she looked, curious heads in pairs looked up at her from hollowed-out holes in the trees where they roosted.

A normal flock of macaws, depending on the species, runs around thirty or so. They all hang out in the morning together. The wingspans are a good three feet, nothing like the harpy eagle, but when they all take to the air, it is a sight unlike any other. In a few moments you'll witness their flight.

He felt her excitement, flowing through her, flowing through him. She had awoken him after centuries of darkness. A part of him would always worry just what she'd managed to awaken. His feelings for her were too intense and too mixed to take out and examine.

Then don't. Let it be, Zacarias. This early morning in the rain forest is glorious. The moon spilling her light over us, the macaws waking and spreading their wings, all blues and golds and scarlet. It's amazing and you've given this to me. I love it.

He looked down at the riot of color, all the shimmering feathers as the macaws slowly stretched and preened, getting ready for their early morning meeting as the moon descended and the sun rose.

How did you get to be so wise?

Women are very wise, Zacarias. You should listen to them more often.

He gave a derisive snort and felt her laughter pour into his mind. She flooded him with happiness. She tightened her fingers around his wrist, her body vibrating with excitement as the birds fluttered wings and, almost as one body, took to the air. Beams of light spilled through the trees, hitting the vibrant colors on the shimmering, iridescent feathers. The colors nearly blinded him, so vivid and intense, making him a little dizzy. He had seen the sight before, but not in living color. Not like this. And not with her.

Marguarita. He breathed her name, a soft whisper on the wind, carrying through the rain forest to the macaws.

The large birds wheeled in the air, a graceful display of living fireworks, a spectacular demonstration of nature at her most beautiful.

Zacarias could barely breathe with the emotions rising like a tidal wave. For her. For Marguarita. He had brought her to this special place to share this very moment. A gift for her, yet in the end, the gift had been from her. The colors. The intensity. The sheer *feeling.*

I need to be inside of you. Right now. Like this.

In the air, in the rain forest, out in the open where he belonged—just at that moment where night turned into day and his heart beat in both places.

Now I know why you forgot my underwear.

She stroked him with love, deep inside his mind, soft caresses that burned through skin and bone, branded him somewhere he thought long gone. She broke him open and poured herself inside of him, filling him up with her light.

She turned, there in his arms, and he stripped them both of clothes, so that it was her skin sliding against his, all warm and soft and lush, her body already ripe for him. He bent his head to find her mouth while she wound one leg around his waist, pressing her inviting entrance tight against him. She tasted of innocence and sin. He bunched her hair in his hand and pulled her head back so he could kiss her again and again, his tongue exploring all that sexy heat.

Her hips rocked invitingly against his. He marveled that she didn't hesitate, didn't deny him anything, not even when she was poised thirty feet in the air with a carpet of macaws spread below them and the branches around them filling with monkeys. She kissed him back, seemingly oblivious to anything but him. Trusting him, giving herself to him without reservation.

He had to let go of her hair to lift her other leg around him. She levered herself up, using her hands on his shoulders, sliding her scorching hot body over his belly to position herself right over the smooth head of his cock. He closed his eyes, savoring the exquisite feeling as she slowly impaled herself, sliding down in an excruciatingly gradual motion, taking his breath with her little circles and the way her tight body reluctantly gave way, stretching around the thick length of him.

She threw her head back and began a slow ride designed to drive him insane. Her muscles gripped and stroked, the friction building like a slow fire when the fierce heat was already surrounding him. She felt velvet soft, moist and tight. Too tight. Strangling him. Sending bolts of lightning streaking through his body. His every nerve ending felt even the tiniest movement she made as she rose up, her body sliding over his, fitting like a glove, a second skin, and then sinking back over him, taking him deep inside her.

Her hair blew around them, cloaking them one moment and sliding away the next to reveal their bodies intertwined. He let her set the pace, watching every expression on her face, her eyes, the happiness, the pleasure, the lust, but mostly, he found himself looking for the love. It was there in her melting eyes. In the way she touched him. In the way she moved, that slow, spiraling lazy ride, as if she wanted to enjoy every last moment with him, wring it out to forever. She savored him.

He realized she had opened the dam of his emotions, and for her, every feeling was more intense, more *everything*. His world centered around her. This world. The one with color. With emotion. With love.

With me. This is the real world, Zacarias. When you're with me. Live here with me. When you go to the other one, you're just hunting in it. But live here with me.

Her hands smoothed his skin, her lips suddenly brushed his shoulder and retreated again as she let her head fall back and her eyes meet his.

Always, avio päläfertiilam—my lifemate. I will always live with you. There is no other way. He took the control back, surging into her over and over, each stroke deep and long and each one telling her what she was to him. He drove her up high and as he tipped her over the edge, she took him with her. They soared across the sky, a dizzying ride, locked together, racing the sun as they made their way home.

16

The thudding was persistent, a drumming annoyance that intruded on her dreams. No matter how many times Marguarita dragged the pillow over her head, pressing it to her ears, the pounding not only continued, but became louder and much more demanding. She wanted desperately to sleep. She was so tired she couldn't find the energy to move. Her arms and legs felt like lead. Even her eyelids didn't want to cooperate.

She lay for a long moment, listening to her heartbeat. The sound was loud, echoing through her head. She could hear the rush of the blood in her veins, and the sounds of insects outside the house in the fields. Through it all was the persistent knocking. Whoever it was at her front door was not going away anytime soon—unless she was having a bizarre nightmare.

The thought of a nightmare didn't alarm her, but the idea that the noises she was hearing so easily were *outside* the walls of the house did. Zacarias had explained, but if she listened, she could hear the murmur of the cattle and they were more than a mile from the house. Coming from the stable was the stamp of horses and even the conversation of two of the men working there. One was very concerned about Ricco.

A strange yelp and more banging on the door convinced her she needed to get up. Experimenting, she tried to lift one arm. She managed about an inch before, sighing, she let it fall onto the mattress. It took some effort, but she rolled over to stare at her ceiling fan slowly turning over her head. More banging on the door and her sluggish mind began to function faster. What if something had happened to Ricco? Maybe that was the reason the workers were discussing him. She should have eavesdropped instead of retreating like a scared baby.

What have you done to me?

Zacarias was deep in the ground far beyond the everyday running of a ranch, while she was at everyone's beck and call. It was well and good to give orders, to demand she stay indoors, try to force her to sleep during the day, but there was work to be done and the ranch was used to her taking part—a big part.

Determined now, Marguarita forced her reluctant body into a sitting position. Light spilled through the small crack in the drapes at her window hitting across her face like a slap. Her eyes burned, an instant painful searing that made her stomach churn ominously and brought tears streaming down her face.

Throwing up her arm to protect her eyes, she slipped from the bed, her legs and body trembling with the effort to find her bones. She wanted to slide to the ground. It took more effort to throw cold water on her face and neck, rinsing her eyes, but she felt much better afterward. Still sluggish, her brain and body tuned to another world, but at least she could drag on her clothes without falling on her face.

Her hair was a wild mess and she did her best to tame it as she hurried through the house on bare feet to get to the front door. The problem with Zacarias's precise instructions regarding the safeguards on the house was, as she had no voice, she couldn't call out to ask who was outside, therefore she had to open the door to see who was there. She tried to peek through the window, but the sun nearly blinded her.

Sun scorch you right back, man of mine, she declared vehemently in her head, a kind of sick amusement creeping in. Where was the man when she was left to deal with the problems he created? She was going to ask him that as soon as sleeping beauty woke up.

Cautiously she cracked the door open. Lea stood outside, her face swollen, one eye closed, the other drooping, her lip cracked and bloody. Tears streamed down her face. She shook her head when Marguarita yanked the door open and reached for her. Pressing her hands to her mouth, she sobbed.

Marguarita caught her arm. The light was so blinding, her sensitive eyes going as red as Lea's, burning and tearing the moment the sun hit them. Even her skin prickled, as if shrinking away from the light. She stepped back instinctively, drawing Lea with her. Lea made a sound, halfway between a groan and a sobbing scream. Behind her, a man loomed, his face a triumphant sneer, and he slammed his hand hard into Lea's back, forcing her forward into the house, propelling her into Marguarita. The two women tumbled to the ground, a tangle of arms and legs, Lea pinning Marguarita to the floor.

The stranger leaped through the door. "Hurry, hurry," he called to Esteban. His face was twisted into a demonic mask, eyes darting around him in a kind of rolling terror even as he leaped over the two women on the floor and whirled around in an effort to see the entire interior at once. Esteban rushed through after him, slamming the door closed and locking it.

A foul odor permeated the air the moment the two men entered. A mixture of heavy garlic, fear and drugs oozed from their pores, nearly gagging Marguarita.

The stranger reached down and caught Lea by her blond hair and yanked. Lea grabbed his wrists in an effort to relieve the pressure on her scalp, struggling to stand, glaring at her brother, anger mixed with fear.

"Get up, bitch," the stranger snapped.

Marguarita assumed she was the bitch, considering Lea was already on her feet. Calm settled over her. There could be only one reason these men were here. Esteban carried a satchel, and it was heavy. Charlie Diaz, in his drunken state, had betrayed the De La Cruz family, and by the silly necklace of garlic hanging around Esteban's neck and the foul garlicky odor pouring off of the stranger, they were planning to kill Zacarias. It was up to her to prevent these men from getting to his resting place.

She took her time, feigning pain as she struggled to her feet. There was a panic button a few feet from her, positioned near the door. If she hit that, her men would come running, armed to the teeth, but they couldn't get in if she didn't open the door to them. Swallowing hard—and it wasn't that difficult to look frightened—she stood, swaying a little, one hand going to her scarred throat, the other searching for the wall as if to hold her up.

Zacarias. Can you hear me? We're in trouble. You have to wake up and hear me.

The panic button was several feet from her, but at least she had her hand on the wall and they were all buying her fear. Now that they were in the house, they were a little less agitated and a little more cocky.

DS threw Lea against the wall beside Marguarita and swaggered over to stand in front of them, so close his garlicky breath blasted their faces in hot, foul puffs as he spoke. He deliberately invaded their space as a terror tactic. Marguarita found, after facing a vampire and Zacarias, DS just didn't scare her as much as she thought he might. The realization that these men couldn't hold a candle to the dangerous beings she had dealt with took her fear down another notch, allowing her to keep her breathing even and steady. Her heart stopped pounding and her mind settled into a quiet, logical machine, working on finding a solution and a backup plan to her present predicament.

Zacarias. She tried again, this time allowing that part of her that sent her spirit soaring free to find him. He came into her fast, a melding of their spirits, strength and courage and total reassurance. There was no panic in him, no thought but destroying the danger to her. He had no thought of himself—only her.

Marguarita hugged that knowledge to herself and it bolstered her courage even more. She wasn't alone trying to control an impossible situation.

I need you to get rid of the safeguards at the doors or windows so Cesaro and the others can come inside. Is that possible?

She tried not to overreact as she shoved her hand into her pocket and pulled out her notepad and pen. Hastily, and in what she hoped was a trembling hand, she scribbled her question.

Who are you? What do you want?

"You know," DS snapped. "You're hiding him. We know he's here."

Lea moistened her swollen lips. "DS thinks Zacarias is a vampire. He plans to kill him."

Marguarita frowned, her eyebrows drawing together in puzzlement.

She scribbled more on the notepad, taking her time, letting Zacarias assess his enemies through her.

He is gone. He left late last night. They never stay long.

DS slapped her hard, so hard the back of her head connected with the wall. The speed was so shocking and the strike so unexpected, Marguarita found herself disoriented for a moment. Beneath her feet, a wave raised the floor. The walls trembled.

"Don't you lie to me, you bitch. You're his guardian. I know he's here and you'll lead us to his resting place."

Call to Julio, Zacarias, and allow the men entry. Marguarita did her best to get the entreaty across to him. She was shaken at the savagery of DS's reaction and his apparent fanaticism.

Esteban giggled, a high-pitched, almost hysterical sound. He didn't necessarily believe in vampires, that much was apparent to her, but DS provided his drugs and an unusual, adrenaline-filled lifestyle. He craved the power DS had, and needed the association, feeling like he was in the inner circle. Marguarita wasn't entirely certain the assessment was hers or Zacarias's.

I am very weak, sívamet. I will strike when I can kill them. I could alert Julio and Cesaro, but they will have to unravel the safeguards and it is very dangerous. If I aid them, I may not have the strength to strike when needed. I am very close to the darkness, more so than most of my kind and the sun takes a toll on me that is not the same as others.

She couldn't hear any note of anxiety in his voice, just that matter-of-fact way that he spoke of everything, but she was locked to him tightly, feeling his emotions when even he couldn't, and his anxiety was all for her.

A Carpathian as close to the darkness as Zacarias suffered the leaden weight of the sun much more than others. The sun was at its highest point. DS had chosen his time well. He must have studied—and believed—all the vampire legends. She let her breath out slowly. Zacarias feared he would have only one chance to strike through her. As it was, *she* was holding the connection between them, not him. He wasn't wasting his energy when she was capable and that told her just how dire the consequence of the afternoon sun really was for him.

Marguarita made a show of pressing her pen to the paper again, taking her time, letting her hand shake, while her mind raced. There was not going to be the opportunity to stall these men until sunset. They were as aware as her just what position the sun was in. She was going to have to keep them away from Zacarias. Charlie had betrayed him, but evidently they didn't know Zacarias's exact location. She could well imagine. Only those serving inside the house knew where the sleeping chambers were located.

I am telling the truth. Señor De La Cruz left late last night to go to one of his other residences. He does not stay in one place long. She knew that would have a ring of truth. Charlie had to have told them that, which was why they hadn't waited. It was obvious Lea had been brutally beaten and yet she hadn't given up Marguarita.

Remembering the ring and the words in the ancient tongue engraved in the antique gold, she plunged her left hand into her skirt pocket. She needed to remove the ring, but Zacarias, being who and what he was, had made it the exact size to snugly fit her finger. It would take a few tugs to slip it off.

Can you do that for me?

She felt his hesitation. He didn't want to waste the energy.

I can stall them for a time to give you time to recoup. It will give me a small chance to convince them you aren't here.

She already knew they weren't going to take her word for it and eventually, after a show of being beaten, she would have to give up some location for them to dig in. If they had any brains, they'd look at her throat and know she would *never* give up his location no matter what they did to her.

Yes, you will. I will not allow them to put another hand on you. Tell them.

Like hell, I'll tell them.

His heart jerked. She felt it. That quiet smoldering rage that built like a volcano beneath the earth. *You will obey me in this.*

Actually, no, I don't think I will. I can handle them. If we get that far, you can destroy them, but I have weapons all over the house. I just need to get a chance at them.

I forbid this.

Forbid away. Did he really think she would give him up to these insane fanatics?

She handed the note to DS. He read it, cursed, crumpled it up and threw it in her face. His fist hit the wall beside her head.

She felt the ring loosen on her finger and slide off into her pocket. The relief was instantaneous. Zacarias might be angry with her, but he still reached out to protect her as best he could. Even that small push of energy drained him. She could feel his weakness—and his frustration. He remained alert, no longer arguing with her, reading her determination just as easily as she could read his anger and silent promise of retaliation. Strangely, that made her shiver, frightening her more than DS and Esteban. But not enough to allow them to get to Zacarias. She would take the consequences as long as she saved his life.

"Do you think I'm kidding around with you? I can hurt you like you've never been hurt."

Lea reached out and took Marguarita's hand in silent camaraderie. "I'm sorry. There was no real way to warn you."

"Shut up," DS snapped. He shoved Lea toward the large family room. "Get in there. Both of you."

Esteban snatched up the satchel and followed. His face beaded with sweat, the smell permeating the room making Marguarita want to gag. Both men were terrified, but so high and elated at the thought of driving a stake through Zacarias's heart that they couldn't stand still.

"Watch them," DS snapped.

He prowled through the house, inspecting every nook and cranny, paying attention to the floors, and closets, opening every door. Marguarita kept the house in perfect order. There were no marks on any of the floors indicating furniture had been moved, or trap doors were installed. The floorboards appeared seamless, even when DS moved throw rugs. She tried not to wince when she heard pottery smashing on the floor, or her dishes being thrown as his frustration and anger grew.

Her heart gave a little thud of protest when he stalked back into the room, fury on his face. His eyes locked onto hers as he marched toward her determinedly. Lea gave a small squeal of fear and moved closer to Marguarita as though she might protect her. Marguarita withdrew immediately from Zacarias, not wanting him to witness or feel what was coming. She heard the sharp echo of his protest, but she broke the contact off anyway.

He was already upset with her for not disclosing his location, so what did it really matter if she could spare him this?

His face was a twisted mask. "You will tell me what I want to know, you little demon bitch." Spittle flew from his mouth. His eyes were maniacal.

DS rained blows on Marguarita without mercy, her face, her stomach, every unprotected part of her body until she went to the floor and he kicked her repeatedly. Marguarita was grateful she couldn't scream. No sound emerged, no matter how much she cried out in pain. She did her best to cover her face and body while the blows continued, curling into the fetal position. The attack continued forever it seemed. She lost track of time, her mind a haze of pain.

"You're going to kill her," Esteban yelled, rushing DS.

"Good. The bitch deserves it." DS yanked his arm away from Esteban and delivered another hard kick to her hip.

"She doesn't know or she would have told you."

"She knows. They protect their masters. They're like dogs, guarding them, with no minds of their own." He continued to rain down punches and kicks, striking anywhere he could, legs, hips, arms and back, even her head.

Esteban grabbed DS again, pulling him away from her. "She won't be able to lead us to the resting place and no one else knows. By the time we tear up the floor, the sun will have set."

DS shoved Esteban away from him with enough force to send him staggering. DS wiped his hand over his face as if clearing his mind. The wild look in his eyes receded. He spit at Marguarita and paced across the floor. There was only the sound of his ragged breathing as he worked to get himself under control. Eventually he dug out a silver vial and dumped white powder on the small table in the corner of the room.

Esteban's eyes lit up. He started over but DS waved him away. "Watch them."

"They aren't going anywhere," Esteban whined. He licked his lips.

Lea slid down the wall, her movements very careful as she positioned herself beside Marguarita. She leaned toward Marguarita, placed her lips against her ear and whispered as softly as she could, "Are you okay?"

Marguarita couldn't catch her breath. There were so many places on her body that hurt and her ribs burned, robbing her of all air. Tears swam in her eyes, obscuring her vision, or maybe it was blood. She could taste it in her mouth. Her lip was swollen and painful. She curled a little tighter in response, praying DS would stay away from her.

Lea put her hand on Marguarita's arm in a gesture of comfort, tears streaming down her face. She looked pleadingly at her brother. His eyes were on the white powder DS was carefully chopping into straight lines on the table. He crept closer, licking his lips repeatedly, his hands shaking in excitement and need. Lea closed her eyes in disgust.

"DS, I need it, come on," Esteban pleaded, his voice shaking.

DS swung around, swearing. "You act like a bitch in heat, you want it so bad, crawl to me, on your hands and knees. Show your high and mighty sister what a bitch dog you are."

"Don't, Esteban," Lea pleaded in a whisper. "Look what he's doing to you."

Esteban didn't turn around. He had eyes for only the white powder. Deliberately, DS took his silver straw and sniffed an entire line up his nose. He threw his head back and howled, as if he was a wolf, howling at the moon. "Damn, that's good shit."

Esteban stumbled forward, and immediately DS's expression changed from rapture to pure contempt. He slapped Esteban and shoved him. "Get away from me, you bitch dog. You want it, you gotta earn it. Crawl across the room on your knees in front of your fuckin' sister."

A sob escaped Lea as Esteban slowly sank to his hands and knees and crawled in front of DS who watched with triumphant, gleaming eyes, his twisted face infused with glee. Laughing, he spat at Esteban, the spit hitting his cheek and slowly dribbling down to his chin.

DS kicked at him when Esteban tried to wipe his face clean. "Leave it. It may remind you who's in charge. Don't interfere again." He turned his back and sniffed another line of the powder.

Esteban crouched on the floor at his feet, looking at him with desperation. He made a single sound of pleading in the back of his throat and tried to slide up to DS.

"Get back. You haven't begged properly yet. Sit up and beg. Come on, little doggie. Sit up and wag your tail like a good little pet."

Marguarita shifted, the subtlest of movements. When she'd fallen, she made certain to fall near the end table where a knife was kept taped beneath the small drawer. She let her hand creep very slowly up the wood, not wanting to draw DS's attention. He was focused on tormenting Esteban and seemed, for the moment, to have forgotten her.

It hurt to move. Everything hurt, just the act of lifting her arm was painful, as if there were minor cracks in her bone. She was certain the damage was all severe bruising, but that small, subtle movement still sent white lightning streaking through her body.

Lea's eyelashes fluttered. She frowned at Marguarita and slowly shook her head, fearing repercussions, but, although she clearly didn't understand what Marguarita's hand was doing sliding so stealthily up the leg of the end table, she valiantly shifted her body just enough to block DS's view should he look. Her eyes went wide when Marguarita's fist came away from under the table with the knife. The blade was four inches long and honed to a razor-sharp edge, tucked inside a smooth leather sheath. Marguarita shoved the knife as deep into the pocket of her skirt as she possibly could.

Her eyes met Lea's. She supposed she looked as bad as her friend. She could tell her eye was swelling, and her mouth hurt. She touched her tongue to her split lip and winced. She had deliberately provoked DS. He would be suspicious if she suddenly gave up Zacarias without a fight. She needed to provide him with an authentic reason to be afraid. She figured if Lea could survive his beating, so could she. He'd been a little more enthusiastic than she'd counted on.

She felt the sudden stirring in her mind, a pouring of ice into her body. She shivered, but hastily reached out to meet Zacarias halfway, trying to take the burden of energy from him.

What are you doing? His voice was very calm—too calm. She felt the edge even though she couldn't hear it.

Dios. She had not expected him to connect with her so soon. She couldn't hide the pain of her bruises from him. He had to be feeling every blow to her body. Seeing inside him and feeling his emotions, she knew it was far worse for him to lie helpless beneath the ground while she was in danger. It was the worst possible situation for a dominant, protective male such as Zacarias. He was trapped. Their enemies had chosen the perfect time to strike, when his body was leaden and he was unable to do anything but stay connected to Marguarita as DS and Esteban did what they wanted to her.

I think the longer I can stall them, the closer we'll get to the sun setting and that will allow you much more strength. It was a logical plan, the best she had. Stall and stall again. Use everything she could think of. Turn them against one another. Whatever it took.

I have stated that I forbid this. I will not have you put yourself in harm's way. Lead them to me immediately.

Marguarita sighed. *You know I can't do that,* she said as gently as possible.

Zacarias didn't respond. She felt his smoldering rage, buried deep, threatening to erupt, but he didn't bother to argue. Like her, he was wound tight through her mind, and he could read her determination.

He didn't have to understand. Marguarita sighed again and tried not to let his disapproval hurt her. This was her decision to make—not his—her life to risk. There was no doubt in her mind that he would risk his life for hers without even considering any other alternative.

It is different. It is my right and duty to protect you.

She could almost see him snapping his teeth like a hungry wolf, impatient with what he considered her defiance. There was no reasoning with him. He was set in his way, certain he was right, and she wouldn't—*couldn't*—give in to him. He made her nervous with that quiet promise of retaliation she sensed, that absolute iron will she knew she wouldn't get around, but he had come up against that side of her that was just as determined and just as certain she was justified.

Zacarias, you were able to darken the sky and emerge before sunset to save Ricco. It was close, but it was still before you should have been able to do so. And when I found you that morning . . . She hated bringing that morning up. He had chosen an honorable death and she had interfered. He had been righteously angry with her. *You should have been dead already, completely incinerated, the sun had been out for a little while. I think you're more resistant to it than you believe. If I stall them and my plan doesn't work, and they get to your resting place, then you'll be that much stronger.*

I have forbidden you to endanger yourself.

She sighed. There was no getting through a brick wall. *We'll have to agree to disagree.*

As long as you understand all consequences are also your choice.

She shivered, blinking back tears when she made the mistake of biting down on her swollen lip. *You're making this worse for me.*

She needed him to retreat, to allow her to concentrate on misleading DS and Esteban. It took courage and Zacarias could sap her courage faster than anyone. Marguarita felt Zacarias's instant, instinctive rejection of her evaluation.

Lea gripped her wrist, distracting her. Her gaze jumped to Esteban as he went up on his knees, his arms curled in the classic begging position.

"Tongue out, faithful Fido," DS laughed. He went back a third time, taking most of the powder.

Esteban cried out and flung himself forward, shoving his face onto the table in desperation. A single sound emerged from Lea, a low keening moan. She buried her face in her hands, unable to watch her brother humiliate himself for the drug.

Marguarita pulled her notepad out of her other pocket and carefully scribbled a message to Lea. It could *not* fall into DS or Esteban's hands.

There is a panic button at the top of the stairs under the picture of my father. If you can open the front door, hit that button. All the men will come running. But they can't enter the house if the door isn't open.

Marguarita snuck a quick peek at DS, who was laughing hysterically at Esteban. She continued, writing as fast as she could, her body covering the movements.

You can't hit the button to call the men if you can't get the door open for them. Too dangerous.

She slid the paper across the floor faceup under Lea's hand, so she could read it. Lea peered through her fingers at the note. Her eyes went wide and she nodded. Before Marguarita could take back the paper, she crumbled it into her fist and brought it to her mouth. Marguarita smiled at her. They were locked forever in that moment of complete camaraderie and understanding. She could count on Lea. They were in it together. Live or die.

DS's maniacal laughter cut off abruptly. Marguarita felt every muscle tense as his gaze settled on the two women.

"What are you lying on the floor for? Get your asses up. If you want this bitch to live through the next five minutes, tell me where he is." He stalked across the room and dragged Lea to her feet, shoving his gun against her left eye.

Marguarita struggled to stand, making a show of pulling herself up the wall, gasping and clutching her ribs. She looked around her for help, and then caved when he pressed the muzzle tight against Lea's eye.

Marguarita indicated the kitchen with her chin, her gaze sliding away from his in a cowed manner. DS stepped close to her, catching her arm, jerking her close to him. The smell of the drug oozed from his pores making her want to gag. She cowered away from him, throwing up her other arm as a shield as if to protect her battered face.

He gripped her tighter, his fingers digging into her skin, wanting to leave bruises, wanting her to feel his strength. Realization of how gently Zacarias touched her flooded her mind, bringing her a warmth she hugged to herself. Zacarias's strength was ten times what this man's was, yet once he'd learned that humans were indeed quite different from Carpathians, his care of her had always been uppermost in his mind. Even when he was a little rough during sex, marking her body, he took the time to ease any soreness after he'd learned her body's responses.

DS was a man who enjoyed inflicting pain and humiliation on others. DS was the monster Zacarias thought himself to be. Zacarias would never prolong suffering for the sake of watching it. He dispensed justice. He eradicated evil, but he didn't enjoy his job. He simply did it to the best of his ability.

"Esteban, get your ass up off the floor."

For the first time, Marguarita allowed herself to look at Lea's brother. DS had knocked the remaining powder from the table onto the floor. Esteban was busily trying to get every speck. His face, when he looked up, was speckled with white. Her heart went out to Lea who made a soft sound of pain.

DS heard her and laughed, enjoying himself even more. "Yeah, Lea, look at him. Your big brother, that's all that matters to him. Not you. You follow him all around the world. You know what he does? He smuggles weapons for me. He traffics women. Children. Whatever I ask. He'd sell his soul for that drug. And this one . . ." He shook Marguarita like a rag doll. "She serves the devil. You really need to have better judgment."

Listen to his voice. He is very angry with her. He obviously belongs to the society that believes in vampires and has targeted my family for death, but there is much more to this.

Marguarita's heart jumped. She hadn't known Zacarias was still in her mind, quiet and careful, a presence watching, but she should have. Once she was in danger, whether she was holding the bridge between them or not, he wouldn't leave her alone. He was that kind of man. Her mind worked quickly to grasp what he was saying.

Lea was in desperate trouble, maybe more than Marguarita was. DS was fanatical about vampires, but this wasn't all about Zacarias. DS had sought out Esteban for a reason, had controlled him out of anger. This was about Lea.

He must have tried to make a move on her first, before all this. She has a natural ability to recognize evil. She probably is not aware of it, but she would definitely resist any advances, because her subconscious would protect her. He is drawn to light and innocence and needs to corrupt and destroy it. He wants her. You can use that. He will not want to kill her. Hurt her—yes—but not kill her.

Marguarita was appalled. *I am not going to put her in danger.*

There was a brief moment of warmth slipping through the ice in her mind. *Silly woman. You want her to run to the door and open it for Cesaro and his men. I am telling you he will not kill her. That should ease your mind, not make you feel guilty. You truly are a little illogical lunatic.*

She knew he was trying to distract her from fear. Fear paralyzed anyone, and with DS dragging her into the kitchen, her heart pounded, accelerating out of control. She could taste the coppery flavor of her own blood in her mouth. This plan had to work. Zacarias had made her feel a little better. At least he wasn't raging at her, making things worse.

She stumbled several times, each tiny delay a second she counted in Zacarias's favor. She pointed very reluctantly to the root cellar door with a trembling hand. The moment DS dropped her arm, she hastily pulled out her notepad.

He will kill me for such a betrayal.

DS wrenched the satchel from Esteban's hands. "He'll be dead when I drive a stake through his heart, cut off his head and fill his mouth with garlic."

"You can't believe Zacarias De La Cruz is sleeping under the ground," Lea burst out. "You're insane to think that."

Marguarita touched her wrist and urgently shook her head, but Lea continued, her voice filled with contempt.

"He's a man, flesh and blood, just like us. I've seen him. He's far too elegant to ever have slept in dirt. He didn't have fangs and I sat at a table with him drinking tea and eating cake."

DS reacted immediately, savagely, swinging out with the heavy satchel, slamming the bag into Lea's stomach, doubling her over. Lea fell into the wall, hitting the back of her head hard. She slid to the floor. DS kicked her hip and spat. He grabbed Marguarita by her long hair and dragged her to the door of the cellar.

"You first, bitch, just in case this is a trap."

Is she dead? Could you tell? Frantically, as she opened the cellar door, she called out to Zacarias. She should have tried harder to stop Lea from taunting DS. Lea didn't seem to realize that she was the trigger.

Turn your head.

She felt Zacarias moving in her and for a moment her vision was strange. She held her breath as DS yanked her back around and nearly shoved her down the stairs. She caught the wall, switching on the light. The stairs were narrow and steep. Only one person at a time could go down them.

She is alive. I saw her chest moving.

Relief swept over her. She let out her breath and began the descent into the root cellar. She took each stair cautiously, trying to count out ten seconds between each step, aware of the sun's position as she never had been before. There was still far too much time before it sank and allowed Zacarias his freedom.

"Esteban, bring your sister down here. If she refuses to walk, drag her down by her feet."

Esteban laughed. "You're one mean son of a bitch, Dan."

"I told you never to call me that," DS snapped.

Furious, he shoved Marguarita between the shoulder blades, sending her flying. She landed hard, facedown in the dirt, the wind knocked out of her. DS stepped over her and looked around with satisfaction. The floor was all dirt. The place was cool and dark, a perfect environment for vampires. He glanced at his watch before toeing Marguarita.

"Get over there, against the wall, away from the stairs."

She scrambled to get out of his reach, wincing when Lea screamed. She was proud of her friend for not pleading with Esteban. It was evident that he was lost to them, in the grip of the drug and deep under DS's influence. Lea sank down beside her and they held hands, the folds of Marguarita's skirt hiding that small act of camaraderie.

"What will happen when they don't find anything," Lea whispered fearfully.

Marguarita shrugged a little helplessly. She tasted dread in her mouth. She would have to act to save Zacarias. She would never give him up. She hadn't betrayed him to the vampire and she wouldn't to such a foul creature as DS.

Both men began to shovel dirt as fast as they could. The soil was rather loose on the top and easy at first, but as they went deeper it became more difficult, packed tight, hard, almost like cement.

"Do you see, Esteban? This is his resting place or it wouldn't be like this." Excitement permeated DS's voice.

"It's damned difficult," Esteban complained.

"Just keep digging."

Marguarita had never known any of their soil to be so hard and she could only surmise that Zacarias had used his energy to change the composition.

Don't. You'll need your strength just in case I fail, she reprimanded.

I am of the earth and Mother Earth protects her own as best she can.

The cryptic reply didn't help her anxiety very much. An hour and a half crept by. Both men had long ago shed their shirts, sweating and swearing. The earth yawned open like a beckoning monster, the gaping hole a good six feet in depth.

DS wiped the sweat from his face and glared at Marguarita, his face once again a mask of fury. "You lied to me."

Esteban screamed, the sound high-pitched and frightened. He pointed toward the hole, backing away.

17

Rats. Little rats digging in the earth. Deep beneath the rich soil, Zacarias could hear the two men sinking their shovels into the ground. Scraping. Slicing. Ripping apart the dirt, digging like the rats they were. The sound echoed through the layers of soil, spreading like a disease, that endless ripping and tearing. Mother Earth shuddered at the vicious attack and he felt her reaching for him, surrounding him with safe arms.

His body was leaden, but his mind raced, trying to figure out a way to overcome the curse of his species. Never in his life had he felt so completely helpless. So frustrated. He had always accepted the weakness that was the price for great strength and power. The night belonged to his kind and the day belonged to humans. That was the way of his world and it was as much a part of him as living on blood.

All those centuries and he had never once railed against that law, but he had been the only one at risk. Just him. His life had been one of duty and acceptance. Had they found him before, it would have mattered little. But this was not about him. This was different. Everything was different.

His woman—his lifemate—was in danger and he could do absolutely nothing. He had no control over the situation. No control over Marguarita. No ability to destroy the men who threatened her. He was forced to lie helpless while she suffered and that was much more difficult to bear than if someone had hammered a stake through his own heart.

DS had put his hands on her—a crime punishable by death—and yet he'd even done worse. He had struck her. Zacarias felt every blow landing on her soft body. He allowed himself to feel, to absorb the pain she experienced. The pounding seemed a lifetime, blows raining down on her face, her breasts, and then her ribs. The kicks struck her hips and legs and arms. The breath had left her lungs in an explosive burst, leaving a desperate burning for air.

Fury swept through him. A rage deeper than anything he'd ever known. He'd *forbidden* her to place herself in such danger and yet she had disobeyed him. She had deliberately led his enemies away from his resting place. They had been digging for a long while and he could tell by the slowing of the shovels that their belief was beginning to wane. They would turn their anger on Marguarita and he would be unable to stop them.

Summoning every ounce of strength he possessed, he sent his will rising through the earth.

"Where the hell is he?" DS demanded, throwing down his shovel in disgust. He glared at Marguarita. "You'd better tell me or, I swear, I'll bury you alive down here."

She slowly got to her feet and scribbled on her notepad. **I told you he never stays long. This is the only place I know that he goes.**

DS slapped the paper from Marguarita's hand, wrenched her around and dragged her toward the open grave.

Marguarita flung herself away from the yawning hole and pointed upstairs frantically.

"You'll take me there this time, or else, do you understand?"

He was angry enough to bury her alive, she could see that. She nodded her head frantically. Deep inside her mind she could hear herself screaming against what she was about to do. Now or never. She had to end this, or die trying.

No. Marguarita, bring him to me. Do not do this.

For the first time, she actually felt panic in Zacarias. He would never understand, but she felt she had no choice. *I love you. I'm sorry, but I will never give you up. Never. Nothing will induce me to do it. Please don't stay with me through this.*

"Stop! Stop this right now." Lea leaped to her feet and rushed DS. "You're crazy. Absolutely out of your mind." She flung herself at DS, pounding on his back.

Esteban giggled, turning away from the pit to lean on his shovel, giggling. "Looks like you've got woman trouble, DS. Did you ever consider there is no such thing as a vampire?"

DS shoved Marguarita hard and turned on Lea. "You fucking bitch. You could have had everything." He gripped the front of her shirt and ripped it down the front, exposing her breasts.

Marguarita gasped and slipped her hand into her pocket, finding the reassuring presence of the knife. She had no choice now. As angry as DS was, he would rape Lea right in front of them.

DS threw Lea to the ground, stepping between her sprawled legs, his hands dropping to the zipper of his jeans. Esteban wiped his mouth and turned back to the pit, his gaze skittering away from the sight of his sister on the ground under a man who would surely rape her. He gripped his shovel and sank it deep. At once the grave erupted with small wiggling bodies, a thousand of them, pouring up from the bottom and out of the four sides. He screamed, jumped back and threw his shovel.

DS whirled around as Esteban stumbled back, screaming away from the empty grave. Esteban ran toward the stairs. DS hissed a low warning, his hold over Esteban strong enough to stop him, but not enough to bring him back to the edge of the deep hole.

Marguarita sank down beside Lea and gripped her hand. Both women edged back as far as they could, trying not to draw DS's attention. Lea's quiet weeping was in her ear, but with her acute hearing, she heard something else, a whisper of sound as thousands of legs brushed dirt.

She hadn't made a mistake had she? Surely Zacarias would have told her if he'd changed his resting place. *I need to know you're safe.*

For a moment there was silence, and she jammed her fist into her mouth to keep from sobbing. Her eyes burned. Lea put her head on Marguarita's shoulder for comfort, trying to hold the edges of her ripped blouse together.

Just as I need to know you are safe. And you are not.

The bite to his voice made her wince, but at least she didn't get the feeling of impending danger. Whatever was in that hole was not Zacarias.

DS approached cautiously and peered down. Where the dirt had appeared brownish in color before, it was now speckled with black dots. Spiders crawled from the sides of the hole, from the bottom, and began filling the grave as he watched in horror. The bodies moved in a mesmerizing way, little legs crawling over one another to get to the top of the writhing pile, building higher as more spiders joined in.

"He's here," DS shouted gleefully. "We're getting close to him. He's got to be using the insects to protect himself."

"I'm not getting near them," Esteban declared. He sank down on the bottom stair, shoving his trembling hands through his hair. "They look hungry and, if they climb out of that hole, I'm getting out of here."

"You'll do what I say." DS studied the mass of bodies. The spiders emerged from tiny holes in the sides of the grave, and began crawling up as though seeking him.

He shuddered and swung around to look at Marguarita and Lea. Marguarita knew her face was pale. She could see the horrible crypt of insects and her entire body recoiled. She pressed her lips together tightly, trying not to show that any second she might get up and run. She was more terrified of the spiders than she was of DS.

She tried to be grateful that Zacarias had sent them. DS believed this was his resting place. As a stalling tactic, it was brilliant. But she was *terrified* of spiders. She closed her eyes and willed them all to go away.

DS caught her wrist and yanked her up. "Now that we know where he is, we don't really need you, do we?" He began to drag her to the edge of the open grave.

She fought like a wild cat, kicking and punching, ignoring his fists as they rained down on her. He managed to get her to side of the yawning hole but she broke away, hysterical now, unable to get her mind to function. She could not go down into that pit of spiders. She wouldn't survive it. Her heart beat out of control until she feared she'd have a heart attack.

Be calm. They will not hurt you.

I can't. I can't do that. Make them go away.

DS wrenched her around and slapped her face hard enough to stun her. "You're going in. We need to find out if they're poisonous, and I have plans for little Lea." He picked her up bodily and threw her into the pit even as Lea launched herself, tackling him at the legs, driving him over the edge into the deep hole along with Marguarita. All three landed heavily, squishing spiders, DS and Lea pushing Marguarita into the very center of the swarm of moving spiders under the weight of the two human bodies.

Marguarita felt the horrible spider legs, thousands of them, crawling over her skin, in her hair, in her mouth. She'd opened it to emit a soundless scream and the spiders swarmed over her as if she were fresh meat. She couldn't breathe, was afraid to swallow. She shut her eyes as tight as possible, willing herself to faint. The ringing in her ears was loud, the scream in her mind loud and long, a wail of sheer terror.

Sívamet. Breathe with me. The spiders will never harm you. Trust me. Come into me and I will hold you safe.

Frantic, she gave herself up to him, following the path to his mind, her spirit leaving her body to the spiders and chaos, giving herself into Zacarias's keeping. Instantly she felt calm, centered. Warm even. She hadn't even known she had been ice cold. He surrounded her with his being, holding her close, sheltering her against the horrendous nightmare she found herself trapped in.

It was Lea's scream that brought her back. Her eyes snapped open as her spirit flowed back into her own body. Esteban frantically shoved dirt into the pit on top of them all, intent on burying the spiders, uncaring that his sister, Marguarita and DS were trapped in the pit. He pushed large piles of soil from the edge of the hole as fast as he could.

Lea screamed and began knocking the dirt from her hair. DS swore at Esteban and made a leap, trying to catch the edges of the pit. Esteban smashed his fingers with the shovel and continued to hysterically push the dirt over all of them. DS, in a rage, caught Lea around her throat and began to strangle her, cutting off her cries, shaking her as he tightened his grip.

Marguarita got her feet under her, plunging her hand in the deep pocket of her skirt, withdrawing the knife. She flung the sheath away, trying not to see the spiders crawling everywhere, running down her arm and clinging to her hair. She stumbled toward DS, feeling the spiders crunching beneath her feet. Her stomach lurched. Dirt rained down on her head and shoulders. She had to wipe her eyes to get the grit out. She kept wholly focused on DS, tunneling her vision, knowing she had moments before he killed Lea.

She took the three steps, closing the distance, unsure where to plunge the blade. His back was to her and she'd never considered having to kill another human being.

He is evil.

The voice was dead calm. Dripped icicles. She stepped closer. Lea's eyes bulged. Her face was scarlet red. The fingers sank deep, cutting off air. Another rain of dirt poured in on them, right over their heads and shoulders. DS didn't loosen his grip for an instant.

Marguarita took a deep breath. Strength poured into her. She slammed the knife as hard as she could, using every ounce of fear she had in her to drive through skin and muscle, deep into DS's kidney.

Turn the blade. The order was delivered in a calm voice.

Pressing her lips together, she did as Zacarias instructed. It was much harder than she thought it would be, even with such power running through her body.

Now pull it out.

She knew blood would pour out with the removal of the blade. She was killing this man. Swallowing hard, she obeyed. The feel of the blade slicing through flesh was a horrendous sensation—one she knew she would never forget—but twisting and then removing it was far worse. She stepped back, choking with bile.

DS stiffened. His eyes went wide as he turned his head to stare at her. His hands fell away from Lea's throat. Lea slid to the spider-covered floor of the hole, coughing, desperate for air. DS staggered backward, half turning toward Marguarita. He reached one hand toward her just as Esteban threw another shovelful of dirt over them.

Marguarita stepped around DS, and tugged at Lea's arm. She had to get her up. She knew she had to get Lea on her feet or they'd never make it out of the grave. They couldn't take the chance of the dirt imprisoning them.

Lea staggered to her feet at the exact moment DS sat abruptly. He looked up at both of them with shock on his face. Marguarita realized she still held the knife and nearly opened her hand to drop it.

Keep it. You may need it. As Esteban shovels in the dirt, step up. You can help each other out of the hole.

She wanted out desperately. DS was dying in front of her. Spiders streamed up his body, covering every inch of him until she couldn't see his face. It was like a scene from a horror movie. She couldn't look at him—or the spiders. She looked up at Esteban. Maybe Lea could get through to him.

Esteban seemed intent on burying them alive, burying the spiders. Looking up at him, she didn't think there was much hope. He had a strange slack-jawed expression and his movements had become mechanical. Lea opened her mouth to call out, coughed and grabbed her throat.

Marguarita shook her head, warning her to stay silent. Something was terribly wrong with Esteban. He didn't look as if he even knew what he was doing any longer. As long as he pushed the dirt back into the pit, she found if they stood to one side and allowed the dirt to pile higher, he created a way out for them. She feared if Lea distracted him, he might try to find another way to kill them.

Eventually some of the spiders made their way to the surface. Instead of dispersing, they crawled to Esteban. He didn't seem to notice even that. He filled his shovel and threw the dirt and returned for more like a robot. The spiders moved over his boots and up his legs, a steady stream of them, silent and stealthy, the numbers growing. Beside her, Lea held her breath and gripped Marguarita's shoulder.

"I have to warn him," she whispered, the words barely audible. She sounded hoarse and immediately went into another coughing fit.

Marguarita shook her head, fearing Esteban would try bashing them over the head with his shovel. She couldn't imagine trying to stab him. DS's body toppled over, a slow-motion action that drew her attention in spite of her resolve not to look. The spiders appeared to be a moving blanket with a second stream steadily climbing out of the pit to swarm up Esteban. Her stomach lurched and she turned away from the hideous sight.

Esteban suddenly frowned and looked down at himself. The spiders were already moving up his neck and face. Every part of his body was covered, weighed down with the sheer mass of small bodies. Hundreds turned to thousands. He dropped the shovel and screamed. The moment he opened his mouth, spiders poured in, rushing down his throat, cramming themselves inside, filling his eyes and nose. Esteban fell backward, his boot heels drumming in dirt.

Stop it. You have to stop. You're killing him.

Of course I am. Zacarias was still so calm. *Did you think I would ever allow such a man to live?*

He's Lea's brother.

She is better off without him. I must rest. Alert Cesaro.

He had already dismissed Esteban from his mind. She knew there was no use in arguing, but she tried anyway. *We don't have the right to take his life. It's murder.*

He attempted to kill you both. He allowed his friend to beat both you and his sister and he would have stood by and allowed his sister—and possibly you—to be raped before you were murdered. I will not argue with you.

He was gone. She felt the loss instantly. After being filled with him, the isolation, the complete sense of being alone was overwhelming. Thankfully, Esteban rolled out of sight and the continuous drumming of his boots faded into silence. The spiders had abandoned both Lea and Marguarita for the two men, leaving the women a little dazed and confused and slightly ill.

"We have to get out of here," Lea said in her hoarse voice. Tears streamed down her swollen face. "We have to help him."

Marguarita wiped DS's blood from the blade and slipped the knife back in the sheath, pushing it down into her pocket just in case. She spat to make certain no spiders were in her mouth and flipped her head upside down and shook it, running her hands through the thick mass to ensure they were gone from her hair, as well.

She climbed onto the pile of dirt Esteban had made. There was a small root looped just above her head and she tugged experimentally. It seemed to hold. She gripped it and pulled hard. Lea moved over and laced her fingers to give Marguarita a foothold. Marguarita raised her head over the edge cautiously. Esteban's body, much like DS's, had a moving blanket swarming over him.

She swallowed rising bile and found a place at the edge of the hole to grab. It took effort to pull up. She hadn't realized how weak she was after the adrenaline had drained away. She felt exhausted, her body almost too heavy to move. She flopped onto her stomach and crawled away from the edge, fighting not to cry. She and Lea had a long day ahead of them and a lot of questions to answer. She'd *killed* a man. All she wanted to do was weep.

Crawling back to the edge, she leaned down to help Lea out. Again, it was a struggle. Lea was as weak as she was. The moment Lea reached the surface she crawled to her brother, trying to get the spiders off his face. It was obvious he wasn't breathing, but Marguarita didn't stop her. She sat on the bottom stair and allowed the tears to stream down her dirty face.

Lea finally sank back on her heels, lifted her face to the ceiling and screamed, a helpless, hopeless sound. She buried her face in her hands and sobbed. Marguarita joined her, but there was no sound and deep inside, she added her own helpless scream.

Neither had any idea of how long they sat in the dimly lit room crying, but eventually, it was Lea who forced herself up and went to Marguarita. They stood, holding one another in an attempt to comfort each other before Lea pulled back and wiped her dirt-streaked face.

"We have to call the authorities."

Marguarita pulled her notepad out. **Zacarias is the authority here. He will return soon. Another hour or so. We have to get Cesaro.**

Lea nodded. Both women went up the stairs, neither looking back, both still with tears streaming down their faces. Marguarita hit the alarm to call the men in and opened the door wide. Fresh air streamed in along with the sunlight. Although it hurt her eyes and seemed to sear her skin, she lifted her face toward the sky and held out her arms. She wasn't certain she'd ever be able to go inside again. She'd *killed* a man.

Horses swept into the yard on a dead run. Julio beat Cesaro by a few inches, leaping from his horse, rifle in hand, taking in both women. Tears and dirt streaked both faces. They were covered in bruises, eyes swelling, lips split and bruises marring skin. Lea's blouse was ripped right down the front. There was a bruise over her left breast. Julio peeled off his jacket as he took the stairs two at a time to gain the porch, his body blocking hers from the other men sweeping into the yard.

"Marguarita, you all right?" he demanded as he wrapped Lea in his jacket.

She shook her head and stepped into his arms, weeping. Lea took the other shoulder, wrapping her arms around his waist, sobbing in unison with Marguarita all over again. Cesaro pushed past him, signaling his men into the house. He touched Marguarita's shoulder. It was Lea who answered.

"Down in the root cellar." She choked on the words. "They're dead."

Julio pulled back to examine her swollen, bruised throat. "Who did this?"

Marguarita was very glad she couldn't speak, leaving Lea to tell the story. Regaining her composure she seated herself in the shade on the porch, grateful for the dark glasses Cesaro brought to her. She drew up her legs and rocked herself as Lea told the men everything that had happened. Lea, of course, thought Zacarias was away from the ranch and both Cesaro and Julio nodded approvingly at the way they had saved themselves—and Zacarias—even though Lea didn't know they had done so.

"We will have to bring the authorities out here to speak with Señor De La Cruz. He will take care of everything," Cesaro reassured Lea. "He will make all the arrangements necessary."

Marguarita shivered. She couldn't imagine Zacarias talking to the authorities. More than likely he would speak and they would be mesmerized by his voice into doing exactly what he wished. He would have no compunction about manipulating minds to believe what he wished them to believe. Right then, it didn't matter to her. She waited there until the sun set, the men milling around and the commander himself had come to the De La Cruz hacienda at the urgent call.

She knew the exact moment that Zacarias rose. He didn't touch her mind, didn't come into her to relieve the terrible isolation and fear. When she touched him, because she couldn't help herself, couldn't stop the need, he had placed a glacier between them. Her warmth didn't seem enough to penetrate that blue ice, thick and hard and impenetrable.

Marguarita shivered and rubbed her hands up and down her arms. He was coming and he was in an ice-cold rage. She felt the slightest tremble in the ground. In the stable, the horses grew restless. Above them, the sky grew a shade darker and clouds rolled in from the south. A wind blew leaves and debris across the yard. The men exchanged quick, uneasy glances.

Dread built in the pit of her stomach. She *felt* his anger charge the air until the clouds became dark towering giants looming above their heads. The slight wind cooled, picked up in velocity, chilling the air. Thunder rolled. Lightning forked inside the churning shadowy clouds, great streaks that shot in all directions, yet never came to earth. Still, they all felt that ominous charge and the biting cold of the wind.

His breath. His mind. All ice. Turbulent and stormy, but held it in tight check. Just as the storm was controlled, so was Zacarias, striding up to the house, tall and dangerous, wide shoulders and thick, muscular chest. Ice blue flames glowed in his midnight black eyes. He was the most intimidating male she'd ever seen, and the police and ranch workers must have felt the same. They went silent as he approached, looking at one another uneasily.

He carried danger with him in the set of his shoulders, the fluid way he moved, the set of his jaw and ice in his eyes. He looked what he was—a dangerous predator—and just as he made the animals uneasy, so did he make humans. He moved in complete silence blending in to his surroundings, and yet he commanded the space around him, filling it completely with his power.

He looked only at her. Focused. Locked on. Those glacial blue flames leaped higher, glittering like dark sapphires of pure ice. The men gathered in the front of the house parted without a word, leaving him a clear path to the front porch—to Marguarita. Her mouth went dry and her stomach somersaulted. Her fingers found the material of her skirt and bunched it in her fist. If she could have screamed, she might have.

He blocked out everything and everybody extending his hand toward her. It seemed a solicitous gesture, but she knew better. Her hand trembled in his as she stood up, facing him. She wanted him to pull her into his arms and hold her. To comfort her. But his expression was as remote as his eyes. Ice flowed in his veins and formed a glacier in his mind far too thick to penetrate.

He was wholly focused on her; she felt his concentrated attention like a spear going through her heart. For Zacarias, no one else existed. He cared nothing for the men standing like statues in his yard. There was only Marguarita—and her disobedience.

His hand moved over her face, fingertips brushing every bruise, her swollen eye and cracked lip. His breath hissed out, a long, slow menace that sent another shiver creeping down her spine. Her heart accelerated and he heard it, but he didn't soothe her. The pain in her face and head lessened with his touch—but that featherlight brush of fingers had been remote, not at all personal.

The sun has seared your skin.

His disapproval of her actions hit like a hard blow to her heart. She had known he had forbidden her actions and he would be angry, but this was more than anger. His remoteness cut her to the bone. Even her soul and heart. He was taking care of her, but there was no comfort in his actions.

She swallowed hard and tried to reach him. *I couldn't stay inside with the bodies and the spiders. It was too much.*

The blue flames leaped, and for a moment his eyes seemed to glow with a strange, frightening fire. *The bodies have been removed and the spiders are gone. Go inside now. I will see to the commander.*

Marguarita refused to cry. She had known all along what she was getting into and Zacarias separated himself from emotions. He had all the long centuries of his existence. She'd put him in touch with feelings, allowing him to tap into them. He had suffered, lying there trapped beneath the earth while she was in danger. She had chosen her own path, disobeyed his direct orders, something probably no one did. She had told him she gave herself into his keeping, and pride and honor refused to allow her to weep.

She nodded her head and swept past him, head up, moving away from the crowd, knowing they thought Zacarias so solicitous of her.

Zacarias went next to Lea, giving her that same featherlight brush of his fingers, and softly whispering, his voice hypnotic, easing her grief a little, as well as the pain of the beating at DS's hands. Marguarita could hear him assuring the girl that he would see to all arrangements and that Julio would take her home and stay just in case to watch over her.

Next came his low voice convincing the commander of everything he wanted the man to believe. Of course the commander went along with it all, half bowing to Zacarias, the elusive billionaire one heard so much about. He would have bragging rights; he met him in person and the De La Cruz legend would only grow.

Eventually everyone was gone and the house was dark and quiet. Marguarita was left to face Zacarias alone. She wanted him there, and yet she was very scared of what he would do. He had warned her numerous times she would face consequences. She couldn't imagine him beating a woman. It simply wasn't his style. He had taken the pain from her face, so he didn't want her to suffer physically, right? She had to be right.

She wrung her hands together. Waiting. Where was he? It was worse waiting in the dark for him to appear and pass sentence on her than not knowing. She sat for a few minutes, her heart pounding and the taste of fear growing. Unable to sit still, she went to the open door and looked out. He was there, big as life, staring into the night.

He turned his head and looked straight at her. Of course he'd known she was there. His eyes burned through the screen, burned like a brand into her heart. She stepped back, her hand moving defensively to her throat. The lines in his face were etched deeper than usual and his jaw was set. There was no mercy in that dark expressionless face. His sensual mouth seemed a little cruel, and his eyes held nothing but all that blue, flaming ice.

He swung around in a swift fluid movement and was on her in a single beat of her heart. The screen never opened and closed. He stood a moment, holding her gaze, drinking in her terror, his mind closed to her, his heart and soul distant—so distant she couldn't reach them. This was not her Zacarias. This was the predator.

I am both, and it is time you learned that lesson.

Without preamble, he gripped her upper arms, dragging her to him, his teeth sinking into her neck. Pain sliced through her, pain that slowly gave way to pure erotic heat. She struggled for one moment, still afraid, knowing his control had slipped dangerously. She couldn't connect, he refused to let her in, yet he was there in her mind, commanding—*demanding*—she give herself to him. This time, she feared what he was asking.

The growing dread didn't cease, even as heat swept through her body and her breasts ached for him, her core heated and wept for him. He didn't stop. Didn't slow down. She found herself sinking into that place, that sort of subspace of mind where Zacarias became her world. Where there was only his strong body and phenomenal strength, his need and hunger. It was a primal place, forged by his will, older than time, where laws of the jungle applied.

In the midst of all that sensual heat a shiver started somewhere and began to increase. She was cold. Growing colder, as if the ice in his veins had poured into her veins and slowly was spreading throughout her body. Her legs turned to rubber, very wobbly as if she could no longer support herself. She caught at Zacarias's neck to anchor herself, but her arms were too weak to hold herself up.

Even as she fell, his arm locked her to him, lifting her from her feet, but he didn't stop. She had the sensation of floating, but her eyes refused to open. Panicked, she tried to struggle.

Stop. It's too much. You have to stop.

I say when it is too much.

Marguarita heard the soft hiss of menace, the need for domination and his iron will that was implacable. She had no chance to save herself. Life or death. Live or die. It was up to him. She gave herself up completely, no longer struggling, not even in her mind.

Choose, then. She had no more strength left to fight him. He was taking her life's blood, as if it was impossible to slake his hunger. There was an edge to his feeding, both sexual and dangerous, as if he'd made a decision he would not back away from. The resolve in him ran so deep, so dark, she couldn't find a way to reach him.

I already have.

The words should have reassured her, but they sent another shiver through her body. It was the way he said them, the pure cold glacier that dripped like icicles from his voice. He carried her through to the master bedroom and laid her on the bed, his body covering hers, all the while draining her of her precious blood. She felt herself fading.

You will stay with me. Come to me, Marguarita. Now. Come to me.

She was too tired, too weak, to do anything but obey. Her spirit reached for his and he surrounded her, held her to him when her body wanted to slip away into another world she didn't recognize.

Only then did he swipe his tongue across the punctures and open his shirt to slash his chest.

You will feed.

It was an absolute command. He was in control, her spirit locked to his. His hand caught the back of her head, forcing her to that dark rich Carpathian blood. Her mouth moved against him. This time, he didn't distance her from the act. The blood flowed into her, his very essence, rushing to do its work, to claim her for all time, to make her his irrevocably. She knew that was uppermost in his mind. *This* was the consequence of her actions. His claiming her. She struggled to understand. He had tied them together in the way of his people. Why such satisfaction? Why this particular show of dominance?

Strength was returning, but he held her spirit captive until she had taken enough of his blood that he deemed satisfactory. His body continued to blanket hers as he lifted his head and stared down into her eyes.

She was missing something. Something important. He looked very expectant. Still cold and distant, but alert and watchful. She touched her tongue to her lip. The split and swelling was gone. Her face didn't hurt, but there was a new, strange pounding in her head. She could not only hear her heart beating, but *feel* it, every single movement, the swish of blood, ebbing and flowing. A ripple of pain moved through her body and her stomach lurched.

18

Marguarita stared at Zacarias with enormous, terrified, *accusing* eyes. She looked very pale, her dark, silken hair spread out all around them.

What have you done?

Zacarias shifted his weight. It was starting then. Her conversion. His blood was working to change her body, reshape her organs, and bring her fully into his world. Satisfaction etched itself into the lines of his face.

"Never again will I be forced by my own lifemate to lie helpless beneath the ground while she endangers herself deliberately. You have disobeyed me for the last time, Marguarita."

His white teeth snapped at her, still slightly lengthened. The flames in his eyes flickered, and still that hot lethal mass of volcanic rage boiled in his gut. *Hours,* he'd lain beneath the surface, stripped of all power, while she risked her life and his soul. For what? There could be no reason good enough for such a decision on her part.

He would be forever dishonored. She even knew the truth about him. She had seen his darkest secret, the one he'd protected for centuries—his legacy of darkness. His own father turning vampire moments after his mother's death. That would have happened to him. If DS had succeeded in killing her, Zacarias would have risen vampire and wiped out the entire ranch.

"Sun scorch you, woman." He spat the curse at her, as fury pounded through his veins, breaking through the ice, a volcanic explosion. He couldn't bear to touch her. Couldn't stay close to inhale her fragrance. His woman. His lifemate. Betrayer. Risking *everything* for the childish whim to prove that she was his equal in strength and power. Risking him. Risking them. Risking his brothers and her family.

He pushed himself off the bed and stalked across the room, a prowling jungle cat, lethal and still very much raging. The tension in the room stretched, but he couldn't find a way to recapture his icy control. His anger had burned its way through the massive glacier and his emotions were a firestorm raging out of control.

He had always known he wouldn't understand a modern woman. He had accepted that his lifemate would never come to him—never accept him as he was. He had been more than prepared to go honorably to the next life. She had changed all of that, destroyed his every plan and she should have realized the enormity of what she'd done. She had no right to risk his soul—*ever.* Not ever. Not in this year and not a hundred years from now.

Marguarita writhed, her eyes going wide with shock, hands flying to her stomach. A ripple of unease slid down his spine. His gaze jumped to her. All attention focused on her. Clearly, she was in pain. In all his centuries, he'd never seen a human turned. He simply didn't associate that closely with them. His brothers had done it, but he'd never bothered to inquire about just what happened. Three blood exchanges were necessary and that should take care of it—as long as she was psychic, which Marguarita clearly was.

Apprehension became knots in the pit of his stomach. Surely nothing could go wrong. He had powerful blood, but the darkness ran deep in him. Shadows crept into the dark room, into his mind, disturbing, haunting possibilities he hadn't considered. Had he made a mistake?

"What is wrong?" he demanded.

She drew her legs up, rolling to her side in the fetal position, her face contorting with pain. She closed her eyes, as if the sight of him was unbearable. Unexpectedly, a pain knifed through his heart. He tasted fear in his mouth.

"What is wrong? When I ask you I want an answer."

He couldn't wait, not when she began writhing in pain, tears streaming down her face and her body contorting wildly. For the very first time in his life, panic welled up, a frightening feeling. This wasn't supposed to happen. He reached for her mind, needing to feel what she was feeling, needing to share her same skin, to know what was happening to her. He reached, but came up against a wall.

She refused him. *Refused* him. His lifemate. His woman. She not only disobeyed him, paving the way for total disaster, but now, she was refusing their most intimate, private path. She'd blocked him out, and judging by the strength of that door, it would take a battering ram to open it.

She had a natural barrier, he knew that, but she had always allowed him through. Now, with his blood flowing in her veins, that shield was even stronger than it had been. He'd been afraid of damaging her before; now, if he destroyed that barrier, he had no idea what would happen to her. And the only way she was going to let him in was if he tore it down.

"Let me in."

She made no reply, stubbornly drawing up her knees to her chest, rocking her body, her hair spilling around her face, shutting him out. She was in pain—that much was more than apparent. He was across the room instantly, reaching down to put his hand on her stomach. There was more than one way to get the information he sought.

She took a deep shuddering breath, as if the pain was receding, and turned her head, her dark eyes glaring at him. Strands of hair fell across her cheek, damp now from sweating. Her body was coated in a fine sheen. When his palm and fingers made contact with her skin, she shuddered and tried to slap at his arm.

Get away from me. I mean it. I don't want you here.

Marguarita couldn't believe he would do this to her. Everyone, every*thing* had known—even the horses—what a monster he was, everyone but her. He was uncaring, a dark, dangerous predator with no real feeling. Everything she'd believed about him had been a fantasy. He'd shattered her heart, and she had nothing left but pride. She couldn't bear to look at him and she wasn't about to let him inside her mind—never again would she willingly share herself with him. He would have to take what he wanted from her. The pain of her shattered heart was far worse than the physical pain he thrust on her.

Zacarias was shocked. He hadn't expected absolute rejection, but she kept him from her mind, and now she thought she could keep him from her body. Before he could say anything else, he saw the next wave building, a sweep of her body, every muscle going rigid, the breath slamming out of her lungs. Her eyes went wide, glazed with pain. Her back bowed, then arched, her body convulsing, nearly thrown from the bed.

He caught her, held her firm, afraid she'd hurt herself more. His hands slid over her skin, now burning with fever. Every organ twisted and threatened to burst inside of her. Her skin was so hot he nearly pulled his hand away. He tried to send healing warmth through her skin, but it seemed to make things worse. Her body jerked nearly into a sitting position, teeth set almost as if in rigor mortis before she was slammed back against the mattress.

Her breath rushed out in silent protest, even as he felt the wave receding. The moment her gaze focused on him, she threw herself away from him, off the bed, putting it between them. She tried to crawl away from him, her body gleaming with sweat, her hair matted to the back of her neck and down her back. Weak, she fell on her stomach.

Zacarias was on her in an instant, his heart pounding as fast as hers, really afraid for her now. He had to figure out what was wrong and how to help her.

"Let me help, Marguarita." In spite of his fear for her, he kept his voice gentle.

His hand settled around her ankle. Marguarita kicked him hard with her other foot and pushed herself up to her hands and knees to escape.

"Stop it. I do not want to have to force your obedience." His fear mounted with the thought of losing her. Something was terribly wrong and he had to fix it.

Why not? She rolled over, her face damp with sweat and beaded with tiny red dots. Her eyes showed both accusation and hurt. *I was so wrong about you. You're exactly what you told me—a monster. And your binding words are a lie. You lied. They mean nothing.*

Marguarita could barely breathe, caught between pain and dissolution.

She'd *loved* those words he'd whispered to her, binding words, he'd said. He'd *married* her in the way of his people with words like *cherish, heart* and *soul.* Things said like *always in my care.* He'd stolen her heart with those glimpses of a man who desperately needed saving, and those tender, amazing words that somehow had bound them together.

There is no care. Certainly nothing like cherish. Take your empty words and keep them. I don't want them.

Zacarias caught his breath, her accusation tearing at him along with the sight of her tears, streaked with pink. Right now nothing could matter to him but her physical condition. He had to find a way to help her. He focused on finding a way through the barrier in her mind.

"Marguarita," he pitched his voice low, velvet soft, bordering on hypnotic. "You could be in trouble, *sívamet.* You have to let me in to see what is happening."

Go away and leave me alone with this. I can get through it myself. I don't want anything to do with . . .

She broke off abruptly. Her eyes went wide and her mouth gaped open in a silent scream. Horror spread across her face. Her stomach seemed alive, rippling, contracting, her muscles knotting in her arms and legs.

Zacarias reached for her again, the need in him bordering now on total insanity. What was wrong? What was going wrong? This made no sense to him. Clearly she was in agony. She had no control, her body struggling to expel toxins, fighting to reshape organs and change her body from human to Carpathian. He was certain if he could share her mind, he would shoulder the pain, but even in the height of the wave, her barrier against him never wavered. He needed another way in without harming her.

Waiting for the surge of pain to pass was agony for him. He breathed through it, trying to take in enough air for both of them. He noticed each bout lasted longer and seemed harder. He waited until he could see recognition in her eyes before he tried again.

"Marguarita. You cannot continue this way. It is getting worse. Let me in. I can take away the pain."

Temper smoldered in her eyes. *I don't want your help. I'd rather suffer. I want to never forget, never ever forget this lesson of yours.*

He needed her to keep talking. Telepathic communication went directly from her mind to his. He found her thread and used a very delicate touch, weaving his thread to hers.

"This was not meant as a lesson, Marguarita. You knew I would bring you into my world. This was consequence. To protect both of us. To protect my brothers from having to hunt me. To protect your family here from a monster unlike any other."

I can do this myself. You can say it isn't a punishment, but you meant it that way.

He shoved both hands through his hair. "You knew I would bring you into my world and you consented," he reiterated, keeping his voice very low, nearly holding his breath as he carefully and very gently wrapped more of himself around that tiny thread she used to access his mind.

I thought you would introduce me with love and care, not in such a cold, unfeeling manner. Not with such pain. She gasped again, her hands flying to her stomach. *I don't want you. Go away.*

Once again she rolled over, struggling to her hands and knees. The vomiting was explosive, horribly wrenching as she expelled all the toxins in her body. Her body convulsed again, contorting, driving her forward until she hit the wall, and rolled over again, drawing her legs up to her belly.

Horrified at her lack of control she buried her face in her hands when she became aware of the mess everywhere. *Please go away.*

His tenacious hold on the thread between them was growing stronger with every contact. It was only a matter of time before he could ease into her mind and seize control without her consent.

"Did you forget what would happen if you were killed, Marguarita?" He asked the question in that same low voice. "You knew my legacy. You uncovered a secret few have knowledge of, my darkest secret, and yet still you persisted in your disobedience."

He couldn't keep the hurt of betrayal from rising. He made every effort not to feel it, to distance himself once again from all overwhelming emotion, but now that the dam had been punctured, he was unable to stem the tide. He cared nothing for the rest of the world. To him, everything and everyone was still separate from him, lost to him, unless he could feel through her. But Marguarita was different. He saw her in full, vivid color. He felt her and through her, his emotions, everything lost to him all those centuries—both good and bad.

She had become his world and he had believed in her. He believed in himself because of her—for the first time thinking he could actually live a life with another. He had spent centuries living only on honor and yet, with a single decision, she could have destroyed and nullified everything he'd ever done—everything he'd ever been.

He didn't remember his father as the man who had raised and shaped his life. He remembered him only as the undead, that rotting, soulless vampire who would have killed his own sons. Marguarita would have made him that same memory for his brothers—the ones who would have had to hunt and kill him. It was more than possible that he would have murdered his own brothers.

A single sound of despair escaped from the back of his throat. He brushed one hand over his face as if he could remove the knowledge of her betrayal so easily.

Just leave me to this.

There was weariness in her voice. She was weakening, the fight between human and Carpathian taking its toll. But even with his reminder, she didn't seem to understand what a terrible betrayal it had been. He couldn't afford to think of himself right now. She was in trouble and he wanted—no, *needed*—to ease her through the change. This terrible, traumatic episode could not continue.

"You know I cannot." Silently he willed her to answer him. Each time she did, she opened her mind just a little more, giving him a stronger hold on the thread that would allow him to seize control without harming her.

I'm too tired to argue. Do what you want. What I want obviously doesn't matter to you.

The weariness in her voice alarmed him. If he knew anything about her with certainty, it was that she was a fighter. In that moment, he sensed she gave up, her life, him, all of it. She was willing to allow it all to slip away.

He was so focused on her that he saw the wave approaching almost before she did. This time was even more intense. Unseen hands picked her up and threw her down like a rag doll. She fell on her back, her hands flying to her throat. Zacarias had to grip her writhing body and turn her over to keep her from choking.

Zacarias couldn't coax her, or plead anymore. He needed this to stop almost more than she did. Waving his hands, he removed all traces of vomit and expelled toxins from her body and the floor. A breeze cleared the room of all scent. Candles sprang up, bringing the soft fragrance of lavender through the entire house.

In desperation, he took control, following those threads straight back into her mind. Complete chaos reigned. Fear uppermost. Hurt. Her sense of betrayal was every bit as strong as his. Her motivation for disobeying him had nothing to do with equality, or asserting her independence. In part it had been a vow imprinted from birth, the lifemate bond and her own character refusing to allow her to take a chance of putting his life in danger.

She had disobeyed out of love for him.

Zacarias groaned aloud, trying to grasp the enormity of what that meant. He still didn't truly understand that emotion. He had felt it long ago—so long ago—but the emotion was so far removed from him that he no longer recognized it for what it was. Marguarita knew how to love. She had given herself into his care, trusting him to do the best thing for her.

Her love enveloped him. Swamped him. Lifted him. Once again, warmth poured through the ice of his mind and body, finding the shadows, bridging the gaps where connections should have been. He felt her inside him—where she belonged—cementing them together with her love. With the essence that was her.

She had made a bad decision in refusing to obey him, yes, but she didn't understand the enormity of the repercussions. He could tell her, but her knowledge wasn't the same as his. He knew evil walked in the world, knew what it could and would do, he had battled it for centuries. She had been raised in a loving environment where vampires were the thing of legends. Yes, she'd faced one, and she had the courage to defy it, but she had never really seen the destruction they could cause on a massive scale.

Zacarias had no time to examine the revelations in her mind. The terrible toll on her body had to be stopped. He pushed away all thoughts of himself and his own reactions to the way her mind worked, the depth of her ability to give and feel. That couldn't matter. Only stopping the crushing pain. He shed his body, flowing as pure spirit into hers, using that delicate thread to find his way.

Just as in her mind, chaos reigned in her body. He could see clearly what was happening, the reformation of her body, the changes taking place in order for her to become Carpathian. He should have realized it would be a near-death experience; she would have to die as a human to be reborn as a Carpathian. And she was fighting it. Refusing. That, too, was unexpected.

He hadn't come to comfort her when she needed it. He'd added to the trauma instead of gathering her into his arms and holding her. She rejected him and his ways as adamantly now as he clung to them. She had closed off access to her mind deliberately, knowing she would suffer, yet not wanting his help to aid her passage. No longer wanting his comfort or him.

He had thought her a lunatic for seeing him as anything but a dangerous predator, too long in the shadows, his soul already blackened, pierced through with a million tiny holes until it was impossible to repair. And yet, she had seen past the dark shadows to the man clinging to life somewhere on the edges. Lost. He'd been so lost. He didn't know anything other than to hunt and kill. She had been the one to give herself freely to him, trusting that he would honor his ritual binding vow.

Zacarias summoned his energy until he was all power and healing light. The reshaping of organs could be speeded up, but the only way to stop the pain was for him to shoulder as much as he could. Share it with her. Feel it with her. She resisted. He knew she would, but she was weak, he was strong and his blood heeded his call.

"Rest as much as possible in between the waves," he said gently as the pain receded from her body. He kept that thread, his one link to her.

She sighed and turned her head away from him as he lifted her into his arms off the floor. The room felt and smelled clean, the scent of lavender and chamomile drifting around them. The bed had cool sheets with the scent woven into them lightly. He placed her in the exact center and lay down beside her, his arms trapping her body to give her an anchor.

"I know you do not want me to help you through this, Marguarita," he said gently, brushing the damp hair from her face. Her lashes lay in two thick crescents, a stark black against the white, almost translucent skin. She shivered continually, uncontrollably. Even her teeth chattered. "But I have to. I know right at this moment you cannot understand, but I have no choice."

The thought was barely out of his mouth before the revelation followed.

Was it possible? Maybe Marguarita had no choice, either. That love she felt, so strong, so deep, sharing parts of him he couldn't even see or touch without her could have made their bond much deeper than he realized. She was *in* him. His mind, yes, but she tapped into his soul. She saw things in him that he didn't. And those traits she'd relied on had to be there or she couldn't have felt such strong emotion for him.

She turned her head toward him. Her lashes fluttered and she looked directly into his eyes. The impact of her gaze hit him like a punch. He could see the change in her eyes already, the color deeper and richer. Before she could speak, her eyes went wide. He felt the wave as it consumed her, faster and harder, a shock to his body when it had been centuries since he'd acknowledged actual pain.

The sensation of a thousand knives stabbing at the insides of his body, slashing and cutting all at once burned through him. His insides felt shredded and tangled, tied into thick, hard knots. The breath left his body and the punch came, a tidal wave like a battering ram, slamming through him. His skull was suddenly too small for his brain, an explosion of shrapnel bursting in his head sending shock waves through his body.

Beside him, Marguarita's body convulsed. He held her to him, skin to skin, sharing the agony, riding on top of it with her, his body sweating tiny beads of blood that smeared over the matching ones dotting her body.

He hadn't known. How could he not have even asked his brothers? Had each of them shared information, told one another just how bad conversion could be?

"It is fading, *sívamet*," he whispered. By sharing the pain with her, at least he had lessened the violence of the seizures. "Try to breathe evenly. Your heart is beating too fast. Let your body follow the rhythm of mine."

Deliberately he matched the frantic, accelerated pounding of her heart, the gasping, ragged breathing of her body, and very slowly, holding her to him, began to slow both their rates. Her gaze clung to his. His heart stuttered for a moment. She looked defeated, not at all like the Marguarita who went alone into a rain forest at night with a predator stalking her. Marguarita who would smile at him when he was at his worst.

Marguarita. He breathed her name, holding her close to him, inside his mind.

She didn't fight him this time, far too weak to make much sense of what was happening to her. He lay there beside her and listened to the rain falling on the roof, amplifying the sound enough that she could hear the soothing sound through the roaring in her head. Deliberately he added small bursts of a breeze to change the pattern of sound against the windows and walls.

Beside him, Marguarita slowly relaxed, the tension easing from sore, knotted muscles enough to allow her to breathe in the soothing mixture of lavender and chamomile scents. She didn't fight him again and Zacarias found the terrible knot in his own gut easing.

He stroked her hair in a gentle caress and murmured nonsense in his own language. Or maybe it wasn't nonsense, maybe he tapped into those feelings of that stranger dwelling deep inside of him, the one who knew he couldn't lose her, not for the burden of his soul, but for the overwhelming emotion that welled like a tsunami he couldn't stop.

She couldn't possibly know what he was saying, he hardly knew. But when the next wave hit, she turned her head and looked at him, focusing on him, rather than turning away. Her eyes went wide, glazed, as the pain hit. This time, Zacarias was prepared and knew exactly how to take most of it from her. Her body was cleansed of all toxins and well on its way to becoming fully Carpathian. As the pain receded, he sensed it would be safe to put her in the healing earth.

"I can send you to sleep, Marguarita. When you awaken you will feel hunger and the need for blood, but you will not be in such pain."

Her gaze jumped to his as his palm wiped those tiny dots of blood from her forehead.

"You will awaken fully Carpathian."

Her tongue touched her dry lower lip in an attempt to moisten it. *It doesn't matter. I just want this over with.*

He *detested* the defeat in her. Marguarita was all fire to his ice, not outwardly, not in the sense of temper and picking fights, in fact, just the opposite. But she was passionate about what she believed in and who and what she loved. She poured herself completely into everything she did, just as she had wholly given herself to him.

She was worn out, her body and mind exhausted. He couldn't blame her. He felt wrung out and he hadn't suffered as she had.

"I do not want you to think I am doing anything else without your knowledge." He waited, but she didn't respond. "I will command your first sleep, and after that, your body will take over and sleep on its own when you command. You have my blood running in your veins. It is ancient blood, very powerful, and you will learn quickly to wield that power." He had to hurry before the next swelling pain came.

"You know the earth will rejuvenate you." He made it a statement.

Her lashes fluttered and fear crept into her eyes, but she nodded. *What do I do if I find myself trapped beneath the earth?*

He brushed another caress through her hair more because he needed to touch her than because it was in her face. "You will it to move. Command it. Picture the soil in your mind, doing what you wish. It may take a few times, but if you do not panic and think as a human, that you are buried alive, then you will be fine."

Her heart accelerated when he used that phrase, *buried alive*, but she nodded.

"I will be with you to ease your way," he assured.

It's coming. She didn't plead with him to take her away. There was no asking, no pleading. Marguarita made it clear, even in her exhausted state, that she would not be asking anything of him.

He felt the swell just as she did and he took command instantly, demanding she sleep deeply, the healing, rejuvenating sleep of his people. Carpathians shut down their hearts and lungs and lay as if dead while Mother Earth used her rich nutrients and minerals to aid them to full recovery and strength. He stopped Marguarita's heart and lungs as gently as possible.

He lifted her into his arms, cradling her gently against his chest, his eyes burning and his heart shredded. She lay limp, her long hair sweeping to one side, revealing the curve of her cheek and her long lashes. She looked so young and innocent, a beautiful woman, ravaged by the conversion, disillusioned by the man sworn to cherish and protect her.

Zacarias carried her through the house to the master bedroom, waving his hand to move the bed out of the way. The hand-woven rug followed and the floor opened to the sleeping chamber deep beneath the structure. Another wave of his hand opened the beckoning soil, almost a black loam rich with minerals. He felt the earth reaching for her as he floated them both down into that warm cocoon of an environment.

Very gently he laid her down, careful of her hair, bending to brush his mouth over hers. She wouldn't feel him—wouldn't know how silly he was acting when she was in a deep sleep, but he felt free to stroke his fingers down her arm to her hand. He threaded his fingers through hers, tenderness welling up unexpectedly.

Could he have lost her? She had pulled away from him. Rebuffed him. It hurt. Plain and simple, her rejection had been so complete, when she'd needed him the most. She would rather have suffered than allowed him into her mind, melding their spirits. His refusal to enter into the modern world could have cost him everything.

He sank down beside her, his eyes burning, his chest aching. He kept possession of her hand, his fingers caressing hers. He'd had everything in Marguarita. She'd offered him a world he could barely conceive of, let alone long for. He hadn't known how much he wanted it. Not the people, not the friends; he knew himself. He was a loner, but he could tolerate others for her sake. He should have paid attention to what those ritual binding words meant. *Her* happiness. *Her* care.

He was a man who was confident for a reason. He couldn't shove his responsibility off on Marguarita. If he expected her to follow where he led, he needed to place blame where it belonged. None of this would have happened if he had taken Solange's blood when it had been offered. He didn't want anything to do with the new world and its modern ways. He wanted to stay where he was comfortable. There would have been no question of taking command of the situation and protecting his lifemate. He didn't have the tools available to him because of sheer stubbornness.

He groaned and shook his head. He had the means right in front of him to provide his woman with protection and happiness, but he'd been too arrogant, too filled with his pride and honor to take advantage of the gifts handed to him. No more.

He was a fighter. That was who he was and Marguarita Fernandez was a woman worth fighting for. He was the one who was meant to walk beside her. Zacarias brought her fingers to his mouth and kissed her hand, little butterfly kisses, his heart aching for both of them.

Stay with me, mića emni kuŋenak minan—my beautiful lunatic. I promise you, I will be a better man, a better lifemate to you. You gave yourself to me once. Do it again. I have learned what cherish means. And I cherish you.

He kissed her hand again and took a deep breath, closed the earth over her and left the chamber to go out into the night. His world. He belonged there. For the first time he felt his affinity for it, the strong kinship of his kind for the night itself. Clouds dimmed the half-moon. The rain was a soft melody, steady and gentle, music to him. The insects and frogs provided a chorus to the symphony. He would make this Marguarita's world, as well. But he needed to at least—for her—take a few steps into the world she loved.

In his lifetime he had never once called for aid from any other. Not his brothers, not those brave enough to call him friend. Asking for help went against his code, yet for Marguarita, for his woman, he knew it had to be done. He stepped off the porch into the night rain, listening to the familiar comfort of the night creatures. Without Marguarita in his mind, bridging all those broken connections and filling all the dark shadows, he no longer saw in color, but the memory of emotion was strong in him. How could it not be? She was on his mind, in his heart, connected to his soul, and he felt his love for her, if not anything else.

Zacarias sent his call into the night. *I have great need, Dominic. Come to me. It is of utmost urgency.*

Part of him was shamed to call to the one Carpathian he loosely thought of as a friend. Men like Dominic and him didn't exactly have friends. Zacarias wasn't altogether certain what that word actually encompassed. He would die to protect Dominic, but that was his way of life, not friendship.

I must get to the Carpathian Mountains as soon as possible. We have news we must carry to the prince.

The reply was faint, as if over a great distance. But at least he had been heard and it meant Dominic was within range that he might meet him and yet he might stay within the night's distance of Marguarita.

I will meet you. Give me a range. I have need of a blood exchange.

Are you injured?

There was a part of him that didn't want to share that he had a lifemate. Marguarita was too important and he feared that every enemy would come after her if word got out. And he had many enemies. He closed his eyes briefly and forced himself to trust. *My lifemate will awaken in need in a few days and it will be necessary to protect her at all times. Already she has been endangered from my refusal of Solange's gift.*

He felt Dominic's shock even over the great distance and it almost made him smile. In that moment, although he accepted that he would always be different, that without Marguarita's presence, he would never feel as others did, he nearly felt true amusement at Dominic's reaction.

This news is—unexpected—but welcomed.

Give me your coordinates. I will meet you and hopefully can make it back before this night ends. She cannot be left unprotected. We have already had a confrontation with human vampire hunters. If one came, there is the possibility of more.

Zacarias was certain that Ruslan was in the area, but he hadn't showed himself, and the small attacks on the ranch had been just probes. It was possible Ruslan had planned to attack the prince even with his army diminished and the attacks on the ranch were merely a diversion, but he was taking no chances.

Dominic sent the necessary information, and Zacarias took to the air.

I will meet you, Dominic said. *My time is very limited as my message is very urgent, but it shouldn't be more than a couple of hours out of our way. Know that we have experimented, Zacarias, and although we can walk in early morning sunlight and evening sunlight, it all depends on the position of the sun. We are not without our Carpathian needs. Your body will still go leaden when the sun is reaching its highest peak. It will stay that way for several hours. We are still vulnerable and there is a great danger of being caught out in the sun when experimenting. I think the closer we are to turning when we take the blood, the less it will work.*

Dominic was warning him, but Zacarias was willing to take the risk. He didn't have a desire to face daylight. That would be Marguarita, and he would be at her side as long as possible, hopefully enjoying her happiness. The moment he knew it was necessary to return to the earth, she would accompany him. He would never be as other Carpathians, comfortable in the world of humans or Carpathians. He would never feel for others as they did. His world would be Marguarita, just as his father's world had been his mother.

I will be careful and learn my limitations, Dominic. Are my brothers well?

Worried about you. Perhaps you should consider bringing your woman to see them. They have waited long for this day.

Zacarias knew he must do so. Part of him even wanted that reunion, but he knew it wouldn't be what his brothers expected and he really didn't want to let them down. He had lost too much in the long centuries of being alone. Marguarita filled him, allowing him to tap into his feelings, allowing him to see color, but even now, as he flew over the rain forest, it was all gray and dull. Colors and emotions wouldn't stay long without her close.

His father had been unable to stand the absence after a time, so he had taken his mother into battle. Now, Zacarias knew somewhat how difficult it must have been, especially after having children and not feeling for them unless his lifemate was near enough to connect with him. Zacarias sent up a silent prayer to any higher power who might be listening, that he had the strength to resist ever taking Marguarita into danger, that he would always keep her safety above his own needs. *Never let me make the mistake of risking her for my own weakness.*

He made the long trip with Dominic flying toward him, in under two hours, which meant he would barely make it back to Marguarita by dawn. They greeted each other in the formal way of the Carpathian warrior, grasping each other's forearms.

"*Bur tule ekämet kuntamak*—well met, brother-kin," Zacarias greeted.

"*Eläsz jeläbam ainaak*—long may you live in the light," Dominic responded, those piercing eyes scrutinizing Zacarias carefully.

Zacarias shook his head. "You will not see what you wish to see. Marguarita enables me to see in color and to feel emotion. Without her in me, I am utterly alone in a stark, gray world." He knew somewhere close, Dominic's warrior woman, Solange, stood ready to defend her chosen lifemate. She was a force to be reckoned with, and he could feel the hairs on the back of his neck alerting him to danger.

Dominic sighed as he dropped his arms and stepped back. "I am sorry, my friend."

Zacarias shrugged. "She has become the center of my universe and I accept and am grateful for a chance I never envisioned. For her, I do this thing."

Dominic kept his eyes on Zacarias. "You are willing to exchange blood with me?"

Hunters gave blood when needed, but an exchange meant a hunter could track another easily. The idea was repulsive to Zacarias. He was a loner. A man apart and safety was paramount. Reclusive, elusive, he took great care to leave no trail when he didn't want to be followed.

For Marguarita he would have to extend that trust. He nodded his head.

Dominic smiled. "It is not necessary." He turned and beckoned to his lifemate. She came out from under cover, a lethal woman who would not hesitate to kill if necessary. She looked happy to see Zacarias.

Already he was feeling a strange crawling sensation in his gut. He needed to get back—to be with her—Marguarita. Being completely alone was no longer something he could bear. He took the extended wrist and once again drank from the powerful woman. Dominic, too, provided for him, giving him the mixture of powerful blood he would pass on to his woman.

"I have fed from your woman before, Dominic, yet still the sun burned me. Do you think this will work for me even as I am?"

Dominic shrugged. "The effect grows stronger each time the blood is taken, but there are limits and the only way to know is to try. Zacarias, have a safety net available to you. Be cautious."

Zacarias nodded. "I cannot be long from her. I thank you both. May the wind grant you fast journey." He gripped Dominic's forearms hard and saluted Solange before taking to the sky once more. His heart soared. Marguarita. He would soon be with her.

19

He was uneasy. When a hunter such as Zacarias De La Cruz was uneasy, it was a good time to go looking for trouble because it had to be near—or approaching.

Three nights. It had to be enough time for Marguarita to fully heal. For three long nights he had lain beside her, holding her in his arms, and yet even then, the world was grim without her filling the empty spaces in him. He was numb. Starkly alone. When one was used to such a thing, when emotions and color faded slowly, it was easier to bear, but losing it all so fast, one moment her warmth filling him, driving out shadow, and the next, being completely alone, was far more difficult than he had ever expected.

Still, Zacarias found himself pacing outside in the night where he could breathe in the night's information instead of waking Marguarita once again. The night was waning, but still he refused to bring her to the surface. Something was just that little bit off kilter. He couldn't find it, not with the wind and not with the insects. Everything appeared normal, but it wasn't. He knew it wasn't. He stepped off the porch and moved out into the yard, his keen sight hunting now—looking for one tiny discrepancy that would alert him to danger.

He needed her. Zacarias De La Cruz who never needed anyone in his life, needed Marguarita. And he needed her happy, giving herself to him, her laughter, her warmth, her soft, sweet body. Was he imagining things because he was he afraid to face her? Fear was an emotion and without Marguarita he didn't have such complications. No, there was something out here, something not right. It was only a matter of time.

His body went on alert, ready for anything. Her horses stamped restlessly in the stables. Missing her. As he was missing her. He moved away from the yard toward the rain forest bordering his land, drawn by an unknown frisson of warning, listening to the night. Insects chorused, the frogs chimed in, the cattle murmured and the horses stamped. Still—there was that note—or lack of one. Maybe it was just him. He felt off. Something not right in the pit of his stomach.

Concern for Marguarita's safety was uppermost in his mind. Things had been relatively quiet on the ranch since Esteban and DS had died. Even Cesaro had stayed away from the main house. He had given blood each time Zacarias had come to him and even seemed a little more at ease with him, but Zacarias had not sought him out for company, only for sustenance. He walked around the fence line to the back of the property, every sense alert.

Zacarias scanned the area for blank spots that might indicate a vampire was near. Absolutely everything seemed in place, perfect, too perfect. He didn't believe it. An attack was imminent, but from which direction? Was this another probe, or the real thing? Wings fluttered up in the trees. Without moving his head, he let his gaze drift to the thick line of trees guarding the rain forest. Eyes shone back at him.

Calm settled over him like a mantle. He stretched his senses. The real thing then. Constant movement in the canopy heralded more and more birds gathering. He wanted to take the fight as far from the hacienda as possible, not willing to risk Marguarita, the workers or her beloved horses. He was grateful she was beneath the ground, that he hadn't yet brought her to the surface where a vampire might detect her presence.

As far as any of his enemies knew, he had no lifemate. He didn't feel the emotions most Carpathian hunters experienced once they found the other half of their soul, so in that regard, he was both lucky and unlucky.

The lack of emotion would aid him in his battle. He kept moving, using the same unhurried, very fluid stride, feeling his muscles loosen in preparation. His breath came evenly, his heart steady and strong.

The wind picked up, the subtlest of movements. The tops of the trees swayed just a little more, leaves fluttering. Along the ground the grass undulated in a slow wave. This was the opening gambit. The battle always felt a little like a chess match to him. Combat was his world and he understood it, every nuance.

Zacarias continued his casual stride, drawing closer to the fence and the trees. The rain forest appeared quiet and dark. The rain fell steadily, soft drops that shifted a bit as the wind blew away from the trees and toward the hacienda. The land sloped down just slightly, the grass a little higher near the fence line. Zacarias walked along the fence, all the while keeping an eye on the birds gathering in the dark of the rain forest. Even as he walked, his arms swinging naturally at his sides, his hands wove a seamless pattern.

He barely noticed the rain. Cool water dripping steadily from the sky, from the rolling clouds above his head. A drop hit his neck and burned through his skin. He shut off the pain instinctively, throwing his woven shield over his head as he ran toward the fence and the forest to take the fight to them and away from Marguarita.

A deluge opened of small acid drops raining from the sky, even as the wind picked up. His shield protected his head, but the wind blew the burning drops into his back and thighs as he sprinted for the cover of the canopy. Fireballs slammed into the earth all around him, several striking his shield with alarming force. Overhead, a towering dark cloud churned with a fiery mass of red and orange threads.

Zacarias took another step and the ground opened up, a long jagged fissure, deep and gaping. He tumbled in, his shield falling a distance away from him. The acid rain and the fiery darts sliced through him. The earth shuddered and moved, closing that foot-wide gap. Zacarias dissolved into tiny molecules, speeding up toward ground level, trying to beat the closing of the fissure. The clap of the two sides of rock and dirt coming together was horrendous, echoing for miles. Birds shrieked and took to the air. Great predators darted down in a frenzy, looking for prey.

The ground shook, a tremor rocking the foundations of the stables and hacienda. Zacarias rose into the air. At once the birds screamed in exaltation, programmed eyes finding those tiny molecules through the rain and wind, diving for them as if streaking for the surface of water to plunge below for fish.

Zacarias had no choice, unless he wanted to be torn apart and consumed by birds. He streaked toward them, meeting the attack, shifting from molecules to a fire-breathing dragon, something he rarely did, but right now, he needed to rid the sky of the predatory birds. He shot through their ranks as they tore at his flanks, pecking like mad so that ruby red droplets dripped from him.

The scent of blood added to the frenzy of the birds. He wheeled and banked, coming above them, sending a stream of fire sweeping through the mass. The stench of burning meat permeated the night as blackened bodies fell from the sky. The remaining birds kept coming, pouncing on the dragon, hundreds multiplying into thousands, pecking and tearing with razor-sharp talons, digging through the tough hide to try to get to the Carpathian inside.

The sheer weight of the birds sent the dragon tumbling toward earth. Torn and bloody, Zacarias burst from the dragon before it hit the ground, the majority of the birds riding the great carcass to the ground, tearing at it in a kind of fury. Calling to the sky, he used the churning cloud of masses of red-orange flames, drawing them down to slam into the birds in great fireballs. Screaming, the vicious creatures tried to rise into the air, but long spears and tiny darts of flames leaped from one to the other until they were all engulfed in fire.

"Do you wish to keep up this silly charade, Ruslan," Zacarias called as he settled in the slight clearing just on the other side of the fence, in the rain forest itself. He continued to edge deeper beneath the canopy of trees, taking the fight farther from Marguarita.

Thunder rolled in answer. The clouds churned and boiled. The black cloud burst upward, a tower of fire and brimstone roiling angrily in the sky. The wind rushed through the trees, yet didn't move the clouds from overhead. Branches swayed, great stick arms reaching almost to the forest floor, as though bowing—or looking to grasp someone with bony fingers.

A dark, hooded figure emerged slowly from the trunk of a large kapok tree. He moved slowly, without any sign of hurry. It was a testament to the power of a master that the tree and surrounding ground didn't recoil from his presence. Nature could not stand the abomination of the undead, yet a true master was so adept at illusion, for brief periods, even Mother Earth could be deceived.

Not a single leaf or blade of grass withered. The figure was tall, imposing, shoulders wide and he walked with complete confidence. Stepping into the grove of trees where the canopy protected the forest floor, he flung off his hood. Long flowing hair was as black as night, his face young and brutally handsome. He smiled and held out his hand to Zacarias.

"Son. We meet again under more pleasant circumstances, I hope."

Zacarias frowned. What was Ruslan playing at? Testing him to see if he had emotions? If he had a lifemate? Every other De La Cruz brother had found his lifemate. Ruslan would hate them all the more for that. He believed himself superior to all of them—so why shouldn't he have the women? Zacarias and his family were unworthy of such things.

"I thought more of you, Ruslan. This is a tired trick. Show yourself and be done with it." For the first time he realized that not feeling emotion without Marguarita locked to him could be more than a curse. Ruslan could not endanger what he did not know of.

Zacarias waved his hand with a true casualness, as if that perfect image of his father didn't bother him at all—and in truth—he felt nothing at all at the sight of the man who had been his childhood hero. His wave removed the illusion and revealed Ruslan's true form. For one second he stood stripped of civility, his body rotted through with a thousand maggots crawling through him. His face was pitted with holes, his eyes sunken and his teeth blackened and serrated, pointed like ice picks sticking up through his gums.

In the time it took Zacarias to blink, that image changed as if it had never been. Ruslan stood before him as he had all those centuries ago. Young. Virile. His face without lines, almost beautiful rather than handsome. Zacarias looked rugged and older in comparison, lines etched into his face and a few scars intersecting here and there.

"I see your vanity has not changed at all," Zacarias greeted. "You did so love your pretty face. I suppose that is half the reason you chose to become vampire."

Ruslan brushed back his long length of hair. "At least you still know pretty from ugly. I have long kept tabs on you, old friend. You refuse to join us and you refuse to die. In all the centuries you have never stayed in one place more than a single night or at best two. Yet here you remain." He swept his arm toward the hacienda and the wind changed course, following his direction, taking with it dozens of small fireballs to rain down across the pastures and structures.

Zacarias sent the rain in a fast deluge, putting out the small fires immediately. He flexed his shoulders, now burned through to bone with a thousand brands from the acid rain and the small, pebble-sized fireballs Ruslan was now using against the ranch.

"We can do this all night, but surely you did not think I would be impressed by such childish games? I play them with your puppets, but they are not really worthy of my attention. I thought at last I might have an opponent of merit."

"You do not heal your wounds."

Had there been a hint of eagerness in Ruslan's tone? Zacarias shrugged again. "I do not feel such things, so how necessary is it really?" He observed Ruslan closely, watching the vampire's nostrils flaring and his tongue continually licking at his lips. "Does the scent of my blood bother you?"

Ruslan shook his head. Shook it again. Much like a twitch he couldn't stop. The licking of his lips continued compulsively. "No more than the scent of any blood I consume. You have not fed this night. I offer my blood."

"How very gentlemanly of you." Zacarias gave a short, mock bow. "What do you want, Ruslan? I grow weary of your games. Have you come for deliverance? Justice? I'll be more than happy to send you from this earth if that is what you wish."

"*Justice* is a good word to use for a betrayer of friendship. Of brotherhood. You turned on us and made an alliance with that brat of a prince. He is worse than his father before him." Ruslan spat a mouthful of wriggling white worms.

Zacarias shrugged. "What is it then?"

"I had long thought to have you join our ranks, but you never came. Then you sent me such an insult, destroying my army to the last puppet."

"They were merely pawns you sent to test me. You expected me to kill them. Cannon fodder, Ruslan, nothing more. Your silly plot to kill the prince didn't work. You had to know testing it on me would prove that to be so."

"You were never supposed to be there." Ruslan's voice rose to a higher note. His beautiful mask slipped a little. The trees shivered as he shrieked out his rising anger. He could barely contain his rage, his fingers curling into tight fists. "You never spend time with your brothers. You never stay in one place. Why? Why would you change your pattern after so many centuries? Did you do so just to irk me?"

"You flatter yourself, Ruslan. I do not give as much thought to you as you give me credit for. I am a hunter—nothing more and nothing less."

All the while he spoke, Zacarias didn't allow himself to focus wholly on Ruslan. The vampire had traps just waiting to be sprung. He noticed every detail, including the rising wind. It was subtle, but the grass bent just that little bit more toward him. The leaves fluttered and spun, a strange grayish when they had been a dull, muddy greenish-brown.

The wind teased the ground around his feet, stirring the leaves and vegetation on the forest floor. Strangler vines shivered. Flowers winding up tree trunks lost petals. To Zacarias they looked like white-gray ash falling to the forest floor.

"You have not told me why you stayed here, old friend," Ruslan coaxed. "It is odd behavior for you."

Zacarias shrugged his shoulders, loosening his muscles. "A bit of an injury, but nothing for you to worry about. Plenty of ready sustenance while I recouped. Have no worries, I am in top condition now."

Ruslan clucked his tongue. "That was not what was reported to me. My men have much to answer for. I was told your injuries are still quite severe."

"Do not believe such tales. I would not want you to worry, Ruslan, about your old friend. I am quite capable of bringing justice to every undead who walks this earth."

Flames leaped to life in Ruslan's eyes. He grimaced and once again that handsome mask slipped revealing blackened, serrated teeth and muddy receding gums. His fingers twitched, and then closed once more into a tight fist.

The wind tugged harder at the debris on the forest floor. Zacarias felt a jab of pain, which he instantly stemmed as something large went through his leg. Glancing down he saw creeper vines rising and writhing together, coiling around and through his leg, starting at his foot and ankle. They grew together, and through his flesh, driving like spears to weave in and out of his leg, making him a part of the new plant.

The vines were covered in moss resembling scales with little hooks. Every scale had snapped up as the thing snaked up and through his leg, hooking into his flesh. He attempted to shift and found his leg was held fast, as the vines growing through his leg locked him in place.

Immediately he knew something alive was being injected into him, tiny bodies running beneath his skin, boring into muscle and tissue, digging deeper still. He ignored the sensation. More than likely the object was to weaken him, bleed him, until he was unable to effectively fight Ruslan while the vine literally held him in place, making him part of its structure.

The master vampire was too experienced to directly challenge him in hand-to-hand combat. He would trade blows from a distance and continue his battle plan of nipping at Zacarias, taking bites out of him until he was certain the hunter was unable to defend himself. Only then would he move in for the kill.

The strategy had one flaw. Zacarias was a single-minded hunter. His body meant nothing to him. Only the kill mattered and he *would* kill Ruslan Malinov. Nothing else in that moment could concern him. Ignoring the vine winding up his leg, now almost to his thigh, he raised his own hands toward the rain forest and called his own weapon.

The wind shifted back toward Ruslan, a swift change, giving him no time to gloat. The sky around the vampire darkened as thousands of tiny biting flies swarmed over and into Ruslan. Every rotting hole provided an entrance, his mouth, eyes and nostrils. Illusions didn't matter, they saw only rotting flesh.

Like tiny missiles they torpedoed deep into Ruslan's body, breeding as they went, depositing larvae and reproducing at a rapid rate. The flies multiplied even as they attacked. Ruslan tore at his chest, sharp nails slashing his face open, giving Zacarias the necessary time to study the vine growing through his leg.

It was a simple enough trap, utilizing what was already in place. The plants were dead, as were the leaves and vegetation lying on the forest floor. In order to breathe life into them, Ruslan had to put some small part of himself into those dead plants. The leaves on the forest floor continued to feed the vines, so that they bored through skin and muscle driving deeper still until they emerged on the other side.

Zacarias let go of his physical self in order for his spirit to enter his body. The vines winding their way through his body, stabbing and spearing through flesh and bone moved toward one thing—the small light of his spirit in him. Granted, without Marguarita, that light was small, but it was there, keeping his honor. The tiny bugs consuming his insides were also sustained by that light. Zacarias took a deep breath and let go of life. All life. He stopped his heart for a moment, refused to allow air through his lungs. The plant loosened immediately, but when he forced his body to work again, the bugs continued to feast.

Zacarias was mostly darkness. Shadows and stains, tainted in a way few if any other hunters were. That darkness was the very thing that allowed him to ignore such wounds, such excruciating pain. He was already part of that world. His father had been legendary with amazing skills in battle, but he was the only Carpathian Zacarias knew of who carried shadows within his soul—until his son had been born.

Now, deliberately, Zacarias reached for those shadows—embraced them—let himself lose all light, drawing on the darkness that seemed to make up so much of him for aid. The moment all light within him was extinguished, the bugs began to die. The shadows were too dark to keep them alive. The plant lost its ability to continue growing, and with an already loosened hold on him, Zacarias was able to sheer off the outer woven branches, leaving the vines still inside his body.

There had to be a source for bringing the dead leaves and vines to life. Zacarias was a hunter and he scented the undead immediately, a small slice of Ruslan giving life to his creation. Ruslan couldn't sustain being in two places at one time, not while fighting off the attack of tiny flies. It took only moments to slay that dark force and take control of the vine within his body. Ignoring Ruslan's scream of fury and promises of retaliation, Zacarias changed the molecules of the remaining plant, reshaping, absorbing, utilizing the thick vines inside him to replace the muscle and tissue lost. He could do nothing about the blood loss, but anything natural and of the earth was within his ability to manipulate.

The moment his body was healed, he attacked without hesitation, a blur of motion, speeding across the distance between the vampire and himself, closing fast. Ruslan shrieked and rushed toward him. Thunder cracked. Shook the earth. Lightning sizzled across the sky in great whips as the two crashed together.

Zacarias drove deep with his fist, piercing the rotted chest. Acid blood poured over him, burning through skin to bone. He hit something solid, abruptly stopping his attack, preventing him from reaching the blackened heart. The jar rode up his arm, and a burning vise fused around his arm sending waves of pain he cut off. The tiny stinging flies took to the air in a black swarm, closing around both vampire and hunter. It was difficult not to breathe them into his lungs. Talons tore at his chest, carving out great chunks of skin and muscle.

Zacarias dissolved, allowing the wind to take him away from Ruslan, giving himself time to temporarily heal injuries and to keep as much blood as possible from leaking onto the ground. Ruslan licked at his fingers, his tongue long and obscenely thick, forked like a serpent's. His face no longer wore his mask of beauty. The real vampire was revealed.

Zacarias had seen his share of rotting corpses, but nothing equaled Ruslan Malinov. Flesh peeled off of him. Worms crawled through gaping holes in his flesh. His mouth was more of a gaping hole, without lips, his eyes sunken. Every living thing shrunk from him, grass withering, ferns and moss going muddy brown. Even the insects scurried away. Only the black flies persisted, feasting on the rotting flesh and depositing as many eggs as possible in the blackened organs.

"You really have let yourself go, old friend," Zacarias observed. "I think your arm is about to fall off."

Ruslan roared, the threat rumbling through the forest, shaking the trees. He raised his arms, up and down, palms pointed to the sky. All around Zacarias the leaves rustled, came to life, whirling and flying with the chaos Ruslan created. It was impossible to see through the whipping leaves as they stacked and formed one creature after another.

He extended his arms and closed his eyes, removing the distraction of thousands of leaves coming alive around him. He reached with his other senses to find the threat within the moving debris. The figures surrounded the entire area, forming a loose ring and adding numbers inside the circle until the forest was populated with great monsters all moving toward him. The shadows in him called to the darkness in them. Ruslan had learned quickly.

"I fear it matters little how I look to you, Zacarias. My little army does not care, either. I have no need to expend energy for your last moments. You should have joined me. In truth, you have always had the darkness in you—far more than I ever had. This was your legacy, the greatest gift of your father yet you refused to embrace it." There was real contempt in Ruslan's voice. "You had greatness handed to you, but you chose to be a martyr, suffering alone while I have whatever I want."

Zacarias slowly opened his eyes, smiling, knowing his white teeth were a stark contrast to Ruslan's blackened, gaping maw and that small detail would prick Ruslan's vanity as nothing else could.

"I cannot fear you, Ruslan. I cannot feel what you do to me. I do not care about anything other than destroying you. You think you have the advantage, but in fact, I do. You want to continue your pitiful existence. You seek power. You wish to rule the world. To destroy the prince. To kill me."

Zacarias's smile turned as cold as ice. "So many wishes, when I have only one. Your death. You are *kuly*—nothing more, an intestinal worm, a demon who devours souls. You are truly *hän ku vie elidet*—a thief of life and for that, I pronounce sentence on you."

The dead and rotting vegetation, collected over hundreds, perhaps thousands of years went into a frenzy, flapping arms and growing teeth as they shuffled toward him. Zacarias sent the wind, but the leaf creatures weren't in the least affected, holding their own against the blast.

Ruslan's laughter grated on the ears of any within hearing range. Joyfully he danced around. "I do not think it will be me who dies this night, hunter."

The creatures closed in, making the air stagnant, oppressive, smelling of dead, rotting things. He needed something completely the opposite to oppose Ruslan's force, giving him the necessary time to kill the vampire. Deliberately Ruslan had preyed on his worst secrets, those shadows cutting through his body, taking his soul.

Now was not the time for pride. Or for fear. He was a hunter and he had no choice but to use every resource possible. Ruslan Malinov was the biggest threat to the Carpathian people. Without him, the army of vampires would diminish, giving Mikhail, the prince, time to bring together his people and shore up all defenses.

He did the unthinkable. *Marguarita. You must wake.*

He could not allow himself to think of her and what she might go through upon waking beneath the ground. She was human and he had already asked so much of her. This vampire was responsible for bringing the Carpathian people to near extinction. He could not escape no matter the cost to the hunter—or his beloved lifemate.

Deep beneath the hacienda, Marguarita became aware of two things: she was buried alive, and Zacarias was in trouble. She came awake instantly, the knowledge flooding her body along with a terrible hunger that clawed and raked her belly. She kept her eyes closed tight, determined not to panic. She knew she would have if she'd simply awakened buried alive, but she *felt* Zacarias.

Strangely, she could hear her heartbeat, but there didn't seem to be air moving through her lungs. The sound echoed eerily through her head. She concentrated on Zacarias, ignoring her need to mindlessly scream, to feel the weight of the earth pushing down on her. Gently, with great stealth, she found the path to his mind. Pain engulfed her—savage—vicious pain, an agony that pushed through her entire body easily rivaling what she had gone through in the conversion. She slipped out of him before she could give herself away, or faint from the horror and pain of what he suffered.

What had he said to her? He had told her how to move the soil from her resting place. *Visualize, Marguarita,* she reminded herself. *Will it to happen.*

Her first attempt got her nowhere, just panic seeping in. Determinedly, she pushed it away. *Use your will. Your father always said you were stubborn enough to move mountains if you really wanted to do it, so move this little bit of earth,* she commanded herself.

Her mind screamed the moment her fingers moved and she was more aware than ever that she was beneath the ground, but she kept her eyes closed tight and forced her mind to picture the dirt above her parting like the Red Sea, pushing up and to either side. When she could draw breath and look up at the ceiling of the chamber, she wiped beads of sweat from her face and sat up.

I am here.

Come to me. Inside me—your way. If this goes wrong, pull out immediately.

She didn't hesitate. No matter how angry or hurt she'd been, a man like Zacarias De La Cruz would never ask such a thing in a time of battle unless it was necessary. She found that now-familiar primitive animal in him and gained entrance, sliding ever so gently into him. The darkness took her breath away. Sheer savagery, kill or be killed. Every part of him seemed dark and shadowed, walls of sheer ice, blocks of it, filling his mind, ice in his veins.

His insides were ravaged. The pain, excruciating, yet somehow he was able to block it, something she didn't understand but was grateful for. She didn't want to know how all that damage had occurred, or how he could remain on his feet, his entire focus on destroying evil. She poured warmth into him. Love. Everything she was. She gave herself up to him, filling him, forcing the dark to recede, spilling her brightness across every shadow.

He made no move to connect with her, but she felt him tap into that flow of warmth—of empathy and understanding. He sent out a call into the rain forest. She felt the summoning. No, not exactly a summoning, more of a request such as she would make. No command. No arrogance. No hint of self. Only that request for aid.

The dead in the forest had to be destroyed by the living. It amazed her how he knew such things—how his mind worked so quickly surrounded by creatures bent on tearing him apart. He needed a clear path to Ruslan and that was all that mattered to him in that moment.

Marguarita took a deep breath as the leaf figures attacked, swinging at Zacarias, slicing through skin and bone as he whirled in the center among them, using every available means to keep them at bay. Fire. Wind. Nothing worked against them and all the while, Ruslan laughed, a shrill, grating sound that set her teeth on edge.

She forced herself to try to stay disconnected from what was happening to Zacarias. He was very calm, his mind working. All this was a distraction. She didn't see how it would help at all, but she couldn't help but be in awe, even as she was terrified for him. He didn't attempt to hide the truth from her—that she was in his mind—but not *on* his mind. She was in him only because he needed another weapon, and he didn't acknowledge she was a flesh and blood woman—his woman. He was not afraid for himself or for her. He felt only the need to destroy evil.

The forest canopy rippled with life and monkeys dropped from the tree branches onto the backs of the creatures, toppling them, tearing them apart and leaping onto the next. It took a moment or two for Marguarita to realize the creatures being destroyed were the ones blocking the path to the exulting Ruslan.

Zacarias sped through the opening the monkeys had carved for him, his entire being focused on one thing only. He knew exactly where Ruslan stood and where his heart was located. He had the time to assess the obstacle he'd met in his earlier attack and he knew how to penetrate that protective coat of armor to reach the withered heart.

He was on Ruslan before the vampire had time to realize he was vulnerable. Zacarias once again changed the molecules in his body, shifting at the last moment to drive through that plating, using split-second timing to open his fist and grasp the heart. His fingers dug through the tendons and muscle, ripping at them in an effort to reach the organ.

Ruslan shrieked, blasting Zacarias in the face with the foul stench of putrid rot. He sank both hands into Zacarias's belly, tearing it open, spilling blood on the ground, insane with rage, dipping his head to the contents, trying to eat the hunter alive with his savage, serrated teeth.

Zacarias ripped the heart from the chest, spinning to try to get the vampire off of him. Powerful Carpathian blood poured over Ruslan's face and down his chin while his own black venom burned through Zacarias's hand and arm to the bone. Zacarias flung the heart from him and clamped both hands over Ruslan's head and jerked, snapping the neck and flinging the vampire away from him.

He clamped both hands over his open belly, his legs going out from under him. He landed hard on his knees, breathing deep, riding out the pain before he could shove it away from him. Ruslan had landed a few feet from him and rolled, his head obscenely lolling to one side.

Zacarias groaned when he saw that Ruslan had fallen over his extracted heart. The vampire caught up his heart and took to the air, black blood dropping and sizzling along the ground. He licked at his fingers in the air, trying to extract every bit of Carpathian blood from his arm and hand before streaking away.

The moment Ruslan had been attacked, he'd pulled his energy from the army of the dead, so that the leaves and branches tumbled back to the forest floor. Monkeys scrambled back into the trees. Zacarias let himself fall, looking up at the rain. Once more it was a gentle drizzle, hitting him in the face. It took great effort to call down the white-hot energy to rid himself of the vampire venom. As soon as it was off of him, he dropped his arms wearily to his sides.

I'm coming to you. Marguarita made it a statement, not a question.

He found himself smiling. His beautiful lunatic. She had every right to despise him, every reason to fear him, yet if he had ordered her to stay away, she would have defied him and come to him anyway. There was no stopping such a quiet force and he was too far gone to try. She never seemed to bother to argue. She just did what she believed was right. His blood was leaking out all over the ground and healing himself was going to be a difficult task.

Do not forget your clothes. Cesaro will be riding this way any moment. I would have to kill him and I am not certain I am up to the task.

She tried to laugh, he'd have to give her that. Her amusement came through her tears. She was crying for him and he knew she would be doing that a lot in the years to come. *I should have converted you with love, Marguarita. With care. I should have held you when you were so afraid. I am so far in the dark, perhaps there is no way to bring me back.*

I don't want to bring you back. I just want to save you. There's a difference. You'll have to do the clothes yourself. I can't manage. There was impatience in her voice. And she was much closer than she had been.

Zacarias lifted his head. Her beloved mare raced toward him with

Marguarita astride her back, and thanks to the good *Dios* the horse had a smooth gait. She was entirely naked. He shook his head. She was slowly filling him back up with her light, pushing the darkness away. He could see his blood was red, pooling on the ground around him.

She was off the horse and running toward him as he waved his hand to clothe her. She nearly tripped over her skirt as she raced to him. Using both hands, she shoved a soft cloth she carried against his belly. *Lie back. Just relax for a moment. And don't let me too far into your mind. I don't want you to feel this.*

He allowed himself to sink back down and just watched her face—that beloved face with so much concern stamped into it. So much love—love he didn't deserve. "What did you mean when you said you didn't want to bring me back from the darkness, that you just wanted to save me? It is the same thing."

She shook her head, digging into the soil to find the richest, untainted earth she could find. She used her own saliva to make a paste. *Actually, it isn't the same thing. The darkness in you that you despise so much is a precious gift and one you have come to rely on. It allows you to hunt the way you do. It keeps you alive when others would die.*

She winced visibly as she packed his wounds tight with the muddy paste she'd made. He touched her lips with gentle fingers. "You think it is a gift not to feel? To be so close to darkness that every moment I exist is a fight?"

Yes. It is that darkness that allows you to instinctively know where your prey is going next, to be one step ahead of them. To endure these kinds of mortal wounds that would kill anyone else. You are already healing yourself, Zacarias. And you are already thinking of where this vampire will be hiding until tomorrow night. It is near dawn and you know he is seeking a resting place. That's what those shadows do for you. They allow you to live and do what you do like no one else can do it. So, no, I don't want to take that from you.

"But you fear I will not come back to you."

She extended her wrist to him. Hunger beat at her, but it was far more important to give him whatever she could to sustain him and help him heal as fast as possible. *You are so good at pushing aside your memories that a small part of me thinks you will one day forget to remember me after the battle.*

He took her wrist and very gently made the cut, allowing her life-giving blood to flow into him. It was the blood of an ancient Carpathian now. Powerful and strong because his blood flowed in her veins. He felt his body reach for it, every organ, all muscle and tissue, each cell.

I will always return to you—always, but I can only be who I am, Marguarita. I want to be gentle for you. I want to give you all the things you deserve. I will always expect you to follow my lead . . .

Her eyebrow shot up. With her free hand she smoothed back his hair. *Do you think I am unaware of this about you? I want who you are, Zacarias, but I expect you to follow the vows you swore to me. I want to be cherished. I want you to have in mind my happiness when you make your decisions. And you have to know I will always be me. I will make up my own mind when I feel you are wrong.*

He glanced up at her face, a smile in his eyes. *I cannot conceive of being wrong. Well—there was that one time . . .*

Her laughter spilled into his mind. *One? I'm going to let that go because after this battle you might just be a little out of your mind.*

He swiped his tongue across the cut on her wrist. "Cesaro comes. He will give you blood and you will have to take it, Marguarita. I need to go."

Her breath caught in her throat. *Go? I don't understand. Go where? You have to go to ground and heal is what you have to do and I can be with you.*

"I must hunt Ruslan."

She shook her head adamantly. *No. You can't do that, not tonight. It's almost dawn and you could be caught out in the sun.*

"You saw my memories of Dominic and his woman sharing their blood with me."

Yes, but I also saw him warn you that you have to be cautious, to test your limits. You haven't done that and you said yourself, the stronger the darkness, the less a Carpathian can take the sun. Don't do this, Zacarias. For me. Don't do this.

He reached out and very gently caressed her long sweep of hair. "This particular vampire is a master unlike any other. I would not get this chance again in another ten thousand years. I am asking you to not ask this of me. Right at this moment, I would give you anything you want—even this, Marguarita. But I need you not to make this request."

She closed her eyes tightly. For a moment she felt she couldn't breathe.

She had to let him go. He couldn't be anything but what he was—a hunter. She would be asking him to be something he was not. *See that you come back to me in one piece.*

Zacarias stood, his clothing in bloody tatters. Lacerations and wounds crisscrossed his body. The bloody cloth fell from his belly, but the wound was closed. He flexed his muscles. "You will take Cesaro's blood from his wrist. He will guard you while I am gone."

Framing her face with his hands, Zacarias leaned down to kiss her upturned mouth. She clung for a moment, uncaring that Cesaro was watching them. Reluctantly, Zacarias put her aside and took to the air. The moment he was away from her, he dismissed her from his mind, pushing her out, trusting her to stay out. There could only be one chance at this. Ruslan Malinov was too dangerous of an adversary to allow him to escape.

Zacarias caught the scent of the vampire's foul stench and he followed, using the droplets as a guide. He had spent centuries patrolling up and down the Amazon crossing borders and going from country to country. He knew every cave, every place a vampire might choose as a resting place. He knew where his enemy would most likely go. More than that, Marguarita was correct in saying the darkness in him allowed him to think like the undead.

Ruslan would want to get as far from Zacarias as possible, but he would want to be able to feed as easily as possible. There were very few towns and ranches in the area near caves. Zacarias knew every one of them. He was convinced Ruslan would choose the most inaccessible, a mere crack in the rock allowing a shapeshifter to flatten his body enough to slide inside that narrow, steep tunnel leading down to the very bowels of the earth. Ruslan would guard it well as only a master vampire could do, so either Zacarias arrived ahead of him—before dawn and secreted himself inside to wait—or it could take hours to unravel the safeguards and he could get caught in the sun.

Ruslan had a head start on Zacarias, but he was cunning and he would know his blood was in the wind and a hunter like Zacarias would scent it as well as any wolf. He would use false trails, backtrack, every trick he had ever learned to hide his true destination from the Carpathian and that would take time. Ruslan would try to use the sun against a hunter, only going to ground at the last moment so there was no risk a hunter could catch him in his lair. Zacarias had to make a decision—go with his gut feeling—depend on the very thing he detested in himself—or follow the trail. Either one could cost him his prey.

Marguarita had said the darkness in him was a gift. She trusted it because it was a part of him. He thought of it as evil. He only remembered his father as evil, never earlier. It was as though that one moment had negated his father's entire life, centuries of honor and duty. His father had taught him every skill he possessed. He had swung his lifemate into the air and laughed readily with her. He had rejoiced as each son was born and mourned, crying bloodred tears unashamedly when his one daughter had lost her battle for survival. His father had not been evil all of his life.

So then, let the darkness guide him. He abandoned the trail and chose the cave deepest in the earth, hurrying now to get there before his prey. If he was wrong, he had lost his chance, but he would be safe from the sun.

Zacarias passed over the rocky ledge where the cracked boulder was the only sign of an entrance to the narrow tunnel. He used stealth, allowing a slight breeze to let him drift, examining the area from every angle. Ruslan didn't appear to have reached the resting place before him. He moved closer, careful not to disturb so much as a pebble, testing the entrance. There was nothing to hinder him going inside.

As smoky vapor, Zacarias slipped inside the mountain, weaving his way through the long crack into the narrow, small tunnel. He followed it deeper and deeper beneath the earth. The sound of dripping water grew in volume as he neared the small chamber. The tunnel had narrowed so that only a small animal might get through to the larger hollowed-out cavern.

Ruslan had not been there before him. There was a certain odor to a vampire, one that even a master could mask only for so long. Did that mean he had never found this particular cave? There was no more time to go looking. He had to trust in his experience. He took his time, examining the small chamber, finding several cracks running through the ceiling and walls. Water dripped steadily from the north wall, but the southern wall was mainly rock. He chose one of the smaller cracks to secrete himself in.

His body desperately needed to go to ground. Shifting took energy, and even with Marguarita's blood, he knew he didn't have much time before it would become critical to heal in the soil or it would be too late. Few Carpathians would be able to survive the mortal wounds he had and continue the hunt. He knew the darkness within him enabled him to never acknowledge what was happening to his body. He fought, he healed himself and he went on without pain or exhaustion. But eventually his body would collapse. If Ruslan did choose this cave, Zacarias could not think about when that collapse would come.

Minutes ticked by. He knew the exact position of the sun and it was very close to rising. He could feel its presence like a burning lamp pressed close against him. He knew the light would always get to him, even if Solange's royal blood really allowed him a few more hours of the day to move in. He would never be comfortable, but if it made Marguarita happier with him, he would endure it, just as he would endure her human companions.

A rock rolled in the dirt. Something scratched along the narrow tunnel wall just outside the chamber. Zacarias stayed relaxed, not expending any of his precious energy. He was in bad shape and if he gave himself away too soon and Ruslan was able to fight, they both would die this night. The foul stench of rotting flesh drifted into the chamber.

Immediately, familiar calm swept through Zacarias. Nothing else mattered now, not him, not anything, but the destruction of this one vampire who had caused the Carpathian people so much pain and damage. This was the reason Zacarias had been born and bred to fight. This was why the darkness in him ran so deep—defending his people against the most vile, evil creature imaginable.

He stayed still, patient, watching as Ruslan prepared his safeguards and staggered to his resting place. His head still listed to one side, which told Zacarias the vampire was as injured as he had been. Ruslan was too vain to allow something like that to go unless he needed to conserve his energy. Zacarias didn't move as Ruslan lay down and folded his arms across his chest, giving himself up to the sleep of the dead. Even then, Zacarias waited until the sun had begun its climb. He wanted to insure Ruslan was in a leaden state.

With infinite stealth he dislodged from the ceiling and made his way to the master vampire's resting place. Instantly Ruslan's eyes snapped open. He hissed, a low sound of hatred. There was no movement, but that didn't mean he wasn't capable. Zacarias stayed out of the strike zone just to be certain.

"What honor is this? Coming to me in my weakest hour?" Ruslan demanded.

Zacarias's eyebrow shot up. "Exterminating vermin is not about honor. Living with a code of conduct is honorable, Ruslan. That is what you always failed to understand. Killing is not honorable. This is my job. Honor demands I use whatever tool possible, whatever weapon, to destroy evil—and you are evil. There is no honor in the method of kill, only the fulfillment of a job that is necessary."

Ruslan's cackle filled his mind. "You can rip out my heart here in this cavern, but you cannot bring the lightning so deep beneath the earth. We will see who survives come nightfall."

"I have no intention of ripping out your heart." Zacarias approached the leaden figure with extreme caution. Ruslan was a powerful vampire and, as a hunter, he respected that power, knowing the master would not go easily to his end.

Ruslan looked puzzled, his hollowed eyes filled with hatred and cunning. Bats dropped without warning, covering Zacarias's body, biting with sharp teeth, trying to drain him for their master. Worms burst through the dirt walls and spiders crept from every crevice, all at the summons of the master. A few rats poked their heads out of the tunnel, beady eyes fixed on Zacarias.

Zacarias dissolved under the weight of the bats, shifting quickly to put himself across the room. He blazed light through the room, a flash bright and terrible, very hot, a concentrated sun that singed the bats and drove the insects and rats away. He needed only a small amount of time.

"You cannot keep that up forever," Ruslan crowed, "and they are mine to command."

"It does not matter." Zacarias was on him instantly, scooping the dead weight into his arms. The foul breath blasting his face disoriented him for just a moment. There was poison in that concentrated breath, but he shifted, taking the vampire's rotting form with him.

What are you doing? Ruslan demanded, switching to the Carpathian common path of communication, for the first time truly alarmed. *Where are you taking me?*

To the surface. Your safeguards keep others out, but they do not keep us in.

Zacarias knew the exact moment Ruslan understood what he was doing. Once through the tunnel and crack, he shifted again, bringing them both into the dawning sun. Ruslan's mouth opened wide in a soundless scream of agony. With sudden effort, driven by sheer will and desperation, he buried talons deep into Zacarias's skin.

If I burn, then so will you.

Zacarias sank with his burden to the ground, his strength nearly gone. He would not be able to enter the cave and he knew by the feel of the sun on his skin that he would not have enough time to unravel the safeguards.

I love you, Marguarita. I am truly sorry for the mistakes I have made with you. Reach for my brothers, they will aid you when I am gone.

Zacarias could not allow himself to think what would happen to her or of all the things he'd done wrong with her. He wanted his last memories of her to be held close, that feeling of complete, unselfish love she'd given him.

Tell me where you are. I will not come to you, have no worries, but show me.

She was calm. Utterly, completely calm. That was Marguarita, and for the first time he believed. She had been sent to him to save him from himself—his own personal miracle. If anyone could save him—she could—but he didn't see how. Even by car, there was no way to reach him in time. He didn't tell her that, what was the point?

He was weary, so exhausted he could barely move.

Don't you dare give up.

He loved that little bite in her voice.

What are you smiling about? Ruslan demanded. *You will die with me. Hurry. I will show you how to unravel the safeguards if you have the strength left to get me out of the sun.*

Zacarias shook his head. "You die this fine morning, Ruslan. No matter the cost to me, your evil will never walk the earth again."

Ruslan's body writhed. Turned lobster red. Heated until he scorched Zacarias's skin. Still those talons remained hooked in his sides, locking them together while the vampire began to sizzle, his rotting skin bubbling.

Smoke rose. The stench of burning meat filled the air. Ruslan screamed, the sound tearing through his chest and throat to startle the birds in the nearby trees into flight.

Zacarias looked up. Vultures began to circle. His own skin burned only because Ruslan's body touched his. He didn't try to fight it. His body hadn't turned to lead as of yet, but his arms and face prickled, wanting to shrink from that mass of red-hot churning threads.

Holes burst through Ruslan's body. The stench increased until Zacarias wanted to gag. The talons loosened, and without the thick plug of those razor-sharp hooked nails, blood began to leak onto the ground, forming a small pool around him.

Stay with me, Zacarias, Marguarita urged.

Her calmness astounded him. She should be in a panic, yet her mind was much clearer than his. He was too tired to think.

Give yourself to me, she whispered. *Trust me to keep you safe.*

He had never trusted anyone. If he did as she asked and passed his spirit into her keeping, there would be nothing she did not know about him. His inability to feel without her shamed him. He would never know the true love of his brothers unless she was anchored in his mind. He would always be uncomfortable in the presence of humans. He could barely tolerate that world and she would know. She would see that he felt nothing even for those serving him. She would see too much. How much could a woman take?

Give yourself to me. Freely—as I gave myself to you.

Losing her to death was perhaps an act of cowardice rather than allowing her to face the true monster that she had given herself to. He had claimed her. Bound them together. Through it all, she had been the one to give herself to him over and over, meeting his every demand.

Ruslan burst into flames, shrieking his hatred of the world. The talons fell from Zacarias's skin, freeing him, and Zacarias dragged himself away from the burning vampire. Black smoke shot into the sky like a beacon.

Zacarias watched until that white-hot heat consumed every inch of the master vampire, until he was certain the heart was gone and not so much as a sliver of him remained anywhere. Only then did he lay his head back and let his body turn into a limp rag doll.

He took a breath and then a leap of faith that she would want him anyway, as dark and shadowed as he was. He sent his spirit outside his physical body, into her keeping. Just before he closed his eyes, he heard the sound of a helicopter and he smiled. That piece of equipment was of the modern world—her world. Maybe there was something to it after all. His resourceful lifemate had obviously used his blood bond with either Julio or Cesaro, and Lea Eldridge was flying them to his rescue.

20

What did it take for a Carpathian to heal such horrific wounds? A week? Two? A month? Marguarita slowly walked through the dark house, toward her own bedroom and bath. She had learned to take blood from Julio and Cesaro, a difficult task. She had learned to part the horrible dirt, wiping frantically at her hair and body, terrified of spiders crawling over her. There was so much she didn't know, so much she needed to learn.

Every evening she went out to the stables to her beloved horses, but even riding her Peruvian Paso, one of her greatest joys, could no longer stop the crush of sorrow welling up in her. It didn't matter how often she told herself Zacarias was safe, was in fact, lying in their sleeping chamber. It didn't matter how many days she lay beside him, holding him, brushing his long hair aside to study every line carved into his face, she still feared for him—mourned for him. At times she feared she might lose her mind.

More than once, waking with Zacarias beside her and spiders crawling over her, she'd smacked him in a fit of temper, remembering the mass of spiders she'd fallen into with no comfort from him. But mostly, she tried not to weep for him, tried not to beg him to wake and be with her. She needed him desperately, but she refused to be weak when he needed to heal.

There were so many things to work on, to occupy her time. She still couldn't quite get the clothing right. She usually took a bath and dressed as she always had. She preferred to take a bath because she couldn't rid herself of the terror of spiders. She slept in the ground for heaven's sake, she knew they crawled across her all night and thought they probably made nests in her hair.

She jumped when arms slid around her and she heard Zacarias laugh softly in her ear.

"I doubt very much that spiders make nests in your hair, my beautiful little lunatic."

Her heart thudded, and for a moment she froze, afraid to believe it was him. Afraid she'd made him up out of sheer desperation. Very slowly she turned and looked up at him. His eyes, always midnight black, had that fantastic sapphire blue sheen to them, the one he got when he looked at her and was particularly aroused. Just the sight of him made her weak.

"I dreamed that you gave me a lecture on spiders and perhaps actually struck me once or twice in retaliation. Could there be truth to that?"

She smiled. *Perhaps. If so, you certainly deserved it.* Her hand went to his flat, hard stomach. Scars crisscrossed where before his skin had been smooth. *I thought this would be gone.*

It was the only thing she could think to say when all she wanted to do was kiss him forever, hold him so tight neither of them could breathe and take him as deep as possible into her body so he would never find his way out.

He touched her throat. "I had hoped you would be able to speak as you wished to so much. I suppose we were both too injured for even powerful Carpathian blood to heal us completely."

He filled the room. Filled her every sense, so that her entire body reached for his, so aware of him. He came into her mind, a soft, gentle flow that surprised her. She almost didn't recognize that light touch. The icy feeling was there, but instead of the familiar glacier, the ice seemed to float through her mind, warming slowly.

She watched his eyes change, desire and hunger slipping through the joy of seeing her. He bent his head to hers and she turned up her mouth. His was hot and dominating, everything and more than she remembered.

Her body belonged to him instantly, melting against him, pliant and soft, making its own demands. He took his time kissing her, over and over.

Zacarias lifted his head slowly, reluctantly, his hands framing her face, looking into her eyes as though searching for something. Satisfaction crept into his gaze; evidently he found whatever he had been looking for.

He waved his hand toward the bathroom. At once the scent of her favorite oils drifted into the room along with a floating steam cloud. "Let's get you in the bath."

You know you don't have to do that. It's a silly ritual when we can just clean ourselves with a thought. That didn't make her feel clean, nor did it overcome her irrational fear of spiders crawling through her hair.

"Your bath is a beautiful ritual and one I hope you keep for many centuries." He corrected gently, "One important to you, and at the same time, it brings me much pleasure." He took her hand and kissed her palm. "I did not see your fear of spiders. It was buried too deep in your childhood memories. I should have taken more care, as I will now. I have every intention of inspecting every inch of you each evening to make certain these pesky creatures do not bother you ever again."

She shuddered, feeling the brush of thousands of hairy legs, rubbing her arms to rid herself of the sensation. Zacarias tipped her chin up so that she had no choice but to drown in his eyes, in those dark, black pools of deep liquid ice—so cold sometimes they burned with a deep midnight blue. He could take her breath away with just one smoldering look. The idea of him inspecting her body so closely every evening sent a million butterflies winging through her stomach.

He took her hand and tugged until she followed him into her now steamy bathroom. Very gently he lifted her, settling her in the deep water of the clawfoot tub. He tipped her head back against the raised, sloped side.

"Close your eyes and let me do this. I want you to know that not a single spider is anywhere near you when I am finished. Do not think about anything, *sívamet.*"

She sank into the depths, noting the water was a lagoon green, and felt like heaven. She closed her eyes and went all the way under at the urging of his hands, soaking her long mass of hair. She let the hot perfumed water and the mesmerizing sound of his voice allow her to drift on a tide of happiness. Zacarias was alive and he was with her. Whatever else happened, she knew now she wanted the man he was—primitive and always alert for trouble. Capable of exploding into violence when needed. A demanding lover. A demanding partner.

Would he be easy? She didn't try to fool herself that he would be. He had entrusted her with his spirit, his very essence, and in doing so, she saw all of him, shared all of him. She knew he wouldn't ever feel as a normal mated Carpathian would unless he was anchored firmly in her—but what he might never understand was that it terrified her to think of him hunting without that darkness in him to give him that extra edge. She wanted that for him. He would never stop his hunt to eradicate evil. Never. Nor would she ever want him to be anything else than who he was.

With her head resting in the curve of the tub, his hands massaging shampoo into her scalp, Marguarita floated in a dream world. He murmured softly in his own language, a dark singsong chant in his rasping velvet voice, and she went out with that tide, giving herself into his care. There was only this moment, Zacarias and the pleasure of the hot water on her body.

She had no idea of the passage of time. The water stayed hot while he rinsed her hair and then began a slow washing of her body, first her face, and then a meticulous and incredibly gentle care of her body. Tears burned in her eyes. She had never imagined him so tender. She doubted that he had known himself capable of such tenderness. Her body began a slow burn, heat building from smoldering embers, his hands going from lingering, memorizing, to claiming. He dried her with the same care, taking his time with her hair, drying it himself while he brushed it out. Only then did he lift her into his arms and carry her to her bed.

Zacarias laid Marguarita down with an exquisite gentleness. There in the darkness, with his extraordinary vision, he inspected her body, once again needing to memorize every inch of her, to see for himself that no hint of the conversion, of DS's assault on her remained. His tongue slid over her mouth, fingertips caressed her breasts, slid down to her ribs, and then over the curve of her hip. He wanted to taste every inch of her, suddenly greedy for her. She was his, the only one who would ever fill his life, fill his heart and repair his soul enough to give him back life.

His mouth returned to suckle at her breast as his hands kneaded and teeth tugged, tongue laving and rolling. Her body heated and he nudged her legs apart with his knee. He wanted to take his time, to drive her so high she would never come down, but he desperately needed to be inside her, to join them, body and soul, skin to skin. He had to feel whole again. The darkness had to recede so far it would take weeks to come back.

Come into me, he invited softly. *Give me your love, Marguarita, all of it. Pour yourself into me and fill me up with you. I need you.*

He had never admitted his need of anyone before. He felt her move in him, that impossible light, so warm, so filled with an emotion he could never hope to understand. The feeling overwhelmed him, and as always he was tempted to push it aside, but not now. Not this night. He slipped his hand between their bodies to feel her welcoming liquid. He was large and entering her was always a stretching burn for her. He didn't want to take a chance of hurting her no matter how eager he was to be inside of her.

He stared down at her face, wanting to watch her every expression as he slowly pushed into her body. He felt her tight sheath, velvet soft, giving way for him as he invaded. All the while she poured warmth into him. Love. He felt surrounded by her. Home. He had truly come home. When he had buried himself to the hilt, touching her cervix, rocking both of them, he stilled, his hands reaching for hers, fingers threading through hers.

"I will make you crazy sometimes, Marguarita, but I swear I will try to please you. I promise you with all my heart, give you my word of honor, that I will always do my best to make you happy. There are some things I am not certain I can change."

She smiled up at him. *I have not asked you to change. Only to merge your life with mine. There are good things about my world if you're open to them.*

He withdrew and plunged deep, watching her eyes glaze. He loved that look on her face, that wild shock of pleasure. He loved knowing he put that there. Once again he went still. "I have brothers, you know that. When we are with them, I will not be able to be far from you. I need you to connect with that emotion I have so long been without."

A slow smile teased her mouth. Teased his mind. *I don't think that will be a problem.*

He was well and truly lost and he was grateful for that feeling. He began a slow, sensual assault on all her senses, sharing his mind, sharing the building pressure, the exquisite pleasure. She would always be his world. He would have to share her with this world she lived in—and loved—but for her, he could manage.

He bent his head and took her breast into his mouth, his weight on his elbows now. *This will be our base, but we must travel, Marguarita. Together.*

I am depending on that. I rather like the things your hands and mouth and body do to me. I'm addicted to you. But more than that, Zacarias, I'm very much in love with you. I want you to take me with you.

He *felt* her love inside of him, bridging all the broken connections for him. Surrounding him. Making it all right to be who he was, damaged and maybe a little broken.

He kissed her as his hands took possession of her hips, lifting her to him in preparation for a wild ride. *You are the only person I will ever love.*

And that was his truth. He finally belonged somewhere—to someone. Marguarita was his home.

Appendix 1

Carpathian Healing Chants

To rightly understand Carpathian healing chants, background is required in several areas:

1. The Carpathian view on healing
2. The Lesser Healing Chant of the Carpathians
3. The Great Healing Chant of the Carpathians
4. Carpathian musical aesthetics
5. Lullaby
6. Song to Heal the Earth
7. Carpathian chanting technique

1. THE CARPATHIAN VIEW ON HEALING

The Carpathians are a nomadic people whose geographic origins can be traced back to at least as far as the Southern Ural Mountains (near the steppes of modern-day Kazakhstan), on the border between Europe and Asia. (For this reason, modern-day linguists call their language "proto-Uralic," without knowing that this is the language of the Carpathians.) Unlike most nomadic peoples, the wandering of the Carpathians was not due to the need to find new grazing lands as the seasons and climate shifted, or the search for better trade. Instead, the Carpathians' movements were driven by a great purpose: to find a land that would have the right earth, a soil with the kind of richness that would greatly enhance their rejuvenative powers.

Over the centuries, they migrated westward (some six thousand years ago), until they at last found their perfect homeland—their *susu*—in the Carpathian Mountains, whose long arc cradled the lush plains of the kingdom of Hungary. (The kingdom of Hungary flourished for over a millennium—making Hungarian the dominant language of the Carpathian Basin—until the kingdom's lands were split among several countries after World War I: Austria, Czechoslovakia, Romania, Yugoslavia and modern Hungary.)

Other peoples from the Southern Urals (who shared the Carpathian language, but were not Carpathians) migrated in different directions. Some ended up in Finland, which accounts for why the modern Hungarian and Finnish languages are among the contemporary descendents of the ancient Carpathian language. Even though they are tied forever

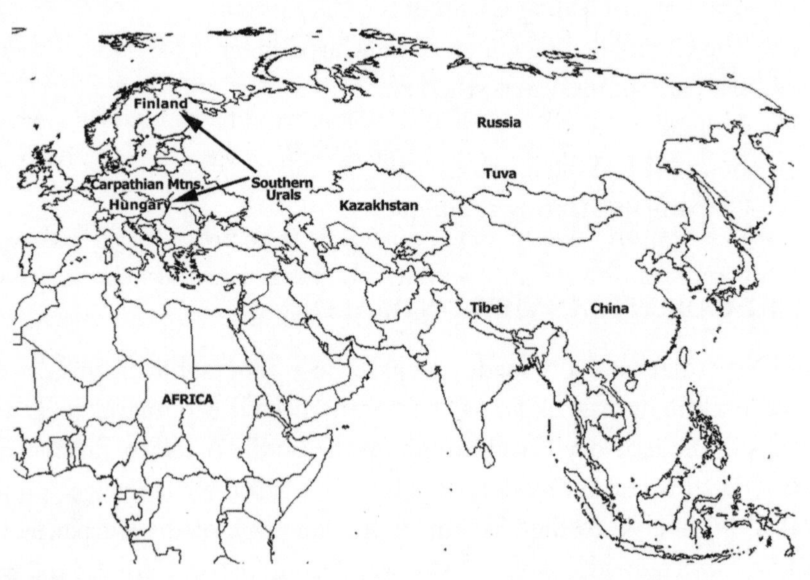

to their chosen Carpathian homeland, the wandering of the Carpathians continues as they search the world for the answers that will enable them to bear and raise their offspring without difficulty.

Because of their geographic origins, the Carpathian views on healing share much with the larger Eurasian shamanistic tradition. Probably the closest modern representative of that tradition is based in Tuva (and is referred to as "Tuvinian Shamanism")—see the map on the previous page.

The Eurasian shamanistic tradition—from the Carpathians to the Siberian shamans—held that illness originated in the human soul, and only later manifested as various physical conditions. Therefore, shamanistic healing, while not neglecting the body, focused on the soul and its healing. The most profound illnesses were understood to be caused by "soul departure," where all or some part of the sick person's soul has wandered away from the body (into the nether realms), or has been captured or possessed by an evil spirit, or both.

The Carpathians belong to this greater Eurasian shamanistic tradition and share its viewpoints. While the Carpathians themselves did not succumb to illness, Carpathian healers understood that the most profound wounds were also accompanied by a similar "soul departure."

Upon reaching the diagnosis of "soul departure," the healer-shaman is then required to make a spiritual journey into the netherworlds to recover the soul. The shaman may have to overcome tremendous challenges along the way, particularly fighting the demon or vampire who has possessed his friend's soul.

"Soul departure" doesn't require a person to be unconscious (although that certainly can be the case as well). It was understood that a person could still appear to be conscious, even talk and interact with others, and yet be missing a part of their soul. The experienced healer or shaman would instantly see the problem nonetheless, in subtle signs that others might miss: the person's attention wandering every now and then, a lessening in their enthusiasm about life, chronic depression, a diminishment in the brightness of their "aura," and the like.

2. THE LESSER HEALING CHANT OF THE CARPATHIANS

***Kepä Sarna Pus* (The Lesser Healing Chant)** is used for wounds that are merely physical in nature. The Carpathian healer leaves his body and enters the wounded Carpathian's body to heal great mortal wounds from the inside out using pure energy. He proclaims, "I offer freely my life for your life," as he gives his blood to the injured Carpathian. Because the Carpathians are of the earth and bound to the soil, they are healed by the soil of their homeland. Their saliva is also often used for its rejuvenative powers.

It is also very common for the Carpathian chants (both the Lesser and the Great) to be accompanied by the use of healing herbs, aromas from Carpathian candles and crystals. The crystals (when combined with the Carpathians' empathic, psychic connection to the entire universe) are used to gather positive energy from their surroundings, which then is used to accelerate the healing. Caves are sometimes used as the setting for the healing.

The Lesser Healing Chant was used by Vikirnoff Von Shrieder and Colby Jansen to heal Rafael De La Cruz, whose heart had been ripped out by a vampire as described in *Dark Secret*.

Kepä Sarna Pus (The Lesser Healing Chant)

The same chant is used for all physical wounds. "Sívadaba" ["into your heart"] would be changed to refer to whatever part of the body is wounded.

Kuńasz, nélkül sivdobbanás, nélkül fesztelen löyly.
You lie as if asleep, without beat of heart, without airy breath.

Ot élidamet andam szabadon élidadért.
I offer freely my life for your life.

O jelä sielam jŏrem ot ainamet és soŋe ot élidadet.
My spirit of light forgets my body and enters your body.

O jelä sielam pukta kinn minden szelemeket belső.
My spirit of light sends all the dark spirits within fleeing without.

Pajńak o susu hanyet és o nyelv nyálamet sívadaba.
I press the earth of our homeland and the spit of my tongue into your heart.

Vii, o verim soŋe o verid andam.
At last, I give you my blood for your blood.

To hear this chant, visit: http://www.christinefeehan.com/members/.

3. THE GREAT HEALING CHANT OF THE CARPATHIANS

The most well-known—and most dramatic—of the Carpathian healing chants was ***En Sarna Pus*** **(The Great Healing Chant)**. This chant was reserved for recovering the wounded or unconscious Carpathian's soul.

Typically a group of men would form a circle around the sick Carpathian (to "encircle him with our care and compassion") and begin the chant. The shaman or healer or leader is the prime actor in this healing ceremony. It is he who will actually make the spiritual journey into the netherworld, aided by his clanspeople. Their purpose is to ecstatically dance, sing, drum and chant, all the while visualizing (through the words of the chant) the journey itself—every step of it, over and over again—to the point where the shaman, in trance, leaves his body, and makes that very journey. (Indeed, the word "ecstasy" is from the Latin *ex statis*, which literally means "out of the body.")

One advantage that the Carpathian healer has over many other shamans is his telepathic link to his lost brother. Most shamans must wander in the dark of the nether realms in search of their lost brother. But the Carpathian healer directly "hears" in his mind the voice of his lost brother calling to him, and can thus "zero in" on his soul like a homing beacon. For this reason, Carpathian healing tends to have a higher success rate than most other traditions of this sort.

Something of the geography of the "other world" is useful for us to examine, in order to fully understand the words of the Great Carpathian Healing Chant. A reference is made to the "Great Tree" (in Carpathian:

En Puwe). Many ancient traditions, including the Carpathian tradition, understood the worlds—the heaven worlds, our world and the nether realms—to be "hung" upon a great pole, or axis, or tree. Here on earth, we are positioned halfway up this tree, on one of its branches. Hence many ancient texts often referred to the material world as "middle earth": midway between heaven and hell. Climbing the tree would lead one to the heaven worlds. Descending the tree to its roots would lead to the nether realms. The shaman was necessarily a master of movement up and down the Great Tree, sometimes moving unaided, and sometimes assisted by (or even mounted upon the back of) an animal spirit guide. In various traditions, this Great Tree was known variously as the *axis mundi* (the "axis of the worlds"), Ygddrasil (in Norse mythology), Mount Meru (the sacred world mountain of Tibetan tradition), etc. The Christian cosmos, with its heaven, purgatory/earth and hell, is also worth comparing. It is even given a similar topography in Dante's *Divine Comedy*: Dante is led on a journey first to hell, at the center of the earth; then upward to Mount Purgatory, which sits on the earth's surface directly opposite Jerusalem; then farther upward first to Eden, the earthly paradise, at the summit of Mount Purgatory; and then upward at last to heaven.

In the shamanistic tradition, it was understood that the small always reflects the large; the personal always reflects the cosmic. A movement in the greater dimensions of the cosmos also coincides with an internal movement. For example, the *axis mundi* of the cosmos also corresponds to the spinal column of the individual. Journeys up and down the *axis mundi* often coincided with the movement of natural and spiritual energies (sometimes called *kundalini* or *shakti*) in the spinal column of the shaman or mystic.

***En Sarna Pus* (The Great Healing Chant)**

In this chant, ekä ("brother") would be replaced by "sister," "father," "mother," depending on the person to be healed.

Ot ekäm ainajanak hany, jama.
My brother's body is a lump of earth, close to death.

Me, ot ekäm kuntajanak, pirädak ekäm, gond és irgalom türe.
We, the clan of my brother, encircle him with our care and compassion.

O pus wäkenkek, ot oma śarnank, és ot pus fünk, álnak ekäm ainajanak, pitänak ekäm ainajanak elävä.
Our healing energies, ancient words of magic and healing herbs bless my brother's body, keep it alive.

Ot ekäm sielanak pälä. Ot omboće päläja juta alatt o jüti, kinta, és szelemek lamtijaknak.
But my brother's soul is only half. His other half wanders in the netherworld.

Ot en mekem ŋamaŋ: kulkedak otti ot ekäm omboće päläjanak.
My great deed is this: I travel to find my brother's other half.

Rekatüre, saradak, tappadak, odam, kaŋa o numa waram, és avaa owe o lewl mahoz.
We dance, we chant, we dream ecstatically, to call my spirit bird, and to open the door to the other world.

Ntak o numa waram, és mozdulak, jomadak.
I mount my spirit bird and we begin to move, we are underway.

Piwtädak ot En Puwe tyvinak, ećidak alatt o jüti, kinta, és szelemek lamtijaknak.
Following the trunk of the Great Tree, we fall into the netherworld.

Fázak, fázak nó o śaro.
It is cold, very cold.

Juttadak ot ekäm o akarataban, o sívaban és o sielaban.
My brother and I are linked in mind, heart and soul.

Ot ekäm sielanak kaŋa engem.
My brother's soul calls to me.

Kuledak és piwtädak ot ekäm.
I hear and follow his track.

Saγedak és tuledak ot ekäm kulyanak.
Encounter I the demon who is devouring my brother's soul.

Nenäm ćoro, o kuly torodak.
In anger, I fight the demon.

O kuly pél engem.
He is afraid of me.

Lejkkadak o kaŋka salamaval.
I strike his throat with a lightning bolt.

Molodak ot ainaja komakamal.
I break his body with my bare hands.

Toja és molanâ.
He is bent over, and falls apart.

Hän ćaδa.
He runs away.

Manedak ot ekäm sielanak.
I rescue my brother's soul.

Alədak ot ekam sielanak o komamban.
I lift my brother's soul in the hollow of my hand.

Aləd am ot ekam numa waramra.
I lift him onto my spirit bird.

Piwtädak ot En Puwe tyvijanak és saγedak jälleen ot elävä ainak majaknak.
Following up the Great Tree, we return to the land of the living.

Ot ekäm elä jälleen.
My brother lives again.

Ot ekäm weńća jälleen.
He is complete again.

To hear this chant, visit: http://www.christinefeehan.com/members/.

4. CARPATHIAN MUSICAL AESTHETICS

In the sung Carpathian pieces (such as the "Lullaby" and the "Song to Heal the Earth"), you'll hear elements that are shared by many of the musical traditions in the Uralic geographical region, some of which still exist—from Eastern European (Bulgarian, Romanian, Hungarian, Croatian, etc.) to Romany ("gypsy"). Some of these elements include:

- the rapid alternation between major and minor modalities, including a sudden switch (called a "Picardy third") from minor to major to end a piece or section (as at the end of the "Lullaby")
- the use of close (tight) harmonies
- the use of *ritardi* (slowing down the piece) and *crescendi* (swelling in volume) for brief periods
- the use of *glissandi* (slides) in the singing tradition
- the use of trills in the singing tradition (as in the final invocation of the "Song to Heal the Earth")—similar to Celtic, a singing tradition more familiar to many of us
- the use of parallel fifths (as in the final invocation of the "Song to Heal the Earth")
- controlled use of dissonance
- "call and response" chanting (typical of many of the world's chanting traditions)

- extending the length of a musical line (by adding a couple of bars) to heighten dramatic effect
- and many more

"Lullaby" and "Song to Heal the Earth" illustrate two rather different forms of Carpathian music (a quiet, intimate piece and an energetic ensemble piece)—but whatever the form, Carpathian music is full of feeling.

5. LULLABY

This song is sung by women while the child is still in the womb or when the threat of a miscarriage is apparent. The baby can hear the song while inside the mother, and the mother can connect with the child telepathically as well. The lullaby is meant to reassure the child, to encourage the baby to hold on, to stay—to reassure the child that he or she will be protected by love even from inside until birth. The last line literally means that the mother's love will protect her child until the child is born ("rise").

Musically, the Carpathian "Lullaby" is in three-quarter time ("waltz time"), as are a significant portion of the world's various traditional lullabies (perhaps the most famous of which is "Brahms' Lullaby"). The arrangement for solo voice is the original context: a mother singing to her child, unaccompanied. The arrangement for chorus and violin ensemble illustrates how musical even the simplest Carpathian pieces often are, and how easily they lend themselves to contemporary instrumental or orchestral arrangements. (A wide range of contemporary composers, including Dvořák and Smetana, have taken advantage of a similar discovery, working other traditional Eastern European music into their symphonic poems.)

***Odam-Sarna Kondak* (Lullaby)**

Tumtesz o wäke ku pitasz belső.
Feel the strength you hold inside.

Hiszasz sívadet. Én olenam gæidnod.
Trust your heart. I'll be your guide.

Sas csecsemõm, kuńasz.
Hush my baby, close your eyes.

Rauho joŋe ted.
Peace will come to you.

Tumtesz o sívdobbanás ku olen lamt3ad belső.
Feel the rhythm deep inside.

Gond-kumpadek ku kim te.
Waves of love that cover you.

Pesänak te, asti o jüti, kidüsz.
Protect, until the night you rise.

To hear this song, visit: http://www.christinefeehan.com/members/.

6. SONG TO HEAL THE EARTH

This is the earth-healing song that is used by the Carpathian women to heal soil filled with various toxins. The women take a position on four sides and call to the universe to draw on the healing energy with love and respect. The soil of the earth is their resting place, the place where they rejuvenate, and they must make it safe not only for themselves but for their unborn children as well as their men and living children. This is a beautiful ritual performed by the women together, raising their voices in harmony and calling on the earth's minerals and healing properties to come forth and help them save their children. They literally dance and sing to heal the earth in a ceremony as old as their species. The dance and notes of the song are adjusted according to the toxins felt through the healer's bare feet. The feet are placed in a certain pattern and the hands gracefully weave a healing spell while the dance is performed. They must be especially careful when the soil is prepared for babies. This is a ceremony of love and healing.

Musically, the ritual is divided into several sections:

- **First verse**: A "call and response" section, where the chant leader sings the "call" solo, and then some or all of the women sing the "response" in the close harmony style typical of the Carpathian musical tradition. The repeated response—*Ai Emä Maγe*—is an invocation of the source of power for the healing ritual: "Oh, Mother Nature."
- **First chorus**: This section is filled with clapping, dancing, ancient horns and other means used to invoke and heighten the energies upon which the ritual is drawing.
- **Second verse**
- **Second chorus**
- **Closing invocation:** In this closing part, two song leaders, in close harmony, take all the energy gathered by the earlier portions of the song/ritual and focus it entirely on the healing purpose.

What you will be listening to are brief tastes of what would typically be a significantly longer ritual, in which the verse and chorus parts are developed and repeated many times, to be closed by a single rendition of the final invocation.

Sarna Pusm O Maγet (Song to Heal the Earth)

First verse
Ai Emä Maγe,
Oh, Mother Nature,

Me sívadbin lańaak.
We are your beloved daughters.

Me tappadak, me pusmak o maγet.
We dance to heal the earth.

Me sarnadak, me pusmak o hanyet.
We sing to heal the earth.

Sielanket jutta tedet it,
We join with you now,

Sívank és akaratank és sielank juttanak.
Our hearts and minds and spirits become one.

Second verse
Ai Emä maγe,
Oh, Mother Nature,

Me sívadbin lańaak.
We are your beloved daughters.

Me andak arwadet emänked és me kaŋank o
We pay homage to our mother and call upon the

Põhi és Lõuna, Ida és Lääs.
North and South, East and West.

Pide és aldyn és myös belső.
Above and below and within as well.

Gondank o maγenak pusm hän ku olen jama.
Our love of the land heals that which is in need.

Juttanak teval it,
We join with you now,

Maγe maγeval.
Earth to earth.

O pirä elidak weńća.
The circle of life is complete.

To hear this chant, visit: http://www.christinefeehan.com/members/.

7. CARPATHIAN CHANTING TECHNIQUE

As with their healing techniques, the actual "chanting technique" of the Carpathians has much in common with the other shamanistic traditions of the Central Asian steppes. The primary mode of chanting was throat chanting using overtones. Modern examples of this manner of singing can still be found in the Mongolian, Tuvan and Tibetan traditions. You can find an audio example of the Gyuto Tibetan Buddhist monks engaged in throat chanting at: http://www.christinefeehan.com/carpathian_chanting/.

As with Tuva, note on the map the geographical proximity of Tibet to Kazakhstan and the Southern Urals.

The beginning part of the Tibetan chant emphasizes synchronizing all the voices around a single tone, aimed at healing a particular "chakra" of the body. This is fairly typical of the Gyuto throat-chanting tradition, but it is not a significant part of the Carpathian tradition. Nonetheless, it serves as an interesting contrast.

The part of the Gyuto chanting example that is most similar to the Carpathian style of chanting is the midsection, where the men are chanting the words together with great force. The purpose here is not to generate a "healing tone" that will affect a particular "chakra," but rather to generate as much power as possible for initiating the "out of body" travel, and for fighting the demonic forces that the healer/traveler must face and overcome.

The songs of the Carpathian women (illustrated by their "Lullaby" and their "Song to Heal the Earth") are part of the same ancient musical and healing tradition as the Lesser and Great Healing Chants of the warrior males. You can hear some of the same instruments in both the male warriors' healing chants and the women's "Song to Heal the Earth." Also, they share the common purpose of generating and directing power. However, the women's songs are distinctively feminine in character. One immediately noticeable difference is that, while the men speak their words in the manner of a chant, the women sing songs with melodies and harmonies, softening the overall performance. A feminine, nurturing quality is especially evident in the "Lullaby."

APPENDIX 2

The Carpathian Language

Like all human languages, the language of the Carpathians contains the richness and nuance that can only come from a long history of use. At best we can only touch on some of the main features of the language in this brief appendix:

1. The history of the Carpathian language
2. Carpathian grammar and other characteristics of the language
3. Examples of the Carpathian language (including the Ritual Words and the Warrior's Chant)
4. A much-abridged Carpathian dictionary

1. THE HISTORY OF THE CARPATHIAN LANGUAGE

The Carpathian language of today is essentially identical to the Carpathian language of thousands of years ago. A "dead" language like the Latin of two thousand years ago has evolved into a significantly different modern language (Italian) because of countless generations of speakers and great historical fluctuations. In contrast, many of the speakers of Carpathian from thousands of years ago are still alive. Their presence—

coupled with the deliberate isolation of the Carpathians from the other major forces of change in the world—has acted (and continues to act) as a stabilizing force that has preserved the integrity of the language over the centuries. Carpathian culture has also acted as a stabilizing force. For instance, the Ritual Words, the various healing chants (see Appendix 1), and other cultural artifacts have been passed down through the centuries with great fidelity.

One small exception should be noted: the splintering of the Carpathians into separate geographic regions has led to some minor dialectization. However the telepathic link among all Carpathians (as well as each Carpathian's regular return to his or her homeland) has ensured that the differences among dialects are relatively superficial (e.g., small numbers of new words, minor differences in pronunciation, etc.), since the deeper, internal language of mind-forms has remained the same because of continuous use across space and time.

The Carpathian language was (and still is) the proto-language for the Uralic (or Finno-Ugrian) family of languages. Today, the Uralic languages are spoken in northern, eastern and central Europe and in Siberia. More than twenty-three million people in the world speak languages that can trace their ancestry to Carpathian. Magyar or Hungarian (about fourteen million speakers), Finnish (about five million speakers) and Estonian (about one million speakers) are the three major contemporary descendents of this proto-language. The only factor that unites the more than twenty languages in the Uralic family is that their ancestry can be traced back to a common proto-language—Carpathian—that split (starting some six thousand years ago) into the various languages in the Uralic family. In the same way, European languages such as English and French belong to the better-known Indo-European family and also evolved from a common proto-language ancestor (a different one from Carpathian).

The following table provides a sense for some of the similarities in the language family.

Note: The Finnic/Carpathian "k" shows up often as Hungarian "h." Similarly, the Finnic/Carpathian "p" often corresponds to the Hungarian "f."

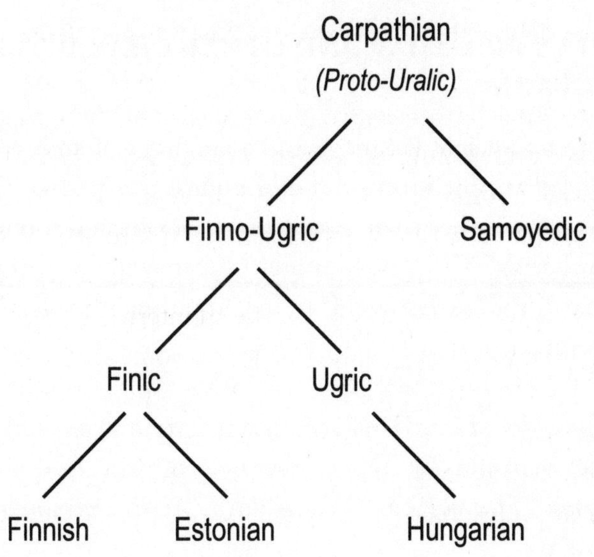

Carpathian *(proto-Uralic)*	**Finnish** *(Suomi)*	**Hungarian** *(Magyar)*
elä—live	*elä*—live	*él*—live
elid—life	*elinikä*—life	*élet*—life
pesä—nest	*pesä*—nest	*fészek*—nest
kola—die	*kuole*—die	*hal*—die
pälä—half, side	*pieltä*—tilt, tip to the side	*fél, fele*—fellow human, friend (half; one side of two) *feleség*—wife
and—give	*anta, antaa*—give	*ad*—give
koje—husband, man	*koira*—dog, the male (of animals)	*here*—drone, testicle
wäke—power	*väki*—folks, people, men; force	*vall-vel*—with (instrumental suffix)
	väkevä—powerful, strong	*vele*—with him/her/it
wete—water	*vesi*—water	*viz*—water

2. CARPATHIAN GRAMMAR AND OTHER CHARACTERISTICS OF THE LANGUAGE

Idioms. As both an ancient language and a language of an earth people, Carpathian is more inclined toward use of idioms constructed from concrete, "earthy" terms, rather than abstractions. For instance, our modern abstraction "to cherish" is expressed more concretely in Carpathian as "to hold in one's heart"; the "netherworld" is, in Carpathian, "the land of night, fog and ghosts"; etc.

Word order. The order of words in a sentence is determined not by syntactic roles (like subject, verb and object) but rather by pragmatic, discourse-driven factors. Examples: *"Tied vagyok."* ("Yours am I."); *"Sivamet andam."* ("My heart I give you.")

Agglutination. The Carpathian language is agglutinative; that is, longer words are constructed from smaller components. An agglutinating language uses suffixes or prefixes whose meaning is generally unique, and which are concatenated one after another without overlap. In Carpathian, words typically consist of a stem that is followed by one or more suffixes. For example, *"sívambam"* derives from the stem *"sív"* ("heart") followed by *"am"* ("my," making it "my heart"), followed by *"bam"* ("in," making it "in my heart"). As you might imagine, agglutination in Carpathian can sometimes produce very long words, or words that are very difficult to pronounce. Vowels often get inserted between suffixes to prevent too many consonants from appearing in a row (which can make the word unpronounceable).

Noun cases. Like all languages, Carpathian has many noun cases; the same noun will be "spelled" differently depending on its role in the sentence. Some of the noun cases include: nominative (when the noun is the subject of the sentence), accusative (when the noun is a direct object of the verb), dative (indirect object), genitive (or possessive), instrumental, final, supressive, inessive, elative, terminative and delative.

We will use the possessive (or genitive) case as an example, to illustrate how all noun cases in Carpathian involve adding standard suffixes to the noun stems. Thus expressing possession in Carpathian—"my lifemate," "your lifemate," "his lifemate," "her lifemate," etc.—involves adding a particular suffix (such as "*-am*") to the noun stem (*"päläfertiil"*), to produce the possessive (*"päläfertiilam"*—"my lifemate"). Which suffix to use depends upon which person ("my," "your," "his," etc.) and whether the noun ends in a consonant or a vowel. The table below shows the suffixes for singular nouns only (not plural), and also shows the similarity to the suffixes used in contemporary Hungarian. (Hungarian is actually a little more complex, in that it also requires "vowel rhyming": which suffix to use also depends on the last vowel in the noun; hence the multiple choices in the cells below, where Carpathian only has a single choice.)

Note: As mentioned earlier, vowels often get inserted between the word

	Carpathian (proto-Uralic)		Contemporary Hungarian	
person	**noun ends in vowel**	**noun ends in consonant**	**noun ends in vowel**	**noun ends in consonant**
1st singular (my)	-m	-am	-m	-om, -em, -öm
2nd singular (your)	-d	-ad	-d	-od, -ed, -öd
3rd singular (his, her, its)	-ja	-a	-ja/-je	-a, -e
1st plural (our)	-nk	-ank	-nk	-unk, -ünk
2nd plural (your)	-tak	-atak	-tok, -tek, -tök	-otok, -etek, -ötök
3rd plural (their)	-jak	-ak	-juk, -jük	-uk, -ük

and its suffix so as to prevent too many consonants from appearing in a row (which would produce unpronounceable words). For example, in the table on the previous page, all nouns that end in a consonant are followed by suffixes beginning with "a."

Verb conjugation. Like its modern descendents (such as Finnish and Hungarian), Carpathian has many verb tenses, far too many to describe here. We will just focus on the conjugation of the present tense. Again, we will place contemporary Hungarian side by side with the Carpathian, because of the marked similarity of the two.

As with the possessive case for nouns, the conjugation of verbs is done by adding a suffix onto the verb stem:

Person	Carpathian (proto-Uralic)	Contemporary Hungarian
1st (I give)	-am (andam), -ak	-ok, -ek, -ök
2nd singular (you give)	-sz (andsz)	-sz
3rd singular (he/she/it gives)	— (and)	—
1st plural (we give)	-ak (andak)	-unk, -ünk
2nd plural (you give)	-tak (andtak)	-tok, -tek, -tök
3rd plural (they give)	-nak (andnak)	-nak, -nek

As with all languages, there are many "irregular verbs" in Carpathian that don't exactly fit this pattern. But the above table is still a useful guideline for most verbs.

3. EXAMPLES OF THE CARPATHIAN LANGUAGE

Here are some brief examples of conversational Carpathian, used in the Dark books. We include the literal translation in square brackets. It is interestingly different from the most appropriate English translation.

Susu.
I am home.
["home/birthplace." "I am" is understood, as is often the case in Carpathian.]

Möért?
What for?

csitri
little one
["little slip of a thing," "little slip of a girl"]

ainaak enyém
forever mine

ainaak sívamet jutta
forever mine (another form)
["forever to-my-heart connected/fixed"]

sívamet
my love
["of-my-heart," "to-my-heart"]

Tet vigyázam.
I love you.
["you-love-I"]

***Sarna Rituaali* (The Ritual Words)** is a longer example, and an example of chanted rather than conversational Carpathian. Note the recurring use of "*andam*" ("I give"), to give the chant musicality and force through repetition.

***Sarna Rituaali* (The Ritual Words)**

Te avio päläfertiilam.
You are my lifemate.

Éntölam kuulua, avio päläfertiilam.
I claim you as my lifemate.

Ted kuuluak, kacad, kojed.
I belong to you.

Élidamet andam.
I offer my life for you.

Pesämet andam.
I give you my protection.

Uskolfertiilamet andam.
I give you my allegiance.

Sívamet andam.
I give you my heart.

Sielamet andam.
I give you my soul.

Ainamet andam.
I give you my body.

Sívamet kuuluak kaik että a ted.
I take into my keeping the same that is yours.

Ainaak olenszal sívambin.
Your life will be cherished by me for all my time.

Te élidet ainaak pide minan.
Your life will be placed above my own for all time.

Te avio päläfertiilam.
You are my lifemate.

Ainaak sívamet jutta oleny.
You are bound to me for all eternity.

Ainaak terád vigyázak.
You are always in my care.

To hear these words pronounced (and for more about Carpathian pronunciation altogether), please visit: http://www.christinefeehan.com/members/.

***Sarna Kontakawk* (The Warriors' Chant)** is another longer example of the Carpathian language. The warriors' council takes place deep beneath the earth in a chamber of crystals with magma far below that, so the steam is natural and the wisdom of their ancestors is clear and focused. This is a sacred place where they bloodswear to their prince and people and affirm their code of honor as warriors and brothers. It is also where battle strategies are born and all dissension is discussed as well as any concerns the warriors have that they wish to bring to the Council and open for discussion.

***Sarna Kontakawk* (The Warriors' Chant)**

Veri isäakank—veri ekäakank.
Blood of our fathers—blood of our brothers.

Veri olen elid.
Blood is life.

Andak veri-elidet Karpatiiakank, és wäke-sarna ku meke arwa-arvo, irgalom, hän ku agba, és wäke kutni, ku manaak verival.
We offer that life to our people with a bloodsworn vow of honor, mercy, integrity and endurance.

Verink sokta; verink kaŋa terád.
Our blood mingles and calls to you.

Akasz énak ku kaŋa és juttasz kuntatak it.
Heed our summons and join with us now.

To hear these words pronounced (and for more about Carpathian pronunciation altogether), please visit: http://www.christinefeehan.com/members/.

See **Appendix 1** for Carpathian healing chants, including the *Kepä Sarna Pus* (The Lesser Healing Chant), the *En Sarna Pus* (The Great Healing Chant), the *Odam-Sarna Kondak* (Lullaby) and the *Sarna Pusm O Maγet* (Song to Heal the Earth).

4. A MUCH-ABRIDGED CARPATHIAN DICTIONARY

This very much abridged Carpathian dictionary contains most of the Carpathian words used in these Dark books. Of course, a full Carpathian dictionary would be as large as the usual dictionary for an entire language (typically more than a hundred thousand words).

Note: The Carpathian nouns and verbs below are word stems. They generally do not appear in their isolated, "stem" form, as below. Instead, they usually appear with suffixes (e.g., "*andam*"—"*I give,*" rather than just the root, "*and*").

a—verb negation (*prefix*).
agba—to be seemly or proper.
ai—oh.
aina—body.
ainaak—forever.
O ainaak jelä peje emnimet ŋamaŋ—Sun scorch that woman forever (*Carpathian swear words*).
ainaakfél—old friend.
ak—suffix added after a noun ending in a consonant to make it plural.
aka—to give heed; to hearken; to listen.
akarat—mind; will.

ál—to bless; to attach to.
alatt—through.
aldyn—under; underneath.
alɘ—to lift; to raise.
alte—to bless; to curse.
and—to give.
and sielet, arwa-arvomet, és jelämet, kuulua huvémet ku feaj és ködet ainaak—to trade soul, honor and salvation, for momentary pleasure and endless damnation.
andasz éntölem irgalomet!—have mercy!
arvo—value; price (*noun*).
arwa—praise (*noun*).
arwa-arvo—honor (*noun*).
arwa-arvod mäne me ködak—may your honor hold back the dark (*greeting*).
arwa-arvo olen gæidnod, ekäm—honor guide you, my brother (*greeting*).
arwa-arvo olen isäntä, ekäm—honor keep you, my brother (*greeting*).
arwa-arvo pile sívadet—may honor light your heart (*greeting*).
aššа—no (*before a noun*); not (*with a verb that is not in the imperative*); not (*with an adjective*).
aššatotello—disobedient.
asti—until.
avaa—to open.
avio—wedded.
avio päläfertiil—lifemate.
avoi—uncover; show; reveal.
belső—within; inside.
bur—good; well.
bur tule ekämet kuntamak—well met brother-kin (*greeting*).
ćaδa—to flee; to run; to escape.
ćoro—to flow; to run like rain.
csecsemõ—baby (*noun*).
csitri—little one (*female*).
diutal—triumph; victory.
eći—to fall.

ek—suffix added after a noun ending in a consonant to make it plural.
ekä—brother.
ekäm—my brother.
elä—to live.
eläsz arwa-arvoval—may you live with honor (*greeting*).
eläsz jeläbam ainaak—long may you live in the light (*greeting*).
elävä—alive.
elävä ainak majaknak—land of the living.
elid—life.
emä—mother (*noun*).
Emä Maγe—Mother Nature.
emäen—grandmother.
embε—if, when.
embε karmasz—please.
emni—wife; woman.
emnim—my wife; my woman.
emni kuηenak ku aššatotello—disobedient lunatic.
én—I.
en—great, many, big.
én jutta félet és ekämet—I greet a friend and brother (*greeting*).
En Puwe—The Great Tree. Related to the legends of Ygddrasil, the axis mundi, Mount Meru, heaven and hell, etc.
engem—of me.
és—and.
ete—before; in front.
että—that.
fáz—to feel cold or chilly.
fél—fellow, friend.
fél ku kuuluaak sívam belső—beloved.
fél ku vigyázak—dear one.
feldolgaz—prepare.
fertiil—fertile one.
fesztelen—airy.
fü—herbs; grass.
gæidno—road, way.

gond—care; worry; love (*noun*).
hän—he; she; it.
hän agba—it is so.
hän ku—prefix: one who; that which.
hän ku agba—truth.
hän ku kaśwa o numamet—sky-owner.
hän ku kuulua sívamet—keeper of my heart.
hän ku lejkka wäke-sarnat—traitor.
hän ku meke pirämet—defender.
hän ku pesä—protector.
hän ku piwtä—predator; hunter; tracker.
hän ku vie elidet—vampire (*literally: thief of life*).
hän ku vigyáz sielamet—keeper of my soul.
hän ku vigyáz sívamet és sielamet—keeper of my heart and soul.
hän ku saa kuć3aket—star-reacher.
hän ku tappa—killer; violent person (*noun*). deadly; violent (*adj.*).
hän ku tuulmahl elidet—vampire (*literally: life-stealer*).
Hän sívamak—Beloved.
hany—clod; lump of earth.
hisz—to believe; to trust.
ida—east.
igazág—justice.
irgalom—compassion; pity; mercy.
isä—father (*noun*).
isäntä—master of the house.
it—now.
jälleen—again.
jama—to be sick, infected, wounded, or dying; to be near death.
jelä—sunlight; day, sun; light.
jelä keje terád—light sear you (*Carpathian swear words*).
o jelä peje terád—sun scorch you (*Carpathian swear words*).
o jelä peje emnimet—sun scorch the woman (*Carpathian swear words*).
o jelä peje kaik hänkanak—sun scorch them all (*Carpathian swear words*).
o jelä peje terád, emni—sun scorch you, woman (*Carpathian swear words*).
o jelä sielamak—light of my soul.

joma—to be underway; to go.
joŋ—to come; to return.
joŋesz arwa-arvoval—return with honor (*greeting*).
jörem—to forget; to lose one's way; to make a mistake.
juo—to drink.
juosz és eläsz—drink and live (*greeting*).
juosz és olen ainaak sielamet jutta—drink and become one with me (*greeting*).
juta—to go; to wander.
jüti—night; evening.
jutta—connected; fixed (*adj.*). to connect; to fix; to bind (*verb*).
k—suffix added after a noun ending in a vowel to make it plural.
kaca—male lover.
kadi—judge.
kaik—all.
kaŋa—to call; to invite; to request; to beg.
kaŋk—windpipe; adam's apple; throat.
kać3—gift.
kaδa—to abandon; to leave; to remain.
kaδa wäkeva óv o köd—stand fast against the dark (*greeting*).
kalma—corpse; death; grave.
karma—want.
Karpatii—Carpathian.
Karpatii ku köd—liar.
käsi—hand (*noun*).
kaśwa—to own.
keje—to cook; to burn; to sear.
kepä—lesser, small, easy, few.
kessa—cat.
kessa ku toro—wildcat.
kessake—little cat.
kidü—to wake up; to arise (*intransitive verb*).
kim—to cover an entire object with some sort of covering.
kinn—out; outdoors; outside; without.
kinta—fog, mist, smoke.

kislány—little girl.
kislány kuŋenak—little lunatic.
kislány kuŋenak minan—my little lunatic.
köd—fog; mist; darkness; evil (*noun*); foggy, dark; evil (*adj.*).
köd elävä és köd nime kutni nimet—evil lives and has a name.
köd alte hän—darkness curse it (*Carpathian swear words*).
o köd belső—darkness take it (*Carpathian swear words*).
köd jutasz belső—shadow take you (*Carpathian swear words*).
koje—man; husband; drone.
kola—to die.
kolasz arwa-arvoval—may you die with honor (*greeting*).
koma—empty hand; bare hand; palm of the hand; hollow of the hand.
kond—all of a family's or clan's children.
kont—warrior.
kont o sívanak—strong heart (*literally: heart of the warrior*).
ku—who; which; that.
kuć3—star.
kuć3ak!—stars! (*exclamation*).
kuja—day, sun.
kuŋe—moon; month.
kule—to hear.
kuly—intestinal worm; tapeworm; demon who possesses and devours souls.
kulke—to go or to travel (on land or water).
kulkesz arwa-arvoval, ekäm—walk with honor, my brother (*greeting*).
kulkesz arwaval—joŋesz arwa arvoval—go with glory—return with honor (*greeting*).
kumpa—wave (*noun*).
kuńa—to lie as if asleep; to close or cover the eyes in a game of hide-and-seek; to die.
kunta—band, clan, tribe, family.
kuras—sword; large knife.
kure—bind; tie.
kutni—to be able to bear, carry, endure, stand, or take.
kutnisz ainaak—long may you endure (*greeting*).
kuulua—to belong; to hold.

lääs—west.
lamti (*or* **lamt3)**—lowland; meadow; deep; depth.
lamti ból jüti, kinta, ja szelem—the netherworld (*literally: the meadow of night, mists, and ghosts*).
lańa—daughter.
lejkka—crack, fissure, split (*noun*). To cut; to hit; to strike forcefully (*verb*).
lewl—spirit (*noun*).
lewl ma—the other world (*literally: spirit land*). *Lewl ma* includes *lamti ból jüti, kinta, ja szelem*: the netherworld, but also includes the worlds higher up *En Puwe*, the Great Tree.
liha—flesh.
lõuna—south.
löyly—breath; steam. (*related to lewl: spirit*).
ma—land; forest.
magköszun—thank.
mana—to abuse; to curse; to ruin.
mäne—to rescue; to save.
maγe—land; earth; territory; place; nature.
me—we.
meke—deed; work (*noun*). To do; to make; to work (*verb*).
mića—beautiful.
mića emni kuŋenak minan—my beautiful lunatic.
minan—mine; my own (*endearment*).
minden—every, all (*adj.*).
möért?—what for? (*exclamation*).
molo—to crush; to break into bits.
molanâ—to crumble; to fall apart.
mozdul—to begin to move, to enter into movement.
muonì—appoint; order; prescribe; command.
muonìak te avoisz te—I command you to reveal yourself.
musta—memory.
myös—also.
nä—for.
nautish—to enjoy.
nélkül—without.

nenä—anger.

nó—like; in the same way as; as.

numa—god; sky; top; upper part; highest (*related to the English word* numinous).

numatorkuld—thunder (literally: sky struggle).

nyelv—tongue.

nyál—saliva; spit. (*related to nyelv: tongue*).

ŋamaŋ—this; this one here; that; that one there.

ńiŋ3—worm; maggot.

odam—to dream; to sleep.

odam-sarna kondak—lullaby (*literally: sleep-song of children*).

olen—to be.

oma—old; ancient; last; previous.

omas—stand.

omboće—other; second (*adj.*).

o—the (*used before a noun beginning with a consonant*).

ot—the (*used before a noun beginning with a vowel*).

otti—to look; to see; to find.

óv—to protect against.

owe—door.

päämoro—aim; target.

pajna—to press.

pälä—half; side.

päläfertiil—mate or wife.

palj3—more.

peje—to burn.

peje terád—get burned (*Carpathian swear words*).

pél—to be afraid; to be scared of.

pesä (n.)—nest (*literal*); protection (*figurative*).

pesä (v.)—nest (*literal*); protect (*figurative*).

pesäd te engemal—you are safe with me.

pesäsz jeläbam ainaak—long may you stay in the light (*greeting*).

pide—above.

pile—to ignite; to light up.

pirä—circle; ring (*noun*). to surround; to enclose (*verb*).

piros—red.
pitä—to keep; to hold; to have; to possess.
pitäam mustaakad sielpesäambam—I hold your memories safe in my soul.
pitäsz baszú, piwtäsz igazáget—no vengeance, only justice.
piwtä—to follow; to follow the track of game; to hunt; to prey upon.
poår—bit; piece.
põhi—north.
pukta—to drive away; to persecutes; to put to flight.
pusm—to be restored to health.
pus—healthy; healing.
puwe—tree; wood.
rauho—peace.
reka—ecstasy; trance.
rituaali—ritual.
sa—sinew; tendon; cord.
sa4—to call; to name.
saa—arrive, come; become; get, receive.
saasz hän ku andam szabadon—take what I freely offer.
salama—lightning; lightning bolt.
sarna—words; speech; magic incantation (*noun*). to chant; to sing; to celebrate (*verb*).
sarna kontakawk—warriors' chant.
śaro—frozen snow.
sas—shoosh (*to a child or baby*).
saγe—to arrive; to come; to reach.
siel—soul.
sieljelä isäntä—purity of soul triumphs.
sisar—sister.
sív—heart.
sív pide köd—love transcends evil.
sívad olen wäkeva, hän ku piwtä—may your heart stay strong, hunter (*greeting*).
sívamet—my heart.
sívam és sielam—my heart and soul.
sívdobbanás—heartbeat (*literal*); rhythm (*figurative*).

sokta—to mix; to stir around.
soŋe—to enter; to penetrate; to compensate; to replace.
susu—home; birthplace (*noun*). at home (*adv.*).
szabadon—freely.
szelem—ghost.
taka—behind; beyond.
tappa—to dance; to stamp with the feet; to kill.
te—you.
Te kalma, te jama ńiŋ3kval, te apitäsz arwa-arvo—You are nothing but a walking maggot-infected corpse, without honor.
Te magköszunam nä ŋamaŋ kać3 taka arvo—Thank you for this gift beyond price.
ted—yours.
terád keje—get scorched (*Carpathian swear words*).
tõd—to know.
Tõdak pitäsz wäke bekimet mekesz kaiket—I know you have the courage to face anything.
tõdhän—knowledge.
tõdhän lõ kuraset agbapäämoroam—knowledge flies the sword true to its aim.
toja—to bend; to bow; to break.
toro—to fight; to quarrel.
torosz wäkeval—fight fiercely (*greeting*).
totello—obey.
tsak—only.
tuhanos—thousand.
tuhanos löylyak türelamak saγe diutalet—a thousand patient breaths bring victory.
tule—to meet; to come.
tumte—to feel; to touch; to touch upon.
türe—full, satiated, accomplished.
türelam—patience.
türelam agba kontsalamaval—patience is the warrior's true weapon.
tyvi—stem; base; trunk.
uskol—faithful.

uskolfertiil—allegiance; loyalty.
varolind—dangerous.
veri—blood.
veri-elidet—blood-life.
veri ekäakank—blood of our brothers.
veri isäakank—blood of our fathers.
veri olen piros, ekäm—literally: blood be red, my brother; figuratively: find your lifemate (*greeting*).
veriak ot en Karpatiiak—by the blood of the Prince (*literally: by the blood of the great Carpathian; Carpathian swear words*).
veridet peje—may your blood burn (*Carpathian swear words*).
vigyáz—to love; to care for; to take care of.
vii—last; at last; finally.
wäke—power; strength.
wäke beki—strength; courage.
wäke kaδa—steadfastness.
wäke kutni—endurance.
wäke-sarna—vow; curse; blessing (*literally: power words*).
wäkeva—powerful.
wara—bird; crow.
weńća—complete; whole.
wete—water (*noun*).